REMEMBRANCE OF THINGS PAST

" When to the sessions of sweet silent thought
I summon up remembrance of things past . . ."

VOLUME VI

THE
GUERMANTES WAY

PART TWO

Of this special edition in twelve volumes of

REMEMBRANCE OF THINGS PAST

one hundred and sixty-five sets have
been printed of which one hundred
and sixty are for sale

N⁰. 56

MARCEL PROUST

THE
GUERMANTES WAY

PART TWO

Translated by
C. K. Scott Moncrieff

ILLUSTRATED BY
PHILIPPE JULLIAN

1949
CHATTO & WINDUS
LONDON

First published in English (cr. 8vo) 1925
First issued in the Phoenix Library 1930
First issued in the Uniform Edition
(12 vols.) 1941
Reprinted 1943, 1949

Printed in Great Britain

CONTENTS

✳

Part 2

LIST OF ETCHINGS

*

THE
GUERMANTES WAY

CHAPTER ONE

W E MADE our way back along the Avenue Gabriel, through the strolling crowd. I left my grandmother to rest on a seat and went in search of a cab. She, in whose heart I always placed myself when I had to form an opinion of the most unimportant person, she was now closed to me, had become part of the world outside, and, more than from any casual passer-by, I was obliged to keep from her what I thought of her condition, to say no word of my uneasiness. I could not have spoken of it to her in greater confidence than to a stranger. She had suddenly handed back to me the thoughts, the griefs which, from the days of my infancy, I had entrusted for all time to her keeping. She was not yet dead. I was already alone. And even those allusions which she had made to the Guermantes, to Mme. de Sévigné, to our conversations about the little clan, assumed an air of being without point or occasion, fantastic, because they sprang from the nullity of this very being who to-morrow possibly would have ceased to exist, for whom they would no longer have any meaning, from that nullity, incapable of conceiving them, which my grandmother would shortly be.

"Well, sir, I don't like to say no, but you have not made an appointment, you have no time fixed. Besides, this is not my day for seeing patients. You surely have a doctor of your own. I cannot interfere with his practice, unless he were to call me in for a consultation. It's a question of professional etiquette . . . "

Just as I was signalling to a cabman, I had caught sight of the famous Professor E——, almost a friend of my father and grandfather, acquainted at any rate with them both, who lived in the Avenue Gabriel, and, with a sudden inspiration, had stopped him just as he was entering his house, thinking that he would perhaps be the very person to advise my grandmother. But he was evidently in a hurry and, after calling for his letters, seemed anxious to get rid of me, so that my only chance of speaking to him lay in going up with him in the lift, of which he begged me to allow him to work the switches himself, this being a mania with him.

" But, sir, I am not asking you to see my grandmother here; you will realise from what I am trying to tell you that she is not in a fit state to come; what I am asking is that you should call at our house in half an hour's time, when I have taken her home."

" Call at your house! Really, sir, you must not expect me to do that. I am dining with the Minister of Commerce. I have a call to pay first. I must change at once, and to make matters worse I have torn my coat and my other one has no buttonholes for my decorations. I beg you, please, to oblige me by not touching the switches. You don't know how the lift works; one can't be too careful. Getting that buttonhole made means more delay. Well, as I am a friend of your people, if your grandmother comes here at once I will see her. But I warn you that I shall be able to give her exactly a quarter of an hour, not a moment more."

I had started off at once, without even getting out of the lift which Professor E—— had himself set in motion to take me down again, casting a suspicious glance at me as he did so.

We may, indeed, say that the hour of death is uncertain, but when we say so we represent that hour to ourselves as situated in a vague and remote expanse of time, it never occurs to us that it can have any connexion with the day that has already dawned, or may signify that death—or its first assault and partial possession of us, after which it will never leave hold of us again—may occur this very afternoon, so far from uncertain, this afternoon every hour of which has already been allotted to some occupation. You make a point of taking your drive every day so that in a month's time you will have had the full benefit of the fresh air; you have hesitated over which cloak you will take, which cabman to call, you are in the cab, the whole day lies before you, short because you have to be at home early, as a friend is coming to see you; you hope that it will be as fine again to-morrow; and you have no suspicion that death, which has been making its way towards you along another plane, shrouded in an impenetrable darkness, has chosen precisely this day of all days to make its appearance, in a few minutes' time, more or less, at the moment when the carriage has reached the Champs-Elysées. Perhaps those who are haunted as a rule by the fear of the utter strangeness of death will find something reassuring in this kind of death—in this kind of first contact with death—because death thus assumes a known, familiar guise of everyday life. A good luncheon has preceded it, and the same outing that people take who are in perfect health. A

3

drive home in an open carriage comes on top of its first onslaught; ill as my grandmother was, there were, after all, several people who could testify that at six o'clock, as we came home from the Champs-Elysées, they had bowed to her as she drove past in an open carriage, in perfect weather. Legrandin, making his way towards the Place de la Concorde, raised his hat to us, stopping to look after us with an air of surprise. I, who was not yet detached from life, asked my grandmother if she had acknowledged his greeting, reminding her of his readiness to take offence. My grandmother, thinking me no doubt very frivolous, raised her hand in the air as though to say: "What does it matter? It is not of the least importance."

Yes, one might have said that, a few minutes earlier, when I was looking for a cab, my grandmother was resting on a seat in the Avenue Gabriel, and that a little later she had driven past in an open carriage. But would that have been really true? The seat, for instance, to maintain its position at the side of an avenue—for all that it may be subjected also to certain conditions of equilibrium—has no need of energy. But in order that a living person may be stable, even when supported by a seat or in a carriage, there is required a tension of forces which we do not ordinarily perceive, any more than we perceive (because its action is universal) atmospheric pressure. Possibly if we were to be hollowed out and then left to support the pressure of the air we might feel, in the moment that preceded our extinction, that terrible weight which there was nothing left in us to neutralise. Similarly when the abyss of sickness and death opens within us, and we have no longer any resistance to offer to the tumult with which the world and our own body rush upon us, then to endure even the tension of our own muscles, the shudder that freezes us to the marrow, then even to keep ourself motionless in what we ordinarily regard as nothing but the simple negative position of a lifeless thing requires, if we wish our head to remain erect and our eyes calm, an expense of vital energy and becomes the object of an exhausting struggle.

And if Legrandin had looked back at us with that astonished air, it was because to him, as to the other people who passed us then, in the cab in which my grandmother was apparently seated she had seemed to be foundering, sliding into the abyss, clinging desperately to the cushions which could barely arrest the downward plunge of her body, her hair in disorder, her eye wild, unable any longer to face the assault of the images which its pupil was not strong enough now to bear. She had appeared to them, although I was still by her side, submerged in that unknown world somewhere in which she had already received the blows, traces of which she still bore when I looked up at her a few minutes earlier in the Champs-Elysées, her hat, her face, her cloak left in disorder by the hand of the invisible angel with whom she had wrestled. I have thought, since, that this moment of her stroke cannot have altogether surprised my grandmother, that indeed she had perhaps foreseen it a long time back, had lived in expectation of it. She had not known, naturally, when this fatal moment would come, had never been certain, any more than those lovers whom a similar doubt leads alternately to found unreasonable hopes and unjustified suspicions on the fidelity of their

5

mistresses. But it is rarely that these grave maladies, like that which now at last had struck her full in the face, do not take up their abode in the sick man for a long time before killing him, during which time they make haste, like a "sociable" neighbour or tenant, to introduce themselves to him. A terrible acquaintance, not so much from the sufferings that it causes as from the strange novelty of the definite restriction which it imposes upon life. A woman sees herself dying, in these cases not at the actual moment of death but months, sometimes years before, when death has hideously come to dwell in her. The sufferer makes the acquaintance of the stranger whom she hears coming and going in her brain. She does not know him by sight, it is true, but from the sounds which she hears him regularly make she can form an idea of his habits. Is he a criminal? One morning, she can no longer hear him. He has gone. Ah! If it were only for ever! In the evening he has returned. What are his plans? Her specialist, put to the question, like an adored mistress, replies with avowals that one day are believed, another day fail to convince her. Or rather it is not the mistress's part but that of the servants one interrogates that the doctor plays. They are only third parties. The person whom we press for an answer, whom we suspect of being about to play us false, is life itself, and although we feel her to be no longer the same we believe in her still or at least remain undecided until the day on which she finally abandons us.

I helped my grandmother into Professor E——'s lift and a moment later he came to us and took us into his consulting room. But there, busy as he was, his bombastic manner changed, such is the force of habit; for

6

his habit was to be friendly, that is to say lively with his patients. Since he knew that my grandmother was a great reader, and was himself one also, he devoted the first few minutes to quoting various favourite passages of poetry appropriate to the glorious summer weather. He had placed her in an armchair and himself with his back to the light so as to have a good view of her. His examination was minute and thorough, even obliging me at one moment to leave the room. He continued it after my return, then, having finished, went on, although the quarter of an hour was almost at an end, repeating various quotations to my grandmother. He even made a few jokes, which were witty enough, though I should have preferred to hear them on some other occasion, but which completely reassured me by the tone of amusement in which he uttered them. I then remembered that M. Fallières, the President of the Senate, had, many years earlier, had a false seizure, and that to the consternation of his political rivals he had returned a few days later to his duties and had begun, it was said, his preparations for a more or less remote succession to the Presidency of the Republic. My confidence in my grandmother's prompt recovery was all the more complete in that, just as I was recalling the example of M. Fallières, I was distracted from following up the similarity by a shout of laughter, which served as conclusion to one of the Professor's jokes. After which he took out his watch, wrinkled his brows petulantly on seeing that he was five minutes late, and while he bade us good-bye rang for his other coat to be brought to him at once. I waited until my grandmother had left the room, closed the door and asked him to tell me the truth.

"There is not the slightest hope," he informed me. "It is a stroke brought on by uraemia. In itself, uraemia is not necessarily fatal, but this case seems to me desperate. I need not tell you that I hope I am mistaken. Anyhow, you have Cottard, you're in excellent hands. Excuse me," he broke off as a maid came into the room with his coat over her arm. "I told you, I'm dining with the Minister of Commerce, and I have a call to pay first. Ah! Life is not all a bed of roses, as one is apt to think at your age."

And he graciously offered me his hand. I had shut the door behind me, and a footman was shewing us into the hall when we heard a loud shout of rage. The maid had forgotten to cut and hem the buttonhole for the decorations. This would take another ten minutes. The Professor continued to storm while I stood on the landing gazing at a grandmother for whom there was not the slightest hope. Each of us is indeed alone. We started for home.

The sun was sinking, it burnished an interminable wall along which our cab had to pass before reaching the street in which we lived, a wall against which the shadow cast by the setting sun of horse and carriage stood out in black on a ruddy background, like a funeral car on some Pompeian terra-cotta. At length we arrived at the house. I made the invalid sit at the foot of the staircase in the hall, and went up to warn my mother. I told her that my grandmother had come home feeling slightly unwell, after an attack of giddiness. As soon as I began to speak, my mother's face was convulsed by the paroxysm of a despair which was yet already so resigned that I realised that for many years she had been holding herself quietly in readiness for an uncalendared but final day. She asked me no question; it seemed that, just as malevolence likes to exaggerate the sufferings of other people, so in her devotion she would not admit that her mother was seriously ill, especially with a disease which might affect the brain. Mamma shuddered, her eyes wept without tears, she ran to give orders for the doctor to be fetched at once; but when Françoise asked who was ill she could not reply, her voice stuck in her throat. She came running downstairs with me, struggling to banish from her face the sob that contracted it. My grandmother was waiting below on the sofa in the hall, but, as soon as she heard us coming, drew herself together, stood up, and waved her hand cheerfully at Mamma. I had partially wrapped her head in a white lace shawl, telling her that it was so that she should not catch cold on the stairs. I had hoped that my mother would not notice the change in her face, the distortion of her mouth; my precaution proved unnecessary; my mother went up to my grandmother, kissed her hand as though it were that of her God, raised her up, carried her to the lift with infinite precautions in which there was, with the fear of hurting her by any clumsy movement, the humility of one who felt herself unworthy to touch the most precious thing, to her, in the world, but never once did she raise her eyes, nor look at the sufferer's face. Perhaps this was in order that my grandmother might not be saddened by the thought that the sight of her could alarm her daughter. Perhaps from fear of a grief so piercing that she dared not face it. Perhaps from reverence, because she did not feel it permissible to herself, without impiety, to remark the trace of any

9

mental weakening on those venerated features. Perhaps to be better able to preserve intact in her memory the image of the true face of my grandmother, radiant with wisdom and goodness. So they went up side by side, my grandmother half hidden by her shawl, my mother turning away her eyes.

Meanwhile there was one person who never took hers from what could be made out of my grandmother's altered features, at which her daughter dared not look, a person who fastened on them a gaze wondering, indiscreet and of evil omen: this was Françoise. Not that she was not sincerely attached to my grandmother (indeed she had been disappointed and almost scandalised by the coldness shewn by Mamma, whom she would have liked to see fling herself weeping into her mother's arms), but she had a certain tendency always to look at the worse side of things, she had retained from her childhood two peculiarities which would seem to be mutually exclusive, but which when combined strengthened one another: the want of restraint common among people of humble origin who make no attempt to conceal the impression, in other words the painful alarm aroused in them by the sight of a physical change which it would be in better taste to appear not to notice, and the unfeeling coarseness of the peasant who begins by tearing the wings off dragonflies until she is allowed to wring the necks of chickens, and lacks that modesty which would make her conceal the interest that she feels in the sight of suffering flesh.

When, thanks to the faultless ministrations of Françoise, my grandmother had been put to bed, she discovered that she could speak much more easily, the little rupture or obstruction of a blood-vessel which had produced the

uraemia having apparently been quite slight. And at once
she was anxious not to fail Mamma in her hour of need,
to assist her in the most cruel moments through which
she had yet had to pass.

" Well, my child," she began, taking my mother's hand
in one of her own, and keeping the other in front of her
lips, so as to account for the slight difficulty which she
still found in uttering certain words. " So this is all the
pity you shew your mother! You look as if you thought
that indigestion was quite a pleasant thing! "

Then for the first time my mother's eyes gazed passionately into those of my grandmother, not wishing to
see the rest of her face, and she replied, beginning the
list of those false promises which we swear but are unable
to fulfil:

" Mamma, you will soon be quite well again, your
daughter will see to that."

And embodying all her dearest love, all her determina-
tion that her mother should recover, in a kiss to which
she entrusted them, and which she followed with her
mind, with her whole being until it flowered upon her
lips, she bent down to lay it humbly, reverently upon
the precious brow. My grandmother complained of a sort
of alluvial deposit of bedclothes which kept gathering
all the time in the same place, over her left leg, and from
which she could never manage to free herself. But she
did not realise that she was herself the cause of this
(so that day after day she accused Françoise unjustly
of not " doing " her bed properly). By a convulsive movement she kept flinging to that side the whole flood of
those billowing blankets of fine wool, which gathered
there like the sand in a bay which is very soon trans-

formed into a beach (unless the inhabitants construct a breakwater) by the successive deposits of the tide.

My mother and I (whose falsehood was exposed before we spoke by the obnoxious perspicacity of Françoise) would not even admit that my grandmother was seriously ill, as though such an admission might give pleasure to her enemies (not that she had any) and it was more loving to feel that she was not so bad as all that, in short from the same instinctive sentiment which had led me to suppose that Andrée was too sorry for Albertine to be really fond of her. The same individual phenomena are reproduced in the mass, in great crises. In a war, the man who does not love his country says nothing against it, but regards it as lost, commiserates it, sees everything in the darkest colours.

Françoise was of infinite value to us owing to her faculty of doing without sleep, of performing the most arduous tasks. And if, when she had gone to bed after several nights spent in the sickroom, we were obliged to call her a quarter of an hour after she had fallen asleep, she was so happy to be able to do the most tiring duties as if they had been the simplest things in the world that, so far from looking cross, her face would light up with a satisfaction tinged with modesty. Only when the time came for mass, or for breakfast, then, had my grandmother been in her death agony, still Françoise would have quietly slipped away so as not to make herself late. She neither could nor would let her place be taken by her young footman. It was true that she had brought from Combray an extremely exalted idea of everyone's duty towards ourselves; she would not have tolerated that any of our servants should " fail " us. This doctrine had made her so noble, so imperious, so efficient an instructor that there had never come to our house any servants, however corrupted, who had not speedily modified, purified their conception of life so far as to refuse to touch the usual commissions from tradesmen and to come rushing—however little they might previously have sought to oblige—to take from my hands and not let me tire myself by carrying the smallest package. But at Combray Françoise had contracted also—and had brought with her to Paris—the habit of not being able to put up with any assistance in her work. The sight of anyone coming to help her seemed to her like receiving a deadly insult, and servants had remained for weeks in the house without receiving from her any response to their morning greeting, had even gone off on their holidays without her bidding them good-bye or their guessing her reason, which was simply and solely that they had offered to do a share of her work on some day when she had not been well. And at this moment when my grandmother was so ill Françoise's duties seemed to her peculiarly her own. She would not allow herself, she, the official incumbent, to be done out of her part in the ritual of these festal days. And so her young footman, sent packing by her, did not know what to do with himself, and not content with having copied the butler's example and supplied himself with note-paper from my desk had begun as well to borrow volumes of poetry from my bookshelves. He sat reading them for a good half of the day, out of admiration for the poets who had written them, but also so as, during the rest of his time, to begem with quotations the letters which he wrote to his friends in his native village. Naturally he expected these to dazzle them. But as there was little sequence in his ideas he had formed the notion that these poems, picked out at random from my shelves, were matters of common knowledge, to which it was customary to refer. So much so that in writing to these peasants, whose stupefaction he discounted, he interspersed his own reflexions with lines from Lamartine, just as he might have said " Who laughs last, laughs longest! " or merely " How are you keeping? "

To ease her pain my grandmother was given morphine. Unfortunately, if this relieved her in other ways, it increased the quantity of albumen. The blows which we aimed at the wicked ogre who had taken up his abode in my grandmother were always wide of the mark, and it was she, her poor interposed body that had to bear them, without her ever uttering more than a faint groan by way of complaint. And the pain that we caused her found no compensation in a benefit which we were unable to give her. The savage ogre whom we were anxious to exterminate we barely succeeded in touching, and all we did was to enrage him still further, and possibly hasten the moment at which he would devour his luckless captive. On certain days when the discharge of albumen had been excessive Cottard, after some hesitation, stopped the morphine. In this man, so insignificant, so common, there was, in these brief moments in which he deliberated, in which the relative dangers of one and another course of treatment presented themselves alternately to his mind until he arrived at a decision, the same sort of greatness as in a general who, vulgar in all the rest of his life, is a great strategist, and in an hour of peril, after a moment's reflexion, decides upon what is from the military point of view the wisest course, and gives the order: "Advance eastwards." Medically, however little hope there might be of setting any limit to this attack of uraemia, it did not do to tire the kidneys. But, on the other hand, when my grandmother did not have morphine, her pain became unbearable; she perpetually attempted a certain movement which it was difficult for her to perform without groaning. To a great extent, suffering is a sort of need felt by the organism to make itself familiar with a new state, which makes it uneasy, to adapt its sensibility to that state. We can discern this origin of pain in the case of certain inconveniences which are not such for everyone. Into a room filled with a pungent smoke two men of a coarse fibre will come and attend to their business; a third, more highly strung, will betray an incessant discomfort. His nostrils will continue to sniff anxiously the odour he ought, one would say, to try not to notice but will keep on attempting to attach, by a more exact apprehension of it, to his troubled sense of smell. One consequence of which may well be that his intense preoccupation will prevent him from complaining of a toothache. When my grandmother was in pain the sweat trickled over the pink expanse of her brow, glueing to it her white locks, and if she thought that none of us was in the room she would cry out: "Oh, it's dreadful!" but if she caught sight of my mother, at once she employed all her energy in banishing from her face every sign of pain, or—an alternative stratagem—repeated the same plaints, accompanying them with explanations which gave a different sense, retrospectively, to those which my mother might have overheard:

"Oh! My dear, it's dreadful to have to stay in bed on

a beautiful sunny day like this when one wants to be out in the air; I am crying with rage at your orders."

But she could not get rid of the look of anguish in her eyes, the sweat on her brow, the convulsive start, checked at once, of her limbs.

" There is nothing wrong. I'm complaining because I'm not lying very comfortably. I feel my hair is untidy, my heart is bad, I knocked myself against the wall."

And my mother, at the foot of the bed, rivetted to that suffering form, as though, by dint of piercing with her gaze that pain-bedewed brow, that body which hid the evil thing within it, she could have succeeded in reaching that evil thing and carrying it away, my mother said:

" No, no, Mamma dear, we won't let you suffer like that, we will find something to take it away, have patience just for a moment; let me give you a kiss, darling—no, you're not to move."

And stooping over the bed, with bended knees, almost kneeling on the ground, as though by an exercise of humility she would have a better chance of making acceptable the impassioned gift of herself, she lowered towards my grandmother her whole life contained in her face as in a ciborium which she extended over her, adorned in relief with dimples and folds so passionate, so sorrowful, so sweet that one knew not whether they had been carved by the chisel of a kiss, a sob or a smile. My grandmother, also, tried to lift up her face to Mamma's. It was so altered that probably, had she been strong enough to go out, she would have been recognised only by the feather in her hat. Her features, like the clay in a sculptor's hands, seemed to be straining, with an effort which distracted her from everything else, to conform to some particular model which we failed to identify. This business of modelling was now almost finished, and if my grandmother's face had shrunk in the process it had at the same time hardened. The veins that ran beneath its surface seemed those not of a piece of marble but of some more rugged stone. Constantly thrust forwards by the difficulty that she found in breathing and as constantly forced back on to her pillow by exhaustion, her face, worn, diminished, terribly expressive, seemed like, in a primitive, almost prehistoric carving, the rude, flushed, purplish, desperate face of some savage guardian of a tomb. But the whole task was not yet accomplished. Next, her resistance must be overcome, and that tomb, the entrance to which she had so painfully guarded, with that tense contraction, entered.

In one of those moments in which, as the saying goes, one does not know what saint to invoke, as my grandmother was coughing and sneezing a good deal, we took the advice of a relative who assured us that if we sent for the specialist X—— he would get rid of all that in a couple of days. People say that sort of thing about their own doctors, and their friends believe them just as Françoise always believed the advertisements in the newspapers. The specialist came with his bag packed with all the colds and coughs of his other patients, like Aeolus's bottle. My grandmother refused point-blank to let herself be examined. And we, out of consideration for the doctor, who had had his trouble for nothing, deferred to the desire that he expressed to inspect each of our noses in turn, albeit there was nothing the matter with any of them. According to him, however, there was; everything, whether headache or colic, heart-disease or diabetes, was a disease of the nose that had been wrongly diagnosed. To each of us he said: " I should like to have another look at that little cornea. Don't put it off too long. I can soon get rid of it for you with a hot needle." We were, of course, thinking of something quite different. And yet we asked ourselves: " Get rid of what? " In a word, every one of our noses was diseased; his mistake lay only in his use of the present tense. For by the following day his examination and provisional treatment had taken effect. Each of us had his or her catarrh. And when in the street he ran into my father doubled up with a cough, he smiled to think that an ignorant layman might suppose the attack to be due to his intervention. He had examined us at a moment when we were already ill.

My grandmother's illness gave occasion to various people to manifest an excess or deficiency of sympathy which surprised us quite as much as the sort of chance which led one or another of them to reveal to us connecting links of circumstances, or of friendship for that matter, which we had never suspected. And the signs of interest shewn by the people who called incessantly at the house to inquire revealed to us the gravity of an illness which, until then, we had not sufficiently detached from the countless painful impressions that we received in my grandmother's room. Summoned by telegram, her sisters declined to leave Combray. They had discovered a musician there who gave them excellent chamber concerts, in listening to which they thought that they could find, better than by the invalid's bedside, food for thought, a melancholy exaltation the form of which was, to say the least of it, unusual. Mme. Sazerat wrote to Mamma, but in the tone of a person whom the sudden breaking off of a betrothal (the cause of the rupture being her Dreyfusism) has parted from one for ever. Bergotte, on the other hand, came every day and spent several hours with me.

He had always made a habit of going regularly for some time to the same house, where, accordingly, he need not stand on ceremony. But formerly it had been in order that he might talk without being interrupted; now it was so that he might sit for as long as he chose in silence, without being expected to talk. For he was very ill, some people said with albuminuria, like my grandmother. According to another version, he had a tumour. He grew steadily weaker; it was with difficulty that he came up our staircase, with greater difficulty still that he went down it. Even though he held on to the banisters he often stumbled, and he would, I believe, have stayed at home had he not been afraid of losing altogether the habit of going out, the capacity to go out, he, the "man with the little beard" whom I had seen so alert, not very long since. He was now quite blind and even his speech was frequently obstructed.

But at the same time, by a directly opposite process, the body of his work, known only to a few literary people at the period when Mme. Swann used to patronise their timid efforts to disseminate it, now grown in stature and strength before the eyes of all, had acquired an extraordinary power of expansion among the general public. The general rule is, no doubt, that only after his death does a writer become famous. But it was while he still lived, and during his slow progress towards a death that he had not yet reached that this writer was able to watch the progress of his works towards Renown. A dead writer can at least be illustrious without any strain on himself. The effulgence of his name is stopped short by the stone upon his grave. In the deafness of the eternal sleep he is not importuned by Glory. But for Bergotte the antithesis was still incomplete. He existed still sufficiently to suffer from the tumult. He was moving still, though with difficulty, while his books, bounding about him, like daughters whom one loves but whose impetuous youthfulness and noisy pleasures tire one, brought day after day, to his very bedside, a crowd of fresh admirers.

The visits which he now began to pay us came for me several years too late, for I had no longer the same admiration for him as of old. Which is not in any sense incompatible with the growth of his reputation. A man's work seldom becomes completely understood and successful before that of another writer, still obscure, has begun in the minds of certain people more difficult to please to substitute a fresh cult for one that has almost ceased to command observance. In the books of Bergotte which I constantly re-read, his sentences stood out as clearly before my eyes as my own thoughts, the furniture in my room and the carriages in the street. All the details were quite easily seen, not perhaps precisely as one had always seen them, but at any rate as one was accustomed to see them now. But a new writer had recently begun to publish work in which the relations between things were so different from those that connected them for me that I could understand hardly anything of what he wrote. He would say, for instance: " The hose-pipes admired the polished tone of the roads " (and so far it

was simple, I followed him smoothly along those roads)
" which started every five minutes from Briand and
Claudel." At that point I ceased to understand, because
I had expected the name of a place and was given that
of a person instead. Only I felt that it was not the
sentence that was badly constructed but I myself that
lacked the strength and ability necessary to reach the
end. I would start afresh striving tooth and nail to
climb to the pinnacle from which I would see things
in their novel relations. And each time, after I had got
about half way through the sentence, I would fall back
again, as later on, when I joined the Army, in my attempts
at the exercise known as the " bridge-ladder ". I felt
nevertheless for the new writer the admiration which an
awkward boy who never receives any marks for gymnastics feels when he watches another more nimble. And
from then onwards I felt less admiration for Bergotte,
whose limpidity began to strike me as insufficient. There
was a time at which people recognised things quite easily
in pictures when it was Fromentin who had painted them,
and could not recognise them at all when it was Renoir.

People of taste and refinement tell us nowadays that
Renoir is one of the great painters of the last century.
But in so saying they forget the element of Time, and
that it took a great deal of time, well into the present
century, before Renoir was hailed as a great artist. To
succeed thus in gaining recognition, the original painter,
the original writer proceeds on the lines adopted by
oculists. The course of treatment they give us by their
painting or by their prose is not always agreeable to
us. When it is at an end the operator says to us: " Now
look ! " And, lo and behold, the world around us (which

was not created once and for all, but is created afresh as often as an original artist is born) appears to us entirely different from the old world, but perfectly clear. Women pass in the street, different from what they used to be, because they are Renoirs, those Renoir types which we persistently refused to see as women. The carriages, too, are Renoirs, and the water, and the sky: we feel tempted to go for a walk in the forest which reminds us of that other which when we first saw it looked like anything in the world except a forest, like for instance a tapestry of innumerable shades but lacking precisely the shades proper to forests. Such is the new and perishable universe which has just been created. It will last until the next geological catastrophe is precipitated by a new painter or writer of original talent.

This writer who had taken Bergotte's place in my affections wearied me not by the incoherence but by the novelty of associations—perfectly coherent—which my mind was not trained to follow. The fact that it was always at the same point that I felt myself relinquish my grasp pointed to a common character in the efforts that I had always to make. Moreover, when once in a thousand times I did succeed in following the writer to the end of his sentence, what I saw there was always of a humour, a truth, a charm similar to those which I had found long ago in reading Bergotte, only more delightful. I reflected that it was not so many years since a similar reconstruction of the world, like that which I was waiting now for his successor to produce, had been wrought for me by Bergotte himself. Until I was led to ask myself whether there was indeed any truth in the distinction which we are always making between art, which is no

more advanced now than in Homer's day, and science with
its continuous progress. Perhaps, on the contrary, art was
in this respect like science; each new writer seemed to
me to have advanced beyond the stage of his immediate
predecessor; and how was I to know that in twenty
years' time, when I should be able to accompany without
strain or effort the newcomer of to-day, another might
not appear at whose approach he in turn would be packed
off to the limbo to which his own coming would have
consigned Bergotte?

I spoke to the latter of the new writer. He gave me
a distaste for him not so much when he said that his art
was uncouth, easy and vacuous, as when he told me that
he had seen him, and had almost mistaken him (so
strong was the likeness) for Bloch. From that moment
my friend's features outlined themselves on the printed
pages, and I no longer felt any obligation to make the
effort necessary to understand them. If Bergotte had
decried him to me it was less, I fancy, out of jealousy
for a success that was yet to come than out of ignorance
of his work. He read scarcely anything. The bulk of
his thought had long since passed from his brain into his
books. He had grown thin, as though they had been
extracted from him by surgical operations. His repro-
ductive instinct no longer impelled him to any activity,
now that he had given an independent existence to almost
all his thoughts. He led the vegetative life of a con-
valescent, of a woman after childbirth; his fine eyes remained motionless, vaguely dazed, like the eyes of a
man who lies on the sea shore and in a vague day-dream
sees only each little breaking wave. However, if it was
less interesting to talk to him now than I should once

have found it, I felt no compunction for that. He was so far a creature of habit that the simplest habits, like the most elaborate, once he had formed them, became indispensable to him for a certain length of time. I do not know what made him come to our house first of all, but after that every day it was simply because he had been there the day before. He would come to the house as he might have gone to a café, so that no one should talk to him, so that he might—very rarely—talk himself; one might in short have found in his conduct a sign that he was moved to sympathise with us in our anxiety, or that he enjoyed my company, had one sought to draw any conclusion from such an assiduity in calling. It did not fail to impress my mother, sensitive to everything that might be regarded as an act of homage to her invalid. And every day she reminded me: " See that you don't forget to thank him nicely."

We had also—a discreet feminine attention like the refreshments that are brought to us in the studio, between sittings, by a painter's mistress—a courteous supplement to those which her husband paid us professionally, a visit from Mme. Cottard. She came to offer us her "waiting-woman", or, if we preferred the services of a man, she would "scour the country" for one, and, best of all, on our declining, said that she did hope this was not just a "put-off" on our part, a word which in her world signifies a false pretext for not accepting an invitation. She assured us that the Professor, who never referred to his patients when he was at home, was as sad about it as if it had been she herself who was ill. We shall see in due course that even if this had been true it would have been at once a very small and a con-

24

siderable admission on the part of the most faithless and the most attentive of husbands.

Offers as helpful and infinitely more touching owing to the form in which they were couched (which was a blend of the highest intelligence, the warmest sympathy, and a rare felicity of expression) were addressed to me by the Hereditary Grand Duke of Luxembourg. I had met him at Balbec where he had come on a visit to one of his aunts, the Princesse de Luxembourg, being himself at that time merely Comte de Nassau. He had married, some months later, the charming daughter of another Luxembourg Princess, extremely rich, because she was the only daughter of a Prince who was the proprietor of an immense flour-mill. Whereupon the Grand Duke of Luxembourg, who had no children of his own and was devoted to his nephew Nassau, had obtained the approval of his Chamber to his declaring the young man his heir. As with all marriages of this nature, the origin of the bride's fortune was the obstacle as it was also the deciding factor. I remembered this Comte de Nassau as one of the most striking young men I had ever met, already devoured, at that time, by a dark and blazing passion for his betrothed. I was deeply touched by the letters which he wrote me, day after day, during my grandmother's illness, and Mamma herself, in her emotion, quoted sadly one of her mother's expressions: "Sévigné would not have put it better."

On the sixth day Mamma, yielding to my grandmother's entreaties, left her for a little and pretended to go and lie down. I should have liked (so that my grandmother might go to sleep) Françoise to sit quite still and not disturb her by moving. In spite of my supplications, she got up and left the room; she was genuinely devoted to my grandmother; with her uncanny insight and her natural pessimism she regarded her as doomed. She would therefore have liked to pay her every possible attention. But word had just come that an electrician was in the house, one of the oldest servants of his firm, the head of which was his brother-in-law, highly esteemed throughout the building, where he had worked for many years, and especially by Jupien. This man had been ordered to come before my grandmother's illness. It seemed to me that he might have been sent away again, or told to wait. But Françoise's code of manners would not permit of this; it would have been a want of courtesy towards this worthy man; my grandmother's condition ceased at once to matter. When, after waiting a quarter of an hour, I lost my patience and went to look for her in the kitchen, I found her talking to him on the landing of the back staircase, the door of which stood open, a device which had the advantage, should any of us come on the scene, of letting it be thought that they were just saying good-bye, but had also the drawback of sending a terrible draught through the house. Françoise tore herself from the workman, not without turning to shout down after him various greetings, forgotten in her haste, to his wife and brother-in-law. A typical Combray scruple, not to be found wanting in politeness, which Françoise extended even to foreign politics. People foolishly imagine that the vast dimensions of social phenomena afford them an excellent opportunity to penetrate farther into the human soul; they ought, on the contrary, to realise that it is by plumbing the depths of a single personality that they might have a chance of understanding those phenomena. A thousand times over had Françoise told the gardener at Combray that war was the most senseless of crimes, that life was the only thing that mattered. Yet, when the Russo-Japanese war broke out, she was quite ashamed, when she thought of the Tsar, that we had not gone to war also to help the " poor Russians ", " since," she reminded us, " we're allianced to them." She felt this abstention to be not quite polite to Nicholas II, who had always " said such nice things about us "; it was a corollary of the same code which would have prevented her from refusing a glass of brandy from Jupien, knowing that it would " upset " her digestion, and which brought it about that now, with my grandmother lying at death's door, the same meanness of which she considered France guilty in remaining neutral with regard to Japan she would have had to admit in herself, had she not gone in person to make her apologies to this good electrician who had been put to so much trouble.

Luckily for ourselves, we were soon rid of Françoise's daughter, who was obliged to be away for some weeks. To the regular stock of advice which people at Combray gave to the family of an invalid: " You haven't tried taking him away for a little . . . the change of air, you know . . . pick up an appetite . . . etc? " she had added the almost unique idea, which she had specially created in her own imagination, and repeated accordingly whenever we saw her, without fail, as though hoping by dint of reiteration to force it through the thickness of people's heads: " She ought to have taken herself in hand *radically* from the first." She did not recommend any one cure rather than another, provided that it were " radical ". As for Françoise herself, she noticed that we were not giving my grandmother many medicines. Since, according to her, they only destroyed the stomach, she was quite glad of this, but at the same time even more humiliated. She had, in the South of France, some cousins—relatively well-to-do—whose daughter, after falling ill just as she was growing up, had died at twenty-three; for several years the father and mother had ruined themselves on drugs, on different doctors, on pilgrimages from one watering-place to another, until her decease. Now all this seemed to Françoise, for the parents in question, a kind of luxury, as though they had owned racehorses, or a place in the country. They themselves, in the midst of their affliction, derived a certain gratification from the thought of such lavish expenditure. They had now nothing left, least of all their most precious possession, their child, but they did enjoy telling people how they had done as much for her and more than the richest in the land. The ultra-violet rays to the action of which, several times a day for months on end, the poor girl had been subjected, delighted them more than anything. The father, elated in his grief by the glory of it all, was led to speak of his daughter at times as of an operatic star for whose sake he had ruined himself. Françoise was not unmoved by this wealth of scenic effect; that which framed my grandmother's sickbed seemed to her a trifle meagre, suited rather to an illness on the stage of a small provincial theatre.

There came a time when her uraemic trouble affected my grandmother's eyes. For some days she could not see at all. Her eyes were not at all like those of a blind person, but remained just the same as before. And I

gathered that she could see nothing only from the strangeness of a certain smile of welcome which she assumed
the moment one opened the door, until one had come up
to her and taken her hand, a smile which began too
soon and remained stereotyped on her lips, fixed, but
always full-faced, and endeavouring to be visible from
all points, because she could no longer rely upon her
sight to regulate it, to indicate the right moment, the
proper direction, to bring it to the point, to make it
vary according to the change of position or of facial
expression of the person who had come in; because it
was left isolated, without the accompanying smile in her
eyes which would have distracted a little from it the
attention of the visitor, it assumed in its awkwardness
an undue importance, giving one the impression of an
exaggerated friendliness. Then her sight was completely
restored; from her eyes the wandering affliction passed
to her ears. For several days my grandmother was deaf.
And as she was afraid of being taken by surprise by the
sudden entry of some one whom she would not have
heard come in, all day long, albeit she was lying with
her face to the wall, she kept turning her head sharply
towards the door. But the movement of her neck was
clumsy, for one cannot adapt oneself in a few days to
this transposition of faculties, so as, if not actually to
see sounds, to listen with one's eyes. Finally her pain
grew less, but the impediment of her speech increased.
We were obliged to ask her to repeat almost everything
that she said.

And now my grandmother, realising that we could no
longer understand her, gave up altogether the attempt
to speak and lay perfectly still. When she caught sight

of me she gave a sort of convulsive start like a person who suddenly finds himself unable to breathe, but could make no intelligible sound. Then, overcome by her sheer powerlessness, she let her head drop on to the pillows, stretched herself out flat in her bed, her face grave, like a face of marble, her hands motionless on the sheet or occupied in some purely physical action such as that of wiping her fingers with her handkerchief. She made no effort to think. Then came a state of perpetual agitation. She was incessantly trying to get up. But we restrained her so far as we could from doing so, for fear of her discovering how paralysed she was. One day when she had been left alone for a moment I found her standing on the floor in her nightgown trying to open the window.

At Balbec, once, when a widow who had jumped into the sea had been rescued against her will, my grandmother had told me (moved perhaps by one of those presentiments which we discern at times in the mystery—so obscure, for all that—of the organic life around us, in which nevertheless it seems that our own future is foreshadowed) that she could think of nothing so cruel as to tear a poor wretch from the death that she had deliberately sought and restore her to her living martyrdom.

We were just in time to catch my grandmother, she put up an almost violent resistance to my mother, then, overpowered, seated forcibly in an armchair, she ceased to wish for death, to regret being alive, her face resumed its impassivity and she began laboriously to pick off the hairs that had been left on her nightgown by a fur cloak which somebody had thrown over her shoulders.

The look in her eyes changed completely; often uneasy, plaintive, haggard, it was no longer the look we knew, it was the sullen expression of a doddering old woman. . . .

By dint of repeatedly asking her whether she would not like her hair done, Françoise managed to persuade herself that the request had come from my grandmother. She armed herself with brushes, combs, eau de Cologne, a wrapper. " It can't hurt Madame Amédée," she said to herself, " if I just comb her; nobody's ever too ill for a good combing." In other words, one was never too weak for another person to be able, for her own satisfaction, to comb one. But when I came into the room I saw between the cruel hands of Françoise, as blissfully happy as though she were in the act of restoring my grandmother to health, beneath a thin rain of aged tresses which had not the strength to resist the action of the comb, a head which, incapable of maintaining the position into which it had been forced, was rolling to and fro with a ceaseless swirling motion in which sheer debility alternated with spasms of pain. I felt that the moment at which Françoise would have finished her task was approaching, and I dared not hasten it by suggesting to her: " That is enough," for fear of her disobeying me. But I did forcibly intervene when, in order that my grandmother might see whether her hair had been done to her liking, Françoise, with innocent savagery, brought her a glass. I was glad for the moment that I had managed to snatch it from her in time, before my grandmother, whom we had carefully kept without a mirror, could catch even a stray glimpse of a face unlike anything she could have imagined. But, alas, when, a moment later, I leaned over her to kiss that dear forehead which had been so harshly treated, she looked up at me with a puzzled, distrustful, shocked expression: she did not know me.

According to our doctor, this was a symptom that the congestion of her brain was increasing. It must be relieved in some way.

Cottard was in two minds. Françoise hoped at first that they were going to apply " clarified cups ". She looked for the effects of this treatment in my dictionary, but could find no reference to it. Even if she had said " scarified " instead of " clarified " she still would not have found any reference to this adjective, since she did not look any more for it under ' S ' than under ' C ', she did indeed say " clarified " but she wrote (and consequently assumed that the printed word was) " esclarified ". Cottard, to her disappointment, gave the preference, though without much hope, to leeches. When, a few hours later, I went into my grandmother's room, fastened to her neck, her temples, her ears, the tiny black serpents were writhing among her bloodstained locks, as on the head of Medusa. But in her pale and peaceful, entirely motionless face I saw wide open, luminous and calm, her own beautiful eyes, as in days gone by (perhaps even more charged with the light of intelligence than they had been before her illness, since, as she could not speak and must not move, it was to her eyes alone that she entrusted her thought, that thought which at one time occupies an immense place in us, offering us undreamed-of treasures, at another time seems reduced to nothing, then may be reborn, as though by spontaneous generation, by the withdrawal of a few drops of blood), her eyes, soft and liquid like two pools of oil in which the rekindled fire that was now burning lighted before the face of the invalid a reconquered universe. Her calm was no longer the wisdom of despair, but that of hope. She realised that she was better, wished to be careful, not to move, and made me the present only of a charming smile so that I should know that she was feeling better, as she gently pressed my hand.

I knew the disgust that my grandmother felt at the sight of certain animals, let alone being touched by them. I knew that it was in consideration of a higher utility that she was enduring the leeches. And so it infuriated me to hear Françoise repeating to her with that laugh which people use to a baby, to make it crow: "Oh, look at the little beasties running about on Madame." This was, moreover, treating our patient with a want of respect, as though she were in her second childhood. But my grandmother, whose face had assumed the calm fortitude of a stoic, did not seem even to hear her.

Alas! No sooner had the leeches been taken off than the congestion returned and grew steadily worse. I was surprised to find that at this stage, when my grandmother was so ill, Françoise was constantly disappearing. The fact was that she had ordered herself a mourning dress, and did not wish to keep her dressmaker waiting. In the lives of most women, everything, even the greatest sorrow, resolves itself into a question of "trying-on".

A few days later, when I was in bed and sleeping, my mother came to call me in the early hours of the morning. With that tender consideration which, in great crises, people who are crushed by grief shew even for the slightest discomfort of others:

" Forgive me for disturbing your sleep," she said to me.

" I was not asleep," I answered as I awoke.

I said this in good faith. The great modification which the act of awakening effects in us is not so much that of introducing us to the clear life of consciousness, as that of making us lose all memory of that other, rather more diffused light in which our mind has been resting, as in the opaline depths of the sea. The tide of thought, half veiled from our perception, over which we were drifting still a moment ago, kept us in a state of motion perfectly sufficient to enable us to refer to it by the name of wakefulness. But then our actual awakenings produce an interruption of memory. A little later we describe these states as sleep because we no longer remember them. And when shines that bright star which at the moment of waking illuminates behind the sleeper the whole expanse of his sleep, it makes him imagine for a few moments that this was not a sleeping but a waking state; a shooting star, it must be added, which blots out with the fading of its light not only the false existence but the very appearance of our dream, and merely enables him who has awoken to say to himself: " I was asleep."

In a voice so gentle that she seemed to be afraid of hurting me, my mother asked whether it would tire me too much to get out of bed, and, stroking my hands, went on:

" My poor boy, you have only your Papa and Mamma to help you now."

We went into the sickroom. Bent in a semi-circle on the bed a creature other than my grandmother, a sort of

34

wild beast which was coated with her hair and couched amid her bedclothes lay panting, groaning, making the blankets heave with its convulsions. The eyelids were closed, and it was because the one nearer me did not shut properly, rather than because it opened at all that it left visible a chink of eye, misty, filmed, reflecting the dimness both of an organic sense of vision and of a hidden, internal pain. All this agitation was not addressed to us, whom she neither saw nor knew. But if this was only a beast that was stirring there, where could my grandmother be? Yes, I could recognise the shape of her nose, which bore no relation now to the rest of her face, but to the corner of which a beauty spot still adhered, and the hand that kept thrusting the blankets aside with a gesture which formerly would have meant that those blankets were pressing upon her, but now meant nothing.

Mamma asked me to go for a little vinegar and water with which to sponge my grandmother's forehead. It was the only thing that refreshed her, thought Mamma, who saw that she was trying to push back her hair. But now one of the servants was signalling to me from the doorway. The news that my grandmother was in the last throes had spread like wildfire through the house. One of those "extra helps" whom people engage at exceptional times to relieve the strain on their servants (a practice which gives deathbeds an air of being social functions) had just opened the front door to the Duc de Guermantes, who was now waiting in the hall and had asked for me: I could not escape him.

"I have just, my dear Sir, heard your tragic news. I should like, as a mark of sympathy, to shake hands with your father." I made the excuse that I could not very well disturb him at the moment. M. de Guermantes was like a caller who turns up just as one is about to start on a journey. But he felt so intensely the importance of the courtesy he was shewing us that it blinded him to all else, and he insisted upon being taken into the drawing-room. As a general rule, he made a point of going resolutely through the formalities with which he had decided to honour anyone, and took little heed that the trunks were packed or the coffin ready.

"Have you sent for Dieulafoy? No? That was a great mistake. And if you had only asked me, I would have got him to come, he never refuses me anything, although he has refused the Duchesse de Chartres before now. You see, I set myself above a Princess of the Blood. However, in the presence of death we are all equal," he added, not that he meant to suggest that my grandmother was becoming his equal, but probably because he felt that a prolonged discussion of his power over Dieulafoy and his pre-eminence over the Duchesse de Chartres would not be in very good taste.

This advice did not in the least surprise me. I knew that, in the Guermantes set, the name of Dieulafoy was regularly quoted (only with slightly more respect) among those of other tradesmen who were "quite the best" in their respective lines. And the old Duchesse de Morte-mart *née* Guermantes (I never could understand, by the way, why, the moment one speaks of a Duchess, one almost invariably says: "The old Duchess of So-and-so," or, alternatively, in a delicate Watteau tone, if she is still young: "The little Duchess of So-and-so,") would prescribe almost automatically, with a droop of the eyelid, in serious cases: "Dieulafoy, Dieulafoy!" as, if one wanted a place for ices, she would advise: "Poiré Blanche," or for small pastry "Rebattet, Rebattet." But I was not aware that my father had, as a matter of fact, just sent for Dieulafoy.

At this point my mother, who was waiting impatiently for some cylinders of oxygen which would help my grandmother to breathe more easily, came out herself to the hall where she little expected to find M. de Guermantes. I should have liked to conceal him, had that been possible. But convinced in his own mind that nothing was more essential, could be more gratifying to her or more indispensable to the maintenance of his reputation as a perfect gentleman, he seized me violently by the arm and, although I defended myself as against an assault with repeated protestations of "Sir, Sir, Sir," dragged me across to Mamma, saying: "Will you do me the great honour of presenting me to your mother?" letting go a little as he came to the last word. And it was so plain to him that the honour was hers that he could not help smiling at her even while he was composing a grave face. There was nothing for it but to mention his name, the sound of which at once started him bowing and scraping, and he was just going to begin the complete ritual of salutation. He apparently proposed to enter into conversation, but my mother, overwhelmed by her grief, told me to come at once and did not reply to the speeches of M. de Guermantes who, expecting to be received as a visitor and finding himself instead left alone in the hall, would have been obliged to retire had he not at that moment caught sight of Saint-Loup who had arrived in Paris that morning and had come to us in haste to

inquire for news. " I say, this is a piece of luck! " cried
the Duke joyfully, catching his nephew by the sleeve,
which he nearly tore off, regardless of the presence of
my mother who was again crossing the hall. Saint-Loup
was not sorry, I fancy, despite his genuine sympathy, at
having missed seeing me, considering his attitude towards
myself. He left the house, carried off by his uncle who,
having had something very important to say to him and
having very nearly gone down to Doncières on purpose
to say it, was beside himself with joy at being able to
save himself so much exertion. " Upon my soul, if anybody had told me I had only to cross the courtyard and
I should find you here, I should have thought it a huge
joke; as your friend M. Bloch would say, it's a regular
farce." And as he disappeared down the stairs with Robert
whom he held by the shoulder: " All the same," he went
on, " it's quite clear I must have touched the hangman's
rope or something; I do have the most astounding luck."
Not that the Duc de Guermantes was ill-bred; far from
it. But he was one of those men who are incapable of
putting themselves in the place of other people, who
resemble in that respect undertakers and the majority
of doctors, and who, after composing their faces and
saying: " This is a very painful occasion," after, if need
be, embracing you and advising you to rest, cease to
regard a deathbed or a funeral as anything but a social
gathering of a more or less restricted kind at which, with
a joviality that has been checked for a moment only,
they scan the room in search of the person whom they
can tell about their own little affairs, or ask to introduce
them to some one else, or offer a " lift " in their carriage
when it is time to go home. The Duc de Guermantes,

while congratulating himself on the "good wind" that had blown him into the arms of his nephew, was still so surprised at the reception—natural as it was—that had been given him by my mother, that he declared later on that she was as disagreeable as my father was civil, that she had "absent fits" during which she seemed literally not to hear a word you said to her, and that in his opinion she had no self-possession and perhaps even was not quite "all there". At the same time he had been quite prepared (according to what I was told) to put this state of mind down, in part at any rate, to the circumstances, and declared that my mother had seemed to him greatly "affected" by the sad event. But he had still stored up in his limbs all the residue of bows and reverences which he had been prevented from using up, and had so little idea of the real nature of Mamma's sorrow that he asked me, the day before the funeral, if I was not doing anything to distract her.

A half-brother of my grandmother, who was in religion, and whom I had never seen, had telegraphed to Austria, where the head of his Order was, and having as a special privilege obtained leave, arrived that day. Bowed down with grief, he sat by the bedside reading prayers and meditations from a book, without, however, taking his gimlet eyes from the invalid's face. At one point, when my grandmother was unconscious, the sight of this cleric's grief began to upset me, and I looked at him tenderly. He appeared surprised by my pity, and then an odd thing happened. He joined his hands in front of his face, like a man absorbed in painful meditation, but, on the assumption that I would then cease to watch him, left, as I observed, a tiny chink between his fingers. And at the moment when my gaze left his face, I saw his sharp eye, which had been making use of its vantage-point behind his hands to observe whether my sympathy were sincere. He was hidden there as in the darkness of a confessional. He saw that I was still looking and at once shut tight the lattice which he had had left ajar. I have met him again since then, but never has any reference been made by either of us to that minute. It was tacitly agreed that I had not noticed that he was spying on me. In the priest as in the alienist, there is always an element of the examining magistrate. Besides, what friend is there, however cherished, in whose and our common past there has not been some such episode which we find it convenient to believe that he must have forgotten?

The doctor gave my grandmother an injection of morphine, and to make her breathing less troublesome ordered cylinders of oxygen. My mother, the doctor, the nursing sister held these in their hands; as soon as one was exhausted another was put in its place. I had left the room for a few minutes. When I returned I found myself face to face with a miracle. Accompanied on a muted instrument by an incessant murmur, my grandmother seemed to be greeting us with a long and blissful chant, which filled the room, rapid and musical. I soon realized that this was scarcely less unconscious, that it was as purely mechanical as the hoarse rattle that I had heard before leaving the room. Perhaps to a slight extent it reflected some improvement brought about by the morphine. Principally it was the result (the air not passing quite in the same way through the bronchial tubes) of a change in the register of her breathing. Released by the twofold action of the oxygen and the morphine, my grandmother's breath no longer laboured, panted, groaned, but, swift and light, shot like a skater along the delicious stream. Perhaps with her breath, unconscious like that of the wind in the hollow stem of a reed, there were blended in this chant some of those more human sighs which, liberated at the approach of death, make us imagine impressions of suffering or happiness in minds which already have ceased to feel, and these sighs came now to add a more melodious accent, but without changing its rhythm, to that long phrase which rose, mounted still higher, then declined, to start forth afresh, from her unburdened bosom in quest of the oxygen. Then, having risen to so high a pitch, having been sustained with so much vigour, the chant, mingled with a murmur of supplication from the midst of her ecstasy, seemed at times to stop altogether like a spring that has ceased to flow.

Françoise, in any great sorrow, felt the need but did not possess the art—as simple as that need was futile—of giving it expression. Regarding my grandmother's case as quite hopeless, it was her own personal impressions that she was impelled to communicate to us. And all that she could do was to repeat: " It makes me feel all queer," in the same tone in which she would say, when she had taken too large a plateful of cabbage broth: " It's like a load on my stomach," sensations both of which were more natural than she seemed to think. Though so feebly expressed, her grief was nevertheless very great, and was aggravated moreover by her annoyance that her daughter, detained at Combray (to which this young Parisian now referred as " the Cambrousse " and where she felt herself growing " *pétrousse* ", in other words fossilised), would not, presumably, be able to return in time for the funeral ceremony, which was certain, Françoise felt, to be a superb spectacle. Knowing that we were not inclined to be expansive, she made Jupien promise at all costs to keep every evening in the week free. She knew that he would be engaged elsewhere at the hour of the funeral. She was determined at least to " go over it all " with him on his return.

For several nights now my father, my grandfather and one of our cousins had been sitting up, and never left the house during the day. Their continuous devotion ended by assuming a mask of indifference, and their interminable leisure round the deathbed made them indulge in that small talk which is an inseparable accompaniment of prolonged confinement in a railway carriage. Anyhow this cousin (a nephew of my great-aunt) aroused in me an antipathy as strong as the esteem which he deserved and generally enjoyed. He was always " sent for " in times of great trouble, and was so assiduous in his attentions to the dying that their mourning families, on the pretext that he was in delicate health, despite his robust appearance, his bass voice and bristling beard, invariably besought him, with the customary euphemisms, not to come to the cemetery. I could tell already that Mamma, who thought of others in the midst of the most crushing grief, would soon be saying to him, in a very different form of words, what he was in the habit of hearing said on all such occasions :

" Promise me that you won't come ' to-morrow '. Please ; for ' her sake '. At any rate, you won't go ' all the way '. It's what she would have wished."

But there was nothing for it; he was always the first to

42

arrive " at the house ", by reason of which he had been given, among another set, the nickname (unknown to us) of " No flowers by request." And before attending everything he had always " attended to everything ", which entitled him to the formula: " We don't know how to thank you."

" What's that? " came in a loud voice from my grandfather, who had grown rather deaf and had failed to catch something which our cousin had just said to my father.

" Nothing," answered the cousin. " I was just saying that I'd heard from Combray this morning. The weather is appalling down there, and here we've got too much sun."

" Yet the barometer is very low," put in my father.

" Where did you say the weather was bad? " asked my grandfather.

" At Combray."

" Ah! I'm not surprised; whenever it's bad here it's fine at Combray, and vice versa. Good gracious! Talking of Combray, has anyone remembered to tell Legrandin? "

" Yes, don't worry about that, it's been done," said my cousin, whose cheeks, bronzed by an irrepressible growth of beard, dimpled faintly with the satisfaction of having " remembered " it.

At this point my father hurried from the room. I supposed that a sudden change, for better or worse, had occurred. It was simply that Dr. Dieulafoy had just arrived. My father went to receive him in the drawing-room, like the actor who is to come next on the stage. We had sent for him not to cure but to certify, in almost a legal capacity. Dr. Dieulafoy might indeed be a great physician, a marvellous professor; to these several parts, in which he excelled, he added a third, in which he remained for forty years without a rival, a part as original as that of the foil, the scaramouch or the noble father, which consisted in coming to certify an agony or a death. The mere sound of his name foreshadowed the dignity with which he would sustain the part, and when the servant announced: "M. Dieulafoy," one imagined oneself at a play by Molière. To the dignity of his attitude was added, without being conspicuous, the suppleness of a perfect figure. A face in itself too good-looking was toned down by the convention due to distressing circumstances. In the sable majesty of his frock coat the Professor entered the room, melancholy without affectation, uttered not the least word of condolence, which might have been thought insincere, nor was he guilty of the slightest infringement of the rules of tact. At the foot of a deathbed it was he and not the Duc de Guermantes who was the great gentleman. Having examined my grandmother, but not so as to tire her, and with an excess of reserve which was an act of courtesy to the doctor who was treating the case, he murmured a few words to my father, bowed respectfully to my mother to whom I felt that my father had positively to restrain himself from saying: "Professor Dieulafoy." But already our visitor had turned away, not wishing to seem to be soliciting an introduction, and left the room in the most polished manner conceivable, simply taking with him the sealed envelope that was slipped into his hand. He had not appeared to see it, and we ourselves were left wondering for a moment whether we had really given it to him, such a conjurer's nimbleness had he put into the act of making it vanish without thereby losing anything of the gravity—

which was increased rather—of the great consultant in his long frock coat with its silken lapels, and his handsome head full of a noble commiseration. The slowness and vivacity of his movements shewed that, even if he had a hundred other visits to pay and patients waiting, he refused to appear hurried. For he was the embodiment of tact, intelligence and kindness. That eminent man is no longer with us. Other physicians, other professors may have rivalled, may indeed have surpassed him. But the "capacity" in which his knowledge, his physical endowments, his distinguished manners made him triumph exists no longer for want of any successor capable of taking his place. Mamma had not even noticed M. Dieulafoy, everything that was not my grandmother having no existence for her. I remember (and here I anticipate) that at the cemetery, where we saw her, like a supernatural apparition, go up timidly to the grave and seem to be gazing in the wake of a flying form that was already far away, my father having remarked to her: "Old Norpois came to the house and to the church and on here; he gave up a most important committee meeting to come; you ought really to say a word to him, he'll be so gratified if you do," my mother, when the Ambassador stood before her and bowed, could do no more than gently incline a face that shewed no tears. A couple of days earlier—to anticipate once again before returning to where we were just now by the bed on which my grandmother lay dying—while they were watching by the body, Françoise, who, not disbelieving entirely in ghosts, was terrified by the least sound, had said: "I believe that's her." But in place of fear it was an ineffable sweetness that her words aroused in my mother, who would have been so glad that the dead should return, to have her mother with her sometimes still.

To return now to those last hours, " You heard about the telegram her sisters sent us? " my grandfather asked the cousin.

" Yes, Beethoven, they told me about it, it's worth framing; still, I'm not surprised."

" My poor wife, who was so fond of them, too," said my grandfather, wiping away a tear. " We mustn't blame them. They're stark mad, both of them, as I've always said. What's the matter now; aren't you going on with the oxygen? "

My mother spoke: " Oh, but then Mamma will be having more trouble with her breathing."

The doctor reassured her: " Oh, no! The effect of the oxygen will last a good while yet; we can begin it again presently."

It seemed to me that he would not have said this of a dying woman, that if this good effect were to last it meant that we could still do something to keep her alive. The hiss of the oxygen ceased for a few moments. But the happy plaint of her breathing poured out steadily, light, troubled, unfinished, without end, beginning afresh. Now and then it seemed that all was over, her breath stopped, whether owing to one of those transpositions to another octave that occur in the breathing of a sleeper, or else from a natural interruption, an effect of unconsciousness, the progress of asphyxia, some failure of the heart. The doctor stooped to feel my grandmother's pulse, but already, as if a tributary were pouring its current into the dried river-bed, a fresh chant broke out from the interrupted measure. And the first was resumed in another

46

pitch with the same inexhaustible force. Who knows whether, without indeed my grandmother's being conscious of them, a countless throng of happy and tender memories compressed by suffering were not escaping from her now, like those lighter gases which had long been compressed in the cylinders? One would have said that everything that she had to tell us was pouring out, that it was to us that she was addressing herself with this prolixity, this earnestness, this effusion. At the foot of the bed, convulsed by every gasp of this agony, not weeping but now and then drenched with tears, my mother presented the unreasoning desolation of a leaf which the rain lashes and the wind twirls on its stem. They made me dry my eyes before I went up to kiss my grandmother.

"But I thought she couldn't see anything now?" said my father.

"One can never be sure," replied the doctor.

When my lips touched her face, my grandmother's hands quivered, a long shudder ran through her whole body, reflex perhaps, perhaps because certain affections have their hyperaesthesia which recognises through the veil of unconsciousness what they barely need senses to enable them to love. Suddenly my grandmother half rose, made a violent effort, as though struggling to resist an attempt on her life. Françoise could not endure this sight and burst out sobbing. Remembering what the doctor had just said I tried to make her leave the room. At that moment my grandmother opened her eyes. I thrust myself hurriedly in front of Françoise to hide her tears, while my parents were speaking to the sufferer. The sound of the oxygen had ceased; the doctor moved away from the bedside. My grandmother was dead.

An hour or two later Françoise was able for the last time, and without causing them any pain, to comb those beautiful tresses which had only begun to turn grey and hitherto had seemed not so old as my grandmother herself. But now on the contrary it was they alone that set the crown of age on a face grown young again, from which had vanished the wrinkles, the contractions, the swellings, the strains, the hollows which in the long course of years had been carved on it by suffering. As at the far-off time when her parents had chosen for her a bridegroom, she had the features delicately traced by purity and submission, the cheeks glowing with a chaste expectation, with a vision of happiness, with an innocent gaiety even, which the years had gradually destroyed. Life in withdrawing from her had taken with it the disillusionments of life. A smile seemed to be hovering on my grandmother's lips. On that funeral couch, death, like a sculptor of the middle ages, had laid her in the form of a young maiden.

CHAPTER TWO

ALBEIT it was simply a Sunday in autumn, I had been born again, life lay intact before me, for that morning, after a succession of mild days, there had been a cold mist which had not cleared until nearly mid-day. A change in the weather is sufficient to create the world and oneself anew. Formerly, when the wind howled in my chimney, I would listen to the blows which it struck on the iron trap with as keen an emotion as if, like the famous bow-taps with which the C Minor Symphony opens, they had been the irresistible appeal of a mysterious destiny. Every change in the aspect of nature offers us a similar transformation by adapting our desires so as to harmonise with the new form of things. The mist, from the moment of my awakening, had made of me, instead of the centrifugal being which one is on fine days, a self-centred man, longing for the chimney corner and the nuptial couch, a shivering Adam in quest of a sedentary Eve, in this different world.

Between the soft grey tint of a morning landscape and the taste of a cup of chocolate I tried to account for all the originality of the physical, intellectual and moral life which I had taken with me, about a year earlier, to Doncières, and which, blazoned with the oblong form of a bare hillside—always present even when it was invisible—formed in me a series of pleasures entirely distinct from all others, incommunicable to my friends, in the sense that the impressions, richly interwoven with one another, which gave them their orchestral accompaniment were a great deal more characteristic of them, to my subconscious mind, than any facts that I might have related. From this point of view the new world in which the mist of this morning had immersed me was a world already known to me (which only made it more real) and forgotten for some time (which restored all its novelty). And I was able to look at several of the pictures of misty landscapes which my memory had acquired, notably a series of "Mornings at Doncières", including my first morning there in barracks and another, in a neighbouring country house, where I had gone with Saint-Loup to spend the night: in which from the windows, whose curtains I had drawn back at daybreak, before getting into bed again, in the first a trooper, in the second (on the thin margin of a pond and a wood, all the rest of which was engulfed in the uniform and liquid softness of the mist) a coachman busy polishing a strap had appeared to me like those rare figures, scarcely visible to the eye obliged to adapt itself to the mysterious vagueness of their half-lights, which emerge from an obliterated fresco.

It was from my bed that I was looking this afternoon at these pictorial memories, for I had gone back to bed to wait until the hour came at which, taking advantage of the absence of my parents, who had gone for a few days to Combray, I proposed to get up and go to a little play which was being given that evening in Mme. de Ville-parisis's drawing-room. Had they been at home I should perhaps not have ventured to go out; my mother, in the delicacy of her respect for my grandmother's memory, wished the tokens of regret that were paid to it to be freely and sincerely given; she would not have forbidden me this outing, she would have disapproved of it. From Combray, on the other hand, had I consulted her wishes, she would not have replied in a melancholy: "Do just as you like; you are old enough now to know what is right or wrong," but, reproaching herself for having left me alone in Paris, and measuring my grief by her own, would have wished for it distractions of a sort which she would have refused to herself, and which she persuaded herself that my grandmother, solicitous above all things for my health and the preservation of my nervous balance, would have advised me to take.

That morning the furnace of the new steam heater had for the first time been lighted. Its disagreeable sound—an intermittent hiccough—had no part whatsoever in my memories of Doncières. But its prolonged encounter, in me this afternoon, with them was to give it so lasting an affinity with them that whenever, after succeeding more or less in forgetting it, I heard the central heater hiccough again it reminded me of them.

There was no one else in the house but Françoise. The grey light, falling like a fine rain on the earth, wove without ceasing a transparent web through which the Sunday holiday-makers appeared in a silvery sheen. I had flung to the foot of my bed the *Figaro,* for which I had been sending out religiously every morning, ever since I had sent in an article which it had not yet printed; despite the absence of the sun, the intensity of the daylight was an indication that we were still only half-way through the afternoon. The tulle window-curtains, vaporous and friable as they would not have been on a fine day, had that same blend of beauty and fragility that dragon-flies' wings have, and Venetian glass. It depressed me all the more that I should be spending this Sunday by myself because I had sent a note that morning to Mlle. de Stermaria. Robert de Saint-Loup, whom his mother had at length

succeeded in parting—after painful and abortive attempts
—from his mistress, and who immediately afterwards had
been sent to Morocco in the hope of his there forgetting
one whom he had already for some little time ceased to
love, had sent me a line, which had reached me the day
before, announcing his arrival, presently, in France for a
short spell of leave. As he would only be passing through
Paris (where his family were doubtless afraid of seeing
him renew relations with Rachel), he informed me, to
shew me that he had been thinking of me, that he had
met at Tangier Mlle. or rather Mme. (for she had di-
vorced her husband three months after their marriage) de
Stermaria. And Robert, remembering what I had told
him at Balbec, had asked her, on my behalf, to arrange a
meeting. She would be delighted to dine with me, she had
told him, on one of the evenings which, before her return
to Brittany, she would be spending in Paris. He warned
me to lose no time in writing to Mme. de Stermaria, for
she would certainly have arrived before I got his letter.
This had come as no surprise to me, even although I had
had no news of him since, at the time of my grandmother's last illness, he had accused me of perfidy and
treachery. It had then been quite easy to see what must
have happened. Rachel, who liked to provoke his jealousy
—she had other reasons also for wishing me harm—had
persuaded her lover that I had made a dastardly attempt
to have relations with her in his absence. It is probable
that he continued to believe in the truth of this allegation,
but he had ceased to be in love with her, which meant
that its truth or falsehood had become a matter of complete indifference to him, and our friendship alone remained. When, on meeting him again, I attempted to

speak to him about his attack on me his sole answer was a cordial and friendly smile, which gave him the air of begging my pardon; then he turned the conversation to something else. All this was not to say that he did not, a little later, see Rachel occasionally when he was in Paris. The fellow-creatures who have played a leading part in one's life very rarely disappear from it suddenly with any finality. They return to take their old place in it at odd moments (so much so as to lead people to believe in a renewal of old love) before leaving it for ever. Saint-Loup's breach with Rachel had very soon become less painful to him, thanks to the soothing pleasure that was given him by her incessant demands for money. Jealousy, which prolongs the course of love, is not capable of containing many more ingredients than are the other forms of imagination. If one takes with one, when one starts on a journey, three or four images which incidentally one is sure to lose on the way (such as the lilies and anemones heaped on the Ponte Vecchio, or the Persian church shrouded in mist), one's trunk is already pretty full. When one parts from a mistress one would be just as glad, until one has begun to forget her, that she should not become the property of three or four potential protectors whom one has in one's mind's eye, of whom, that is to say, one is jealous: all those whom one does not so picture count for nothing. Now frequent demands for money from a cast-off mistress no more give one a complete idea of her life than charts shewing a high temperature would of her illness. But the latter would at any rate be an indication that she was ill, and the former furnish a presumption, vague enough, it is true, that the forsaken one, or forsaker (whichever she be) cannot have found anything very remarkable in the way of rich protectors. And so each demand is welcomed with the joy which a lull produces in the jealous one's sufferings, while he responds to it at once by dispatching money, for naturally he does not like to think of her being in want of anything, except lovers (one of the three lovers he has in his mind's eye), until time has enabled him to regain his composure and he can learn without the slightest emotion the name of his successor. Sometimes Rachel came in so late at night that she could ask her former lover's permission to lie down beside him until the morning. This was a great comfort to Robert, for it refreshed his memory of how they had, after all, lived in intimacy together merely to see that even if he took the greater part of the bed for himself it did not in the least interfere with her sleep. He realised that she was more comfortable, lying close to his body, than she would have been elsewhere, that she felt herself, by his side—even in an hotel—to be in a bedroom known of old, in which the force of habit prevails and one sleeps better. He felt that his shoulders, his limbs, all of him were for her, even when he was unduly restless, from sleeplessness or from having to get up in the night, things so entirely usual that they could not disturb her, and that the perception of them added still further to her sense of repose.

To revert to where we were, I had been all the more disquieted by Robert's letter in that I could read between the lines what he had not ventured to write more explicitly. "You can most certainly ask her to dine in a private room," he told me. "She is a charming young person, a delightful nature, you will get on splendidly with her, and I am sure you will have a capital evening together." As my parents were returning at the end of the week, on Saturday or Sunday, and as after that I should be forced to dine every evening at home, I had written at once to Mme. de Stermaria, proposing any evening that might suit her, up to Friday. A message was brought back that I should hear from her in writing the same evening, about eight o'clock. The time would have passed quickly enough if I had had, during the afternoon that separated me from her letter, the help of a visit from anyone else. When the hours pass wrapped in conversation one ceases to count, or indeed to notice them, they vanish, and suddenly it is a long way beyond the point at which it escaped you that there reappears the nimble truant time. But if we are alone, our preoccupation, by bringing before us the still distant and incessantly awaited moment with the frequency and uniformity of a ticking pendulum, divides, or rather multiplies the hours by all the minutes which, had we been with friends, we should not have counted. And confronted, by the incessant return of my desire, with the ardent pleasure which I was going to taste—not for some days though, alas!—in Mme. de Stermaria's company, this afternoon, which I should have to spend by myself, seemed to me very empty and very melancholy.

Every now and then I heard the sound of the lift coming up, but it was followed by a second sound, not that for which I was hoping, namely the sound of its coming to a halt at our landing, but another very different sound which the lift made in continuing its progress to the floors above and which, because it so often meant the desertion of my floor when I was expecting a visitor, remained for me at other times, even when I had no wish to see anyone, a sound lugubrious in itself, in which there echoed, as it were, a sentence of solitary confinement. Weary, resigned, busy for several hours still over its immemorial task, the grey day stitched its shimmering needlework of light and shade, and it saddened me to think that I was to be left alone with a thing that knew me no more than would a seamstress who, installed by the window so as to see better while she finished her work, paid no attention to the person present with her in the room. Suddenly, although I had heard no bell, Françoise opened the door to let in Albertine, who came forward smiling, silent, plump, containing in the fulness of her body, made ready so that I might continue living them, come in search of me, the days we had spent together at that Balbec to which I had never since returned. No doubt, whenever we see again a person with whom our relations—however trivial they may have been—are altered, it is like a juxtaposition of two different periods. For this, we do not require that a former mistress should come to call upon us as a friend, all that we need is the visit to Paris of a person whom we had known in the daily round of some particular kind of life, and that this life should have ceased for us, were it no more than a week ago. On each of Albertine's smiling, questioning, blushing features I could read the questions: "And Madame de Villeparisis? And the dancing-master? And the pastry-cook?" When she sat down her back seemed to be saying: "Gracious! There's no cliff here; you don't mind if I sit down beside you, all the same, as I used to do at Balbec?" She was like an enchantress handing me a mirror that reflected time. In this she was like all the people whom we seldom see now but with whom at one time we lived on more intimate terms. With Albertine, however, there was something more than this. Certainly, even at Balbec, in our daily encounters, I had always been surprised when she came in sight, so variable was her appearance from day to day. But now it was difficult to recognise her. Cleared of the pink vapour that used to bathe them, her features had emerged like those of a statue. She had another face, or rather she had a face at last; her body too had grown. There remained scarcely anything now of the shell in which she had been enclosed and on the surface of which, at Balbec, her future outline had been barely visible.

This time, Albertine had returned to Paris earlier than usual. As a rule she came only in the spring, which meant that, already disturbed for some weeks past by the storms that were beating down the first flowers, I did not distinguish, in the elements of the pleasure that I felt, the return of Albertine from that of the fine weather. It was enough that I should be told that she was in Paris and that she had called at the house, for me to see her again like a rose flowering by the sea. I cannot say whether it was the desire for Balbec or for herself that overcame me at such moments; possibly my desire for her was itself a lazy, cowardly, and incomplete method of possessing Balbec, as if to possess a thing materially, to take up one's abode in a town, were equivalent to possessing it spiritually. Besides, even materially, when she was no longer posed by my imagination before a horizon of sea, but sitting still in a room with me, she seemed to me often a very poor specimen of a rose, so poor, indeed, that I would gladly have shut my eyes in order not to observe this or that blemish of its petals, and to imagine instead that I was inhaling the salt air on the beach.

I must say it at this point, albeit I was not then aware of what was to happen only later on. Certainly, it is more reasonable to devote one's life to women than to postage stamps or old snuff-boxes, even to pictures or statues. Only the example of other collectors should be a warning to us to make changes, to have not one woman only but several. Those charming suggestions in which a girl abounds of a sea-beach, of the braided hair of a statue in church, of an old print, of everything that makes one see and admire in her, whenever she appears, a charming composition, those suggestions are not very stable. Live with a woman altogether and you will soon cease to see any of the things that made you love her; though I must add that these two sundered elements can be reunited by jealousy. If, after a long period of life in common, I was to end by seeing nothing more in Albertine than an ordinary woman, an intrigue between her and some person whom she had loved at Balbec would still suffice, perhaps, to reincorporate in her, to amalgamate the beach and the unrolling of the tide. Only, as these secondary suggestions no longer captivate our eyes, it is to the heart that they are perceptible and fatal. We cannot, under so dangerous a form, regard the repetition of the miracle as a thing to be desired. But I am anticipating the course of years. And here I need only state my regret that I did not have the sense simply to have kept my collection of women as people keep their collections of old quizzing glasses, never so complete, in their cabinet, that there is not room always for another and rarer still.

Departing from the customary order of her holiday movements, this year she had come straight from Balbec, where furthermore she had not stayed nearly so late as usual. It was a long time since I had seen her, and as I did not know even by name the people with whom she was in the habit of mixing in Paris, I could form no impression of her during the periods in which she abstained from coming to see me. These lasted often for quite a time. Then, one fine day, in would burst Albertine whose rosy apparitions and silent visits left me little if any better informed as to what she might have been doing in an interval which remained plunged in that darkness of her hidden life which my eyes felt little anxiety to pierce.

This time, however, certain signs seemed to indicate that some new experience must have entered into that life. And yet, perhaps, all that one was entitled to conclude from them was that girls change very rapidly at the age which Albertine had now reached. For instance, her intellect was now more in evidence, and on my reminding her of the day when she had insisted with so much ardour on the superiority of her idea of making Sophocles write: "My dear Racine," she was the first to laugh, quite whole-heartedly, at her own stupidity. "Andrée was quite right; it was stupid of me," she admitted. "Sophocles ought to have begun: 'Sir.'" I replied that the "Sir," and "Dear Sir," of Andrée were no less comic than her own "My dear Racine," or Gisèle's "My dear Friend," but that after all the really stupid people were the Professors who still went on making Sophocles write letters to Racine. Here, however, Albertine was unable to follow me. She could not see in what the silliness consisted; her intelligence was dawning, but had not fully developed. There were other more attractive novelties in her; I felt, in this same pretty girl who had just sat down by my bed, something that was different; and in those lines which, in one's eyes and other features, express one's general attitude towards life, a change of front, a partial conversion, as though there had now been shattered those resistances against which I had hurled my strength in vain at Balbec, one evening, now remote in time, on which we formed a couple symmetrical with but the converse of our present arrangement, since then it had been she who was lying down and I who sat by her bedside. Wishing and not venturing to make certain whether now she would let herself be kissed, every time that she rose to go I asked her to stay beside me a little longer. This was a concession not very easy to obtain, for albeit she had nothing to do (otherwise she would have rushed from the house) she was a person methodical in her habits and moreover not very gracious towards me, seeming scarcely to be at ease in my company, and yet each time, after looking at her watch, she sat down again at my request until finally she had spent several hours with me without my having asked her for anything; the things I was saying to her followed logically those that I had said during the hours before, and bore no relation to what I was thinking about, what I desired from her, remained indefinitely parallel. There is nothing like desire for preventing the thing one says from bearing any resemblance to what one has in one's mind. Time presses, and yet it seems as though we were seeking to gain time by speaking of subjects absolutely alien to that by which we are obsessed. We then arrange that the sentence which we should like to utter shall be accompanied, or rather preluded by a gesture, supposing that is to say that we have not (to give ourself the pleasure of an immediate demonstration and to gratify the curiosity we feel as to the reactions which will follow it, without a word said, without even a "By your leave") already made this gesture. Certainly I was not in the least in love with Albertine; child of the mists outside, she could merely content the imaginative desire which the change of weather had awakened in me and which was midway between the desires that are satisfied by the arts of the kitchen and of monumental sculpture respectively, for it made me dream simultaneously of mingling with my flesh a substance different and warm, and of attaching at some point to my outstretched body a body divergent, as the body of Eve barely holds by the feet to the side of Adam, to whose body hers is almost perpendicular, in those romanesque bas-reliefs on the church at Balbec which represent in so noble and so reposeful a fashion, still almost like a classical frieze, the Creation of Woman; God in them is everywhere followed, as by two ministers, by two little angels in whom the visitor recognises—like winged, swarming summer creatures which winter has surprised and spared—cupids from Herculaneum, still surviving well into the thirteenth century, and winging their last slow flight, weary but never failing in the grace that might be expected of them, over the whole front of the porch.

As for this pleasure which by accomplishing my desire would have set me free from these meditations and which I should have sought quite as readily from any other pretty woman, had I been asked upon what—in the course of this endless flow of talk throughout which I took care to keep from Albertine the one thing that was in my mind —was based my optimistic hypothesis with regard to her possible complaisances, I should perhaps have answered that this hypothesis was due (while the forgotten outlines of Albertine's voice retraced for me the contour of her personality) to the apparition of certain words which did not form part of her vocabulary, or at least not in the acceptation which she now gave them. Thus she said to me that Elstir was stupid, and, on my protesting:

"You don't understand," she replied, smiling, "I mean that it was stupid of him to behave like that; of course I know he's quite a distinguished person, really."

Similarly, wishing to say of the Fontainebleau golf club that it was smart, she declared: "They are quite a selection."

Speaking of a duel that I had fought, she said of my seconds: "What very choice seconds," and looking at my face confessed that she would like to see me "wear a moustache". She even went so far (and my chances appeared then enormous) as to announce, in a phrase of which I would have sworn that she was ignorant a year earlier, that since she had last seen Gisèle there had passed a certain "lapse of time". This was not to say that Albertine had not already possessed, when I was at Balbec, a quite adequate assortment of those expressions which reveal at once that one's people are in easy circumstances, and which, year by year, a mother passes on to her daughter just as she bestows on her, gradually, as the girl grows up, on important occasions, her own jewels. It was evident that Albertine had ceased to be a little girl when one day, to express her thanks for a present which a strange lady had given her, she had said: "I am quite confused." Mme. Bontemps could not help looking across at her husband, whose comment was:

"Gad, she's old for fourteen."

The approach of nubility had been more strongly

marked still when Albertine, speaking of another girl whose tone was bad, said: " One can't even tell whether she's pretty, she paints her face a foot thick." Finally, though still a schoolgirl, she already displayed the manner of a grown woman of her upbringing and station when she said, of some one whose face twitched: " I can't look at him, because it makes me want to do the same," or, if some one else were being imitated: " The absurd thing about it is that when you imitate her voice you look exactly like her." All these are drawn from the social treasury. But it did not seem to me possible that Albertine's natural environment could have supplied her with " distinguished ", used in the sense in which my father would say of a colleague whom he had not actually met, but whose intellectual attainments he had heard praised: " It appears he's quite a distinguished person." " Selection ", even when used of a golf club, seemed to me as incompatible with the Simonet family as it would be, if preceded by the adjective " Natural ", with a text published centuries before the researches of Darwin. " Lapse of time " struck me as being of better augury still. Finally there appeared the evidence of certain upheavals, the nature of which was unknown to me, but sufficient to justify me in all my hopes when Albertine announced, with the satisfaction of a person whose opinion is by no means to be despised:

" To my mind, that is the best thing that could possibly happen. I regard it as the best solution, the stylish way out."

This was so novel, so manifestly an alluvial deposit giving one to suspect such capricious wanderings over soil hitherto unknown to her, that on hearing the words "to my mind" I drew Albertine towards me, and at "I regard" made her sit on the side of my bed.

No doubt it does happen that women of moderate culture, on marrying well-read men, receive such expressions as part of their paraphernalia. And shortly after the metamorphosis which follows the wedding night, when they begin to pay calls, and talk shyly to the friends of their girlhood, one notices with surprise that they have turned into matrons if, in deciding that some person is intelligent, they sound both ' l's in the word; but that is precisely the sign of a change of state, and I could see a difference when I thought of the vocabulary of the Albertine I had known of old—a vocabulary in which the most daring flights were to say of any unusual person: "He's a type," or, if you suggested a game of cards to her: "I've no money to lose," or again, if any of her friends were to reproach her, in terms which she felt to be undeserved: "That really is magnificent!" an expression dictated in such cases by a sort of middle-class tradition almost as old as the *Magnificat* itself, and one which a girl slightly out of temper and confident that she is in the right employs, as the saying is, "quite naturally", that is to say because she has learned the words from her mother, just as she has learned to say her prayers or to greet a friend. All these expressions Mme. Bontemps had imparted to her at the same time as her hatred of the Jews and her feeling for black, which was always suitable and becoming, indeed without any formal instruction, but as the piping of the parent goldfinches serves as a model for that of the young ones, recently hatched, so that they in turn grow into true goldfinches also. But when all was said,

" selection " appeared to me of alien growth and " I regard " encouraging. Albertine was no longer the same; which meant that she would not perhaps act, would not react in the same way.

Not only did I no longer feel any love for her, but I had no longer to consider, as I should have had at Balbec, the risk of shattering in her an affection for myself, which no longer existed. There could be no doubt that she had long since become quite indifferent to me. I was well aware that to her I was in no sense a member now of the " little band " into which I had at one time so anxiously sought and had then been so happy to have secured admission. Besides, as she had no longer even, as in Balbec days, an air of frank good nature, I felt no serious scruples: still I believe that what made me finally decide was another philological discovery. As, continuing to add fresh links to the external chain of talk behind which I hid my intimate desire, I spoke, having Albertine secure now on the corner of my bed, of one of the girls of the little band, one smaller than the rest, whom, nevertheless, I had thought quite pretty, " Yes," answered Albertine, " she reminds me of a little *mousmé*." There had been nothing in the world to shew, when I first knew Albertine, that she had ever heard the word *mousmé*. It was probable that, had things followed their normal course, she would never have learned it, and for my part I should have seen no cause for regret in that, for there is no more horrible word in the language. The mere sound of it makes one's teeth ache as they do when one has put too large a spoonful of ice in one's mouth. But coming from Albertine, as she sat there looking so pretty, not even *"mousmé"* could strike me as unpleasant. On the contrary, I felt it to be a revelation, if not of an outward initiation, at any rate of an inward evolution. Unfortunately it was now time for me to bid her good-bye if I wished her to reach home in time for her dinner, and myself to be out of bed and dressed in time for my own. It was Françoise who was getting it ready; she did not like having to keep it back, and must already have found it an infringement of one of the articles of her code that Albertine, in the absence of my parents, should be paying me so prolonged a visit, and one which was going to make everything late. But before *" mousmé "* all these arguments fell to the ground and I hastened to say:

" Just fancy; I'm not in the least ticklish; you can go on tickling me for an hour on end and I won't even feel it."

" Really? "

" I assure you."

She understood, doubtless, that this was the awkward expression of a desire on my part, for, like a person who offers to give you an introduction for which you have not ventured to ask him, though what you have said has shewn him that it would be of great service to you:

" Would you like me to try? " she inquired, with womanly meekness.

" Just as you like, but you would be more comfortable if you lay down properly on the bed."

" Like that? "

" No; get right on top."

" You're sure I'm not too heavy? "

As she uttered these words the door opened and

66

Françoise, carrying a lamp, came in. Albertine had just time to fling herself back upon her chair. Perhaps Françoise had chosen this moment to confound us, having been listening at the door or even peeping through the keyhole. But there was no need to suppose anything of the sort; she might have scorned to assure herself, by the use of her eyes, of what her instinct must plainly enough have detected, for by dint of living with me and my parents her fears, her prudence, her alertness, her cunning had ended by giving her that instinctive and almost prophetic knowledge of us all that the mariner has of the sea, the quarry of the hunter, and, of the malady, if not the physician, often at any rate the patient. The amount of knowledge that she managed to acquire would have astounded a stranger, and with as good reason as does the advanced state of certain arts and sciences among the ancients, seeing that there was practically no source of information open to them. (Her sources were no larger. They were a few casual remarks forming barely a twentieth part of our conversation at dinner, caught on the wing by the butler and inaccurately transmitted to the kitchen.) Again, her mistakes were due, like theirs, like the fables in which Plato believed, rather to a false conception of the world and to pre-conceived ideas than to the insufficiency of the materials at her disposal. Only the other day, has it not been possible for the most important discoveries as to the habits of insects to be made by a scientist who had access to no laboratory and used no instruments of any sort? But if the drawbacks arising from her menial position had not prevented her from acquiring a stock of learning indispensable to the art which was its ultimate goal—

and which consisted in putting us to confusion by communicating to us the results of her discoveries—the limitations under which she worked had done more; in this case the impediment, not content with merely not paralysing the flight of her imagination, had greatly strengthened it. Of course Françoise never let slip any artificial device, those for example of diction and attitude. Since (if she never believed what we said to her, hoping that she would believe it) she admitted without any shadow of doubt the truth of anything that any person of her own condition in life might tell her, however absurd, which might at the same time prove shocking to our ideas, just as her way of listening to our assertions bore witness to her incredulity, so the accents in which she reported (the use of indirect speech enabling her to hurl the most deadly insults at us with impunity) the narrative of a cook who had told her how she had threatened her employers, and won from them, by treating them before all the world like dirt, any number of privileges and concessions, shewed that the story was to her as gospel. Françoise went so far as to add: " I'm sure, if I had been the mistress I should have been quite vexed." In vain might we, despite our scant sympathy at first with the lady on the fourth floor, shrug our shoulders, as though at an unlikely fable, at this report of so shocking an example; in making it the teller was able to speak with the crushing, the lacerating force of the most unquestionable, most irritating affirmation.

But above all, just as great writers often attain to a power of concentration from which they would have been dispensed under a system of political liberty or literary anarchy, when they are bound by the tyranny of a monarch or of a school of poetry, by the severity of prosodic laws or of a state religion, so Françoise, not being able to reply to us in an explicit fashion, spoke like Tiresias and would have written like Tacitus. She managed to embody everything that she could not express directly in a sentence for which we could not find fault with her without accusing ourselves, indeed in less than a sentence, in a silence, in the way in which she placed a thing in a room.

Thus when I happened to leave, by accident, on my table, among a pile of other letters, one which it was imperative that she should not see, because, let us say, it referred to her with a dislike which afforded a presumption of the same feeling towards her in the recipient as in the writer, that evening, if I came home with a troubled conscience and went straight to my room, there on top of my letters, neatly arranged in a symmetrical pile, the compromising document caught my eye as it could not possibly have failed to catch the eye of Françoise, placed by her right at the top, almost separated from the rest, in a prominence that was a form of speech, that had an eloquence all its own, and, as I stood in the doorway, made me shudder like a cry. She excelled in the preparation of these scenic effects, intended so to enlighten the spectator, in her absence, that he already knew that she knew everything when in due course she made her appearance. She possessed, for thus making an inanimate object speak, the art, at once inspired and painstaking, of Irving or Frédéric Lemaître. On this occasion, holding over Albertine and myself the lighted lamp whose searching beams missed none of the still visible depressions which the girl's body had hollowed in the counterpane, Françoise made one think of a picture of " Justice throwing light upon Crime." Albertine's face did not suffer by this illumination. It revealed on her cheeks the same sunny burnish that had charmed me at Balbec. This face of Albertine, the general effect of which sometimes was, out of doors, a sort of milky pallor, now shewed, according as the lamp shone on them, surfaces so dazzlingly, so uniformly coloured, so firm, so glowing that one might have compared them to the sustained flesh tints of certain flowers. Taken aback meanwhile by the unexpected entry of Françoise, I exclaimed:

" What? The lamp already? I say, the light is strong! "

My object, as may be imagined, was by the second of these ejaculations to account for my confusion, by the first to excuse my lateness in rising. Françoise replied with a cruel ambiguity:

" Do you want me to extinglish it? "

"—guish! " Albertine slipped into my ear, leaving me charmed by the familiar vivacity with which, taking me at once for teacher and for accomplice, she insinuated this psychological affirmation as though asking a grammatical question.

When Françoise had left the room and Albertine was seated once again on my bed:

" Do you know what I'm afraid of? " I asked her. " It is that if we go on like this I may not be able to resist the temptation to kiss you.

" That would be a fine pity."

I did not respond at once to this invitation, which another man might even have found superfluous, for Albertine's way of pronouncing her words was so carnal,

so seductive that merely in speaking to you she seemed
to be caressing you. A word from her was a favour,
and her conversation covered you with kisses. And yet
it was highly attractive to me, this invitation. It would
have been so, indeed, coming from any pretty girl of
Albertine's age; but that Albertine should be now so
accessible to me gave me more than pleasure, brought
before my eyes a series of images that bore the stamp
of beauty. I recalled the original Albertine standing between me and the beach, almost painted upon a background of sea, having for me no more real existence
than those figures seen on the stage, when one knows
not whether one is looking at the actress herself who
is supposed to appear, at an understudy who for the
moment is taking her principal's part, or at a mere
projection from a lantern. Then the real woman had
detached herself from the luminous mass, had come
towards me, with the sole result that I had been able
to see that she had nothing in real life of that amorous
facility which one supposed to be stamped upon her in
the magic pictures. I had learned that it was not possible
to touch her, to embrace her, that one might only talk
to her, that for me she was no more a woman than the
jade grapes, an inedible decoration at one time in fashion
on dinner tables, were really fruit. And now she was
appearing to me in a third plane, real as in the second
experience that I had had of her but facile as in the
first; facile, and all the more deliciously so in that I had
so long imagined that she was not. My surplus knowledge of life (of a life less uniform, less simple than I
had at first supposed it to be) inclined me provisionally
towards agnosticism. What can one positively affirm,

when the thing that one thought probable at first has then shewn itself to be false and in the third instance turns out true? And alas, I was not yet at the end of my discoveries with regard to Albertine. In any case, even if there had not been the romantic attraction of this disclosure of a greater wealth of planes revealed one after another by life (an attraction the opposite of that which Saint-Loup had felt during our dinners at Rivebelle on recognising beneath the mask with which the course of existence had overlaid them, in a calm face, features to which his lips had once been pressed), the knowledge that to kiss Albertine's cheeks was a possible thing was a pleasure perhaps greater even than that of kissing them. What a difference between possessing a woman to whom one applies one's body alone, because she is no more than a piece of flesh, and possessing the girl whom one used to see on the beach with her friends on certain days without even knowing why one saw her on those days and not on others, which made one tremble to think that one might not see her again. Life had obligingly revealed to one in its whole extent the romance of this little girl, had lent one, for the study of her, first one optical instrument, then another, and had added to one's carnal desire an accompaniment which multiplied it an hundredfold and diversified it with those other desires, more spiritual and less easily assuaged, which do not emerge from their torpor, leaving carnal desire to move by itself, when it aims only at the conquest of a piece of flesh, but which to gain possession of a whole tract of memories, whence they have felt the wretchedness of exile, rise in a tempest round about it, enlarge, extend it, are unable to follow it to the accomplishment, the assimilation, impossible in the form in which it is looked for, of an immaterial reality, but wait for this desire half way and at the moment of recollection, of return furnish it afresh with their escort; to kiss, instead of the cheeks of the first comer, however cool and fresh they might be, but anonymous, with no secret, with no distinction, those of which I had so long been dreaming, would be to know the taste, the savour of a colour on which I had endlessly gazed. One has seen a woman, a mere image in the decorative setting of life, like Albertine, outlined against the sea, and then one has been able to take that image, to detach it, to bring it close to oneself, gradually to discern its solidity, its colours, as though one had placed it behind the glasses of a stereoscope. It is for this reason that the women who are a little difficult, whose resistance one does not at once overcome, of whom one does not indeed know at first whether one ever will overcome it, are alone interesting. For to know them, to approach them, to conquer them is to make fluctuate in form, in dimensions, in relief the human image, is an example of relativity in the appreciation of an image which it is delightful to see afresh when it has resumed the slender proportions of a silhouette in the setting of one's life. The women one meets first of all in a brothel are of no interest because they remain invariable.

In addition, Albertine preserved, inseparably attached to her, all my impressions of a series of seascapes of which I was particularly fond. I felt that it was possible for me, on the girl's two cheeks, to kiss the whole of the beach at Balbec.

" If you really don't mind my kissing you, I would

rather put it off for a little and choose a good moment. Only you mustn't forget that you've said I may. I shall want a voucher: 'Valid for one kiss.'"

" Shall I have to sign it? "

" But if I took it now, should I be entitled to another later on? "

" You do make me laugh with your vouchers; I shall issue a new one every now and then."

" Tell me; just one thing more. You know, at Balbec, before I had been introduced to you, you used often to have a hard, calculating look; you can't tell me what you were thinking about when you looked like that? "

" No; I don't remember at all."

" Wait; this may remind you: one day your friend Gisèle put her feet together and jumped over the chair an old gentleman was sitting in. Try to remember what was in your mind at that moment."

" Gisèle was the one we saw least of; she did belong to the band, I suppose, but not properly. I expect I thought that she was very ill-bred and common."

" Oh, is that all? "

I should certainly have liked, before kissing her, to be able to fill her afresh with the mystery which she had had for me on the beach before I knew her, to find latent in her the place in which she had lived earlier still; for that, at any rate, if I knew nothing of it, I could substitute all my memories of our life at Balbec, the sound of the waves rolling up and breaking beneath my window, the shouts of the children. But when I let my eyes glide over the charming pink globe of her cheeks, the gently curving surfaces of which ran up to expire beneath the first foothills of her piled black tresses which

ran in undulating mountain chains, thrust out escarped
ramparts and moulded the hollows of deep valleys, I
could not help saying to myself: " Now at last, after
failing at Balbec, I am going to learn the fragrance of
the secret rose that blooms in Albertine's cheeks, and,
since the cycles through which we are able to make
things and people pass in the course of our existence
are comparatively few, perhaps I ought now to regard
mine as nearing its end when, having made to emerge
from its remoteness the flowering face that I had chosen
from among all others, I shall have brought it into this
new plane in which I shall at last acquire a tactual experience of it with my lips." I told myself this because
I believed that there was such a thing as knowledge
acquired by the lips; I told myself that I was going
to know the taste of this fleshly rose, because I had
never stopped to think that man, a creature obviously
less rudimentary in structure than the sea-urchin or
even the whale, is nevertheless still unprovided with a
certain number of essential organs, and notably possesses
none that will serve for kissing. The place of this absent
organ he supplies with his lips, and thereby arrives perhaps at a slightly more satisfying result than if he were
reduced to caressing the beloved with a horny tusk.
But a pair of lips, designed to convey to the palate
the taste of whatever whets the appetite, must be content, without ever realising their mistake or admitting
their disappointment, with roaming over the surface
and with coming to a halt at the barrier of the impenetrable but irresistible cheek. Besides, at such moments,
at the actual contact between flesh and flesh, the lips,
even supposing them to become more expert and better

endowed, could taste no better probably the savour which nature prevents their ever actually grasping, for in that desolate zone in which they are unable to find their proper nourishment, they are alone; the sense of sight, then that of smell have long since deserted them. To begin with, as my mouth began gradually to approach the cheeks which my eyes had suggested to it that it should kiss, my eyes, changing their position, saw a different pair of cheeks; the throat, studied at closer range and as though through a magnifying glass shewed in its coarse grain a robustness which modified the character of the face.

Apart from the most recent applications of the art of photography—which set crouching at the foot of a cathedral all the houses which, time and again, when we stood near them, have appeared to us to reach almost to the height of the towers, drill and deploy like a regiment, in file, in open order, in mass, the same famous and familiar structures, bring into actual contact the two columns on the Piazzetta which a moment ago were so far apart, thrust away the adjoining dome of the Salute, and in a pale and toneless background manage to include a whole immense horizon within the span of a bridge, in the embrasure of a window, among the leaves of a tree that stands in the foreground and is portrayed in a more vigorous tone, give successively as setting to the same church the arched walls of all the others—I can think of nothing that can so effectively as a kiss evoke from what we believe to be a thing with one definite aspect, the hundred other things which it may equally well be since each is related to a view of it no less legitimate. In short, just as at Balbec Albertine had often appeared to me different, so now, as if, wildly accelerating the speed of the changes of aspect and changes of colouring which a person presents to us in the course of our various encounters, I had sought to contain them all in the space of a few seconds so as to reproduce experimentally the phenomenon which diversifies the individuality of a fellow creature, and to draw out one from another, like a nest of boxes, all the possibilities that it contains, in this brief passage of my lips towards her cheek it was ten Albertines that I saw; this single girl being like a goddess with several heads, that which I had last seen, if I tried to approach it, gave place to another. At least so long as I had not touched it, that head, I could still see it, a faint perfume reached me from it. But alas—for in this matter of kissing our nostrils and eyes are as ill placed as our lips are shaped—suddenly my eyes ceased to see; next, my nose, crushed by the collision, no longer perceived any fragrance, and, without thereby gaining any clearer idea of the taste of the rose of my desire, I learned, from these unpleasant signs, that at last I was in the act of kissing Albertine's cheek.

Was it because we were enacting—as may be illustrated by the rotation of a solid body—the converse of our scene together at Balbec, because it was I, now, who was lying in bed and she who sat beside me, capable of evading any brutal attack and of dictating her pleasure to me, that she allowed me to take so easily now what she had refused me on the former occasion with so forbidding a frown? (No doubt from that same frown the voluptuous expression which her face assumed now at the approach of my lips differed only by a deviation of its lines immeasurably minute but one in which may be contained all the disparity that there is between the gesture of " finishing off " a wounded man and that of bringing him relief, between a sublime and a hideous portrait.) Not knowing whether I had to give the credit, and to feel grateful for this change of attitude to some unwitting benefactor who in these last months, in Paris or at Balbec, had been working on my behalf, I supposed that the respective positions in which we were now placed might account for it. It was quite another explanation, however, that Albertine offered me; this, in short: " Oh, well, you see, that time at Balbec I didn't know you properly. For all I knew, you might have meant mischief." This argument left me in perplexity. Albertine was no doubt sincere in advancing it. So difficult is it for a woman to recognise in the movements of her limbs, in the sensations felt by her body in the course of an intimate conversation with a friend, the unknown sin into which she would tremble to think that a stranger was planning her fall.

In any case, whatever the modifications that had occurred at some recent time in her life, which might perhaps have explained why it was that she now readily accorded to my momentary and purely physical desire what at Balbec she had with horror refused to allow to my love, another far more surprising manifested itself in Albertine that same evening as soon as her caresses had procured in me the satisfaction which she could not have failed to notice, which, indeed, I had been afraid might provoke in her the instinctive movement of revulsion and offended modesty which Gilberte had given at a corresponding moment behind the laurel shrubbery in the Champs-Elysées.

The exact opposite happened. Already, when I had first made her lie on my bed and had begun to fondle her, Albertine had assumed an air which I did not remember in her, of docile good will, of an almost childish simplicity. Obliterating every trace of her customary anxieties and interests, the moment preceding pleasure, similar in this respect to the moment after death, had restored to her rejuvenated features what seemed like the innocence of earliest childhood. And no doubt everyone whose special talent is suddenly brought into play becomes modest, devoted, charming; especially if by this talent he knows that he is giving us a great pleasure, he is himself happy in the display of it, anxious to present it to us in as complete a form as possible. But in this new expression on Albertine's face there was more than a mere profession of disinterestedness, conscience, generosity, a sort of conventional and unexpected devotion; and it was farther than to her own childhood, it was to the infancy of the race that she had reverted. Very different from myself who had looked for nothing more than a physical alleviation, which I had finally secured, Albertine seemed to feel that it would indicate a certain coarseness on her part were she to seem to believe that this material pleasure could be unaccompanied by a moral sentiment or was to be regarded as terminating anything. She, who had been in so great a hurry a moment ago, now, presumably because she felt that kisses implied love and that love took precedence of all other duties, said when I reminded her of her dinner:

"Oh, but that doesn't matter in the least; I have plenty of time."

She seemed embarrassed by the idea of getting up and

going immediately after what had happened, embarrassed by good manners, just as Françoise when, without feeling thirsty, she had felt herself bound to accept with a seemly gaiety the glass of wine which Jupien offered her, would never have dared to leave him as soon as the last drops were drained, however urgent the call of duty. Albertine—and this was perhaps, with another which the reader will learn in due course, one of the reasons which had made me unconsciously desire her—was one of the incarnations of the little French peasant whose type may be seen in stone at Saint-André-des-Champs. As in Françoise, who presently nevertheless was to become her deadly enemy, I recognised in her a courtesy towards friend and stranger, a sense of decency, of respect for the bedside.

Françoise who, after the death of my aunt, felt obliged to speak only in a plaintive tone, would, in the months that preceded her daughter's marriage, have been quite shocked if, when the young couple walked out together, the girl had not taken her lover's arm. Albertine lying motionless beside me said:

"What nice hair you have; what nice eyes; you are a dear boy."

When, after pointing out to her that it was getting late, I added: "You don't believe me?" she replied, what was perhaps true but could be so only since the minute before and for the next few hours:

"I always believe you."

She spoke to me of myself, my family, my social position. She said: "Oh, I know your parents know some very nice people. You are a friend of Robert Forestier and Suzanne Delage." For the moment these names conveyed absolutely nothing to me. But suddenly I remembered that I had indeed played as a child in the Champs-Elysées with Robert Forestier, whom I had never seen since then. As for Suzanne Delage, she was the great-niece of Mme. Blatin, and I had once been going to a dancing lesson, and had even promised to take a small part in a play that was being acted in her mother's drawing-room. But the fear of being sent into fits of laughter, and of a bleeding nose, had made me decline, so that I had never set eyes on her. I had at the most a vague idea that I had once heard that the Swanns' governess with the feather in her hat had at one time been with the Delages, but perhaps it was only a sister of this governess, or a friend. I protested to Albertine that Robert Forestier and Suzanne Delage occupied a very small place in my life. " That may be; but your mothers are friends, I can place you by that. I often pass Suzanne Delage in the Avenue de Messine, I admire her style." Our mothers were acquainted only in the imagination of Mme. Bontemps, who having heard that I had at one time played with Robert Forestier, to whom, it appeared, I used to recite poetry, had concluded from that that we were bound by family ties. She could never, I gathered, hear my mother's name mentioned without observing: " Oh yes, she is in the Delage Forestier set," giving my parents a good mark which they had done nothing to deserve.

Apart from this, Albertine's social ideas were fatuous in the extreme. She regarded the Simonnets with a double ' n ' as inferior not only to the Simonets with a single ' n ' but to everyone in the world. That some one else should bear the same name as yourself without belonging to your family is an excellent reason for despising him. Of course there are exceptions. It may happen that two Simonnets (introduced to one another at one of those gatherings where one feels the need to converse, no matter on what subject, and where moreover one is instinctively well disposed towards strangers, for instance in a funeral procession on its way to the cemetery), finding that they have the same name, will seek with a mutual friendliness though without success to discover a possible connexion. But that is only an exception. Plenty of people are of dubious character, but we either know nothing or care nothing about them. If, however, a similarity of names brings to our door letters addressed to them, or vice versa, we at once feel a mistrust, often justified, as to their moral worth. We are afraid of being confused with them, we forestall the mistake by a grimace of disgust when any-one refers to them in our hearing. When we read our own name, as borne by them, in the newspaper, they seem to have usurped it. The transgressions of other members of the social organism leave us cold. We lay the burden of them more heavily upon our namesakes. The hatred which we bear towards the other Simonnets is all the stronger in that it is not a personal feeling but has been trasmitted by heredity. After the second generation we remember only the expression of disgust with which our grandparents used to refer to the other Simonnets, we know nothing of the reason, we should not be surprised to learn that it had begun with a murder. Until, as is not uncommon, the time comes when a male and female Simonnet, who are not related in any way, are joined together in matrimony and so repair the breach.

Not only did Albertine speak to me of Robert Forestier and Suzanne Delage, but spontaneously, with that impulse to confide which the approximation of two human bodies creates, that is to say at first, before it has engendered a special duplicity and reticence in one person towards the other, she told me a story about her own family and one of Andrée's uncles, as to which, at Balbec, she had refused to utter a word; thinking that now she ought not to appear to have any secrets in which I might not share. From this moment, had her dearest friend said anything to her against me, she would have made it her duty to inform me. I insisted upon her going home, and finally she did go, but so ashamed on my account at my discourtesy that she laughed almost as though to apologise for me, as a hostess to whose party you have gone without dressing makes the best of you but is offended nevertheless.

"Are you laughing at me?" I inquired.

"I am not laughing, I am smiling at you," she replied lovingly. "When am I going to see you again?" she went on, as though declining to admit that what had just happened between us, since it is generally the crowning consummation, might not be at least the prelude to a great friendship, a friendship already existing which we should have to discover, to confess, and which alone could account for the surrender we had made of ourselves.

"Since you give me leave, I shall send for you when I can." I dared not let her know that I was subordinating everything else to the chance of seeing Mme. de Stermaria. "It will have to be at short notice, unfortunately," I went on, "I never know beforehand. Would it be possible for me to send round for you in the evenings, when I am free?"

"It will be quite possible in a little while, I am going to have a latch-key of my own. But just at present it can't be done. Anyhow I shall come round to-morrow or next day in the afternoon. You needn't see me if you're busy."

On reaching the door, surprised that I had not anticipated her, she offered me her cheek, feeling that there was no need now for any coarse physical desire to prompt us to kiss one another. The brief relations in which we had just indulged being of the sort to which an absolute intimacy and a heartfelt choice often tend, Albertine had felt it incumbent upon her to improvise and add provisionally to the kisses which we had exchanged on my bed the sentiment of which those kisses would have been the symbol for a knight and his lady such as they might have been conceived in the mind of a gothic minstrel.

When she had left me, this young Picard, who might have been carved on his porch by the image-maker of Saint-André-des-Champs, Françoise brought me a letter which filled me with joy, for it was from Mme. de Stermaria, who accepted my invitation to dinner. From Mme. de Stermaria, that was to say for me not so much from the real Mme. de Stermaria as from her of whom I had been thinking all day before Albertine's arrival. It is the terrible deception of love that it begins by engaging us in play not with a woman of the external world but with a puppet fashioned and kept in our brain, the only form of her moreover that we have always at our disposal, the only one that we shall ever possess, one which the arbitrary power of memory, almost as

84

absolute as that of imagination, may have made as different from the real woman as had been from the real Balbec the Balbec of my dreams; an artificial creation to which by degrees, and to our own hurt, we shall force the real woman into resemblance.

Albertine had made me so late that the play had just finished when I entered Mme. de Villeparisis's drawing-room; and having little desire to be caught in the stream of guests who were pouring out, discussing the great piece of news, the separation, said to be already effected, of the Duc de Guermantes from his wife, I had, until I should have an opportunity of shaking hands with my hostess, taken my seat on an empty sofa in the outer room, when from the other, in which she had no doubt had her chair in the very front row of all, I saw emerging, majestic, ample and tall in a flowing gown of yellow satin upon which stood out in relief huge black poppies, the Duchess herself. The sight of her no longer disturbed me in the least. There had been a day when, laying her hands on my forehead (as was her habit when she was afraid of hurting my feelings) and saying: "You really must stop hanging about trying to meet Mme. de Guermantes. All the neighbours are talking about you. Besides, look how ill your grandmother is, you really have something more serious to think about than waylaying a woman who only laughs at you," in a moment, like a hypnotist who brings one back from the distant country in which one imagined oneself to be, and opens one's eyes for one, or like the doctor who, by recalling one to a sense of duty and reality, cures one of an imaginary disease in which one has been indulging one's fancy, my mother had awakened me from an unduly

protracted dream. The rest of the day had been consecrated to a last farewell to this malady which I was
renouncing; I had sung, for hours on end and weeping
as I sang, the sad words of Schubert's *Adieu*:

> Farewell, strange voices call thee
> Away from me, dear sister of the angels.

And then it had finished. I had given up my morning
walks, and with so little difficulty that I thought myself
justified in the prophecy (which we shall see was to
prove false later on) that I should easily grow accustomed
in the course of my life to ceasing to see a woman. And
when, shortly afterwards, Françoise had reported to me
that Jupien, anxious to enlarge his business, was looking
for a shop in the neighbourhood, wishing to find one
for him (quite happy, moreover, when strolling along
a street which already from my bed I had heard luminously vociferous like a peopled beach, to see behind the
raised iron shutters of the dairies the young milk-girls
with their white sleeves), I had been able to begin these
excursions again. Nor did I feel the slightest constraint;
for I was conscious that I was no longer going out with
the object of seeing Mme. de Guermantes; much as a
married woman who takes endless precautions so long
as she has a lover, from the day on which she has broken
with him leaves his letters lying about, at the risk of
disclosing to her husband an infidelity which ceased to
alarm her the moment she ceased to be guilty of it. What
troubled me now was the discovery that almost every
house sheltered some unhappy person. In one the wife
was always in tears because her husband was unfaithful
to her. In the next it was the other way about. In

another a hardworking mother, beaten black and blue by a drunkard son, was endeavouring to conceal her sufferings from the eyes of the neighbours. Quite half of the human race was in tears. And when I came to know the people who composed it I saw that they were so exasperating that I asked myself whether it might not be the adulterous husband and wife (who were so simply because their lawful happiness had been withheld from them, and shewed themselves charming and faithful to everyone but their respective wife and husband) who were in the right. Presently I ceased to have even the excuse of being useful to Jupien for continuing my morning wanderings. For we learned that the cabinet-maker in our courtyard, whose workrooms were separated from Jupien's shop only by the flimsiest of partitions, was shortly to be " given notice " by the Duke's agent because his hammering made too much noise. Jupien could have hoped for nothing better; the workrooms had a basement for storing timber, which communicated with our cellars. He could keep his coal in this, he could knock down the partition, and would then have a huge shop all in one room. But even without the amusement of house-hunting on his behalf I had continued to go out every day before luncheon, just as Jupien himself, finding the rent that M. de Guermantes was asking him exorbitant, was allowing the premises to be inspected in the hope that, discouraged by his failure to find a tenant, the Duke would resign himself to accepting a lower offer. Françoise, noticing that, even at an hour when no prospective tenant was likely to call, the porter left the door of the empty shop on the latch, scented a trap laid by him to entice the young woman who was engaged to the

Guermantes footman (they would find a lovers' retreat there) and to catch them red-handed.

However that might be, and for all that I had no longer to find Jupien a new shop, I still went out before luncheon. Often, on these excursions, I met M. de Norpois. It would happen that, conversing as he walked with a colleague, he cast at me a glance which after making a thorough scrutiny of my person returned to his companion without his having smiled at me or given me any more sign of recognition than if he had never set eyes on me before. For, with these eminent diplomats, looking at you in a certain way is intended to let you know not that they have seen you but that they have not seen you and that they have some serious question to discuss with the colleague who is accompanying them. A tall woman whom I frequently encountered near the house was less discreet with me. For in spite of the fact that I did not know her, she would turn round to look at me, would wait for me, unavailingly, before shop windows, smile at me as though she were going to kiss me, make gestures indicative of a complete surrender. She resumed an icy coldness towards me if anyone appeared whom she knew. For a long time now in these morning walks, thinking only of what I had to do, were it but the most trivial purchase of a newspaper, I had chosen the shortest way, with no regret were it outside the ordinary course which the Duchess followed in her walks, and if on the other hand it lay along that course, without either compunction or concealment, because it no longer appeared to me the forbidden way on which I should snatch from an ungrateful woman the favour of setting eyes on her against her will. But it had never

occurred to me that my recovery, when it restored me to
a normal attitude towards Mme. de Guermantes, would
have a corresponding effect on her, and so render possible
a friendliness, even a friendship in which I no longer
felt any interest. Until then, the efforts of the entire
world banded together to bring me into touch with her
would have been powerless to counteract the evil spell
that is cast by an ill-starred love. Fairies more powerful
than mankind have decreed that in such cases nothing
can avail us until the day on which we have uttered
sincerely and from our hearts the formula: "I am no
longer in love." I had been vexed with Saint-Loup for
not having taken me to see his aunt. But he was no more
capable than anyone else of breaking an enchantment.
So long as I was in love with Mme. de Guermantes, the
marks of politeness that I received from others, their
compliments actually distressed me, not only because they
did not come from her but because she would never hear
of them. And yet even if she had known of them it would
not have been of the slightest use to me. Indeed, among
the lesser auxiliaries to success in love, an absence, the
declining of an invitation to dinner, an unintentional,
unconscious harshness are of more service than all the
cosmetics and fine clothes in the world. There would be
plenty of social success, were people taught upon these
lines the art of succeeding.

As she swept through the room in which I was sitting,
her mind filled with thoughts of friends whom I did not
know and whom she would perhaps be meeting presently
at some other party, Mme. de Guermantes caught sight
of me on my sofa, genuinely indifferent and seeking only
to be polite whereas while I was in love I had tried so

desperately, without ever succeeding, to assume an air of indifference; she swerved aside, came towards me and, reproducing the smile she had worn that evening at the Opéra-Comique, which the unpleasant feeling of being cared for by some one for whom she did not care was no longer there to obliterate: " No, don't move; you don't mind if I sit down beside you for a moment? " she asked, gracefully gathering in her immense skirt which otherwise would have covered the entire sofa.

Of less stature than she, who was further expanded by the volume of her gown, I was almost brushed by her exquisite bare arm round which a faint, innumerable down rose in perpetual smoke like a golden mist, and by the fringe of her fair tresses which wafted their fragrance over me. Having barely room to sit down, she could not turn easily to face me, and so, obliged to look straight before her rather than in my direction, assumed the sort of dreamy, sweet expression one sees in a portrait.

" Have you any news of Robert? " she inquired.

At that moment Mme. de Villeparisis entered the room.

" Well, sir, you arrive at a fine time, when we do see you here for once in a way! " And noticing that I was talking to her niece, concluding, perhaps, that we were more intimate than she had supposed: " But don't let me interrupt your conversation with Oriane," she went on, and (for these good offices as pander are part of the duties of the perfect hostess): " You wouldn't care to dine with her here on Thursday? "

It was the day on which I was to entertain Mme. de Stermaria, so I declined.

" Saturday, then? "

As my mother was returning on Saturday or Sunday,

it would never do for me not to stay at home every evening to dine with her; I therefore declined this invitation also.

" Ah, you're not an easy person to get hold of."

" Why do you never come to see me? " inquired Mme. de Guermantes when Mme. de Villeparisis had left us to go and congratulate the performers and present the leading lady with a bunch of roses upon which the hand that offered it conferred all its value, for it had cost no more than twenty francs. (This, incidentally, was as high as she ever went when an artist had performed only once. Those who gave their services at all her afternoons and evenings throughout the season received roses painted by the Marquise.)

" It's such a bore that we never see each other except in other people's houses. Since you won't meet me at dinner at my aunt's, why not come and dine with me? " Various people who had stayed to the last possible moment, upon one pretext or another, but were at length preparing to leave, seeing that the Duchess had sat down to talk to a young man on a seat so narrow as just to contain them both, thought that they must have been misinformed, that it was the Duchess, and not the Duke, who was seeking a separation, and on my account. Whereupon they hastened to spread abroad this intelligence. I had better grounds than anyone to be aware of its falsehood. But I was myself surprised that at one of those difficult periods in which a separation that is not yet completed is beginning to take effect, the Duchess, instead of withdrawing from society, should go out of her way to invite a person whom she knew so slightly. The suspicion crossed my mind that it had been the

Duke alone who had been opposed to her having me in the house, and that now that he was leaving her she saw no further obstacle to her surrounding herself with the people that she liked.

A minute earlier I should have been stupefied had anyone told me that Mme. de Guermantes was going to ask me to call on her, let alone to dine with her. I might be perfectly aware that the Guermantes drawing-room could not furnish those particular refinements which I had extracted from the name of its occupants, the fact that it had been forbidden ground to me, by obliging me to give it the same kind of existence that we give to the drawing-rooms of which we have read the description in a novel, or seen the image in a dream, made me, even when I was certain that it was just like any other, imagine it as quite different. Between myself and it was the barrier at which reality ends. To dine with the Guermantes was like travelling to a place I had long wished to see, making a desire emerge from my brain and take shape before my eyes, forming acquaintance with a dream. At the most, I might have supposed that it would be one of those dinners to which one's hosts invite one with: "Do come; there'll be *absolutely* nobody but ourselves," pretending to attribute to the pariah the alarm which they themselves feel at the thought of his mixing with their other friends, seeking indeed to convert into an enviable privilege, reserved for their intimates alone, the quarantine of the outsider, hopelessly uncouth, whom they are befriending. I felt on the contrary that Mme. de Guermantes was anxious for me to enjoy the most delightful society that she had to offer me when she went on, projecting as she spoke before my eyes as it were the

violet-hued loveliness of a visit to Fabrice's aunt with
the miracle of an introduction to Count Mosca:

"On Friday, now, couldn't you? There are just a few
people coming; the Princesse de Parme, who is charming,
not that I'ld ask you to meet anyone who wasn't nice."

Discarded in the intermediate social grades which are
engaged in a perpetual upward movement, the family
still plays an important part in certain stationary grades,
such as the lower middle class and the semi-royal aristocracy, which latter cannot seek to raise itself since
above it, from its own special point of view, there exists
nothing higher. The friendship shewn me by her "aunt
Villeparisis" and Robert had perhaps made me, for
Mme. de Guermantes and her friends, living always
upon themselves and in the same little circle, the object
of a curious interest of which I had no suspicion.

She had of those two relatives a familiar, everyday,
homely knowledge, of a sort, utterly different from what
we imagine, in which if we happen to be comprised in it,
so far from our actions being at once ejected, like the
grain of dust from the eye or the drop of water from
the windpipe, they are capable of remaining engraved,
and will still be related and discussed years after we
ourselves have forgotten them, in the palace in which
we are astonished to find them preserved, like a letter
in our own handwriting among a priceless collection of
autographs.

People who are merely fashionable may set a guard
upon doors which are too freely invaded. But the Guermantes door was not that. Hardly ever did a stranger
have occasion to pass by it. If, for once in a way, the
Duchess had one pointed out to her, she never dreamed

of troubling herself about the social increment that he would bring, since this was a thing that she conferred and could not receive. She thought only of his real merits. Both Mme. de Villeparisis and Saint-Loup had testified to mine. Doubtless she might not have believed them if she had not at the same time observed that they could never manage to secure me when they wanted me. and therefore that I attached no importance to worldly things, which seemed to the Duchess a sign that the stranger was to be numbered among what she called "nice people".

It was worth seeing, when one spoke to her of women for whom she did not care, how her face changed as soon as one named, in connexion with one of these, let us say, her sister-in-law. "Oh, she is charming!" the Duchess would exclaim in a judicious, confident tone. The only reason that she gave was that this lady had declined to be introduced to the Marquise de Chaussegros and the Princesse de Silistrie. She did not add that the lady had declined also an introduction to herself, the Duchesse de Guermantes. This had, nevertheless, been the case, and ever since the mind of the Duchess had been at work trying to unravel the motives of a woman who was so hard to know. She was dying to be invited to call on her. People in society are so accustomed to be sought after that the person who shuns them seems to them a phoenix and at once monopolises their attention.

Was the true motive in the mind of Mme. de Guermantes for thus inviting me (now that I was no longer in love with her) that I did not run after her relatives, although apparently run after myself by them? I cannot say. In any case, having made up her mind to invite me, she was anxious to do me the honours of the best company at her disposal and to keep away those of her friends whose presence might have dissuaded me from coming again, those whom she knew to be boring. I had not known to what to attribute her change of direction, when I had seen her deviate from her stellar path, come to sit down beside me and had heard her invite me to dinner, the effect of causes unknown for want of a special sense to enlighten us in this respect. We picture to ourselves the people who know us but slightly—such as, in my case, the Duchesse de Guermantes—as thinking of us only at the rare moments at which they set eyes on us. As a matter of fact this ideal oblivion in which we picture them as holding us is a purely arbitrary conception on our part. So that while, in our solitary silence, like that of a cloudless night, we imagine the various queens of society pursuing their course in the heavens at an infinite distance, we cannot help an involuntary start of dismay or pleasure if there falls upon us from that starry height, like a meteorite engraved with our name which we supposed to be unknown on Venus or Cassiopeia, an invitation to dinner or a piece of malicious gossip.

Perhaps now and then when, following the example of the Persian princes who, according to the Book of Esther, made their scribes read out to them the registers in which were enrolled the names of those of their subjects who had shewn zeal in their service, Mme. de Guermantes consulted her list of the well-disposed, she had said to herself, on coming to my name: "A man we must ask to dine some day." But other thoughts had distracted her

(Beset by surging cares, a Prince's mind
Towards fresh matters ever is inclined)

95

until the moment when she had caught sight of me sitting alone like Mordecai at the palace gate; and, the sight of me having refreshed her memory, sought, like Ahasuerus, to lavish her gifts upon me.

I must at the same time add that a surprise of a totally different sort was to follow that which I had felt on hearing Mme. de Guermantes ask me to dine with her. Since I had decided that it would shew greater modesty, on my part, and gratitude also not to conceal this initial surprise, but rather to exaggerate my expression of the delight that it gave me, Mme. de Guermantes, who was getting ready to go on to another, final party, had said to me, almost as a justification and for fear of my not being quite certain who she was, since I appeared so astonished at being invited to dine with her: "You know I'm the aunt of Robert de Saint-Loup, who is such a friend of yours; besides we have met before." In replying that I was aware of this I added that I knew also M. de Charlus, "who had been very good to me at Balbec and in Paris." Mme. de Guermantes appeared dumbfoundered, and her eyes seemed to turn, as though for a verification of this statement, to some page, already filled and turned, of her internal register of events. "What, so you know Palamède, do you?" This name assumed on the lips of Mme. de Guermantes a great charm, due to the instinctive simplicity with which she spoke of a man who was socially so brilliant a figure, but for her was no more than her brother-in-law and the cousin with whom she had grown up. And on the confused greyness which the life of the Duchesse de Guermantes was for me this name, Palamède, shed as it were the radiance of long summer days on which she had played with him as a girl, at Guermantes, in the garden. Moreover, in this long outgrown period in their lives, Oriane de Guermantes and her cousin Palamède had been very different from what they had since become; M. de Charlus in particular, entirely absorbed in the artistic pursuits from which he had so effectively restrained himself in later life that I was stupefied to learn that it was he who had painted the huge fan with black and yellow irises which the Duchess was at this moment unfurling. She could also have shewn me a little sonatina which he had once composed for her. I was completely unaware that the Baron possessed all these talents, of which he never spoke. Let me remark in passing that M. de Charlus did not at all relish being called " Palamède " by his family. That the form " Mémé " might not please him one could easily understand. These stupid abbreviations are a sign of the utter inability of the aristocracy to appreciate its own poetic beauty (in Jewry, too, we may see the same defect, since a nephew of Lady Israels, whose name was Moses, was commonly known as " Momo ") concurrently with its anxiety not to appear to attach any importance to what is aristocratic. Now M. de Charlus had, in this connexion, a greater wealth of poetic imagination and a more blatant pride. But the reason for his distaste for " Mémé " could not be this, since it extended also to the fine name Palamède. The truth was that, considering, knowing himself to come of a princely stock, he would have liked his brother and sister-in-law to refer to him as " Charlus ", just as Queen Marie-Amélie and Duc d'Orléans might have spoken of their sons and grandsons, brothers and nephews as " Joinville, Nemours, Chartres, Paris."

" What a humbug Mémé is ! " she exclaimed. " We

talked to him about you for hours; he told us that he would be delighted to make your acquaintance, just as if he had never set eyes on you. You must admit he's odd, and — though it's not very nice of me to say such a thing about a brother-in-law I'm devoted to, and really do admire immensely — a trifle mad at times."

I was struck by the application of this last epithet to M. de Charlus, and said to myself that this half-madness might perhaps account for certain things, such as his having appeared so delighted by his own proposal that I should ask Bloch to castigate his mother. I decided that, by reason not only of the things he said but of the way in which he said them, M. de Charlus must be a little mad. The first time that one listens to a barrister or an actor, one is surprised by his tone, so different from the conversational. But, observing that everyone else seems to find this quite natural, one says nothing about it to other people, one says nothing in fact to oneself, one is content with appreciating the degree of talent shewn. At the most, one may think, of an actor at the Théâtre-Français: "Why, instead of letting his raised arm fall naturally, did he make it drop in a series of little jerks broken by pauses for at least ten minutes?" or of a Labori: "Why, whenever he opened his mouth, did he utter those tragic, unexpected sounds to express the simplest things?" But as everybody admits these actions to be necessary and obvious one is not shocked by them. So, upon thinking it over, one said to oneself that M. de Charlus spoke of himself with undue emphasis in a tone which was not in the least that of ordinary speech. It seemed as though one might have at any moment interrupted him with: "But why do you shout so? Why are you so offensive?"

only everyone seemed to have tacitly agreed that it was all right. And one took one's place in the circle which applauded his outbursts. But certainly, at certain moments, a stranger might have thought that he was listening to the ravings of a maniac.

" But are you sure you're not thinking of some one else? Do you really mean my brother-in-law Palamède? " went on the Duchess, a trace of impertinence grafted upon her natural simplicity.

I replied that I was absolutely sure, and that M. de Charlus must have failed to catch my name.

" Oh well! I shall leave you now," said Mme. de Guermantes, as though she regretted the parting. " I must look in for a moment at the Princesse de Ligne's. You aren't going on there? No? You don't care for parties? You're very wise, they are too boring for words. If only I hadn't got to go. But she's my cousin; it wouldn't be polite. I am sorry, selfishly, for my own sake, because I could have taken you there, and brought you back afterwards, too. So I shall say good-bye now, and look forward to Friday."

That M. de Charlus should have blushed to be seen with me by M. d'Argencourt was all very well. But that to his own sister-in-law, who had so high an opinion of him besides, he should deny all knowledge of me, knowledge which was perfectly natural seeing that I was a friend of both his aunt and his nephew, was a thing that I could not understand.

I shall end my account of this incident with the remark that from one point of view there was in Mme. de Guermantes a true greatness which consisted in her entirely obliterating from her memory what other people would have only partially forgotten. Had she never seen me waylaying her, following her, tracking her down as she took her morning walks, had she never responded to my daily salute with an angry impatience, had she never refused Saint-Loup when he begged her to invite me to her house, she could not have greeted me now in a nobler or more gracious manner. Not only did she waste no time in retrospective explanations, in hints, allusions or ambiguous smiles, not only was there in her present affability, without any harking back to the past, without any reticence, something as proudly rectilinear as her majestic stature, but the resentment which she might have felt against anyone in the past was so entirely reduced to ashes, the ashes were themselves cast so utterly from her memory, or at least from her manner, that on studying her face whenever she had occasion to treat with the most exquisite simplification what in so many other people would have been a pretext for reviving stale antipathies and recriminations one had the impression of an intense purity of mind.

But if I was surprised by the modification that had occurred in her opinion of me, how much more did it surprise me to find a similar but ever so much greater change in my feeling for her. Had there not been a time during which I could regain life and strength only if —always building new castles in the air!—I had found some one who would obtain for me an invitation to her house and, after this initial boon, would procure many others for my increasingly exacting heart? It was the impossibility of finding any avenue there that had made me leave Paris for Doncières to visit Robert de Saint-Loup. And now it was indeed by the consequence of a

letter from him that I was agitated, but on account this
time of Mme. de Stermaria, not of Mme. de Guermantes.

Let me add further, to conclude my account of this
party, that there occurred at it an incident, contradicted
a few days later, which continued to puzzle me, interrupted
for some time my friendship with Bloch, and constitutes
in itself one of those curious paradoxes the explanation
of which will be found in the next part of this work. At
this party at Mme. de Villeparisis's, Bloch kept on boasting to me about the friendly attentions shewn him by M.
de Charlus, who, when he passed him in the street, looked
him straight in the face as though he recognised him,
was anxious to know him personally, knew quite well who
he was. I smiled at first, Bloch having expressed so
vehemently at Balbec his contempt for the said M. de
Charlus. And I supposed merely that Bloch, like his
father in the case of Bergotte, knew the Baron " without
actually knowing him ", and that what he took for a
friendly glance was due to absent-mindedness. But finally
Bloch became so precise and appeared so confident that
on two or three occasions M. de Charlus had wished to
address him that, remembering that I had spoken of my
friend to the Baron, who had, as we walked away together from this very house, as it happened, asked me
various questions about him, I came to the conclusion that
Bloch was not lying, that M. de Charlus had heard his
name, realised that he was my friend, and so forth. And
so, a little later, at the theatre one evening, I asked M. de
Charlus if I might introduce Bloch to him, and, on his
assenting, went in search of my friend. But as soon as M.
de Charlus caught sight of him an expression of astonishment, instantly repressed, appeared on his face, where it

gave way to a blazing fury. Not only did he not offer
Bloch his hand but whenever Bloch spoke to him he replied in the most insolent manner, in an angry and wound-
ing tone. So that Bloch, who, according to his version, had
received nothing until then from the Baron but smiles,
assumed that I had not indeed commended but disparaged
him in the short speech in which, knowing M. de Charlus's
liking for formal procedure, I had told him about my
friend before bringing him up to be introduced. Bloch left
us, his spirit broken, like a man who has been trying to
mount a horse which is always ready to take the bit in
its teeth, or to swim against waves which continually dash
him back on the shingle, and did not speak to me again
for six months.

The days that preceded my dinner with Mme. de Stermaria were for me by no means delightful, in fact it was
all I could do to live through them. For as a general
rule, the shorter the interval is that separates us from our
planned objective, the longer it seems to us, because we
apply to it a more minute scale of measurement, or simply
because it occurs to us to measure it at all. The Papacy,
we are told, reckons by centuries, and indeed may not
think perhaps of reckoning time at all, since its goal is in
eternity. Mine was no more than three days off; I
counted by seconds, I gave myself up to those imaginings
which are the first movements of caresses, of caresses
which it maddens us not to be able to make the woman
herself reciprocate and complete—those identical caresses,
to the exclusion of all others. And, as a matter of fact,
it is true that, generally speaking, the difficulty of attain-
ing to the object of a desire enhances that desire (the
difficulty, not the impossibility, for that suppresses it

altogether), yet in the case of a desire that is wholly physical the certainty that it will be realised, at a fixed and not distant point in time, is scarcely less exciting than uncertainty; almost as much as an anxious doubt, the absence of doubt makes intolerable the period of waiting for the pleasure that is bound to come, because it makes of that suspense an innumerably rehearsed accomplishment and by the frequency of our proleptic representations divides time into sections as minute as could be carved by agony. What I required was to possess Mme. de Stermaria, for during the last few days, with an incessant activity, my desires had been preparing this pleasure, in my imagination, and this pleasure alone, for any other kind (pleasure, that is, taken with another woman) would not have been ready, pleasure being but the realisation of a previous wish, and of one which is not always the same, but changes according to the endless combinations of one's fancies, the accidents of one's memory, the state of one's temperament, the variability of one's desires, the most recently granted of which lie dormant until the disappointment of their satisfaction has been to some extent forgotten; I should not have been prepared, I had already turned from the main road of general desires and had ventured along the bridle-path of a particular desire; I should have had—in order to wish for a different assignation—to retrace my steps too far before rejoining the main road and taking another path. To take possession of Mme. de Stermaria on the island in the Bois de Boulogne where I had asked her to dine with me, this was the pleasure that I imagined to myself afresh every moment. It would have automatically perished if I had dined on that island without

Mme. de Stermaria; but perhaps as greatly diminished had I dined, even with her, somewhere else. Besides, the attitudes in which one pictures a pleasure to oneself exist previously to the woman, to the type of woman required to give one that pleasure. They dictate the pleasure, and the place as well, and on that account bring to the fore alternatively, in our capricious fancy, this or that woman, this or that scene, this or that room, which in other weeks we should have dismissed with contempt. Child of the attitude that produced her, one woman will not appeal to us without the large bed in which we find peace by her side, while others, to be caressed with a more secret intention, require leaves blown by the wind, water rippling in the night, are as frail and fleeting as they.

No doubt in the past, long before I received Saint-Loup's letter and when there was as yet no question of Mme. de Stermaria, the island in the Bois had seemed to me to be specially designed for pleasure, because I had found myself going there to taste the bitterness of having no pleasure to enjoy in its shelter. It is to the shores of the lake from which one goes to that island, and along which, in the last weeks of summer, those ladies of Paris who have not yet left for the country take the air, that, not knowing where to look for her, or if indeed she has not already left Paris, one wanders in the hope of seeing the girl go by with whom one fell in love at the last ball of the season, whom one will not have a chance of meeting again in any drawing-room until the following spring. Feeling it to be at least the eve, if not the morrow, of the beloved's departure, one follows along the brink of the shivering water those attractive paths by which already a first red leaf is blooming like a last rose, one scans that horizon where, by a device the opposite of that employed in those panoramas beneath whose domed roofs the wax figures in the foreground impart to the painted canvas beyond them the illusory appearance of depth and mass, our eyes, passing without any transition from the cultivated park to the natural heights of Meudon and the Mont Valérien, do not know where to set the boundary, and make the natural country trespass upon the handiwork of the gardener, of which they project far beyond its own limits the artificial charm; like those rare birds reared in the open in a botanical garden which every day in the liberty of their winged excursions sally forth to strike, among the surrounding woods, an exotic note. Between the last festivity of summer and one's winter exile, one ranges anxiously that romantic world of chance encounters and lover's melancholy, and one would be no more surprised to learn that it was situated outside the mapped universe than if, at Versailles, looking down from the terrace, an observatory round which the clouds are massed against a blue sky in the manner of Van der Meulen, after having thus risen above the bounds of nature, one were informed that, there where nature begins again at the end of the great canal, the villages which one just could not make out, on a horizon as dazzling as the sea, were called Fleurus or Nimègue.

And then, the last carriage having rolled by, when one feels with a throb of pain that she will not come now, one goes to dine on the island; above the shivering poplars which suggest endless mysteries of evening though without response, a pink cloud paints a last touch of life in the tranquil sky. A few drops of rain fall without noise on the water, ancient but still in its divine infancy coloured always by the weather and continually forgetting the reflexions of clouds and flowers. And after the geraniums have vainly striven, by intensifying the brilliance of their scarlet, to resist the gathering darkness, a mist rises to envelop the now slumbering island; one walks in the moist dimness along the water's edge, where at the most the silent passage of a swan startles one like, in a bed, at night, the eyes, for a moment wide open, and the swift smile of a child whom one did not suppose to be awake. Then one would like to have with one a loving companion, all the more as one feels oneself to be alone and can imagine oneself to be far away from the world.

But to this island, where even in summer there was often a mist, how much more gladly would I have brought Mme. de Stermaria now that the cold season, the back end of autumn had come. If the weather that had prevailed since Sunday had not by itself rendered grey and maritime the scenes in which my imagination was living—as other seasons made them balmy, luminous, Italian—the hope of, in a few days' time, making Mme. de Stermaria mine would have been quite enough to raise, twenty times in an hour, a curtain of mist in my monotonously love-sick imagination. In any event the mist, which since yesterday had risen even in Paris, not only made me think incessantly of the native place of the young woman whom I had invited to dine with me, but, since it was probable that, far more thickly than in the streets of the town, it must after sunset be invading the Bois, especially the shores of the lake, I thought that it would make the Swans' Island, for me, something like that Breton island

the marine and misty atmosphere of which had always
enwrapped in my mind like a garment the pale outline
of Mme. de Stermaria. Of course when we are young,
at the age I had reached at the period of my walks along
the Méséglise way, our desires, our faith bestow on a
woman's clothing an individual personality, an ultimate
quintessence. We pursue reality. But by dint of allowing
it to escape we end by noticing that, after all those vain
endeavours which have led to nothing, something solid
subsists, which is what we have been seeking. We begin
to separate, to recognise what we love, we try to procure
it for ourselves, be it only by a stratagem. Then, in the
absence of our vanished faith, costume fills the gap, by
means of a deliberate illusion. I knew quite well that
within half an hour of home I should not find myself in
Brittany. But in walking arm in arm with Mme. de
Stermaria in the dusk of the island, by the water's edge,
I should be acting like other men who, unable to penetrate
the walls of a convent, do at least, before enjoying a
woman, clothe her in the habit of a nun.

I could even look forward to hearing, as I sat with the
lady, the lapping of waves, for, on the day before our
dinner, a storm broke over Paris. I was beginning to
shave myself before going to the island to engage the
room (albeit at this time of year the island was empty
and the restaurant deserted) and order the food for
our dinner next day when Françoise came in to tell me
that Albertine had called. I made her come in at once,
indifferent to her finding me disfigured by a bristling
chin, her for whom at Balbec I had never felt smart
enough and who had cost me then as much agitation and
distress as Mme. de Stermaria was costing me now. The

latter, I was determined, must go away with the best possible impression from our evening together. Accordingly I asked Albertine to come with me there and then to the island to order the food. She to whom one gives everything is so quickly replaced by another that one is surprised to find oneself giving all that one has, afresh, at every moment, without any hope of future reward. At my suggestion the smiling rosy face beneath Albertine's flat cap, which came down very low, to her eyebrows, seemed to hesitate. She had probably other plans; if so she sacrificed them willingly, to my great satisfaction, for I attached the utmost importance to my having with me a young housewife who would know a great deal more than myself about ordering dinner.

It is quite true that she had represented something utterly different for me at Balbec. But our intimacy, even when we do not consider it close enough at the time, with a woman with whom we are in love creates between her and us, in spite of the shortcomings that pain us while our love lasts, social ties which outlast our love and even the memory of our love. Then, in her who is nothing more for us than a means of approach, an avenue towards others, we are just as astonished and amused to learn from our memory what her name meant originally to that other creature which we then were as if, after giving a cabman an address in the Boulevard des Capucines or the Rue du Bac, thinking only of the person whom we are going to see there, we remind ourself that the names were once those of, respectively, the Capuchin nuns whose convent stood on the site and the ferry across the Seine.

At the same time, my Balbec desires had so generously ripened Albertine's body, had gathered and stored in it

savours so fresh and sweet that, as we drove through the
Bois, while the wind like a careful gardener shook the
trees, brought down the fruit, swept up the fallen leaves,
I said to myself that had there been any risk of Saint-
Loup's being mistaken, or of my having misunderstood
his letter, so that my dinner with Mme. de Stermaria
might lead to no satisfactory result, I should have made
an appointment for the same evening, later on, with
Albertine, so as to forget, for a purely voluptuous hour,
as I held in my arms a body of which my curiosity had
long since computed, weighed up all the possible charms
in which now it abounded, the emotions and perhaps the
regrets of this first phase of love for Mme. de Stermaria.
And certainly if I could have supposed that Mme. de
Stermaria would not grant me any of her favours at our
first meeting, I should have formed a slightly depressing
picture of my evening with her. I knew too well from
experience how the two stages which occur in us in the
first phase of our love for a woman whom we have
desired without knowing her, loving in her rather the
particular kind of existence in which she is steeped than
her still unfamiliar self—how distorted is the reflexion of
those two stages in the world of facts, that is to say not
in ourself any longer but in our meetings with her. We
have, without ever having talked to her, hesitated,
tempted as we were by the poetic charm which she represented for us. Shall it be this woman or another? And
lo, our dreams become fixed round about her, cease to
have any separate existence from her. The first meeting
with her which will shortly follow should reflect this
dawning love. Nothing of the sort. As if it were necessary that our material life should have its first period

also, in love with her already, we talk to her in the most trivial fashion: " I asked you to dine on this island because I thought the surroundings would amuse you. I've nothing particular to say to you, don't you know. But it's rather damp, I'm afraid, and you may find it cold——" " Oh, no, not at all! " " You just say that out of politeness. Very well, Madame, I shall allow you to battle against the cold for another quarter of an hour, as I don't want to bother you, but in fifteen minutes I shall carry you off by force. I don't want to have you catching a chill." And without another word said we take her home, remembering nothing about her, at the most a certain look in her eyes, but thinking only of seeing her again. Well, at our second meeting (when we do not find even that look, our sole memory of her, but nevertheless have been thinking only of seeing her again), the first stage is passed. Nothing has happened in the interval. And yet, instead of talking about the comfort or want of comfort of the restaurant, we say, without our words' appearing to surprise the new person, who seems to us positively plain but to whom we should like to think that people were talking about us at every moment in her life: " We are going to have our work cut out to overcome all the obstacles in our way. Do you think we shall be successful? Do you suppose that we can triumph over our enemies—live happily ever afterwards, and all that sort of thing? " But these conversational openings, trivial to begin with, then hinting at love, would not be required; I could trust Saint-Loup's letter for that. Mme. de Stermaria would yield herself to me from the first, I should have no need therefore to engage Albertine to come to me, as a makeshift, later in the evening. It would be superfluous;

Robert never exaggerated, and his letter was explicit.

Albertine spoke hardly at all, conscious that my thoughts were elsewhere. We went a little way on foot into the greenish, almost submarine grotto of a dense mass of trees, on the domed tops of which we heard the wind sweep and the rain pelt. I trod underfoot dead leaves which, like shells, were trampled into the soil, and poked with my stick at fallen chestnuts prickly as sea-urchins.

On the boughs the last clinging leaves, shaken by the wind, followed it only as far as their stems would allow, but sometimes these broke, and they fell to the ground, along which they coursed to overtake it. I thought with joy how much more remote still, if this weather lasted, the island would be on the morrow—and in any case quite deserted. We returned to our carriage and, as the storm had passed off, Albertine asked me to take her on to Saint-Cloud. As on the ground the drifting leaves so up above the clouds were chasing the wind. And a stream of migrant evenings, of which a sort of conic section cut through the sky made visible the successive layers, pink, blue and green, were gathered in readiness for departure to warmer climes. To obtain a closer view of a marble goddess who had been carved in the act of leaping from her pedestal and, alone in a great wood which seemed to be consecrated to her, filled it with the mythological terror, half animal, half divine, of her frenzied bounding, Albertine climbed a grassy slope while I waited for her in the road. She herself, seen thus from below, no longer coarse and plump as, a few days earlier, on my bed when the grain of her throat became apparent in the lens of my eye as it approached her person, but chiselled and delicate, seemed a little statue on which our happy hours together at Balbec had left their patina. When I found myself alone again at home, and remembered that I had taken a drive that afternoon with Albertine, that I was to dine in two days' time with Mme. de Guermantes and that I had to answer a letter from Gilberte, three women each of whom I had once loved, I said to myself that our social existence is, like an artist's studio, filled with abandoned sketches in which we have fancied for a moment that we could set down in permanent form our need of a great love, but it did not occur to me that sometimes, if the sketch be not too old, it may happen that we return to it and make of it a work wholly different, and possibly more important than what we had originally planned.

The next day was cold and fine; winter was in the air—indeed the season was so far advanced that it had seemed miraculous that we should find in the already pillaged Bois a few domes of gilded green. When I awoke I saw, as from the window of the barracks at Doncières, a uniform, dead white mist which hung gaily in the sunlight, consistent and sweet as a web of spun sugar. Then the sun withdrew, and the mist thickened still further in the afternoon. Night fell early, I made ready for dinner, but it was still too soon to start; I decided to send a carriage for Mme. de Stermaria. I did not like to go for her in it myself, not wishing to force my company on her, but I gave the driver a note for her in which I asked whether she would mind my coming to call for her. While I waited for her answer I lay down on my bed, shut my eyes for a moment, then opened them again. Over the top of the curtains there was nothing now but a thin strip of daylight which grew steadily fainter. I recognised that wasted hour, the large ante-room of pleasure, the dark, delicious emptiness of which I had learned at Balbec to know and to enjoy when, alone in my room as I was now, while all the rest were at dinner, I saw without regret the daylight fade from above my curtains, knowing that, presently, after a night of arctic brevity, it was to be resuscitated in a more dazzling brightness in the lighted rooms of Rivebelle. I sprang from my bed, tied my black necktie, passed a brush over my hair, final gestures of a belated tidying carried out at Balbec with my mind not on myself but on the women whom I should see at Rivebelle, while I smiled at them in anticipation in the mirror that stood across a corner of my room, gestures which, on that account, had continued to herald a form of entertainment in which music and lights would be mingled. Like magic signs they summoned, nay rather presented this entertainment already; thanks to them I had, of its intoxicating frivolous charm, as complete an enjoyment as I had had at Combray, in the month of July, when I heard the hammer-blows ring on the packing cases and enjoyed, in the coolness of my darkened room, a sense of warmth and sunshine.

Also, it was no longer exactly Mme. de Stermaria that I should have wished most to see. Forced now to spend my evening with her, I should have preferred, as it was almost the last before the return of my parents, that it should remain free and myself try instead to find some of the women from Rivebelle. I gave my hands one more final wash and, my sense of pleasure keeping me on the move, dried them as I walked through the shuttered dining-room. It appeared to have a door open on to the lighted hall, but what I had taken for the bright chink of the door, which as a matter of fact was closed, was only the gleaming reflexion of my towel in a mirror that had been laid against the wall in readiness to be fixed in its place before Mamma's return. I thought of all the other illusions of the sort which I had discovered in different parts of the house, and which were not optical only, for when we first came there I had supposed that our next door neighbour kept a dog on account of the continuous, almost human yapping which came from a certain pipe in the kitchen whenever the tap was turned on. And the door on to the outer landing never closed by itself, very gently, caught by a draught on the staircase, without rendering those broken, voluptuous, whimpering passages which sound over the chant of the pilgrims towards the end of the Overture to *Tannhäuser*. I had, moreover, just as I had put my towel back on its rail, an opportunity of hearing a fresh rendering of this brilliant symphonic fragment, for at a peal of the bell I hurried out to open the door to the driver who had come with Mme. de Stermaria's answer. I thought that his message would be: " The lady is downstairs," or " The lady is waiting." But he had a letter in his hand. I hesitated for a moment before looking to see what Mme. de Stermaria had written, who, while she held the pen in her hand, might have been anything but was now, detached from herself, an engine of fate, pursuing a course alone, which she was utterly powerless to alter. I asked the driver to wait downstairs for a moment, although he was cursing the fog. As soon as he had gone I opened the envelope. On her card, inscribed *Vicomtesse Alix de Stermaria,* my guest had written: " Am so sorry—am unfortunately prevented from dining with you this evening on the island in the Bois. Had been so looking forward to it. Will write you a proper letter from Stermaria. Very sorry. Kindest regards." I stood motionless, stunned by the shock that I had received. At my feet lay the card and envelope, fallen like the spent cartridge from a gun when the shot has been fired. I picked them up, tried to analyse her message. " She says that she cannot dine with me on the island in the Bois. One might gather from that that she would dine with me somewhere else. I shall not be so indiscreet as to go and fetch her, but, after all, that is quite a reasonable interpretation." And from that island in the Bois, as for the last few days my thoughts had been installed there beforehand with Mme. de Stermaria, I could not succeed in bringing them back to where I was. My desire responded automatically to the gravitational force which had been pulling it now for so many hours on end, and in spite of this message, too recent to counteract that force, I went on instinctively getting ready to start, just as a student, although ploughed by the examiners, tries to answer one question more. At last I decided to tell Françoise to go down and pay the driver. I went along the passage without finding her, I passed through the dining-room, where suddenly my feet ceased to sound on the bare boards as they had been doing and were hushed to a silence which, even before I had realised the explanation of it, gave me a feeling of suffocation and confinement. It was the carpets which, in view of my parents' return, the servants had begun to put down again, those carpets which look so well on bright mornings when amid their disorder the sun stays and waits for you like a friend come to take you out to luncheon in the country, and casts over them the dappled light and shade of the forest, but which now on the contrary were the first installation of the wintry prison from which, obliged as I should be to live, to take my meals at home, I should no longer be free now to escape when I chose.

"Take care you don't slip, Sir; they're not tacked yet," Françoise called to me. "I ought to have lighted up. Oh, dear, it's the end of 'Sectember' already, the fine days are over." In no time, winter; at the corner of a window, as in a Gallé glass, a vein of crusted snow; and even in the Champs-Élysées, instead of the girls one waits to see, nothing but solitary sparrows.

What added to my distress at not seeing Mme. de Stermaria was that her answer led me to suppose that whereas, hour by hour, since Sunday, I had been living for this dinner alone, she had presumably never given it a second thought. Later on I learned of an absurd love match that she had suddenly made with a young man whom she must already have been seeing at this time, and who had presumably made her forget my invitation. For if she had remembered it she would surely never have waited for the carriage which I was not, for that matter, supposed to be sending for her, to inform me that she was otherwise engaged. My dreams of a young feudal maiden on a misty island had cleared the way to a still non-existent love. Now my disappointment, my rage, my desperate desire to recapture her who had just refused me were able, by bringing my sensibility into play, to make definite the possible love which until then my imagination alone had—and that more loosely—offered me.

How many are there in our memories, how many more have we forgotten, of these faces of girls and young women, all different, to which we have added a certain charm and a frenzied desire to see them again only because at the last moment they eluded us? In the case of Mme. de Stermaria there was a good deal more than this, and it was enough now to make me love her for me to see her again so that I might refresh those impressions, so vivid but all too brief, which my memory would not, without such refreshment, have the strength to keep alive when we were apart. Circumstances decided against me; I did not see her again. It was not she that I loved, but it might well have been. And one of the things that made most cruel, perhaps, the great love which was presently to come to me was that when I thought of this evening I used to say to myself that my love might, given a slight modification of very ordinary circumstances, have been directed elsewhere, to Mme. de Stermaria; its application to her who inspired it in me so soon afterwards was not therefore—as I so longed, so needed to believe—absolutely necessary and predestined.

Françoise had left me by myself in the dining-room with the remark that it was foolish of me to stay there before she had lighted the fire. She went to get me some dinner, for even before the return of my parents, from this very evening, my seclusion was to begin. I caught sight of a huge bundle of carpets, still rolled up, and leaning against one end of the sideboard, and burying my head in it, swallowing its dust with my own tears, as the Jews used to cover their heads with ashes in times of mourning, I began to sob. I shuddered not only be-cause the room was cold, but because a distinct lowering of temperature (against the danger and—I should add, perhaps—the by no means disagreeable sensation of which we make no attempt to react) is brought about by a certain kind of tears which fall from our eyes, drop by drop, like a fine, penetrating, icy rain, and seem as though never would they cease to flow. Suddenly I heard a voice:

"May I come in? Françoise told me you would be in the dining-room. I looked in to see whether you would care to come out and dine somewhere, if it isn't bad for your throat—there's a fog outside you could cut with a knife."

It was—arrived in Paris that morning, when I imagined him to be still in Morocco or on the sea—Robert de Saint-Loup.

I have already said (as a matter of fact, it was Robert himself who, at Balbec, had helped me, quite without meaning it, to arrive at this conclusion) what I think about friendship: to wit that it is so small a thing that I find it hard to understand how men with some claim to genius—Nietzsche, for instance—can have been such simpletons as to ascribe to it a certain intellectual value, and consequently to deny themselves friendships in which intellectual esteem would have no part. Yes, it has always been a surprise to me to find a man who carried sincerity towards himself to so high a pitch as to cut himself off, by a scruple of conscience, from Wagner's music imagining that the truth could ever be attained by the mode of expression, naturally vague and inadequate, which our actions in general and acts of friendship in particular furnish, or that there could be any kind of significance in the fact of one's leaving one's work to go and see a friend

118

and shed tears with him on hearing the false report that the Louvre was burned. I had got so far, at Balbec, as to find that the pleasure of playing with a troop of girls is less destructive of the spiritual life, to which at least it remains alien, than friendship, the whole effort of which is directed towards making us sacrifice the one real and (save by the channel of art) incommunicable part of ourself to a superficial self which finds—not, like the other, any joy in itself, but rather a vague, senti-mental attraction in the feeling that it is being supported by external props, hospitably entertained by a strange personality, through which, happy in the protection that is afforded it there, it makes its own comfort radiate in warm approval, and marvels at qualities which it would denounce as faults and seek to correct in itself. More-over the scorners of friendship can, without illusion and not without remorse, be the finest friends in the world, just as an artist carrying in his brain a masterpiece and feeling that his duty is rather to live and carry on his work, nevertheless, so as not to be thought or to run the risk of actually being selfish, gives his life for a vain cause, and gives it all the more gallantly in that the reasons for which he would have preferred not to give it were disinterested. But whatever might be my opinion of friendship, to mention only the pleasure that it procured me, of a quality so mediocre as to be like something half-way between physical exhaustion and mental boredom, there is no brew so deadly that it can-not at certain moments become precious and invigorating by giving us just the stimulus that was necessary, the warmth that we cannot generate in ourself.

The thought of course never entered my mind now of

asking Saint-Loup to take me (as, an hour earlier, I had been longing to go) to see some of the Rivebelle women; the scar left by my disappointment with Mme. de Stermaria was too recent still to be so easily healed, but at the moment when I had ceased to feel in my heart any reason for happiness Saint-Loup's bursting in upon me was like a sudden apparition of kindness, mirth, life, which were external to me, no doubt, but offered themselves to me, asked only to be made mine. He did not himself understand my shout of gratitude, my tears of affection. And yet is there anything more unaccountably affecting than one of those friends, be he diplomat, explorer, airman or soldier like Saint-Loup, who, having to start next day for the country, from where they will go on heaven knows where, seem to form for themselves, in the evening which they devote to us, an impression which we are astonished both to find, so rare and fleeting is it, can be so pleasant to them, and, since it does so delight them, not to see them prolong farther or repeat more often. A meal with us, an event so natural in itself, affords these travellers the same strange and exquisite pleasure as our boulevards give to an Asiatic. We set off together to dine, and as I went downstairs I thought of Doncières where every evening I used to meet Robert at his restaurant, and the little dining-rooms there that I had forgotten. I remembered one of these to which I had never given a thought, and which was not in the hotel where Saint-Loup dined but in another, far humbler, a cross between an inn and a boarding-house, where the waiting was done by the landlady and one of her servants. I had been forced to take shelter there once from a snow-storm. Besides, Robert was not to be dining at the hotel

that evening and I had not cared to go any farther.
My food was brought to me, upstairs, in a little room
with bare wooden walls. The lamp went out during
dinner and the servant lighted a couple of candles. I,
pretending that I could not see very well as I held out
my plate, while she helped me to potatoes, took her
bare fore-arm in my hand, as though to guide her. Seeing
that she did not withdraw it, I began to fondle it, then,
without saying a word, pulled her bodily to me, blew out
the candles and told her to feel in my pocket for some
money. For the next few days physical pleasure seemed
to me to require, to be properly enjoyed, not only this
servant but the timbered dining-room, so remote and
lonely. And yet it was to the other, in which Saint-Loup
and his friends dined, that I returned every evening,
from force of habit and in friendship for them, until I
left Doncières. But even of this hotel, where he took
his meals with his friends, I had long ceased to think;
we make little use of our experience, we leave uncon-
sumed in the summer dusk or precocious nights of winter
the hours in which it had seemed to us that there might
nevertheless be contained some element of tranquillity or
pleasure. But those hours are not altogether wasted.
When, in their turn, come and sing to us fresh moments
of pleasure, which by themselves would pass by equally
bare in outline, the others recur, bringing them the
groundwork, the solid consistency of a rich orchestration.
They are in this way prolonged into one of those types
of happiness which we recapture only now and again
but which continue to exist; in the present instance the
type was that of forsaking everything else to dine in comfortable surroundings, which by the help of memory em-

body in a scene from nature suggestions of the rewards of travel, with a friend who is going to stir our dormant life with all his energy, his affection, to communicate to us an emotional pleasure, very different from anything that we could derive from our own efforts or from social distractions; we are going to exist solely for him, to utter vows of friendship which, born within the confines of the hour, remaining imprisoned in it, will perhaps not be kept on the morrow but which I need have no scruple in taking before Saint-Loup since, with a courage into which there entered a great deal of common sense and the presentiment that friendship cannot explore its own depths, on the morrow he would be gone.

If as I came downstairs I lived over again the evenings at Doncières, when we reached the street, in a moment the darkness, now almost total, in which the fog seemed to have put out the lamps, which one could make out, glimmering very faintly, only when close at hand, took me back to I could not say what arrival, by night, at Combray, when the streets there were still lighted only at long intervals and one felt one's way through a darkness moist, warm, consecrated, like that of a Christmas manger, just visibly starred here and there by a wick that burned no brightlier than a candle. Between that year—to which I could ascribe no precise date—of my Combray life and the evenings at Rivebelle which had, an hour earlier, been reflected above my drawn curtains, what a world of differences! I felt on perceiving them an enthusiasm which might have borne fruit had I been left alone and would then have saved me the unnecessary round of many wasted years through which I was yet to pass before there was revealed to me that invisible vocation of which these

volumes are the history. Had the revelation come to me
this evening, the carriage in which I sat would have
deserved to rank as more memorable with me than Dr.
Percepied's, on the box seat of which I had composed
that little sketch—on which, as it happened, I had recently
laid my hands, altered it and sent it in vain to the *Figaro*
—of the spires of Martinville. Is it because we live over
our past years not in their continuous sequence, day by
day, but in a memory that fastens upon the coolness or
sun-parched heat of some morning or afternoon, receives
the shadow of some solitary place, is enclosed, immovable,
arrested, lost, remote from all others, because, therefore,
the changes gradually wrought not only in the world outside but in our dreams and our evolving character,
(changes which have imperceptibly carried us through
life from one to another, wholly different time) are of
necessity eliminated, that, if we revive another memory
taken from a different year, we find between the two,
thanks to lacunae, to vast stretches of oblivion, as it
were the gulf of a difference in altitude or the incompatibility of two divers qualities, that of the air we breathe
and the colour of the scene before our eyes? But between
one and another of the memories that had now come to
me in turn of Combray, of Doncières and of Rivebelle,
I was conscious at the moment of more than a distance
in time, of the distance that there would be between two
separate universes the material elements in which were
not the same. If I had sought to reproduce the element
in which appeared carven my most trivial memories of
Rivebelle, I should have had to streak with rosy veins,
to render at once translucent, compact, refreshing,
resonant a substance hitherto analogous to the coarse

dark sandstone walls of Combray. But Robert having finished giving his instructions to the driver joined me now in the carriage. The ideas that had appeared before me took flight. Ideas are goddesses who deign at times to make themselves visible to a solitary mortal, at a turning in the road, even in his bedroom while he sleeps, when they, standing framed in the doorway, bring him the annunciation of their tidings. But as soon as a companion joins him they vanish, in the society of his fellows no man has ever beheld them. And I found myself cast back upon friendship. When he first appeared Robert had indeed warned me that there was a good deal of fog outside, but while we were indoors, talking, it had grown steadily thicker. It was no longer merely the light mist which I had looked forward to seeing rise from the island and envelop Mme. de Stermaria and myself. A few feet away from us the street lamps were blotted out and then it was night, as dark as in the open fields, in a forest, or rather on a mild Breton island whither I would fain have gone; I lost myself, as on the stark coast of some Northern sea where one risks one's life twenty times over before coming to the solitary inn; ceasing to be a mirage for which one seeks, the fog became one of those dangers against which one has to fight, so that we had, in finding our way and reaching a safe haven, the difficulties, the anxiety and finally the joy which safety, so little perceived by him who is not threatened with the loss of it, gives to the perplexed and benighted traveller. One thing only came near to destroying my pleasure during our adventurous ride, owing to the angry astonishment into which it flung me for a moment. "You know, I told Bloch," Saint-Loup suddenly informed me, "that you

didn't really think all that of him, that you found him
rather vulgar at times. I'm like that, you see, I want
people to know where they stand," he wound up with
a satisfied air and in a tone which brooked no reply.
I was astounded. Not only had I the most absolute confidence in Saint-Loup, in the loyalty of his friendship,
and he had betrayed it by what he had said to Bloch,
but it seemed to me that he of all men ought to have
been restrained from doing so, by his defects as well
as by his good qualities, by that astonishing veneer of
breeding which was capable of carrying politeness to
what was positively a want of frankness. His triumphant
air, was it what we assume to cloak a certain embarrass-
ment in admitting a thing which we know that we ought
not to have done, or did it mean complete unconsciousness; stupidity making a virtue out of a defect which I
had not associated with him; a passing fit of ill humour
towards me, prompting him to make an end of our
friendship, or the notation in words of a passing fit of
ill humour in the company of Bloch to whom he had felt
that he must say something disagreeable, even although
I should be compromised by it? However that might be,
his face was seared, while he uttered this vulgar speech,
by a frightful sinuosity which I saw on it once or
twice only in all the time I knew him, and which,
beginning by running more or less down the middle of
his face, when it came to his lips twisted them, gave them
a hideous expression of baseness, almost of bestiality,
quite transitory and no doubt inherited. There must
have been at such moments, which recurred probably
not more than once every other year, a partial eclipse
of his true self by the passage across it of the personality

of some ancestor whose shadow fell on him. Fully as
much as his satisfied air, the words: " I want people to
know where they stand," encouraged the same doubt and
should have incurred a similar condemnation. I felt inclined to say to him that if one wants people to know
where they stand one ought to confine these outbursts
of frankness to one's own affairs and not to acquire a
too easy merit at the expense of others. But by this time
the carriage had stopped outside the restaurant, the huge
front of which, glazed and streaming with light, alone
succeeded in piercing the darkness. The fog itself, beside
the comfortable brightness of the lighted interior, seemed
to be waiting outside on the pavement to shew one the
way in with the joy of servants whose faces reflect the
hospitable instincts of their master; shot with the most
delicate shades of light, it pointed the way like the pillar
of fire which guided the Children of Israel. Many of
whom, as it happened, were to be found inside. For this
was the place to which Bloch and his friends had long
been in the habit, maddened by a hunger as famishing
as the Ritual Fast, which at least occurs only once a
year, for coffee and the satisfaction of political curiosity,
of repairing in the evenings. Every mental excitement
creating a value that overrides others, a quality superior
to the rest of one's habits, there is no taste at all keenly
developed that does not thus gather round it a society
which it unites and in which the esteem of his fellows
is what each of its members seeks before anything else
from life. Here, in their café, be it in a little provincial
town, you will find impassioned music-lovers; the greater
part of their time, all their spare cash is spent in chamber-
concerts, in meetings for musical discussion, in cafés where

one finds oneself among musical people and rubs shoulders
with the members of the orchestra. Others, keen upon
flying, seek to stand well with the old waiter in the glazed
bar perched on top of the aerodrome; sheltered from the
wind as in the glass cage of a lighthouse, they can follow
in the company of an airman who is not going up that
day the evolutions of a pilot practising loops, while another, invisible a moment ago, comes suddenly swooping
down to land with the great winged roar of an Arabian
roc. The little group which met to try to perpetuate, to
explore the fugitive emotions aroused by the Zola trial
attached a similar importance to this particular café.
But they were not viewed with favour by the young
nobles who composed the rest of its patrons and had
taken possession of a second room, separated from the
other only by a flimsy parapet topped with a row of
plants. These looked upon Dreyfus and his supporters
as traitors, albeit twenty-five years later, ideas having
had time to classify themselves and Dreyfusism to acquire, in the light of history, a certain distinction, the
sons, dance-mad Bolshevists, of these same young nobles
were to declare to the " intellectuals " who questioned
them that undoubtedly, had they been alive at the time,
they would have stood up for Dreyfus, without having
any clearer idea of what the great Case had been about
than Comtesse Edmond de Pourtalès or the Marquise
de Galliffet, other luminaries already extinct at the date
of their birth. For on the night of the fog the noblemen
of the café, who were in due course to become the fathers
of these young intellectuals, Dreyfusards in retrospect,
were still bachelors. Naturally the idea of a rich marriage
was present in the minds of all their families, but none

of them had yet brought such a marriage off. While still potential, the only effect of this rich marriage, the simultaneous ambition of several of them (there were indeed several heiresses in view, but after all the number of big dowries was considerably below that of the aspirants to them), was to create among these young men a certain amount of rivalry.

As ill luck would have it, Saint-Loup remaining outside for a minute to explain to the driver that he was to call for us again after dinner, I had to make my way in by myself. In the first place, once I had involved myself in the spinning door, to which I was not accustomed, I began to fear that I should never succeed in escaping from it. (Let me note here for the benefit of lovers of verbal accuracy that the contrivance in question, despite its peaceful appearance, is known as a " revolver ", from the English " revolving door ".) This evening the proprietor, not venturing either to brave the elements outside or to desert his customers, remained standing near the entrance so as to have the pleasure of listening to the joyful complaints of the new arrivals, all aglow with the satisfaction of people who have had difficulty in reaching a place and have been afraid of losing their way. The smiling cordiality of his welcome was, however, dissipated by the sight of a stranger incapable of disengaging himself from the rotating sheets of glass. This flagrant sign of social ignorance made him knit his brows like an examiner who has a good mind not to utter the formula: *Dignus est intrare*. As a crowning error I went to look for a seat in the room set apart for the nobility, from which he at once expelled me, indicating to me, with a rudeness to which all the waiters at once conformed, a place in the other room. This was all the less to my liking because the seat was in the middle of a crowded row and I had opposite me the door reserved for the Hebrews which, as it did not revolve, opening and shutting at every moment kept me in a horrible draught. But the proprietor declined to move me, saying: " No, sir, I cannot have the whole place upset for you." Presently, however, he forgot this belated and troublesome guest, captivated as he was by the arrival of each newcomer who, before calling for his beer, his wing of cold chicken or his hot grog (it was by now long past dinner-time), must first, as in the old romances, pay his scot by relating his adventure at the moment of his entry into this asylum of warmth and security where the contrast with the perils just escaped made that gaiety and sense of comradeship prevail which create a cheerful harmony round the camp fire.

One reported that his carriage, thinking it had got to the Pont de la Concorde had circled three times round the Invalides, another that his, in trying to make its way down the Avenue des Champs-Élysées, had driven into a clump of trees at the Rond Point, from which it had taken him three quarters of an hour to get clear. Then followed lamentations upon the fog, the cold, the deathly stillness of the streets, uttered and received with the same exceptionally jovial air, which was accounted for by the pleasant atmosphere of the room which, except where I sat, was warm, the dazzling light which set blinking eyes already accustomed to not seeing, and the buzz of talk which restored their activity to deafened ears.

It was all the newcomers could do to keep silence.

The singularity of the mishaps which each of them thought unique burned their tongues, and their eyes roved in search of some one to engage in conversation. The proprietor himself lost all sense of social distinction. "M. le Prince de Foix lost his way three times coming from the Porte Saint-Martin," he was not afraid to say with a laugh, actually pointing out, as though introducing one to the other, the illustrious nobleman to an Israelite barrister, who, on any evening but this, would have been divided from him by a barrier far harder to surmount than the ledge of greenery. "Three times—fancy that!" said the barrister, touching his hat. This note of personal interest was not at all to the Prince's liking. He formed one of an aristocratic group for whom the practice of impertinence, even at the expense of their fellow-nobles when these were not of the very highest rank, seemed the sole possible occupation. Not to acknowledge a bow, and, if the polite stranger repeated the offence, to titter with sneering contempt or fling back one's head with a look of fury, to pretend not to know some elderly man who might have done them a service, to reserve their handclasp for dukes and the really intimate friends of dukes whom the latter introduced to them, such was the attitude of these young men, and especially of the Prince de Foix. Such an attitude was encouraged by the ill-balanced mentality of early manhood (a period in which, even in the middle class, one appears ungrateful and behaves like a cad because, having forgotten for months to write to a benefactor after he has lost his wife, one then ceases to nod to him in the street so as to simplify matters), but it was inspired above all by an over-acute caste snobbishness. It is true that, after the fashion of certain nervous affections the symptoms of which grow less pronounced in later life, this snobbishness was on the whole to cease to express itself in so offensive a form in these men who had been so intolerable when young. Once youth is outgrown, it is seldom that anyone remains hidebound by insolence. He had supposed it to be the only thing in the world; suddenly he discovers, for all the Prince that he is, that there also are such things as music, literature, even standing for parliament. The scale of human values is correspondingly altered and he joins in conversation with people whom at one time he would have slain with a glare of lightning. Which is fortunate for those of the latter who have had the patience to wait, and whose character is sufficiently formed—if one may so put it—for them to feel pleasure in receiving in their forties the civility and welcome that had been coldly withheld from them at twenty.

As I have mentioned the Prince de Foix, it may not be inconsequent here to add that he belonged to a set of a dozen or fifteen young men and to an inner group of four. The dozen or fifteen shared this characteristic (which the Prince lacked, I fancy) that each of them faced the world in a dual aspect. Up to their own eyes in debt, they were of no account in those of their trades-men, notwithstanding the pleasure these took in address-ing them as " Monsieur le Comte," " Monsieur le Mar-quis," " Monsieur le Duc." They hoped to retrieve their fortunes by means of the famous rich marriage (" money-bags " as the expression still was) and, as the fat dowries which they coveted numbered at the most four or five, several of them would be silently training their batteries on the same damsel. And the secret would be so well kept that when one of them, on arriving at the café, announced: "My dear fellows, I am too fond of you all not to tell you of my engagement to Mlle. d'Ambresac," there was a general outburst, more than one of the others imagining that the marriage was as good as settled already between Mlle. d'Ambresac and himself, and not having enough self-control to stifle a spontaneous cry of stupefaction and rage. "So you like the idea of marriage, do you, Bibi?" the Prince de Châtellerault could not help exclaiming, letting his fork drop in his surprise and despair, for he had been fully expecting the engagement of this identical Mlle. d'Ambresac to be announced, but with himself, Châtellerault, as her bridegroom. And heaven only knew all that his father had cunningly hinted to the Ambresacs against Bibi's mother. "So you think it'll be fun, being married, do you?" he was impelled to repeat his question to Bibi, who, better prepared to meet it, for he had had plenty of time to decide on the right attitude to adopt since the engagement had reached the semi-official stage, replied with a smile: "What pleases me is not the idea of marriage, which never appealed much to me, but marrying Daisy d'Ambresac, whom I think charming." In the time taken up by this response M. de Châtellerault had recovered his composure, but he was thinking that he must at the earliest possible moment execute a change of front in the direction of Mlle. de la Canourque or Miss Foster, numbers two and three on the list of heiresses, pacify somehow the creditors who were expecting the Ambresac marriage and finally explain to the people to whom he too had declared that Mlle. d'Ambresac was charming that this marriage was all very well for Bibi, but that he himself would have had all his family down on him like a ton of bricks if he had married her. Mme. Soléon (he decided to say) had actually announced that she would not have them in her house.

But if in the eyes of tradesmen, proprietors of restaurants and the like they seemed of little account, conversely, being creatures of dual personality, the moment they appeared in society they ceased to be judged by the decay of their fortunes and the sordid occupations by which they sought to repair them. They became once more M. le Prince this, M. le Duc that, and were reckoned only in terms of their quarterings. A duke who was practically a multi-millionaire and seemed to combine in his own person every possible distinction gave precedence to them because, the heads of their various houses, they were by descent sovereign princes of minute territories in which they were entitled to coin money and so forth. Often in this café one of them lowered his eyes when another came in so as not to oblige the newcomer to greet him. This was because in his imaginative pursuit of riches he had invited a banker to dine. Every time that a man about town enters into relations, on this footing, with a banker, the latter leaves him the poorer by a hundred thousand francs, which does not prevent the man about town from at once repeating the process with another. We continue to burn candles in churches and to consult doctors.

But the Prince de Foix, who was rich already, belonged not only to this fashionable set of fifteen or so young men, but to a more exclusive and inseparable group of four which included Saint-Loup. These were never asked anywhere separately, they were known as the four *gigo-*

los, they were always to be seen riding together, in country houses their hostesses gave them communicating bedrooms, with the result that, especially as they were all four extremely good looking, rumours were current as to the extent of their intimacy. I was in a position to give these the lie direct so far as Saint-Loup was concerned. But the curious thing is that if, later on, one was to learn that these rumours were true of all four, each of the quartet had been entirely in the dark as to the other three. And yet each of them had done his utmost to find out about the others, to gratify a desire or (more probably) a resentment, to prevent a marriage or to secure a hold over the friend whose secret he discovered. A fifth (for in these groups of four there are never four only) had joined this Platonic party who was more so than any of the others. But religious scruples restrained him until long after the group had broken up, and he himself was a married man, the father of a family, fervently praying at Lourdes that the next baby might be a boy or a girl, and spending the intervals of procreation in the pursuit of soldiers.

Despite the Prince's code of manners, the fact that the barrister's comment, though uttered in his hearing, had not been directly addressed to him made him less angry than he would otherwise have been. Besides, this evening was somewhat exceptional. Finally, the barrister had no more prospect of coming to know the Prince de Foix than the cabman who had driven that noble lord to the restaurant. The Prince felt, accordingly, that he might allow himself to reply, in an arrogant tone, as though speaking to some one "off stage", to this stranger who, thanks to the fog, was in the position of a travelling companion whom one meets at some seaside place at the ends of the earth, scoured by all the winds of heaven or shrouded in mist: "Losing your way's nothing; the trouble is, you can't find it again." The wisdom of this aphorism impressed the proprietor, for· he had already heard it several times in the course of the evening.

He was, in fact, in the habit of always comparing what he heard or read with an already familiar canon, and felt his admiration aroused if he could detect no difference. This state of mind is by no means to be ignored, for, applied to political conversations, to the reading of newspapers, it forms public opinion and thereby makes possible the greatest events in history. An aggregation of German landlords, simply by being impressed by a customer or a newspaper when he or it said that France, England and Russia were "out to crush" Germany, made war, at the time of Agadir, possible, even if no war occurred. Historians, if they have not been wrong to abandon the practice of attributing the actions of peoples to the will of kings, ought to substitute for the latter the psychology of the person of no importance.

In politics the proprietor of this particular café had for some time now concentrated his pupil-teacher's mind on certain particular details of the Dreyfus case. If he did not find the terms that were familiar to him in the conversation of a customer or the columns of a newspaper he would pronounce the article boring or the speaker insincere. The Prince de Foix, however, impressed him so forcibly that he barely gave him time to finish what he was saying. "That's right, Prince, that's right," (which meant neither more nor less than "repeated without a mistake") "that's exactly how it is!" he exclaimed, expanding, like people in the Arabian Nights "to the limit of repletion". But the Prince had by this time vanished into the smaller room. Then, as life resumes its normal course after even the most sensational happenings, those who had emerged from the sea of fog began to order whatever they wanted to eat or drink; among them a party of young men from the Jockey Club who, in view of the abnormality of the situation, had no hesitation in taking their places at a couple of tables in the big room, and were thus quite close to me. So the cataclysm had established even between the smaller room and the bigger, among all these people stimulated by the comfort of the restaurant after their long wanderings across the ocean of fog, a familiarity from which I alone was excluded, not unlike the spirit that must have prevailed in Noah's ark. Suddenly I saw the landlord's body whipped into a series of bows, the head waiters hurrying to support him in a full muster which drew every eye towards the door. "Quick, send Cyprien here, lay a table for M. le Marquis de Saint-Loup," cried the proprietor, for whom Robert was not merely a great nobleman possessing a real importance even in the eyes of the Prince de Foix, but a client who drove through life four-in-hand, so to speak, and spent a great deal of money in this restaurant. The customers in the big room looked on with interest, those in the small room shouted simultaneous greetings to their friend as he finished wiping his shoes. But just as he was about to make his way into the small room he caught sight of me in the big one. "Good God," he exclaimed, "what on earth are you doing there? And with the door wide open too?" he went on, with an angry glance at the proprietor, who ran to shut it, throwing the blame on his staff: " I'm always telling them to keep it shut."

I had been obliged to shift my own table and to disturb others which stood in the way in order to reach him. " Why did you move? Would you sooner dine here than in the little room? Why, my poor fellow, you're freezing. You will oblige me by keeping that door locked;" he turned to the proprietor. " This very instant, M. le Marquis; the gentlemen will have to go out of this room through the other, that is all." And the better to shew his zeal he detailed for this operation a head waiter and several satellites, vociferating the most terrible threats of punishment were it not properly carried out. He began to shew me exaggerated marks of respect, so as to make me forget that these had begun not upon my arrival but only after that of Saint-Loup, while, lest I should think them to have been prompted by the friendliness shewn me by his rich and noble client, he gave me now and again a surreptitious little smile which seemed to indicate a regard that was wholly personal.

Something said by one of the diners behind me made me turn my head for a moment. I had caught, instead of the words: " Wing of chicken, excellent; and a glass of champagne, only not too dry," the unexpected: " I should prefer glycerine. Yes, hot, excellent." I wanted to see who the ascetic was that was inflicting upon himself such a diet. I turned quickly back to Saint-Loup so as not to be recognised by the man of strange appetite. It was simply a doctor, whom I happened to know, and of whom another customer, taking advantage of the fog to buttonhole him here in the café, was asking his professional advice. Like stockbrokers, doctors employ the first person singular.

Meanwhile I was studying Saint-Loup, and my thoughts took a line of their own. There were in this café, I had myself known at other times plently of foreigners, intellectuals, budding geniuses of all sorts, resigned to the laughter excited by their pretentious capes, their 1830 neckties and still more by the clumsiness of their movements, going so far as to provoke that laughter in order to shew that they paid no heed to it, who yet were men of real intellectual and moral worth, of an extreme sensibility. They repelled—the Jews among them principally, the unassimilated Jews, that is to say, for with the other kind we are not concerned—those who could not endure any oddity or eccentricity of appearance (as Bloch repelled Albertine). Generally speaking, one realised afterwards that if they had against them hair worn too long, noses and eyes that were too big, stilted theatrical gestures, it was puerile to judge them by these only, they had plenty of intelligence and spirit and were men to whom, in the long run, one could become closely attached. Among the Jews especially there were few whose parents and kinsfolk had not a warmth of heart, a breadth of mind in comparison with which Saint-Loup's mother and the Duc de Guermantes cut the poorest of figures by their sereness, their skin-deep religiosity which denounced only the most open scandals, their apology for a Christianity which led invariably (by the unexpected channel of a purely calculating mind) to an enormously wealthy marriage. But in Saint-Loup, when all was said, however the faults of his relatives might be combined in a fresh creation of character, there reigned the most charming openness of mind and heart. And whenever (it must be frankly admitted, to the undying glory of France) these qualities are found in a man who is purely French, be he noble or plebeian, they flower—flourish would be too strong a word, for a sense of proportion persists and also a certain restraint—with a grace which the foreign visitor, however estimable he may be, does not present to us. Of these intellectual and moral qualities others undoubtedly have their share, and if we have first to overcome what repels us and what makes us smile they remain no less precious. But it is all the same a pleasant thing, and one which is perhaps exclusively French that what is fine from the standpoint of equity, what is of value to the heart and mind should be first of all attractive to the eyes, charmingly coloured, consummately chiselled, should express outwardly as well in substance as in form an inward perfection. I studied Saint-Loup's features and said to myself that it is a thing to be glad of when there is no lack of bodily grace to prepare one for the graces within, and when the winged nostrils are spread as delicately and with as perfect a design as the wings of the little butterflies that hover over the field-flowers round Combray ; and that the true *opus francigenum*, the secret of which was not lost in the thirteenth century, the beauty of which would not be lost with the destruction of our churches, consists not so much in the stone angels of Saint-André-des-Champs as in the young sons of France, noble, citizen or peasant, whose faces are carved with that delicacy and boldness which have remained as traditional there as on the famous porch, but are creative still as well.

After leaving us for a moment in order to supervise personally the barring of the door and the ordering of our dinner (he laid great stress on our choosing "butcher's meat", the fowls being presumably nothing to boast of) the proprietor came back to inform us that M. le Prince de Foix would esteem it a favour if M. le Marquis would allow him to dine at a table next to ours. "But they are all taken," objected Robert, casting an eye over the tables which blocked the way to mine. "That doesn't matter in the least, if M. le Marquis would like it, I can easily ask these people to move to another table. It is always a pleasure to do anything for M. le Marquis!" "But you must decide," said Saint-Loup to me. "Foix is a good fellow, he may bore you or he may not; anyhow he's not such a fool as most of them." I told Robert that of course I should like to meet his friend but that now that I was for once in a way dining with him and was so entirely happy, I should be just as well pleased to have him all to myself. "He's got a very fine cloak, the Prince has," the proprietor broke in upon our deliberation. "Yes, I know," said Saint-Loup. I wanted to tell Robert that M. de Charlus had disclaimed all knowledge of me to his sister-in-law, and to ask him what could be the reason of this, but was prevented by the arrival of M. de Foix. Come to see whether his request had been favourably received, we caught sight of him standing beside our table. Robert introduced us, but did not hide from his friend that as we had things to talk about he would prefer not to be disturbed. The Prince withdrew, adding to the farewell bow which he made me a smile which, pointed at Saint-Loup, seemed to transfer to him the responsibility for the shortness of a meeting which the Prince himself would have liked to see prolonged. As he turned to go, Robert, struck, it appeared, by a sudden idea, dashed off after his friend, with a " Stay where you are and get on with your dinner, I shall be back in a moment," to me; and vanished into the smaller room. I was pained to hear the smart young men sitting near me, whom I did not know, repeat the most absurd and malicious stories about the young Hereditary Grand Duke of Luxembourg (formerly Comte de Nassau) whom I had met at Balbec and who had shewn me such delicate marks of sympathy at the time of my grandmother's illness. According to one of these young men, he had said to the Duchesse de Guermantes: " I expect everyone to get up when my wife passes," to which the Duchess had retorted (with as little truth, had she said any such thing, as humour, the grandmother of the young Princess having always been the very pink of propriety): " Get up when your wife passes, do they? Well, that's a change from her grandmother's day. She expected the gentlemen to lie down." Then some one alleged that, having gone down to see his aunt the Princesse de Luxembourg at Balbec, and put up at the Grand Hotel, he had complained to the manager there (my friend) that the royal standard of Luxembourg was not flown in front of the hotel, over the sea. And that this flag being less familiar and less generally in use than the British or Italian, it had taken him several days to procure one, greatly to the young Grand Duke's annoyance. I did not believe a word of this story, but made up my mind, as soon as I went to Balbec, to inquire of the manager, so as to make certain that it was a pure invention. While waiting for Saint-Loup to return I asked the proprietor to get me some bread. " Certainly, Monsieur le Baron! " " I am

REMEMBRANCE OF THINGS PAST

not a Baron," I told him. "Oh, beg pardon, Monsieur
le Comte!" I had no time to lodge a second protest
which would certainly have promoted me to the rank
of marquis; faithful to his promise of an immediate
return, Saint-Loup reappeared in the doorway carrying
over his arm the thick vicuna cloak of the Prince de
Foix, from whom I guessed that he had borrowed it
in order to keep me warm. He signed to me not to get
up, and came towards me, but either my table would
have to be moved again or I must change my seat if
he was to get to his. Entering the big room he sprang
lightly on to one of the red plush benches which ran
round its walls and on which, apart from myself, there
were sitting only three or four of the young men from
the Jockey Club, friends of his own, who had not managed
to find places in the other room. Between the tables
and the wall electric wires were stretched at a certain
height; without the least hesitation Saint-Loup jumped
nimbly over them like a horse in a steeplechase; embarrassed that it should be done wholly for my benefit and to
save me the trouble of a slight movement, I was at the
same time amazed at the precision with which my friend
performed this exercise in levitation; and in this I was
not alone; for, albeit they would probably have had but
little admiration for a similar display on the part of a
more humbly born and less generous client, the proprietor and his staff stood fascinated, like race-goers in
the enclosure; one underling, apparently rooted to the
ground, stood there gaping with a dish in his hand for
which a party close beside him were waiting; and when
Saint-Loup, having to get past his friends, climbed on
the narrow ledge behind them and ran along it, bal-

ancing himself with his arms, discreet applause broke
from the body of the room. On coming to where I
was sitting he stopped short in his advance with the
precision of a tributary chieftain before the throne of
a sovereign, and, stooping down, handed to me with an
air of courtesy and submission the vicuna cloak which,
a moment later, having taken his place beside me, without my having to make a single movement he arranged
as a light but warm shawl about my shoulders.

"By the way, while I think of it, my uncle Charlus
has something to say to you. I promised I'ld send you
round to him to-morrow evening."

"I was just going to speak to you about him. But
to-morrow evening I am dining with your aunt Guermantes."

"Yes there's a regular beanfeast to-morrow at Oriane's.
I'm not asked. But my uncle Palamède don't want you
to go there. You can't get out of it, I suppose? Well,
anyhow, go on to my uncle's afterwards. I'm sure he
really does want to see you. Look here, you can easily
manage to get there by eleven. Eleven o'clock; don't
forget; I'll let him know. He's very touchy. If you don't
turn up he'll never forgive you. And Oriane's parties
are always over quite early. If you are only going to
dine there you can quite easily be at my uncle's by eleven.
I ought really to go and see Oriane, about getting shifted
from Morocco; I want an exchange. She is so nice about
all that sort of thing, and she can get anything she likes
out of General de Saint-Joseph, who runs that branch.
But don't say anything about it to her. I've mentioned
it to the Princesse de Parme, everything will be all right.
Interesting place, Morocco. I could tell you all sorts of

things. Very fine lot of men out there. One feels they're on one's own level, mentally."

" You don't think the Germans are going to go to war about it? "

" No; they're annoyed with us, as after all they have every right to be. But the Emperor is out for peace. They are always making us think they want war, to force us to give in. Pure bluff, you know, like poker. The Prince of Monaco, one of Wilhelm's agents, comes and tells us in confidence that Germany will attack us. Then we give way. But if we didn't give way, there wouldn't be war in any shape or form. You have only to think what a comic spectacle a war would be in these days. It'ld be a bigger catastrophe than the Flood and the *Götterdämmerung* rolled in one. Only it wouldn't last so long."

He spoke to me of friendship, affection, regret, albeit like all visitors of his sort he was going off the next morning for some months, which he was to spend in the country, and would only be staying a couple of nights in Paris on his way back to Morocco (or elsewhere); but the words which he thus let fall into the heated furnace which my heart was this evening kindled a pleasant glow there. Our infrequent meetings, this one in particular, have since formed a distinct episode in my memories. For him, as for me, this was the evening of friendship. And yet the friendship that I felt for him at this moment was scarcely, I feared (and felt therefore some remorse at the thought), what he would have liked to inspire. Filled still with the pleasure that I had had in seeing him come bounding towards me and gracefully pause on arriving at his goal, I felt that this pleasure lay in my recognising that each of the series of movements which he had developed against the wall, along the bench, had its meaning, its cause in Saint-Loup's own personal nature, possibly, but even more in that which by birth and upbringing he had inherited from his race.

A certainty of taste in the region not of beauty but manners, which when he was faced by a novel combination of circumstances enabled the man of breeding to grasp at once—like a musician who has been asked to play a piece he has never seen—the feeling, the motions that were required, and to apply the appropriate mechanism and technique; which then allowed this taste to display itself without the constraint of any other consideration, by which the average young man of the middle class would have been paralysed, from fear as well of making himself ridiculous in the eyes of strangers by his disregard of convention as of appearing too deferential in the eyes of his friends; the place of this constraint being taken in Robert by a lofty disdain which certainly he had never felt in his heart but which he had received by inheritance in his body, and which had moulded the attitudes of his ancestors to a familiarity with their inferiors which, they imagined, could only flatter and enchant those to whom it was displayed; lastly, a noble liberality which, taking no account of his boundless natural advantages (lavish expenditure in this restaurant had succeeded in making him, here as elsewhere, the most fashionable customer and the general favourite, a position which was underlined by the deference shewn him throughout the place not only by the waiters but by all its most exclusive young patrons), led him to trample them underfoot, just as he had, actually and symbolically, trodden upon those benches decked with purple, like a triumphal way which pleased my friend only because it enabled him more gracefully and swiftly to arrive at my side; such were the qualities, essential to aristocracy, which through the husk of this body, not opaque and vague as mine would have been, but significant and limpid, transmitted as through a work of art the industrious, energetic force which had created it and rendered the movements of this lightfoot course which Robert had pursued along the wall intelligible and charming as those of a row of knights upon a marble frieze. "Alas!" Robert might have thought, "was it worth while to have grown up despising birth, honouring only justice and intellect, choosing outside the ranks of the friends provided for me companions who were awkward and ill-dressed, provided they had the gift of eloquence, only for the sole personality apparent in me, which is to remain a treasured memory, to be not that which my will, with the most praiseworthy effort, has fashioned in my likeness, but one which is not of my making, which is not even myself, which I have always disliked and striven to overcome; was it worth while to love my chosen friend as I have loved him, for the greatest pleasure that he can find in me to be that of discovering something far more general than myself, a pleasure which is not in the least (as he says, though he cannot seriously believe it) one of the pleasures of friendship, but an intellectual and detached, a sort of artistic pleasure?" This is what I am now afraid that Saint-Loup may at times have thought. If so, he was mistaken. If he had not (as he steadfastly had) cherished something more lofty than the suppleness innate in his body, if he had not kept aloof for so long from the pride that goes with noble birth, there would have been something more studied, a certain heaviness in his very agility, a self-important vulgarity in his manners. As with Mme. de Villeparisis a strong vein of seriousness had been necessary for her to give in her conversation and in her Memoirs a sense of the frivolous, which is intellectual, so, in order that Saint-Loup's body might be indwelt by so much nobility, the latter had first to desert a mind that was aiming at higher things, and, reabsorbed into his body, to be fixed there in unconscious, noble lines. In this way his distinction of mind was not absent from a bodily distinction which otherwise would not have been complete. An artist has no need to express his mind directly in his work for it to express the quality of that mind; it has indeed been said that the highest praise of God consists in the denial of Him by the atheist, who finds creation so perfect that it can dispense with a creator. And I was quite well aware that it was not merely a work of art that I was admiring in this young man unfolding along the wall the frieze of his flying course; the young Prince (a descendant of Catherine de Foix, Queen of Navarre and grand-daughter of Charles VII) whom he had just left for my sake, the endowments, by birth and fortune, which he was laying at my feet, the proud and shapely ancestors who survived in the assurance, the agility, the courtesy with which he now arranged about my shivering body the warm woollen cloak, were not all these like friends of longer standing in his life, by whom I might have expected that we should be permanently kept apart, and whom, on the contrary, he was sacrificing to me by a choice which one can make only in the loftiest places of the mind, with that sovereign liberty of which Robert's movements were the presentment and in which is realised perfect friendship?

How much familiar intercourse with a Guermantes—in place of the distinction that it had in Robert, because there the inherited scorn of humanity was but the outer garment, become an unconscious charm, of a real moral humility—could disclose of vulgar arrogance I had had an opportunity of seeing, not in M. de Charlus, in whom certain characteristic faults, for which I had been unable, so far, to account, were overlaid upon his aristocratic habits, but in the Duc de Guermantes. And yet he too, in the general impression of commonness which had so strongly repelled my grandmother when she had met him once, years earlier, at Mme. de Villeparisis's, included glimpses of historic grandeur of which I became conscious when I went to dine in his house, on the evening following that which I had spent with Saint-Loup.

They had not been apparent to me either in himself or in the Duchess when I had met them first in their aunt's drawing-room, any more than I had discerned, on first seeing her, the differences that set Berma apart from her fellow-players, all the more that in her the individuality was infinitely more striking than in any social celebrity, such distinctions becoming more marked in proportion as the objects are more real, more conceivable by the intellect. And yet, however slight the shades of social distinction may be (and so slight are they that when an accurate portrayer like Sainte-Beuve tries to indicate the shades of difference between the salons of Mme. Geoffrin, Mme. Récamier and Mme. de Boigne, they appear so much alike that the cardinal truth which, unknown to the author, emerges from his investigations is the vacuity of that form of life), with them, and for the same reason as with Berma, when the Guermantes had ceased to impress me and the tiny drop of their originality was no longer vaporised by my imagination, I was able to distil and analyse it, imponderable as it was.

The Duchess having made no reference to her husband when she talked to me at her aunt's party, I wondered whether, in view of the rumours of a divorce that were current, he would be present at the dinner. But my doubts were speedily set at rest, for through the crowd of footmen who stood about in the hall and who (since they must until then have regarded me much as they regarded the children of the evicted cabinet-maker, that is to say with more fellow-feeling perhaps than their master but as a person incapable of being admitted to his house) must have been asking themselves to what this social revolution could be due, I saw slip towards me M. de Guermantes himself, who had been watching for my arrival so as to receive me upon his threshold and take off my greatcoat with his own hands.

" Mme. de Guermantes will be as pleased as punch," he greeted me in a glibly persuasive tone. " Let me help you off with your duds." (He felt it to be at once companionable and comic to employ the speech of the people.) " My wife was just the least bit afraid you might fail us, although you had fixed a date. We've been saying to each other all day long: ' Depend upon it, he'll never turn up.' I am bound to say, Mme. de Guermantes was a better prophet than I was. You are not an easy man to get hold of, and I was quite sure you were going to play

us false." And the Duke was so bad a husband, so brutal
even (people said), that one felt grateful to him, as one
feels grateful to wicked people for their occasional kindness of heart, for those words "Mme. de Guermantes"
with which he appeared to be spreading out over the
Duchess a protecting wing, that she might be but one
flesh with him. Meanwhile, taking me familiarly by the
hand, he began to lead the way, to introduce me into his
household. Just as some casual phrase may delight us
coming from the lips of a peasant if it points to the survival of a local tradition, shews the trace of some historic
event unknown, it may be, to him who thus alludes to it;
so this politeness on the part of M. de Guermantes, which,
moreover, he was to continue to shew me throughout the
evening, charmed me as a survival of habits of many
centuries' growth, habits of the seventeenth century in
particular. The people of bygone ages seem to us infinitely remote. We do not feel justified in ascribing to
them any underlying intention apart from those to which
they give formal expression; we are amazed when we
come upon a sentiment more or less akin to what we are
feeling to-day in a Homeric hero, or upon a skilful tactical
feint in Hannibal, during the battle of Cannae, where he
let his flank be driven back in order to take the enemy
by surprise and surround him; it would seem that we
imagined the epic poet and the Punic general as being as
remote from ourselves as an animal seen in a zoological
garden. Even in certain personages of the court of Louis
XIV, when we find signs of courtesy in the letters written
by them to some man of inferior rank who could be of no
service to them whatever, they leave us bewildered because they reveal to us suddenly, as existing among these

great gentlemen, a whole world of beliefs to which they never give any direct expression but which govern their conduct, and especially the belief that they are bound in politeness to feign certain sentiments and to carry out with the most scrupulous care certain obligations of friendship.

This imagined remoteness of the past is perhaps one of the things that enable us to understand how even great writers have found an inspired beauty in the works of mediocre mystifiers, such as Macpherson's *Ossian.* We so little expected to learn that bards long dead could have modern ideas that we marvel if in what we believe to be an ancient Gaelic ode we come upon one which we should have thought, at the most, ingenious in a contemporary. A translator of talent has simply to add to an ancient writer whom he presents to us more or less faithfully reproduced fragments which, signed with a contemporary name and published separately, would seem entertaining only; at once he imparts a moving grandeur to his poet, who is thus made to play upon the keyboards of several ages at once. This translator was capable only of a mediocre book, if that book had been published as his original work. Given out as a translation, it seems that of a masterpiece. The past not merely is not fugitive, it remains present. It is not within a few months only after the outbreak of a war that laws passed without haste can effectively influence its course, it is not within fifteen years only after a crime which has remained obscure that a magistrate can still find the vital evidence which will throw a light on it; after hundreds and thousands of years the scholar who has been studying in a distant land the place-names, the customs of the inhabitants, may still extract from them some legend long anterior to the Christian era, already unintelligible, if not actually forgotten, at the time of Herodotus, which in the name given to a rock, in a religious rite, dwells surrounded by the present, like an emanation of greater density, immemorial and stable. There was similarly an emanation, though far less ancient, of the life of the court, if not in the manners of M. de Guermantes, which were often vulgar, at least in the mind that controlled them. I was to breathe this again, like the odour of antiquity, when I joined him a little later in the drawing-room. For I did not go there at once.

As we left the outer hall, I had mentioned to M. de Guermantes that I was extremely anxious to see his Elstirs. " I am at your service. Is M. Elstir a friend of yours, then? If so, it is most vexing, for I know him slightly; he is a pleasant fellow, what our fathers used to call an ' honest fellow ', I might have asked him to honour us with his company, and to dine to-night. I am sure he would have been highly flattered at being invited to spend the evening in your society." Very little suggestive of the old order when he tried thus to assume its manner, the Duke relapsed unconsciously into it. After inquiring whether I wished him to shew me the pictures, he conducted me to them, gracefully standing aside for me at each door, apologising when, to shew me the way, he was obliged to precede me, a little scene which (since the days when Saint-Simon relates that an ancestor of the Guermantes did him the honours of his town house with the same punctilious exactitude in the performance of the frivolous duties of a gentleman) must, before coming gradually down to us, have been enacted by many other

Guermantes for numberless other visitors. And as I had said to the Duke that I would like very much to be left alone for a few minutes with the pictures, he discreetly withdrew, telling me that I should find him in the drawing-room when I was ready.

Only, once I was face to face with the Elstirs, I completely forgot about dinner and the time; here again as at Balbec I had before me fragments of that strangely coloured world which was no more than the projection, the way of seeing things peculiar to that great painter, which his speech in no way expressed. The parts of the walls that were covered by paintings from his brush, all homogeneous with one another, were like the luminous images of a magic lantern, which would have been in this instance the brain of the artist, and the strangeness of which one could never have suspected so long as one had known only the man, which was like seeing the iron lantern boxing its lamp before any coloured slide had been slid into its groove. Among these pictures several of the kind that seemed most absurd to ordinary people interested me more than the rest because they recreated those optical illusions which prove to us that we should never succeed in identifying objects if we did not make some process of reasoning intervene. How often, when driving in the dark, do we not come upon a long, lighted street which begins a few feet away from us, when what we have actually before our eyes is nothing but a rectangular patch of wall with a bright light falling on it, which has given us the mirage of depth. In view of which is it not logical, not by any artifice of symbolism but by a sincere return to the very root of the impression, to represent one thing by that other for which, in the flash of a first illusion, we mistook it? Surfaces and volumes are in reality independent of the names of objects which our memory imposes on them after we have recognised them. Elstir attempted to wrest from what he had just felt what he already knew, his effort had often been to break up that aggregate of impressions which we call vision.

The people who detested these "horrors" were aston-ished to find that Elstir admired Chardin, Perroneau, any number of painters whom they, the ordinary men and women of society, liked. They did not take into account that Elstir had had to make, for his own part, in striving to reproduce reality (with the particular index of his taste for certain lines of approach), the same effort as a Chardin or a Perroneau and that consequently, when he ceased to work for himself, he admired in them at-tempts of the same order, fragments anticipatory so to speak of works of his own. Nor did these society people include in their conception of Elstir's work that temporal perspective which enabled them to like, or at least to look without discomfort at Chardin's painting. And yet the older among them might have reminded themselves that in the course of their lives they had seen gradually, as the years bore them away from it, the unbridgeable gulf between what they considered a masterpiece by Ingres and what, they had supposed, must remain for ever a " horror " (Manet's *Olympia,* for example) shrink until the two canvases seemed like twins. But we learn nothing from any lesson because we have not the wisdom to work backwards from the particular to the general, and imagine ourselves always to be going through an experience which is without precedents in the past.

I was moved by the discovery in two of the pictures

(more realistic, these, and in an earlier manner) of the same person, in one in evening dress in his own drawing-room, in the other wearing a frock coat and tall hat at some popular regatta where he had evidently no business to be, which proved that for Elstir he was not only a regular sitter but a friend, perhaps a patron whom it pleased him (just as Carpaccio used to introduce prominent figures, and in speaking likenesses, from contemporary life in Venice) to introduce into his pictures, just as Beethoven, too, found pleasure in inscribing at the top of a favourite work the beloved name of the Archduke Rudolph. There was something enchanting about this waterside carnival. The river, the women's dresses, the sails of the boats, the innumerable reflexions of one thing and another came crowding into this little square panel of beauty which Elstir had cut out of a marvellous afternoon. What delighted one in the dress of a woman who had stopped for a moment in the dance because it was hot and she was out of breath was irresistible also in the same way in the canvas of a motionless sail, in the water of the little harbour, in the wooden bridge, in the leaves of the trees and in the sky. As in one of the pictures that I had seen at Balbec, the hospital, as beautiful beneath its sky of lapis lazuli as the cathedral itself, seemed (more bold than Elstir the theorician, than Elstir the man of taste, the lover of things mediaeval) to be intoning: "There is no such thing as gothic, there is no such thing as a masterpiece; this tasteless hospital is just as good as the glorious porch," so I now heard: "The slightly vulgar lady at whom a man of discernment would refrain from glancing as he passed her by, would except her from the poetical composition which nature has set before him—

her dress is receiving the same light as the sail of that boat, and there are no degrees of value and beauty; the commonplace dress and the sail, beautiful in itself, are two mirrors reflecting the same gleam; the value is all in the painter's eye." This eye had had the skill to arrest for all time the motion of the hours at this luminous instant, when the lady had felt hot and had stopped dancing, when the tree was fringed with a belt of shadow, when the sails seemed to be slipping over a golden glaze. But just because the depicted moment pressed on one with so much force, this so permanent canvas gave one the most fleeting impression, one felt that the lady would presently move out of it, the boats drift away, the night draw on, that pleasure comes to an end, that life passes and that the moments illuminated by the convergence, at once, of so many lights do not recur. I recognised yet another aspect, quite different it is true, of what the moment means in a series of water-colours of mythological subjects, dating from Elstir's first period, which also adorned this room. Society people who held " advanced " views on art went " as far as " this earliest manner, but no farther. These were certainly not the best work that he had done, but already the sincerity with which the subject had been thought out melted its natural coldness. Thus the Muses, for instance, were represented as it might be creatures belonging to a species now fossilised, but creatures which it would not have been surprising in mythological times to see pass in the evening, in twos or threes, along some mountain path. Here and there a poet, of a race that had also a peculiar interest for the zoologist (characterised by a certain sexlessness) strolled with a Muse, as one sees in nature creatures of different but of kindred species consort together. In one of these water-colours one saw a poet wearied by long wanderings on the mountains, whom a Centaur, meeting him and moved to pity by his weakness, had taken on his back and was carrying home. In more than one other, the vast landscape (in which the mythical scene, the fabulous heroes occupied a minute place and were almost lost) was rendered, from the mountain tops to the sea, with an exactitude which told one more than the hour, told one to the very minute what time of day it was, thanks to the precise angle of the setting sun, to the fleeting fidelity of the shadows. In this way the artist managed to give, by making it instantaneous, a sort of historical reality, as of a thing actually lived, to the symbol of his fable, painted it and set it at a definite point in the past.

While I was examining Elstir's paintings the bell, rung by arriving guests, had been pealing uninterruptedly, and had lulled me into a pleasing unconsciousness. But the silence which followed its clangour and had already lasted for some time succeeded — less rapidly, it is true — in awakening me from my dream, as the silence that follows Lindor's music arouses Bartolo from his sleep. I was afraid that I had been forgotten, that they had sat down to dinner, and hurried to the drawing-room. At the door of the Elstir gallery I found a servant waiting for me, white-haired, though whether with age or powder I cannot say, with the air of a Spanish Minister, but treating me with the same respect that he would have shewn to a King. I felt from his manner that he must have been waiting for at least an hour, and I thought with alarm of the delay I had caused in the service of dinner, especially as I had promised to be at M. de Charlus's by eleven.

The Spanish Minister (though I also met on the way the footman persecuted by the porter, who, radiant with delight when I inquired after his girl, told me that the very next day they were both to be off duty, so that he would be able to spend the whole day with her, and extolled the generosity of Madame la Duchesse) conducted me to the drawing-room, where I was afraid of finding M. de Guermantes in an ill humour. He welcomed me, on the contrary, with a joy that was evidently to a certain extent artificial and dictated by politeness, but was also sincere, prompted both by his stomach which so long a delay had begun to famish, and his consciousness of a similar impatience in all his other guests, who completely filled the room. Indeed I heard afterwards that I had kept them waiting for nearly three-quarters of an hour. The Duc de Guermantes probably thought that to prolong the general torment for two minutes more would not intensify it and that, politeness having driven him to postpone for so long the moment of moving into the dining-room, this politeness would be more complete if, by not having dinner announced immediately, he could succeed in persuading me that I was not late, and that they had not been waiting for me. And so he asked me, as if we had still an hour before dinner and some of the party had not yet arrived, what I thought of his Elstirs. But at the same time, and without letting the cravings of his stomach become apparent, so as not to lose another moment, he, in concert with the Duchess, proceeded to the ceremony of introduction. Then only I perceived that there had occurred round about me, me who until this evening, save for my novitiate in Mme. Swann's drawing-room, had been accustomed, in my mother's homes, at

Combray and in Paris, to the manners, either protecting or defensive, of the grim ladies of our middle-world, who treated me as a child, a change of surroundings comparable to that which introduces Parsifal suddenly into the midst of the Flower-Maidens. Those who surrounded me now, their bosoms entirely bare (the naked flesh appeared on either side of a sinuous spray of mimosa or behind the broad petals of a rose) could not murmur a word of greeting without at the same time bathing me in long, caressing glances, as though shyness alone restrained them from kissing me. Many of them were nevertheless highly respectable from the moral standpoint; many, not all, for the most virtuous had not for those of a lighter vein the same repulsion that my mother would have felt. The caprices of one's conduct, denied by saintlier friends, in the face of the evidence, seemed in the Guermantes world to matter far less than the relations which one had been able to maintain. One pretended not to know that the body of one's hostess was at the disposal of all comers, provided that her visiting list showed no gaps. As the Duke put himself out not at all for his other guests (of whom he had long known everything that there was to know, and they of him) but quite markedly for me, whose kind of superiority, being outside his experience, inspired in him something akin to the respect which the great noblemen of the court of Louis XIV used to feel for his plebeian Ministers, he evidently considered that the fact of my not knowing his other guests mattered not at all— to me at least, though it might to them—and while I was anxious, on his account, as to the impression that I was going to make on them he was thinking only of how his friends would impress me.

At the very outset I found myself completely bewildered. No sooner had I entered the drawing-room than M. de Guermantes, without even allowing me time to shake hands with the Duchess, had led me, as though I were a delightful surprise to the person in question to whom he seemed to be saying: "Here's your friend! You see, I'm bringing him to you by the scruff of his neck," towards a lady of smallish stature. Whereupon, long before, thrust forward by the Duke, I had reached her chair, the lady had begun to flash at me continuously from her large, soft, dark eyes the thousand smiles of understanding which we address to an old friend who perhaps has not recognised us. As this was precisely my case and I could not succeed in calling to mind who she was I averted my eyes from her as I approached so as not to have to respond until our introduction should have released me from my predicament. Meanwhile the lady continued to maintain in unstable equilibrium the smile intended for myself. She looked as though she were anxious to be relieved of it and to hear me say: "Oh, but this is a pleasure! Mamma will be pleased when I tell her I've met you!" I was as impatient to learn her name as she was to see that I did finally greet her, fully aware of what I was doing, so that the smile which she was holding on indefinitely, like the note of a tuning-fork, might at length be let go. But M. de Guermantes managed things so badly (to my mind, at least) that I seemed to have heard only my own name uttered and was given no clue to the identity of my unknown friend, to whom it never occurred to tell me herself what her name was, so obvious did the grounds of our intimacy, which baffled me completely, seem to her. Indeed, as soon as I

THE PRINCESSE DE PARME

THE PRINCESSE DE PARME

had come within reach, she did not offer me her hand, but took mine in a familiar clasp, and spoke to me exactly as though I had been equally conscious with herself of the pleasant memories to which her mind reverted. She told me how sorry Albert (who, I gathered, was her son) would be to have missed seeing me. I tried to remember who, among the people I had known as boys, was called Albert, and could think only of Bloch, but this could not be Bloch's mother that I saw before me since she had been dead for some time. In vain I struggled to identify the past experience common to herself and me to which her thoughts had been carried back. But I could no more distinguish it through the translucent jet of her large, soft pupils which allowed only her smile to pierce their surface than one can distinguish a landscape that lies on the other side of a smoked glass, even when the sun is blazing on it. She asked me whether my father was not working too hard, if I would not come to the theatre some evening with Albert, if I was stronger now, and as my replies, stumbling through the mental darkness in which I was plunged, became distinct only to explain that I was not feeling well that evening, she pushed forward a chair for me herself, going to all sorts of trouble which I was not accustomed to see taken by my parents' friends. At length the clue to the riddle was furnished me by the Duke: "She thinks you're charming," he murmured in my ear, which felt somehow that it had heard these words before. They were what Mme. de Villeparisis had said to my grandmother and myself after we had made the acquaintance of the Princesse de Luxembourg. Everything became clear; the lady I now saw had nothing in common with Mme. de Luxembourg, but from the language of him who thus served me with her I could discern the nature of the animal. It was a Royalty. She had never before heard of either my family or myself, but, a scion of the noblest race and endowed with the greatest fortune in the world (for, a daughter of the Prince de Parme, she had married a cousin of equal princelihood), she sought always, in gratitude to her Creator, to testify to her neighbour, however poor or lowly he might be, that she did not look down upon him. Really, I might have guessed this from her smile. I had seen the Princesse de Luxembourg buy little rye-cakes on the beach at Balbec to give to my grandmother, as though to a caged deer in the zoological gardens. But this was only the second Princess of the Blood Royal to whom I had been presented, and I might be excused my failure to discern in her the common factors of the friendliness of the great. Besides, had not they themselves gone out of their way to warn me not to count too much on this friendliness, since the Duchesse de Guermantes, who had waved me so effusive a greeting with her gloved hand at the Opéra-Comique, had appeared furious when I bowed to her in the street, like people who, having once given somebody a sovereign, feel that this has set them free from any further obligation towards him. As for M. de Charlus, his ups and downs were even more sharply contrasted. While in the sequel I have known, as the reader will learn, Highnesses and Majesties of another sort altogether, Queens who play the Queen and speak not after the conventions of their kind but like the Queens in Sardou's plays.

If M. de Guermantes had been in such haste to present me, it was because the presence at a party of anyone not personally known to a Royal Personage is an intolerable state of things which must not be prolonged for a single instant. It was similar to the haste which Saint-Loup had shewn in making me introduce him to my grandmother. By the same token, by a fragmentary survival of the old life of the court which is called social courtesy and is not superficial, in which, rather, by a centripetal reversion, it is the surface that becomes essential and profound, the Duc and Duchesse de Guermantes regarded as a duty more essential than those (which one at least of the pair neglected often enough) of charity, chastity, pity and justice, as a more unalterable law that of never addressing the Princesse de Parme save in the third person.

Having never yet in my life been to Parma (a pilgrimage I had been anxious to make ever since certain Easter holidays long ago), to meet its Princess, who, I knew, owned the finest palace in that matchless city, where, moreover, everything must be in keeping, isolated as it was from the rest of the world, within the polished walls, in the atmosphere, stifling as a breathless summer evening on the Piazza of a small town in Italy, of its compact and almost cloying name, would surely have substituted in a flash for what I had so often tried to imagine all that did really exist at Parma in a sort of partial arrival there, without my having to stir from Paris, of myself; it was in the algebraical expression of a journey to the city of Correggio a simple equation, so to speak, of that unknown quantity. But if I had for many years past—like a perfumer impregnating a solid mass of grease with scent—made this name, Princesse de Parme, absorb the fragrance of thousands of violets, in return, when I set eyes on the Princess, who, until then I should have sworn, must be the Sanseverina herself, a second process began which was not, I may say, completed until several months had passed, and consisted in expelling, by means of fresh chemical combinations, all the essential oil of violets and all the Stendhalian fragrance from the name of the Princess, and in implanting there, in their place, the image of a little dark woman, taken up with good works, of a friendliness so humble that one felt at once in how exalted a pride that friendliness had its roots. Moreover, while, barring a few points of difference, she was exactly like any other great lady, she was as little Stendhalian as is, for example, in Paris, in the Europe quarter, the Rue de Parme, which bears far less resemblance to the name of Parma than to any or all of the neighbouring streets, and reminds one not nearly so much of the Charterhouse in which Fabrice ends his days as of the waiting room in the Saint-Lazare station.

Her friendliness sprang from two causes. The first and more general was the education which this daughter of Kings had received. Her mother (not merely allied by blood to all the royal families of Europe but furthermore —in contrast to the Ducal House of Parma—richer than any reigning Princess) had instilled into her from her earliest childhood the arrogantly humble precepts of an evangelical snobbery; and to-day every line of the daughter's face, the curve of her shoulders, the movements of her arms seemed to repeat the lesson: " Remember that if God has caused you to be born on the steps of a throne you ought not to make that a reason for looking down upon those to whom Divine Providence has willed (wherefore His Name be praised) that you should be superior by birth and fortune. On the contrary, you must suffer the little ones. Your ancestors were Princes of Treves and

Juliers from the year 647: God has decreed in His bounty
that you should hold practically all the shares in the Suez
Canal and three times as many Royal Dutch as Edmond
de Rothschild; your pedigree in a direct line has been
established by genealogists from the year 63 of the Christian Era; you have as sisters-in-law two Empresses.
Therefore never seem, in your speech, to be recalling
these great privileges, not that they are precarious (for
nothing can alter antiquity of race, while the world will
always need petrol), but because it is useless to point out
that you are better born than other people or that your
investments are all gilt-edged, since everyone knows these
facts already. Be helpful to the needy. Furnish to all
those whom the bounty of heaven has done you the
favour of placing beneath you as much as you can give
them without forfeiture of your rank, that is to say help
in the form of money, even your personal service by their
sickbeds, but never (bear well in mind) invite them to
your parties, which would do them no possible good and,
by weakening your own position, would diminish the effi-
cacy of your benevolent activities."

And so even at the moments when she could not do
good the Princess endeavoured to shew, or rather to let it
be thought, by all the external signs of dumb language,
that she did not consider herself superior to the people
among whom she found herself thrown. She treated each
of them with that charming courtesy with which well-
bred people treat their inferiors and was continually,
to make herself useful, pushing back her chair so as to
leave more room, holding my gloves, offering me all those
services which would demean the proud spirit of a commoner but are very willingly rendered by sovereign ladies

or, instinctively and by force of professional habit, by retired servants.

But already the Duke, who seemed in a hurry to complete the round of introduction, had led me off to another of the flower-maidens. On hearing her name I told her that I had passed by her country house, not far from Balbec. " Oh, I should have been so pleased to take you over it," she informed me, almost in a whisper, to enhance her modesty, but in a tone of deep feeling, steeped in regret for the loss of an opportunity to enjoy a quite exceptional pleasure; and went on, with a meaning glance: " I do hope you will come again some day. But I must say that what would interest you more still would be my aunt Brancas's place. It was built by Mansard; it is the jewel of the province." It was not only she herself who would have been glad to shew me over her house, but her aunt Brancas would have been no less delighted to do me the honours of hers, or so I was assured by this lady who thought evidently that, especially at a time when the land shewed a tendency to pass into the hands of financiers who had no knowledge of the world, it was important that the great should keep up the exalted traditions of lordly hospitality, by speeches which involved them in nothing. It was also because she sought, like everyone in her world, to say the things which would give most pleasure to the person she was addressing, to give him the highest idea of himself, to make him think that he flattered people by writing to them, that he honoured those who entertained him, that everyone was burning to know him. The desire to give other people this comforting idea of themselves does, it must be admitted, exist even among the middle classes. We find there that kindly disposition,

166

in the form of an individual merit compensating for some
other defect, not alas among the most trusty male friends
but at any rate among the most agreeable female companions. But there anyhow it blooms only in isolated
patches. In an important section of the aristocracy, on
the other hand, this characteristic has ceased to be individual; cultivated by education, sustained by the idea
of a personal greatness which can fear no humiliation,
which knows no rival, is aware that by being pleasant it
can make people happy and delights in doing so, it has
become the generic feature of a class. And even those
whom personal defects of too incompatible a kind prevent
from keeping it in their hearts bear the unconscious trace
of it in their vocabulary or their gesticulation.

"She is a very good creature," said the Duc de Guermantes, of the Princesse de Parme, "and she can play
the 'great lady' when she likes, better than anyone."

While I was being introduced to the ladies, one of the
gentlemen of the party had been shewing various signs
of agitation: this was Comte Hannibal de Bréauté-Consalvi. Arriving late, he had not had time to investigate
the composition of the party, and when I entered the
room, seeing in me a guest who was not one of the
Duchess's regular circle and must therefore have some
quite extraordinary claim to admission, installed his monocle beneath the groined arch of his eyebrow, thinking
that this would be a great help to him in discovering
what manner of man I was. He knew that Mme. de Guermantes possessed (the priceless appanage of truly superior
women) what was called a "salon", that is to say added
occasionally to the people of her own set some celebrity
who had recently come into prominence by the discovery

of a new cure for something or the production of a masterpiece. The Faubourg Saint-Germain had not yet recovered from the shock of learning that, to the reception which she had given to meet the King and Queen of England, the Duchess had not been afraid to invite M. Detaille. The clever women of the Faubourg who had not been invited were inconsolable, so deliciously thrilling would it have been to come into contact with that strange genius. Mme. de Courvoisier made out that M. Ribot had been there as well, but this was a pure invention, designed to make people believe that Oriane was aiming at an Embassy for her husband. Finally, a last straw of scandal, M. de Guermantes, with a gallantry that would have done credit to Marshal Saxe, had repaired to the green-room of the Comédie Française, and had begged Mlle. Reichemberg to come and recite before the King, which having come to pass constituted an event without precedent in the annals of routs. Remembering all these surprises, which, moreover, had his entire approval, his own presence being not merely an ornament but, in the same way as that of the Duchesse de Guermantes, a consecration to any drawing-room, M. de Bréauté, when he asked himself who I could be, felt that the field of exploration was very wide. For a moment the name of M. Widor flashed before his mind, but he decided that I was not old enough to be an organist, and M. Widor not striking enough to be "asked out". It seemed on the whole more plausible to regard me simply as the new Attaché at the Swedish Legation of whom he had heard, and he was preparing to ask me for the latest news of King Oscar, by whom he had several times been very hospitably received; but when the Duke, in introducing me, had mentioned my name to M. de Bréauté, the latter, finding that name to be completely unknown to him, had no longer any doubt that, being where I was, I must be a celebrity of some sort. Oriane would certainly never invite anyone who was not, and had the art of attracting men who were in the public eye to her house, in a ratio that of course never exceeded one per cent., otherwise she would have lowered its tone. M. de Bréauté began, therefore, to lick his chops and to sniff the air greedily, his appetite whetted not only by the good dinner upon which he could count, but by the character of the party, which my presence could not fail to make interesting, and which would furnish him with a topic for brilliant conversation next day at the Duc de Chartres's luncheon-table. He had not yet settled in his own mind whether I was the man who had just been making those experiments with a serum to cure cancer, or the author of the new " curtain-raiser " then in rehearsal at the Théâtre Français; but, a great intellectual, a great collector of " travellers' tales ", he continued an ever increasing display of reverences, signs of mutual understanding, smiles filtered through the glass of his monocle; either in the mistaken idea that a man of my standing would esteem him more highly if he could manage to instil into me the illusion that for him, the Comte de Bréauté-Consalvi, the privileges of the mind were no less deserving of respect than those of birth; or simply from the need to express and difficulty of expressing his satisfaction, in his ignorance of the language in which he ought to address me, just as if, in fact, he had found himself face to face with one of the " natives " of an undiscovered country on which his keel had grounded, natives from whom, in the hope of ultimate profit, he would endeavour, observing with interest the while their quaint customs and without interrupting his demonstrations of friendship, or like them uttering loud cries, to obtain ostrich eggs and spices in exchange for his glass beads. Having responded as best I could to his joy, I shook hands next with the Duc de Châtellerault, whom I had already met at Mme. de Villeparisis's, who, he informed me, was "as cunning as they made 'em". He was typically Guermantes in the fairness of his hair, his arched profile, the points where the skin of his cheeks lost colour, all of which may be seen in the portraits of that family which have come down to us from the sixteenth and seventeenth centuries. But, as I was no longer in love with the Duchess, her reincarnation in the person of a young man offered me no attraction. I interpreted the hook made by the Duc de Châtellerault's nose, as if it had been the signature of a painter whose work I had long studied but who no longer interested me in the least. Next, I said good evening also to the Prince de Foix, and to the detriment of my knuckles, which emerged crushed and mangled, let them be caught in a vice which was the German handclasp, accompanied by an ironical or good-natured smile, of the Prince von Faffenheim, M. de Norpois's friend, who, by virtue of the mania for nicknames which prevailed in this set, was known so universally as Prince Von that he himself used to sign his letters " Prince Von ", or, when he wrote to his intimates, " Von ". And yet this abbreviation was understandable, in view of his triple-barrelled name. It was less easy to grasp the reasons which made " Elizabeth " be replaced, now by " Lili ", now by " Bebeth ", just as another world swarmed with " Kikis ". One can realise that these people, albeit in most respects idle and light-minded enough, might have come to adopt " Quiou " in order not to waste the precious time that it would have taken them to pronounce "Montes-quiou". But it is not so easy to see what they saved by naming one of their cousins " Dinand " instead of " Fer-dinand". It must not be thought, however, that in the invention of nicknames the Guermantes invariably pro-ceed to curtail or reduplicate syllables. Thus two sisters, the Comtesse de Montpeyroux and the Vicomtesse de Vélude, who were both of them enormously stout, in-variably heard themselves addressed, without the least trace of annoyance on their part or of amusement on other people's, so long established was the custom, as " Petite " and " Mignonne ". Mme. de Guermantes, who adored Mme. de Montpeyroux, would, if her friend had been seri-ously ill, have flown to the sister with tears in her eyes and exclaimed: " I hear Petite is dreadfully bad! " Mme. de l'Eclin, who wore her hair in bands that entirely hid her ears, was never called anything but " The Empty Stomach"; in some cases people simply added an ' a ' to the last or first name of the husband to indicate the wife. The most miserly, most sordid, most inhuman man in the Faubourg having been christened Raphael, his charmer, his flower springing also from the rock always signed herself " Raphaela "—but these are merely a few speci-mens taken from innumerable rules, to which we can always return later on, if the occasion offers, and explain some of them. I then asked the Duke to present me to the Prince d'Agrigente. " What! Do you mean to say you don't know our excellent Gri-gri! " cried M. de Guer-mantes, and gave M. d'Agrigente my name. His own, so often quoted by Françoise, had always appeared to me like a transparent sheet of coloured glass through which I beheld, struck, on the shore of the violet sea, by the slanting rays of a golden sun, the rosy marble cubes of an ancient city of which I had not the least doubt that the Prince—happening for a miraculous moment to be passing through Paris—was himself, as luminously Sicilian and gloriously mellowed, the absolute sovereign. Alas, the vulgar drone to whom I was introduced, and who wheeled round to bid me good evening with a ponderous ease which he considered elegant, was as independent of his name as of any work of art that he might have owned without bearing upon his person any trace of its beauty, without, perhaps, ever having stopped to examine it. The Prince d'Agrigente was so entirely devoid of anything princely, anything that might make one think of Girgenti that one was led to suppose that his name, entirely distinct from himself, bound by no ties to his person, had had the power of attracting to itself the whole of whatever vague poetical element there might have been in this man as in any other, and isolating it, after the operation, in the enchanted syllables. If any such operation had been performed, it had certainly been done most efficiently, for there remained not an atom of charm to be drawn from this kinsman of the Guermantes. With the result that he found himself at one and the same time the only man in the world who was Prince d'Agrigente and the man who, of all the men in the world was, perhaps, least so. He was, for all that, very glad to be what he was, but as a banker is glad to hold a number of shares in a mine without caring whether the said mine answers to the charming name of Ivanhoe or Primrose, or is called merely the Premier. Meanwhile, as these introductions, which it has taken me so long to recount but which, beginning as I entered the room, had lasted only a few seconds, were coming to an end, and Mme. de Guermantes, in an almost suppliant tone, was saying to me: " I am sure Basin is tiring you, dragging you round like that; we are anxious for you to know our friends, but we are a great deal more anxious not to tire you, so that you may come again often," the Duke, with a somewhat awkward and timid wave of the hand, gave (as he would gladly have given it at any time during the last hour, filled for me by the contemplation of his Elstirs) the signal that dinner might now be served.

I should add that one of the guests was still missing, M. de Grouchy, whose wife, a Guermantes by birth, had arrived by herself, her husband being due to come straight from the country, where he had been shooting all day. This M. de Grouchy, a descendent of his namesake of the First Empire, of whom it has been said, quite wrongly, that his absence at the start of the Battle of Waterloo was the principal cause of Napoleon's defeat, came of an excellent family which, however, was not good enough in the eyes of certain fanatics for blue blood. Thus the Prince de Guermantes, whose own tastes, in later life, were to prove more easily satisfied, had been in the habit of saying to his nieces: " What a misfortune for that poor Mme. de Guermantes " (the Vicomtesse de Guermantes, Mme. de Grouchy's mother) " that she has never succeeded in marrying any of her children." " But, uncle, the eldest girl married M. de Grouchy." " I do not call that a husband! However, they say that your uncle François has proposed for the youngest one, so perhaps they won't all die old maids." No sooner was the order to serve dinner given than with a vast gyratory whirr, multiple and simultaneous, the double doors of the dining-room swung apart; a chamberlain with the air of a Lord Chamberlain bowed before the Princesse de Parme and announced the tidings "Madame is served," in a tone such as he would have employed to say "Madame is dead," which, however, cast no gloom over the assembly for it was with an air of unrestrained gaiety and as, in summer, at "Robinson" that the couples moved forward one behind another to the dining-room, separating when they had reached their places where footmen thrust their chairs in behind them; last of all, Mme. de Guermantes advanced upon me, that I might lead her to the table, and without my feeling the least shadow of the timidity that I might have feared, for, like a huntress to whom her great muscular prowess has made graceful motion an easy thing, observing no doubt that I had placed myself on the wrong side of her, she pivoted with such accuracy round me that I found her arm resting on mine and attuned in the most natural way to a rhythm of precise and noble movements. I yielded to these with all the more readiness in that the Guermantes attached no more importance to them than does to learning a truly learned man in whose company one is less alarmed than in that of a dunce; other doors opened through which there entered the steaming soup, as though the dinner were being held in a puppet-theatre of skilful mechanism where the belated arrival of the young guest set, on a signal from the puppet-master, all the machinery in motion.

Timid and not majestically sovereign had been this signal from the Duke, to which had responded the unlocking of that vast, ingenious, subservient and sumptuous clockwork, mechanical and human. The indecision of his gesture did not spoil for me the effect of the spectacle that was attendant upon it. For I could feel that what had made it hesitating and embarrassed was the fear of letting me see that they were waiting only for myself to begin dinner and that they had been waiting for some time, just as Mme. de Guermantes was afraid that after looking at so many pictures I would find it tiring and would be hindered from taking my ease among them if her husband engaged me in a continuous flow of introductions. So that it was the absence of grandeur in this gesture that disclosed its true grandeur. As, also, did that indifference shewn by the Duke to the splendour of his surroundings, in contrast to his deference towards a guest, however insignificant, whom he desired to honour.

Not that M. de Guermantes was not in certain respects thoroughly commonplace, shewing indeed some of the absurd weaknesses of a man with too much money, the arrogance of an upstart, which he certainly was not. But just as a public official or a priest sees his own humble talents multiplied to infinity (as a wave is by the whole mass of the sea which presses behind it) by those forces on which they can rely, the Government of France and the Catholic Church, so M. de Guermantes was borne on by that other force, aristocratic courtesy in its truest form. This courtesy drew the line at any number of people. Mme. de Guermantes would not have asked to her house Mme. de Cambremer, or M. de Forcheville. But the moment that anyone (as was the case with me) appeared eligible for admission into the Guermantes world, this courtesy revealed treasures of hospitable simplicity more splendid still, were that possible, than those historic rooms, or the marvellous furniture that had remained in them.

When he wished to give pleasure to anyone, M. de Guermantes possessed, in this way, for making his guest for the moment the principal person present, an art which made the most of the circumstances and the place. No doubt at Guermantes his "distinctions" and "favours" would have assumed another form. He would have ordered his carriage to take me for a drive, alone with himself, before dinner. Such as they were, one could not help feeling touched by his manners as one is in reading memoirs of the period by those of Louis XIV when he replies good-naturedly, smiling and almost with a bow, to some one who has come to solicit his favour. It must however in both instances be borne in mind that this "politeness" did not go beyond the strict meaning of the word.

Louis XIV (with whom the sticklers for pure nobility of his day find fault, nevertheless, for his scant regard for etiquette, so much so that, according to Saint-Simon, he was only a very minor king, as kings go, when compared with such monarchs as Philippe de Valois or Charles V), has the most minute instructions drawn up so that Princes of the Blood and Ambassadors may know to what sovereigns they ought to give precedence. In certain cases, in view of the impossibility of arriving at a decision, a compromise is arranged by which the son of Louis XIV, Monseigneur, shall entertain certain foreign sovereigns only out of doors, in the open air, so that it may not be said that in entering the house one has preceded the other; and the Elector Palatine, entertaining the Duc de Chevreuse at dinner, pretends, so as not to have to make way for his guest, to be taken ill, and dines with him indeed, but dines lying down, thus avoiding the difficulty. M. le Duc evading opportunities of paying his duty to Monsieur, the latter, on the advice of the King, his brother, who is moreover extremely attached to him, seizes an excuse for making his cousin attend his levee and forcing him to pass him his shirt. But as soon as the feeling is deep, when the heart is involved, this rule of duty, so inflexible when politeness only is at stake, changes entirely. A few hours after the death of this brother, one of the people whom he most dearly loved, when Monsieur, in the words of the Duc de Montfort, is "still warm", we find Louis XIV singing snatches from operas, astonished that the Duchesse de Bourgogne, who has difficulty in concealing her grief, should be looking so woe-begone, and, desiring that the gaiety of the court shall be at once resumed, so that his courtiers may be encouraged to sit down to the tables, ordering the Duc de Bourgogne to start a game of *brelan*. Well, not only in his social and concentrated activities, but in the most spontaneous utterances, the ordinary preoccupations of M. de Guermantes, the use he made of his time, one found a similar contrast; the Guermantes were no more susceptible than other mortals to grief; one might indeed say that their actual sensibility was lower; on the other hand one saw their names every day in the social columns of the *Gaulois* on account of the prodigious number of funerals at which they would have felt it a neglect of duty not to have their presence recorded. As the traveller discovers, almost unaltered, the houses roofed with turf, the terraces which may have met the eyes of Xenophon or Saint Paul, so in the manners of M. de Guermantes, a man who melted

one's heart by his courtesy and revolted it by his harshness, I found still intact after the lapse of more than two
centuries that deviation typical of court life under Louis
XIV which transfers all scruples of conscience from
matters of the affections and morality and applies them
to purely formal questions.

The other reason for the friendliness shewn me by
the Princesse de Parme was of a more personal kind. It
was that she was convinced beforehand that everything
that she saw at the Duchesse de Guermantes's, people and
things alike, was of a quality superior to that of anything
that she had at home. It is true that in all the other
houses of her acquaintance she behaved as if this had
been the case; over the simplest dish, the most ordinary
flowers, she was not satisfied with going into ecstasies,
she would ask leave to send round next morning, to copy
the recipe or to examine the variety of blossom, her head
cook or head gardener, gentlemen with large salaries who
kept their own carriages and were deeply humiliated at
having to come to inquire after a dish they despised or
to take notes of a kind of carnation that was not half
so fine, had not such ornamental streaks, did not produce
so large a blossom as those which they had long been
growing for her at home. But if in the Princess, wherever
she went, this astonishment at the sight of the most commonplace things was assumed, and intended to shew that
she did not derive from the superiority of her rank and
riches a pride forbidden by her early instructors, habitually dissembled by her mother and intolerable in the sight
of her Creator, it was, on the other hand, in all sincerity
that she regarded the drawing-room of the Duchesse de
Guermantes as a privileged place in which she could pass

only from surprise to delight. To a certain extent, for that matter, though not nearly enough to justify this state of mind, the Guermantes were different from the rest of noble society, they were rarer and more refined. They had given me at first sight the opposite impression; I had found them vulgar, similar to all other men and women, but because before meeting them I had seen in them, as in Balbec, in Florence, in Parma, only names. Evidently, in this drawing-room, all the women whom I had imagined as being like porcelain figures were even more like the great majority of women. But, in the same way as Balbec or Florence, the Guermantes, after first disappointing the imagination because they resembled their fellow-creatures rather than their name, could subsequently, though to a less degree, appeal to the intellect by certain distinctive characteristics. Their bodily structure, the colour — a peculiar pink that merged at times into violet—of their skins, a certain almost flashing fairness of the finely spun hair, even in the men, on whom it was massed in soft golden tufts, half a wall-growing lichen, half a catlike fur (a luminous sparkle to which corresponded a certain brilliance of intellect, for if people spoke of the Guermantes complexion, the Guermantes hair, they spoke also of the wit of the Guermantes, as of the wit of the Mortemarts— a certain social quality whose superior fineness was famed even before the days of Louis XIV and all the more universally recognised since they published the fame of it themselves), all this meant that in the material itself, precious as that might be, in which one found them embedded here and there, the Guermantes remained recognisable, easy to detect and to follow, like the veins whose paleness streaks a block of jasper or onyx, or, better still, like the pliant waving of those tresses of light whose loosened hairs run like flexible rays along the sides of a moss-agate.

The Guermantes—those at least who were worthy of the name—were not only of a quality of flesh, or hair, of transparency of gaze that was exquisite, but had a way of holding themselves, of walking, of bowing, of looking at one before they shook one's hand, of shaking hands, which made them as different in all these respects from an ordinary person in society as he in turn was from a peasant in a smock. And despite their friendliness one asked oneself: "Have they not indeed the right, though they waive it, when they see us walk, bow, leave a room, do any of those things which when performed by them become as graceful as the flight of a swallow or the bending of a rose on its stem, to think: 'These people are of another race than ours, and we are, we, the true lords of creation.' ?" Later on, I realised that the Guermantes did indeed regard me as being of another race, but one that aroused their envy because I possessed merits of which I knew nothing and which they professed to regard as alone important. Later still I came to feel that this profession of faith was only half sincere and that in them scorn or surprise could be coexistent with admiration and envy. The physical flexibility essential to the Guermantes was twofold; thanks to one of its forms, constantly in action, at any moment and if, for example, a male Guermantes were about to salute a lady, he produced a silhouette of himself made from the unstable equilibrium of a series of asymmetrical movements with nervous compensations, one leg dragging a little, either on purpose or because, having been broken so often in the hunting-field,

it imparted to his trunk in its effort to keep pace with
the other a deviation to which the upward thrust of one
shoulder gave a counterpoise, while the monocle settled
itself before his eye, raising an eyebrow just as the tuft
of hair on the forehead was lowered in the formal bow;
the other flexibility, like the form of the wave, the wind
or the ocean track which is preserved on the shell or the
vessel, was so to speak stereotyped in a sort of fixed
mobility, curving the arched nose which, beneath the blue,
protruding eyes, above the over-thin lips, from which, in
the women, there emerged a raucous voice, recalled the
fabulous origin attributed in the sixteenth century by the
complaisance of parasitic and Hellenising genealogists to
his race, ancient beyond dispute, but not to the degree of
antiquity which they claimed when they gave as its
source the mythological impregnation of a nymph by
a divine Bird.

The Guermantes were just as idiomatic from the intellectual as from the physical point of view. With the
exception of Prince Gilbert (the husband with antiquated
ideas of " Marie-Gilbert ", who made his wife sit on his
left when they drove out together because her blood,
though royal, was inferior to his own), but he was an
exception and furnished, behind his back, a perpetual
laughing-stock to the rest of the family, who had always
fresh anecdotes to tell of him, the Guermantes, while living
in the pure cream of aristocracy, affected to take no
account of nobility. The theories of the Duchesse de
Guermantes, who, to tell the truth, by dint of being a
Guermantes, became to a certain extent something different and more attractive, subordinated everything else so
completely to intellect, and were in politics so socialistic

that one asked oneself where in her mansion could be hiding the familiar spirit whose duty it was to ensure the maintenance of the aristocratic standard of living, and which, always invisible but evidently crouching at one moment in the entrance hall, at another in the drawing-room, at a third in her dressing-room, reminded the servants of this woman who did not believe in titles to address her as Mme. la Duchesse, reminding also herself who cared only for reading and had no respect for persons to go out to dinner with her sister-in-law when eight o'clock struck, and to put on a low gown.

The same familiar spirit represented to Mme. de Guermantes the social duties of duchesses, of the foremost among them, that was, who like herself were multi-millionaires, the sacrifice to boring tea, dinner and evening parties of hours in which she might have read interesting books, as unpleasant necessities like rain, which Mme. de Guermantes accepted, letting play on them her biting humour, but without seeking in any way to justify her acceptance of them. The curious accident by which the butler of Mme. de Guermantes invariably said "Madame la Duchesse" to this woman who believed only in the intellect did not however appear to shock her. Never had it entered her head to request him to address her simply as "Madame". Giving her the utmost benefit of the doubt one might have supposed that, thinking of something else at the time, she had heard only the word " Madame " and that the suffix appended to it had not caught her attention. Only, though she might feign deafness, she was not dumb. In fact, whenever she had a message to give to her husband she would say to the butler: "Remind Monsieur le Duc——"

The familiar spirit had other occupations as well, one of which was to inspire them to talk morality. It is true that there were Guermantes who went in for intellect and Guermantes who went in for morals, and that these two classes did not as a rule coincide. But the former kind—including a Guermantes who had forged cheques, who cheated at cards and was the most delightful of them all, with a mind open to every new and sound idea—spoke even more eloquently upon morals than the others, and in the same strain as Mme. de Villeparisis, at the moments in which the familiar spirit expressed itself through the lips of the old lady. At corresponding moments one saw the Guermantes adopt suddenly a tone almost as old-lady-like, as genial and (as they themselves had more charm) more touching than that of the Marquise, to say of a servant: "One feels that she has a thoroughly sound nature, she's not at all a common girl, she must come of decent parents, she is certainly a girl who has never gone astray." At such moments the familiar spirit took the form of an intonation. But at times it could be bearing also, the expression on a face, the same in the Duchess as in her grandfather the Marshal, a sort of undefinable convulsion (like that of the Serpent, the genius of the Carthaginian family of Barca) by which my heart had more than once been set throbbing, on my morning walks, when before I had recognized Mme. de Guermantes I felt her eyes fastened upon me from the inside of a little dairy. This familiar spirit had intervened in a situation which was far from immaterial not merely to the Guermantes but to the Courvoisiers, the rival faction of the family and, though of as good blood as the Guermantes (it was, indeed, through his Courvoisier grandmother that the Guermantes explained the obsession which led the Prince de Guermantes always to speak of birth and titles as though those were the only things that mattered), their opposite in every respect. Not only did the Courvoisiers not assign to intelligence the same importance as the Guermantes, they had not the same idea of it. For a Guermantes (even were he a fool) to be intelligent meant to have a sharp tongue, to be capable of saying cutting things, to " get away with it "; but it meant also the capacity to hold one's own equally in painting, music, architecture, to speak English. The Courvoisiers had formed a less favourable impression of intelligence, and unless one were actually of their world being intelligent was almost tantamount to " having probably murdered one's father and mother ". For them intelligence was the sort of burglar's jemmy by means of which people one did not know from Adam forced the doors of the most reputable drawing-rooms, and it was common knowledge among the Courvoisiers that you always had to pay in the long run for having " those sort " of people in your house. To the most trivial statements made by intelligent people who were not " in society " the Courvoisiers opposed a systematic distrust. Some one having on one occasion remarked: " But Swann is younger than Palamède,"—" He says so, at any rate, and if he says it you may be sure it's because he thinks it is to his interest! " had been Mme. de Gallardon's retort. Better still, when some one said of two highly distinguished foreigners whom the Guermantes had entertained that one of them had been sent in first because she was the elder: " But is she really the elder? " Mme. de Gallardon had inquired, not positively as though that sort of person did not have any age, but as if presumably devoid of civil or religious status, of definite traditions, they were both more or less young, like two kittens of the same litter between which only a veterinary surgeon was competent to decide. The Courvoisiers, more than the Guermantes, maintained also in a certain sense the integrity of the titled class thanks at once to the narrowness of their minds and the bitterness of their hearts. Just as the Guermantes (for whom, below the royal families and a few others like the Lignes, the La Trémoïlles and so forth, all the rest were lost in a common rubbish-heap) were insolent towards various people of long descent who lived round Guermantes, simply because they paid no attention to those secondary distinctions by which the Courvoisiers were enormously impressed, so the absence of such distinctions affected them little. Certain women who did not hold any specially exalted rank in their native provinces but, brilliantly married, rich, good-looking, beloved of Duchesses, were for Paris, where people are never very well up in who one's " father and mother " were, an excellent and exclusive piece of " imported goods ". It might happen, though not commonly, that such women were, through the channel of the Princesse de Parme or by virtue of their own attractions, received by certain Guermantes. But with regard to these the indignation of the Courvoisiers knew no bounds. Having to meet, between five and six in the afternoon, at their cousin's, people with whose relatives their own relatives did not care to be seen mixing down in the Perche became for them an ever-increasing source of rage and an inexhaustible fount of rhetoric. The moment, for instance, when the charming Comtesse G—— entered the Guermantes drawing-room, the face of Mme.

de Villebon assumed exactly the expression that would have befitted it had she been called to recite the line:

And should but one stand fast, that one were surely I,

a line which for that matter was unknown to her. This Courvoisier had consumed almost every Monday an *éclair* stuffed with cream within a few feet of the Comtesse G——, but to no consequence. And Mme. de Villebon confessed in secret that she could not conceive how her cousin Guermantes could allow a woman into her house who was not even in the second-best society of Château-dun. " I really fail to see why my cousin should make such a fuss about whom she knows; it's making a perfect farce of society! " concluded Mme. de Villebon with a change of facial expression, this time a sly smile of despair, which, in a charade, would have been interpreted rather as indicating another line of poetry, though one with which she was no more familiar than with the first:

Grâce aux Dieux mon malheur passe mon espérance.

We may here anticipate events to explain that the *persévérance* (which rhymes, in the following line, with *espérance*) shewn by Mme. de Villebon in snubbing Mme. G—— was not entirely wasted. In the eyes of Mme. G—— it invested Mme. de Villebon with a distinction so supreme, though purely imaginary, that when the time came for Mme. G——'s daughter, who was the prettiest girl and the greatest heiress in the ballrooms of that season, to marry, people were astonished to see her refuse all the Dukes in succession. The fact was that her mother, remembering the weekly humiliations she had had to endure in the Rue de Grenelle on account of Châteaudun could think of only one possible husband for her daughter —a Villebon son.

A single point at which Guermantes and Courvoisiers converged was the art (one, for that matter, of infinite variety) of marking distances. The Guermantes manners were not absolutely uniform towards everyone. And yet, to take an example, all the Guermantes, all those who really were Guermantes, when you were introduced to them proceeded to perform a sort of ceremony almost as though the fact that they held out their hands to you had been as important as the conferring of an order of knighthood. At the moment when a Guermantes, were he no more than twenty, but treading already in the footsteps of his ancestors, heard your name uttered by the person who introduced you, he let fall on you as though he had by no means made up his mind to say "How d'ye do?" a gaze generally blue, always of the coldness of a steel blade which he seemed ready to plunge into the deepest recesses of your heart. Which was as a matter of fact what the Guermantes imagined themselves to be doing, each of them regarding himself as a psychologist of the highest order. They thought moreover that they increased by this inspection the affability of the salute which was to follow it, and would not be rendered you without full knowledge of your deserts. All this occurred at a distance from yourself which, little enough had it been a question of a passage of arms, seemed immense for a handclasp, and had as chilling an effect in this connexion as in the other, so that when the Guermantes, after a rapid twisting thrust that explored the most intimate secrets of your soul and laid bare your title to honour, had deemed you worthy to associate with him thereafter, his hand, directed towards you at the end of an arm stretched out to its fullest extent, appeared to be presenting a rapier at you for a single combat, and that hand was in fact placed so far in advance of the Guermantes himself at that moment that when he afterwards bowed his head it was difficult to distinguish whether it was yourself or his own hand that he was saluting. Certain Guermantes, lacking the sense of proportion, or being incapable of refraining from repeating themselves incessantly, went farther and repeated this ceremony afresh every time that they met you. Seeing that they had no longer any need to conduct the preliminary psychological investigation for which the "familiar spirit" had delegated its powers to them and the result of which they had presumably kept in mind, the insistence of the perforating gaze preceding the handclasp could be explained only by the automatism which their gaze had acquired or by some power of fascination which they believed themselves to possess. The Courvoisiers, whose physique was different, had tried in vain to assimilate that searching gaze and had had to fall back upon a lordly stiffness or a rapid indifference. On the other hand, it was from the Courvoisiers that certain very exceptional Guermantes of the gentler sex seemed to have borrowed the feminine form of greeting. At the moment when you were presented to one of these, she made you a sweeping bow in which she carried towards you, almost to an angle of forty-five degrees, her head and bust, the rest of her body (which came very high, up to the belt which formed a pivot)

remaining stationary. But no sooner had she projected
thus towards you the upper part of her person than she
flung it backwards beyond the vertical line by a sudden
retirement through almost the same angle. This subsequent withdrawal neutralised what appeared to have
been conceded to you; the ground which you believed
yourself to have gained did not even remain a conquest,
as in a duel; the original positions were retained. This
same annulment of affability by the resumption of
distance (which was Courvoisier in origin and intended
to shew that the advances made in the first movement
were no more than a momentary feint) displayed itself
equally clearly, in the Courvoisier ladies as in the Guermantes, in the letters which you received from them, at
any rate in the first period of your acquaintance. The
" body " of the letter might contain sentences such as
one writes only (you would suppose) to a friend, but
in vain might you have thought yourself entitled to boast
of being in that relation to the lady, since the letter began
with " Monsieur," and ended with " Croyez monsieur à
mes sentiments distingués." After which, between this
cold opening and frigid conclusion which altered the
meaning of all the rest, there might come in succession
(were it a reply to a letter of condolence from yourself)
the most touching pictures of the grief which the Guermantes lady had felt on losing her sister, of the intimacy
that had existed between them, of the beauty of the
place in which she was staying, of the consolation that
she found in the charm of her young children, all this
amounted to no more than a letter such as one finds in
printed collections, the intimate character of which implied, however, no more intimacy between yourself and

the writer than if she had been the Younger Pliny or
Mme. de Simiane.

It is true that certain Guermantes ladies wrote to you
from the first as " My dear friend," or " My friend,"
these were not always the most simple natured among
them, but rather those who, living only in the society of
kings and being at the same time " light ", assumed in
their pride the certainty that everything which came from
themselves gave pleasure and in their corruption the
habit of setting no price upon any of the satisfactions
that they had to offer. However, since to have had a common ancestor in the reign of Louis XIII was enough to
make a young Guermantes say, in speaking of the Marquise de Guermantes: " My aunt Adam," the Guermantes
were so numerous a clan that, even among these simple
rites, that for example of the bow upon introduction to
a stranger, there existed a wide divergence. Each subsection of any refinement had its own, which was handed
down from parents to children like the prescription for
a liniment or a special way of making jam. Thus it was
that we saw Saint-Loup's handclasp thrust out as though
involuntarily at the moment of his hearing one's name,
without any participation by his eyes, without the addition of a bow. Any unfortunate commoner who for a
particular reason—which, for that matter, very rarely
occurred—was presented to anyone of the Saint-Loup
subsection racked his brains over this abrupt minimum
of a greeting, which deliberately assumed the appearance
of non-recognition, to discover what in the world the
Guermantes—male or female—could have against him.
And he was highly surprised to learn that the said Guermantes had thought fit to write specially to the intro-

ducer to tell him how delighted he or she had been with the stranger, whom he or she looked forward to meeting again. As specialised as the mechanical gestures of Saint-Loup were the complicated and rapid capers (which M. de Charlus condemned as ridiculous) of the Marquis de Fierbois, the grave and measured paces of the Prince de Guermantes. But it is impossible to describe here the richness of the choreography of the Guermantes ballet owing to the sheer length of the cast.

To return to the antipathy which animated the Courvoisiers against the Duchesse de Guermantes, they might have had the consolation of feeling sorry for her so long as she was still unmarried, for she was then comparatively poor. Unfortunately, at all times and seasons, a sort of fuliginous emanation, quite *sui generis,* enveloped, hid from the eye the wealth of the Courvoisiers which, however great it might be, remained obscure. In vain might a young Courvoisier with an ample dowry find a most eligible bridegroom; it invariably happened that the young couple had no house of their own in Paris, " came up to stay " in the season with his parents, and for the rest of the year lived down in the country in the thick of a society that may have been unadulterated but was also quite undistinguished. Whereas a Saint-Loup who was up to the eyes in debt dazzled Doncières with his carriage-horses, a Courvoisier who was extremely rich always went in the tram. Similarly (though of course many years earlier) Mlle. de Guermantes (Oriane), who had scarcely a penny to her name, created more stir with her clothes than all the Courvoisiers put together. The really scandalous things she said gave a sort of advertisement to her style of dressing and doing her hair. She

had had the audacity to say to the Russian Grand Duke:
" Well, Sir, I hear you would like to have Tolstoy murdered? " at a dinner-party to which none of the Courvoisiers, not that any of them knew very much about
Tolstoy, had been asked. They knew little more about
Greek writers, if we may judge by the Dowager Duchesse
de Gallardon (mother-in-law of the Princesse de Gallardon who at that time was still a girl) who, not having
been honoured by Oriane with a single visit in five years,
replied to some one who asked her the reason for this
abstention: " It seems she recites Aristotle " (meaning
Aristophanes) " in society. I cannot allow that sort of
thing in my house! "

One can imagine how greatly this " sally " by Mlle.
de Guermantes upon Tolstoy, if it enraged the Courvoisiers, delighted the Guermantes, and by derivation
everyone who was not merely closely but even remotely
attached to them. The Dowager Comtesse d'Argencourt
(*née* Seineport), who entertained a little of everything,
because she was a blue-stocking and in spite of her son's
being a terrible snob, repeated the saying before her
literary friends with the comment: " Oriane de Guermantes, you know; she's as fine as amber, as mischievous
as a monkey, there's nothing she couldn't do if she chose,
her water-colours are worthy of a great painter and she
writes better verses than most of the great poets, and
as for family, don't you know, you couldn't imagine anything better, her grandmother was Mlle. de Montpensier,
and she is the eighteenth Oriane de Guermantes in succession, without a single misalliance; it's the purest blood,
the oldest in the whole of France." And so the sham men
of letters, those demi-intellectuals who went to Mme.

d'Argencourt's, forming a mental picture of Oriane de Guermantes, whom they would never have an opportunity to know personally, as something more wonderful and more extraordinary than Princess Badroulbadour, not only felt themselves ready to die for her on learning that so noble a person glorified Tolstoy above all others, but felt also quickening with a fresh strength in their minds their own love of Tolstoy, their longing to fight against Tsarism. These liberal ideas might have grown faint in them, they might have begun to doubt their importance, no longer venturing to confess to holding them, when suddenly from Mlle. de Guermantes herself, that is to say from a girl so indisputably cultured and authorised to speak, who wore her hair flat on her brow (a thing that no Courvoisier would ever have consented to do), came this vehement support. A certain number of realities, good or bad in themselves, gain enormously in this way by receiving the adhesion of people who are in authority over us. For instance among the Courvoisiers the rites of affability in a public thoroughfare consisted in a certain bow, very ugly and far from affable in itself but which people knew to be the distinguished way of bidding a person good day, with the result that everyone else, suppressing the instinctive smile of welcome on his own face, endeavoured to imitate these frigid gymnastics. But the Guermantes in general and Oriane in particular, while better conversant than anyone with these rites, did not hesitate, if they caught sight of you from a carriage, to greet you with a sprightly wave of the hand, and in a drawing-room, leaving the Courvoisiers to make their stiff and imitative bows, sketched charming reverences in the air, held out their hands as though to a comrade with a smile from their blue eyes, so that suddenly, thanks to the Guermantes, there entered into the substance of smartness, until then a little hollow and dry, everything that you would naturally have liked and had compelled yourself to forego, a genuine welcome, the effusion of a true friendliness, spontaneity. It is in a similar fashion (but by a rehabilitation which this time is scarcely justified) that people who carry in themselves an instinctive taste for bad music and for melodies, however commonplace, which have in them something easy and caressing, succeed, by dint of education in symphonic culture, in mortifying that appetite. But once they have arrived at this point, when, dazzled—and rightly so—by the brilliant orchestral colouring of Richard Strauss, they see that musician adopt with an indulgence worthy of Auber the most vulgar motifs, what those people originally admired finds suddenly in so high an authority a justification which delights them, and they let themselves be enchanted without scruple and with a twofold gratitude, when they listen to *Salomé,* by what it would have been impossible for them to admire in *Les Diamants de la Couronne.*

Authentic or not, the retort made by Mlle. de Guermantes to the Grand Duke, retailed from house to house, furnished an opportunity to relate the excessive smartness with which Oriane had been turned out at the dinner-party in question. But if such splendour (and this is precisely what rendered it unattainable by the Courvoisiers) springs not from wealth but from prodigality, the latter does nevertheless last longer if it enjoys the constant support of the former, which allows it to spend all its fire. Given the principles openly advertised not

only by Oriane but by Mme. de Villeparisis, namely that
nobility does not count, that it is ridiculous to bother one's
head about rank, that wealth does not necessarily mean
happiness, that intellect, heart, talent are alone of importance, the Courvoisiers were justified in hoping that,
as a result of the training she had received from the Marquise, Oriane would marry some one who was not in
society, an artist, a fugitive from justice, a scalliwag, a
free-thinker, that she would pass definitely into the
category of what the Courvoisiers called " detrimentals ".
They were all the more justified in this hope since,
inasmuch as Mme. de Villeparisis was at this very
moment, from the social point of view, passing through
an awkward crisis (none of the few bright stars whom I
was to meet in her drawing-room had as yet reappeared
there), she professed an intense horror of the society
which was thus holding her aloof. Even when she referred
to her nephew the Prince de Guermantes, whom she did
still see, she could never make an end of mocking at him
because he was so infatuated about his pedigree. But
the moment it became a question of finding a husband for
Oriane, it had been no longer the principles publicly
advertised by aunt and niece that had controlled the
operations, it had been the mysterious " familiar spirit "
of their race. As unerringly as if Mme. de Villeparisis
and Oriane had never spoken of anything but rent-rolls
and pedigrees in place of literary merit and depth of
character, and as if the Marquise, for the space of a few
days, had been—as she would ultimately be—dead and
on her bier, in the church of Combray, where each member of the family would be reduced to a mere Guermantes,
with a forfeiture of individuality and baptismal names to

which there testified on the voluminous black drapery
of the pall the single 'G' in purple surmounted by the
ducal coronet, it was on the wealthiest man and the
most nobly born, on the most eligible bachelor of the
Faubourg Saint-Germain, on the eldest son of the Duc
de Guermantes, the Prince des Laumes, that the familiar
spirit had let fall the choice of the intellectual, the
critical, the evangelical Mme. de Villeparisis. And for a
couple of hours, on the day of the wedding, Mme. de
Villeparisis received in her drawing-room all the noble
persons at whom she had been in the habit of sneering,
at whom she indeed sneered still to the various plebeian
intimates whom she had invited and on whom the Prince
des Laumes promptly left cards, preparatory to " cutting
the cable " in the following year. And then, making the
Courvoisiers' cup of bitterness overflow, the same old
maxims, which made out intellect and talent to be the
sole claims to social pre-eminence, resumed their doc-
trinal force in the household of the Princesse des Laumes
immediately after her marriage. And in this respect,
be it said in passing, the point of view which Saint-Loup
upheld when he lived with Rachel, frequented the friends
of Rachel, would have liked to marry Rachel, implied—
whatever the horror that it inspired in the family—less
falsehood than that of the Guermantes young ladies in
general, preaching the virtues of intellect, barely admitting
the possibility of anyone's questioning the equality of
mankind, all of which ended at a given point in the same
result as if they had professed the opposite principles,
that is to say in marriage to an extremely wealthy duke.
Saint-Loup did, on the contrary, act in conformity with
his theories, which led people to say that he was treading

in evil ways. Certainly from the moral standpoint Rachel
was not altogether satisfactory. But it is by no means
certain whether, if she had been some person no more
worthy but a duchess or the heiress to many millions,
Mme. de Marsantes would not have been in favour of
the match.

Well, to return to Mme. des Laumes (shortly afterwards Duchesse de Guermantes, on the death of her
father-in-law), it was the last agonising straw upon the
backs of the Courvoisiers that the theories of the young
Princess, remaining thus lodged in her speech, should
not in any sense be guiding her conduct; with the result
that this philosophy (if one may so call it) in no way
impaired the aristocratic smartness of the Guermantes
drawing-room. No doubt all the people whom Mme. de
Guermantes did not invite imagined that it was because
they were not clever enough, and some rich American
lady who had never had any book in her possession except a little old copy, never opened, of Parny's poems,
arranged because it was of the " period " upon one of
the tables in her inner room, shewed how much importance she attached to the things of the mind by the
devouring gaze which she fastened on the Duchesse de
Guermantes when that lady made her appearance at the
Opera. No doubt, also, Mme. de Guermantes was sincere
when she selected a person on account of his or her
intellect. When she said of a woman: " It appears, she's
quite charming! " or of a man that he was the " cleverest
person in the world," she imagined herself to have no
other reason for consenting to receive them than this
charm or cleverness, the familiar spirit not interposing
itself at this last moment; more deeply-rooted, stationed

at the obscure entry of the region in which the Guermantes exercised their judgment, this vigilant spirit precluded them from finding the man clever or the woman charming if they had no social value, actual or potential. The man was pronounced learned, but like a dictionary, or, on the contrary, common, with the mind of a commercial traveller, the woman pretty, but with a terribly bad style, or too talkative. As for the people who had no definite position, they were simply dreadful—such snobs! M. de Bréauté, whose country house was quite close to Guermantes, mixed with no one below the rank of Highness. But he laughed at them in his heart and longed only to spend his days in museums. Accordingly Mme. de Guermantes was indignant when anyone spoke of M. de Bréauté as a snob. "A snob! Babal! But, my poor friend, you must be mad, it's just the opposite. He loathes smart people; he won't let himself be introduced to anyone. Even in my house! If I ask him to meet some one he doesn't know, he swears at me all the time." This was not to say that, even in practice, the Guermantes did not adopt an entirely different attitude towards cleverness from the Courvoisiers. In a positive sense, this difference between the Guermantes and the Courvoisiers had begun already to bear very promising fruit. Thus the Duchesse de Guermantes, enveloped moreover in a mystery which had set so many poets dreaming of her at a respectful distance, had given that party to which I have already referred, at which the King of England had enjoyed himself more thoroughly than anywhere else, for she had had the idea, which would never have occurred to a Courvoisier mind, of inviting, and the audacity, from which a Courvoisier courage would have recoiled, to invite, apart from the personages already mentioned, the musician Gaston Lemaire and the dramatist Grandmougin. But it was pre-eminently from the negative point of view that intellectuality made itself felt. If the necessary coefficient of cleverness and charm declined steadily as the rank of the person who sought an invitation from the Princesse des Laumes became more exalted, vanishing into zero when he or she was one of the principal Crowned Heads of Europe, conversely the farther they fell below this royal level the higher the coefficient rose. For instance at the Princesse de Parme's parties there were a number of people whom her Royal Highness invited because she had known them as children, or because they were related to some duchess, or attached to the person of some Sovereign, they themselves being quite possibly ugly, boring or stupid; well, with a Courvoisier any of the reasons: " a favourite of the Princesse de Parme," " a niece on the mother's side of the Duchesse d'Arpajon," " spends three months every year with the Queen of Spain," would have been sufficient to make her invite such people to her house, but Mme. de Guermantes, who had politely acknowledged their bows for ten years at the Princesse de Parme's, had never once allowed them to cross her threshold, considering that the same rule applied to a drawing-room in a social as in a material sense, where it only needed a few pieces of furniture which had no particular beauty but were left there to fill the room and as a sign of the owner's wealth, to render it hideous. Such a drawing-room resembled a book in which the author could not refrain from the use of language advertising his own learning, brilliance, fluency.

Like a book, like a house, the quality of a "salon", thought Mme. de Guermantes—and rightly—is based on the corner-stone of sacrifice.

Many of the friends of the Princesse de Parme, with whom the Duchesse de Guermantes had confined herself for years past to the same conventional greeting, or to returning their cards, without ever inviting them to her parties or going to theirs, complained discreetly of these omissions to her Highness who, on days when M. de Guermantes came by himself to see her, passed on a hint to him. But the wily nobleman, a bad husband to the Duchess in so far as he kept mistresses, but her most tried and trusty friend in everything that concerned the good order of her drawing-room (and her own wit, which formed its chief attraction), replied: "But does my wife know her? Indeed! Oh, well, I daresay she does. But the truth is, Ma'am, that Oriane does not care for women's conversation. She lives surrounded by a court of superior minds—I am not her husband, I am only the first footman. Except for quite a small number, who are all of them very clever indeed, women bore her. Surely, Ma'am, your Highness with all her fine judgment is not going to tell me that the Marquise de Souvré has any brains. Yes, I quite understand, the Princess receives her out of kindness. Besides, your Highness knows her. You tell me that Oriane has met her; it is quite possible, but once or twice at the most, I assure you. And then, I must explain to your Highness, it is really a little my fault as well. My wife is very easily tired, and she is so anxious to be friendly always that if I allowed her she would never stop going to see people. Only yesterday evening she had a temperature, she was afraid of hurting the Duchesse de Bourbon's feelings by not going to see her. I had to shew my teeth, I assure you; I positively forbade them to bring the carriage round. Do you know, Ma'am, I should really prefer not to mention to Oriane that you have spoken to me about Mme. de Souvré. My wife is so devoted to your Highness, she will go round at once to invite Mme. de Souvré to the house; that will mean another call to be paid, it will oblige us to make friends with the sister, whose husband I know quite well. I think I shall say nothing at all about it to Oriane, if the Princess has no objection. That will save her a great deal of strain and excitement. And I assure you that it will be no loss to Mme. de Souvré. She goes everywhere, moves in the most brilliant circles. You know, we don't entertain at all, really, just a few little friendly dinners, Mme. de Souvré would be bored to death." The Princesse de Parme, innocently convinced that the Duc de Guermantes would not transmit her request to his Duchess, and dismayed by her failure to procure the invitation that Mme. de Souvré sought, was all the more flattered to think that she herself was one of the regular frequenters of so exclusive a household. No doubt this satisfaction had its drawbacks also. Thus whenever the Princesse de Parme invited Mme. de Guermantes to her own parties she had to rack her brains to be sure that there was no one else on her list whose presence might offend the Duchess and make her refuse to come again.

On ordinary evenings (after dinner, at which she invariably entertained at a very early hour, for she clung to old customs, a small party) the drawing-room of the Princesse de Parme was thrown open to her regular guests, and, generally speaking, to all the higher ranks of the aristocracy, French and foreign. The order of her receptions was as follows: on issuing from the dining-room the Princess sat down on a sofa before a large round table and chatted with the two most important of the ladies who had dined with her, or else cast her eyes over a magazine, or sometimes played cards (or pretended to play, adopting a German court custom), either a game of patience by herself or selecting as her real or pretended partner some prominent personage. By nine o'clock the double doors of the big drawing-room were in a state of perpetual agitation, opening and shutting and opening again to admit the visitors who had dined quietly at home (or if they had dined in town hurried from their café promising to return later, since they intended only to go in at one door and out at the other) in order to conform with the Princess's time-table. She, meanwhile, her mind fixed on her game or conversation, made a show of not seeing the new arrivals, and it was not until they were actually within reach of her that she rose graciously from her seat, with a friendly smile for the women. The latter thereupon sank before the upright Presence in a courtesy which was tantamount to a genuflexion, so as to bring their lips down to the level of the beautiful hand which hung very low, and to kiss it. But at that moment the Princess, just as if she had been every time surprised by a formality with which nevertheless she was perfectly familiar, raised the kneeling figure as though by main force, and with incomparable grace and sweetness, and kissed her on both cheeks. A grace and sweetness that were conditional, you may say, upon the meekness with which the arriving guest inclined her knee. Very likely; and it seems that in a society without distinctions of rank politeness would vanish, not, as is generally supposed, from want of breeding, but because from one class would have vanished the deference due to a distinction which must be imaginary to be effective, and, more completely still, from the other class the affability in the distribution of which one is prodigal so long as one knows it to be, to the recipient, of an untold value which, in a world based on equality, would at once fall to nothing like everything that has only a promissory worth. But this disappearance of politeness in a reconstructed society is by no means certain, and we are at times too ready to believe that the present is the only possible state of things. People of first-rate intelligence have held the opinion that a Republic could not have any diplomacy or foreign alliances, and, more recently, that the peasant class would not tolerate the separation of Church and State. After all, the survival of politeness in a society levelled to uniformity would be no more miraculous than the practical success of the railway or the use of the aeroplane in war. Besides, even if politeness were to vanish, there is nothing to shew that this would be a misfortune. Lastly, would not society become secretly more hierarchical as it became outwardly more democratic. This seems highly probable. The political power of the Popes has grown enormously since they ceased to possess either States or an Army; our cathedrals meant far less to a devout Catholic of the seventeenth century than they mean to an atheist of the twentieth, and if the Princesse de Parme had been the sovereign ruler of a State, no doubt I should have felt myself impelled to speak of her almost as I should speak of a President of the Republic, that is to say not at all.

As soon as the postulant had been raised from the ground and embraced by the Princess, the latter resumed her seat and returned to her game of patience, but first of all, if the newcomer were of any importance, held her for a moment in conversation, making her sit down in an armchair.

When the room became too crowded the lady in waiting who had to control the traffic cleared the floor by leading the regular guests into an immense hall on to which the drawing-room opened, a hall filled with portraits and minor trophies of the House of Bourbon. The intimate friends of the Princess would then volunteer for the part of guide and would repeat interesting anecdotes, to which the young people had not the patience to listen, more interested in the spectacle of living Royalties (with the possibility of having themselves presented to them by the lady in waiting and the maids of honour) than in examining the relics of dead Sovereigns. Too much occupied with the acquaintances which they would be able to form and the invitations it might perhaps be possible to secure, they knew absolutely nothing, even in after-years, of what there was in this priceless museum of the archives of the Monarchy, and could only recall confusedly that it was decorated with cacti and giant palms which gave this centre of social elegance a look of the palmarium in the Jardin d'Acclimatation.

Naturally the Duchesse de Guermantes, by way of self-mortification, did occasionally appear on these evenings to pay an " after dinner " call on the Princess, who kept her all the time by her side, while she rallied the Duke. But on evenings when the Duchess came to dine, the Princess took care not to invite her regular party, and closed her doors to the world on rising from table, for fear lest a too liberal selection of guests might offend the exacting Duchess. On such evenings, were any of the faithful who had not received warning to present themselves on the royal doorstep, they would be informed by the porter: "Her Royal Highness is not at home this evening," and would turn away. But, long before this, many of the Princess's friends had known that, on the day in question, they would not be asked to her house. These were a special set of parties, a privilege barred to so many who must have longed for admission. The excluded could, with a practical certainty, enumerate the roll of the elect, and would say irritably among themselves: "You know, of course, that Oriane de Guermantes never goes anywhere without her entire staff." With the help of this body the Princesse de Parme sought to surround the Duchess as with a protecting rampart against those persons the chance of whose making a good impression on her was at all doubtful. But with several of the Duchess's favourites, with several members of this glittering " staff " the Princesse de Parme resented having to go out of her way to shew them attentions, seeing that they paid little or no attention to herself. No doubt the Princess was fully prepared to admit that it was possible to derive more enjoyment in the company of the Duchesse de Guermantes than in her own. She could not deny that there was always a "crush" on the Duchess's at-home days, or that she herself often met there three or four royal personages who thought it sufficient to leave their cards upon her. And in vain might she commit to memory Oriane's witty sayings, copy her gowns, serve at her own tea-parties the same strawberry tarts, there were occasions on which she was left by herself all afternoon with a lady in waiting and some foreign Counsellor of Legation. And so whenever (as had been the case with Swann, for instance, at an earlier period) there was anyone who never let a day pass without going to spend an hour or two at the Duchess's and paid a call once in two years on the Princesse de Parme, the latter felt no great desire, even for the sake of amusing Oriane, to make to this Swann or whoever he was the " advances " of an invitation to dinner. In a word, having the Duchess in her house was for the Princess a source of endless perplexity, so haunted was she by the fear that Oriane would find fault with everything. But in return, and for the same reason, when the Princesse de Parme came to dine with Mme. de Guermantes she could be certain beforehand that everything would be perfect, delightful, she had only one fear which was that of her own inability to understand, remember, give satisfaction, her inability to assimilate new ideas and people. On this account my presence aroused her attention and excited her cupidity, just as might a new way of decorating the dinner-table with festoons of fruit, uncertain as she was which of the two it might be—the table decorations or my presence—that was the more distinctively one of those charms, the secret of the success of Oriane's parties, and in her uncertainty firmly resolved to try at her own next dinner-party to introduce them both. What for that matter fully justified the enraptured curiosity which the Princesse de Parme brought to the Duchess's house was that element—amusing, dangerous, exciting—into which the Princess used to plunge with a combination of anxiety, shock and delight (as

at the seaside on one of those days of " big waves " of
the danger of which the bathing-masters warn us, simply
and solely because none of them knows how to swim),
from which she used to emerge terrified, happy, rejuvenated, and which was known as the wit of the Guermantes. The wit of the Guermantes—a thing as non-
existent as the squared circle, according to the Duchess
who regarded herself as the sole Guermantes to possess
it—was a family reputation like that of the pork pies of
Tours or the biscuits of Rheims. No doubt (since an intellectual peculiarity does not employ for its perpetuation
the same channels as a shade of hair or complexion)
certain intimate friends of the Duchess who were not
of her blood were nevertheless endowed with this wit,
which on the other hand had failed to permeate the minds
of various Guermantes, too refractory to assimilate wit
of any kind. The holders, not related to the Duchess, of
this Guermantes wit had generally the characteristic
feature of having been brilliant men, fitted for a career
to which, whether it were in the arts, diplomacy, parliamentary eloquence or the army, they had preferred the
life of a small and intimate group. Possibly this preference could be explained by a certain want of originality,
of initiative, of will power, of health or of luck, or possibly
by snobbishness.

With certain people (though these, it must be admitted, were the exception) if the Guermantes drawing-
room had been the stumbling-block in their careers, it
had been without their knowledge. Thus a doctor, a
painter and a diplomat of great promise had failed to
achieve success in the careers for which they were nevertheless more brilliantly endowed than most of their com-

petitors because their friendship with the Guermantes had the result that the two former were regarded as men of fashion and the third as a reactionary, which had prevented each of the three from winning the recognition of his colleagues. The mediaeval gown and red cap which are still donned by the electoral colleges of the Faculties are (or were at least, not so long since) something more than a purely outward survival from a narrow-minded past, from a rigid sectarianism. Under the cap with its golden tassels, like the High Priest in the conical mitre of the Jews, the " Professors " were still, in the years that preceded the Dreyfus Case, fast rooted in rigorously pharisaical ideas. Du Boulbon was at heart an artist, but was safe because he did not care for society. Cottard was always at the Verdurins'. But Mme. Verdurin was a patient; besides, he was protected by his vulgarity; finally, at his own house he entertained no one outside the Faculty, at banquets over which there floated an aroma of carbolic. But in powerful corporations, where more-over the rigidity of their prejudices is but the price that must be paid for the noblest integrity, the most lofty conceptions of morality, which weaken in an atmosphere that, more tolerant, freer at first, becomes very soon dissolute, a Professor in his gown of scarlet satin faced with ermine, like that of a Doge (which is to say a Duke) of Venice enshrined in the Ducal Palace, was as virtuous, as deeply attached to noble principles, but as unsparing of any alien element as that other Duke, excellent but terrible, whom we know as M. de Saint-Simon. The alien, here, was the worldly doctor, with other manners, other social relations. To make good, the unfortunate of whom we are now speaking, so as not to be accused by his colleagues of looking down on them (the strange ideas of a man of fashion!) if he concealed from them his Duchesse de Guermantes, hoped to disarm them by giving mixed dinner-parties in which the medical element was merged in the fashionable. He was unaware that in so doing he signed his own death-warrant, or rather he discovered this later, when the Council of Ten had to fill a vacant chair, and it was invariably the name of another doctor, more normal, it might be obviously inferior, that leaped from the fatal urn, when their "Veto" thundered from the ancient Faculty, as solemn, as absurd and as terrible as the "Juro" that spelt the death of Molière. So too with the painter permanently labelled man of fashion, when fashionable people who dabbled in art had succeeded in making themselves be labelled artists; so with the diplomat who had too many reactionary associations.

But this case was the rarest of all. The type of distinguished man who formed the main substance of the Guermantes drawing-room was that of people who had voluntarily (or so at least they supposed) renounced all else, everything that was incompatible with the wit of the Guermantes, with the courtesy of the Guermantes, with that indefinable charm odious to any "Corporation" however little centralised.

And the people who were aware that in days gone by one of these frequenters of the Duchess's drawing-room had been awarded the gold medal of the Salon, that another, Secretary to the Bar Council, had made a brilliant start in the Chamber, that a third had ably served France as Chargé d'Affaires, might have been led to regard as "failures" people who had done nothing more now for twenty years. But there were few who were thus "well-informed", and the parties concerned would themselves have been the last to remind people, finding these old distinctions to be now valueless, in the light of this very Guermantes spirit of wit: for did not this condemn respectively as a bore or an usher, and as a counter-jumper a pair of eminent Ministers, one a trifle solemn the other addicted to puns, of whose praises the news-papers were always full but in whose company Mme. de Guermantes would begin to yawn and shew signs of impatience if the imprudence of a hostess had placed either of them next to her at the dinner-table. Since being a statesman of the first rank was in no sense a recommendation to the Duchess's favour, those of her friends who had definitely abandoned the "Career" or the "Service", who had never stood for the Chamber, felt, as they came day after day to have luncheon and talk with their great friend, or when they met her in the houses of Royal Personages, of whom for that matter they thought very little (or at least they said so), that they themselves had chosen the better part, albeit their melancholy air, even in the midst of the gaiety, seemed somehow to challenge the soundness of this opinion.

It must be recognised also that the refinement of social life, the subtlety of conversation at the Guermantes' did also contain, exiguous as it may have been, an element of reality. No official title was equivalent to the approval of certain chosen friends of Mme. de Guermantes, whom the most powerful Ministers had been unable to attract to their houses. If in this drawing-room so many intel-lectual ambitions, such noble efforts even had been for ever buried, still at least from their dust the rarest blos-

soms of civilised society had taken life. Certainly men
of wit, Swann for instance, regarded themselves as superior to men of genuine worth, whom they despised,
but that was because what the Duchesse de Guermantes
valued above everything else was not intellect; it was,
according to her, that superior, more exquisite form of
the human intellect exalted to a verbal variety of talent—
wit. And long ago at the Verdurins' when Swann condemned Brichot and Elstir, one as a pedant and the other
as a clown, despite all the learning of one and the other's
genius, it was the infiltration of the Guermantes spirit that
had led him to classify them so. Never would he have
dared to present either of them to the Duchess, conscious
instinctively of the air with which she would have listened
to Brichot's monologues and Elstir's hair-splittings, the
Guermantes spirit regarding pretentious and prolix speech,
whether in a serious or a farcical vein, as alike of the
most intolerable imbecility.

As for the Guermantes of the true flesh and blood, if
the Guermantes spirit had not absorbed them as completely as we see occur in, to take an example, those
literary circles in which everyone shares a common way
of pronouncing his words, of expressing his thoughts,
and consequently of thinking, it was certainly not because
originality is stronger in purely social groups or presents
any obstacle there to imitation. But imitation depends
not merely upon the absence of any unconquerable originality but also demands a relative fineness of ear which
enables one first of all to discern what one is afterwards
to imitate. Whereas there were several Guermantes in
whom this musical sense was as entirely lacking as in
the Courvoisiers.

To take as an instance what is called, in another sense of the word imitation, "giving imitations" (or among the Guermantes was called "taking off"), Mme. de Guermantes might succeed in this to perfection, the Courvoisiers were as incapable of appreciating her as if they had been a tribe of rabbits instead of men and women, because they had never had the sense to observe the particular defect or accent that the Duchess was endeavouring to copy. When she "gave an imitation" of the Duc de Limoges, the Courvoisiers would protest: "Oh, no, he doesn't really speak like that; I met him again only yesterday at dinner at Bebeth's; he talked to me all evening and he didn't speak like that at all!" whereas the Guermantes of any degree of culture exclaimed: "Gad, what fun Oriane is! The odd part of it is that when she is copying him she looks exactly like him! I feel I'm listening to him. Oriane, do give us a little more Limoges!" Now these Guermantes (and not necessarily the few really outstanding members of the clan who, when the Duchess imitated the Duc de Limoges, would say admiringly: "Oh, you really have got him," or "You do get him,") might indeed be devoid of wit according to Mme. de Guermantes (and in this respect she was right); yet, by dint of hearing and repeating her sayings they had come to imitate more or less her way of expressing herself, of criticising people, of what Swann, like the Duke himself, used to call her "phrasing" of things, so that they presented in their conversation something which to the Courvoisiers appeared "fearfully like" Oriane's wit and was treated by them collectively as the "wit of the Guermantes". As these Guermantes were to her not merely kinsfolk but admirers, Oriane (who kept the rest of the family rigorously at arm's-length and now avenged by her disdain the insults that they had heaped upon her in her girlhood) went to call on them now and then, generally in company with the Duke, in the season, when she drove out with him. These visits were historic events. The heart began to beat more rapidly in the bosom of the Princesse d'Epinay, who was " at home " in her big drawing-room on the ground floor, when she perceived afar off, like the first glow of an innocuous fire, or the " reconnaissances " of an unexpected invasion, making her way across the courtyard slowly, in a diagonal course, the Duchess crowned with a ravishing hat and holding atilt a sunshade from which there rained down a summer fragrance. " Why, here comes Oriane," she would say, like an " On guard! " intended to convey a prudent warning to her visitors, so that they should have time to beat an orderly retreat, to clear the rooms without panic. Half of those present dared not remain, and rose at once to go. " But no, why? Sit down again, I insist on keeping you a little longer," said the Princess in a careless tone and seemingly at her ease (to shew herself the great lady) but in a voice that suddenly rang false. " But you may want to talk to each other." " Really, you're in a hurry? Oh, very well, I shall come and see you," replied the lady of the house to those whom she was just as well pleased to see depart. The Duke and Duchess gave a very civil greeting to people whom they had seen there regularly for years, without for that reason coming to know them any better, while these in return barely said good day to them, thinking this more discreet. Scarcely had they left the room before the Duke began asking good-naturedly who they were, so as to appear to be taking an interest in the intrinsic quality of people whom he himself, owing to the cross-purposes of fate or the wretched state of Oriane's nerves, never saw in his own house. " Tell me, who was that little woman in the pink hat? " " Why, my dear cousin, you have seen her hundreds of times, she's the Vicomtesse de Tours, who was a Lamarzelle." " But, do you know, she's quite good-looking; she seems clever too; if it weren't for a little flaw in her upper lip she'ld be a regular charmer. If there's a Vicomte de Tours, he can't have any too bad a time. Oriane, do you know what those eyebrows and the way her hair grows reminded me of? Your cousin Hedwige de Ligne." The Duchesse de Guermantes, who languished whenever people spoke of the beauty of any woman other than herself, let the conversation drop. She had reckoned without the weakness her husband had for letting it be seen that he knew all about the people who did not come to his house, whereby he believed that he shewed himself to be more seriously minded than his wife. " But," he resumed suddenly with emphasis, " You mentioned the name Lamarzelle. I remember, when I was in the Chamber, hearing a really remarkable speech made . . ." " That was the uncle of the young woman you saw just now." " Indeed! What talent! No, my dear girl," he assured the Vicomtesse d'Egremont, whom Mme. de Guermantes could not endure, but who, refusing to stir from the Princesse d'Epinay's drawing-room where she willingly humbled herself to play the part of parlour-maid (and was ready to slap her own parlour-maid on returning home), stayed there, confused, tearful, but stayed when the ducal couple were in the room, took their cloaks, tried to make herself useful, offered discreetly to withdraw into the next room, "you are not to make tea for us, let us just sit and talk quietly, we are simple souls, really, honestly. Besides," he went on, turning to the Princesse d'Epinay (leaving the Egremont lady blushing, humble, ambitious and full of zeal), "we can only give you a quarter of an hour." This quarter of an hour was entirely taken up with a sort of exhibition of the witty things which the Duchess had said during the previous week, and to which she herself would certainly not have referred had not her husband, with great adroitness, by appearing to be rebuking her with reference to the incidents that had provoked them, obliged her as though against her will to repeat them.

The Princesse d'Epinay, who was fond of her cousin and knew that she had a weakness for compliments, went into ecstasies over her hat, her sunshade, her wit. "Talk to her as much as you like about her clothes," said the Duke in the sullen tone which he had adopted and now tempered with a sardonic smile so that his resentment should not be taken seriously, "but for heaven's sake don't speak of her wit, I should be only too glad not to have so witty a wife. You are probably alluding to the shocking pun she made about my brother Palamède," he went on, knowing quite well that the Princess and the rest of the family had not yet heard this pun, and delighted to have an opportunity of shewing off his wife. "In the first place I consider it unworthy of a person who has occasionally, I must admit, said some quite good things, to make bad puns, but especially about my brother, who is very susceptible, and if it is going to lead to his quarrelling with me, that would really be too much of

a good thing." "But we never heard a word about it!
One of Oriane's puns! It's sure to be delicious. Oh,
do tell us!" "No, no," the Duke went on, still sulking
though with a broader smile, "I'm so glad you haven't
heard it. Seriously, I'm very fond of my brother."
"Listen, Basin," broke in the Duchess, the moment
having come for her to take up her husband's cue, "I
can't think why you should say that it might annoy
Palamède, you know quite well it would do nothing of
the sort. He is far too intelligent to be vexed by a stupid
joke which has nothing offensive about it. You are making
them think I said something nasty; I simply uttered a
remark which was not in the least funny, it is you who
make it seem important by losing your temper over it.
I don't understand you." "You are making us terribly
excited, what is it all about?" "Oh, obviously nothing
serious!" cried M. de Guermantes. "You may have
heard that my brother offered to give Brézé, the place
he got from his wife, to his sister Marsantes." "Yes, but
we were told that she didn't want it, she didn't care for
that part of the country, the climate didn't suit her."
"Very well, some one had been telling my wife all that
and saying that if my brother was giving this place to
our sister it was not so much to please her as to tease
her. 'He's such a teaser, Charlus,' was what they actually
said. Well, you know Brézé, it's a royal domain, I should
say it's worth millions, it used to be part of the crown
lands, it includes one of the finest forests in the whole of
France. There are plenty of people who would be only
too delighted to be teased to that tune. And so when she
heard the word 'teaser' applied to Charlus because he
was giving away such a magnificent property, Oriane

could not help exclaiming, without meaning anything, I must admit, there wasn't a trace of ill-nature about it, for it came like a flash of lightning: ' Teaser, teaser? Then he must be Teaser Augustus!' You understand," he went on, resuming his sulky tone, having first cast a sweeping glance round the room in order to judge the effect of his wife's witticism—and in some doubt as to the extent of Mme. d'Epinay's acquaintance with ancient history, " you understand, it's an allusion to Augustus Caesar, the Roman Emperor; it's too stupid, a bad play on words, quite unworthy of Oriane. And then, you see, I am more circumspect than my wife, if I haven't her wit, I think of the consequences; if anyone should be so ill-advised as to repeat the remark to my brother there'll be the devil to pay. All the more," he went on, " because as you know Palamède is very high and mighty, and very fussy also, given to gossip and all that sort of thing, so that quite apart from the question of his giving away Brézé you must admit that ' Teaser Augustus ' suits him down to the ground. That is what justifies my wife's remarks; even when she is inclined to stoop to what is almost vulgar, she is always witty and does really describe people."

And so, thanks on one occasion to " Teaser Augustus", on another to something else, the visits paid by the Duke and Duchess to their kinsfolk replenished the stock of anecdotes, and the emotion which these visits aroused lasted long after the departure of the sparkling lady and her " producer ". Her hostess would begin by going over again with the privileged persons who had been at the entertainment (those who had remained in the room) the clever things that Oriane had said. " You hadn't

heard 'Teaser Augustus'?" asked the Princesse
d'Epinay. "Yes," replied the Marquise de Baveno, blushing as she spoke, "the Princesse de Sarsina (the La
Rochefoucauld one) mentioned it to me, not quite in
the same words. But of course it was far more interesting
to hear it repeated like that with my cousin in the room,"
she went on, as though speaking of a song that had been
accompanied by the composer himself. "We were speaking of Oriane's latest—she was here just now," her
hostess greeted a visitor who would be plunged in despair
at not having arrived an hour earlier. "What! Has
Oriane been here?" "Yes, you ought to have come a
little sooner," the Princesse d'Epinay informed her, not
in reproach but letting her understand all that her clumsiness had made her miss. It was her fault alone if she had
not been present at the Creation of the World or at
Mme. Carvalho's last performance. "What do you think
of Oriane's latest? I must say, I do enjoy 'Teaser
Augustus'," and the "saying" would be served up again
cold next day at luncheon before a few intimate friends
who were invited on purpose, and would reappear under
various sauces throughout the week. Indeed the Princess happening in the course of that week to pay her
annual visit to the Princesse de Parme seized the opportunity to ask whether her Royal Highness had heard the
pun, and repeated it to her. "Ah! Teaser Augustus,"
said the Princesse de Parme, her eyes bulging with an
instinctive admiration, which begged however for a com-
plementary elucidation which Mme. d'Epinay was not
loath to furnish. "I must say, 'Teaser Augustus' pleases
me enormously as a piece of 'phrasing'," she concluded.
As a matter of fact the word "phrasing" was not in the

least applicable to this pun, but the Princesse d'Epinay, who claimed to have assimilated her share of the Guermantes spirit, had borrowed from Oriane the expressions "phrased" and "phrasing" and employed them without much discrimination. Now the Princesse de Parme, who was not at all fond of Mme. d'Epinay, whom she considered plain, knew to be miserly and believed, on the authority of the Courvoisiers, to be malicious, recognised this word "phrasing" which she had heard used by Mme. de Guermantes but would not by herself have known how or when to apply. She received the impression that it was in fact its "phrasing" that formed the charm of "Teaser Augustus" and, without altogether forgetting her antipathy towards the plain and miserly lady, could not repress a burst of admiration for a person endowed to such a degree with the Guermantes spirit, so strong that she was on the point of inviting the Princesse d'Epinay to the Opera. She was held in check only by the reflexion that it would be wiser perhaps to consult Mme. de Guermantes first. As for Mme. d'Epinay, who, unlike the Courvoisiers, paid endless attentions to Oriane and was genuinely fond of her but was jealous of her exalted friends and slightly irritated by the fun which the Duchess used to make of her before everyone on account of her meanness, she reported on her return home what an effort it had required to make the Princesse de Parme grasp the point of "Teaser Augustus", and declared what a snob Oriane must be to number such a goose among her friends. "I should never have been able to see much of the Princesse de Parme even if I had cared to," she informed the friends who were dining with her. "M. d'Epinay would not have allowed it for a moment, because of her immorality," she explained, alluding to certain purely imaginary excesses on the part of the Princess. "But even if I had had a husband less strict in his views, I must say I could never have made friends with her. I don't know how Oriane can bear to see her every other day, as she does. I go there once a year, and it's all I can do to sit out my call." As for those of the Courvoisiers who happened to be at Victurnienne's on the day of Mme. de Guermantes's visit, the arrival of the Duchess generally put them to flight owing to the exasperation they felt at the "ridiculous salaams" that were made to her there. One alone remained on the afternoon of of "Teaser Augustus". He did not entirely see the point, but he did see part of it, being an educated man. And the Courvoisiers went about repeating that Oriane had called uncle Palamède "Caesar Augustus", which was, according to them, a good enough description of him, but why all this endless talk about Oriane, they went on. People couldn't make more fuss about a queen. "After all, what is Oriane? I don't say that the Guermantes aren't an old family, but the Courvoisiers are every bit as good in rank, antiquity, marriages. We mustn't forget that on the Field of the Cloth of Gold, when the King of England asked François I who was the noblest of the lords there present, 'Sire,' said the King of France, 'Courvoisier.'" But even if all the Courvoisiers had stayed in the room to hear them, Oriane's sayings would have fallen on deaf ears, since the incidents that usually gave occasion for those sayings would have been regarded by them from a totally different point of view. If, for instance, a Courvoisier found herself running short of chairs, in the middle of a party, or if she used the wrong name in greeting a guest whose face she did not remember, or if one of her servants said something stupid, the Courvoisier, extremely annoyed, flushed, quivering with excitement, would deplore so unfortunate an occurrence. And when she had a visitor in the room and Oriane was expected, she would say in a tone anxiously and imperiously questioning: " Do you know her? ", fearing that if the visitor did not know her his presence might make an unfortunate impression on Oriane. But Mme. de Guermantes on the contrary extracted from such incidents opportunities for stories which made the Guermantes laugh until the tears streamed down their cheeks, so that one was obliged to envy her, her having run short of chairs, having herself made or having allowed her servant to make a blunder, having had at her party some one whom nobody knew, as one is obliged to be thankful that great writers have been kept at a distance by men and betrayed by women when their humiliations and their sufferings have been if not the direct stimulus of their genius, at any rate the subject matter of their works.

The Courvoisiers were incapable of rising to the level of the spirit of innovation which the Duchesse de Guermantes introduced into the life of society and, by adapting it, following an unerring instinct, to the necessities of the moment, made into something artistic where the purely rational application of cut and dried rules would have given as unfortunate results as would greet a man who, anxious to succeed in love or in politics, was to reproduce in his own daily life the exploits of Bussy d'Amboise. If the Courvoisiers gave a family dinner or a dinner to meet some prince, the addition of a recognised wit, of some friend of their son seemed to them an anomaly capable of producing the direst consequences. A Courvoisier whose father had been a Minister of the Empire having to give an afternoon party to meet Princesse Mathilde deduced by a geometrical formula that she could invite no one but Bonapartists. Of whom she knew practically none. All the smart women of her acquaintance, all the amusing men were ruthlessly barred because, from their Legitimist views or connexions, they might easily, according to Courvoisier logic, give offence to the Imperial Highness. The latter, who in her own house entertained the flower of the Faubourg Saint-Germain, was quite surprised when she found at Mme. de Courvoisier's only a notorious old sponger whose husband had been an Imperial Prefect, the widow of the Director of Posts and sundry others known for their loyalty to Napoleon, their stupidity and their dullness. Princesse Mathilde, however, in no way stinted the generous and refreshing shower of her sovereign grace over these miserable scarecrows whom the Duchesse de Guermantes, for her part, took good care not to invite when it was her turn to entertain the Princess, but substituted for them without any abstract reasoning about Bonapartism the most brilliant coruscation of all the beauties, all the talents, all the celebrities, who, the exercise of some subtle sixth sense made her feel, would be acceptable to the niece of the Emperor even when they belonged actually to the Royal House. There was not lacking indeed the Duc d'Aumale, and when on withdrawing the Princess, raising Mme. de Guermantes from the ground where she had sunk in a curtsey and was trying to kiss the august hand, embraced her on both cheeks, it was from the bottom of her heart that she was able to assure the Duchess that never had she spent a happier afternoon nor seen so delightful a party. The Princesse de Parme was Courvoisier in her incapacity for innovation in social matters, but unlike the Courvoisiers the surprise that was perpetually caused her by the Duchesse de Guermantes engendered in her not, as in them, antipathy but admiration. This astonishment was still farther enhanced by the infinitely backward state of the Princess's education. Mme. de Guermantes was herself a great deal less advanced than she supposed. But it was enough for her to have gone a little beyond Madame de Parme to stupefy that lady, and, as the critics of each generation confine themselves to maintaining the direct opposite of the truths admitted by their predecessors, she had only to say that Flaubert, that arch-enemy of the bourgeois, had been bourgeois through and through, or that there was a great deal of Italian music in Wagner, to open before the Princess, at the cost of a nervous exhaustion which recurred every time, as before the eyes of a swimmer in a stormy sea, horizons that seemed to her unimaginable and remained for ever vague. A stupefaction caused also by the paradoxes uttered with relation not only to works of art but to persons of their acquaintance and to current social events. No doubt the incapacity that prevented Mme. de Parme from distinguishing the true wit of the Guermantes from certain rudimentarily acquired forms of that wit (which made her believe in the high intellectual worth of certain, especially certain female Guermantes, of whom she was bewildered on hearing the Duchess confide to her with a smile that they were mere blockheads) was one of the causes of the astonishment which the Princess always felt on hearing Mme. de Guermantes criticise other people. But there was another cause also, one which I, who knew at this time more books than people and literature better than life, explained to myself by thinking that the Duchess, living this worldly life the idleness and sterility of which are to a true social activity what criticism, in art, is to creation, extended to the persons who surrounded her the instability of point of view, the uneasy thirst of the reasoner who to assuage a mind that has grown too dry goes in search of no matter what paradox that is still fairly new, and will make no bones about upholding the refreshing opinion that the really great *Iphigénie* is Piccini's and not Gluck's, at a pinch the true *Phèdre* that of Pradon.

When a woman who was intelligent, educated, witty had married a shy bumpkin whom one saw but seldom and never heard, Mme. de Guermantes one fine day would find a rare intellectual pleasure not only in decrying the wife but in " discovering " the husband. In the Cambremer household, for example, if she had lived in that section of society at the time, she would have decreed that Mme. de Cambremer was stupid, and that the really interesting person, misunderstood, delightful, condemned to silence by a chattering wife but himself worth a thousand of her, was the Marquis, and the Duchess would have felt on declaring this the same kind of refreshment as the critic who, after people have for seventy years been admiring *Hernani,* confesses to a preference for *Le Lion Amoureux.* And from this same morbid need of arbitrary novelties, if from her girlhood everyone had been pitying a model wife, a true saint, for being married to a scoundrel, one fine day Mme. de Guermantes would assert that this scoundrel was perhaps a frivolous man but one with a heart of gold, whom the implacable harshness of his wife had driven to do the most inconsistent things. I knew that it is not only over different works, in the long course of centuries, but over different parts of the same work that criticism plays, thrusting back into the shadow what for too long has been thought brilliant, and making emerge what has appeared to be doomed to permanent obscurity. I had not only seen Bellini, Winterhalter, the Jesuit architects, a Restoration cabinet-maker come to take the place of men of genius who were called "worn out", simply because they had worn out the lazy minds of the intellectuals, as neurasthenics are always worn out and always changing; I had seen preferred in Sainte-Beuve alternately the critic and the poet, Musset rejected so far as his poetry went save for a few quite unimportant little pieces. No doubt certain essayists are mistaken when they set above the most famous scenes in *Le Cid* or *Polyeucte* some speech from *Le Menteur* which, like an old plan, furnishes information about the Paris of the day, but their predilection, justified if not by considerations of beauty at least by a documentary interest, is still too rational for our criticism run mad. It will barter the whole of Molière for a line from *L'Etourdi*, and even when it pronounces Wagner's *Tristan* a bore will except a "charming note on the horns" at the point where the hunt goes by. This depravation of taste helped me to understand that of which Mme. de Guermantes gave proof when she decided that a man of their world, recognised as a good fellow but a fool, was a monster of egoism, sharper than people thought—that another widely known for his generosity might be the personification of avarice, that a good mother paid no attention to her children, and that a woman generally supposed to be vicious was really actuated by the noblest feelings. As though spoiled by the nullity of life in society, the intelligence and perception of Mme. de Guermantes were too vacillating for disgust not to follow pretty swiftly in the wake of infatuation (leaving her still ready to feel herself attracted afresh by the kind of cleverness which she had in turn sought out and abandoned) and for the charm which she had felt in some warm-hearted man not to change, if he came too often to see her, sought too freely from her directions which she was incapable of giving him, into an irritation which she believed to be produced by her admirer but which was in fact due to the utter impossibility of finding pleasure when one does nothing else than seek it. The variations of the Duchess's judgment spared no one, except her husband. He alone had never been in love with her, in him she had always felt an iron character, indifferent to the caprices that she displayed, contemptuous of her beauty, violent, of a will that would never bend, the sort under which alone nervous people can find tranquillity. M. de Guermantes on the other hand, pursuing a single type of feminine beauty but seeking it in mistresses whom he constantly replaced, had, once he had left them, and to express derision of them, only an associate, permanent and identical, who irritated him often by her chatter but as to whom he knew that everyone regarded her as the most beautiful, the most virtuous, the cleverest, the best-read member of the aristocracy, as a wife whom he, M. de Guermantes, was only too fortunate to have found, who cloaked all his irregularities, entertained like no one else in the world, and upheld for their drawing-room its position as the premier in the Faubourg Saint-Germain. This common opinion he himself shared; often moved to ill-humour against her, he was proud of her. If, being as niggardly as he was fastidious, he refused her the most trifling sums for her charities or for the servants, yet he insisted upon her wearing the most sumptuous clothes and driving behind the best horses in Paris. Whenever Mme. de Guermantes had just perpetrated, with reference to the merits and defects, which she suddenly transposed, of one of their friends, a new and succulent paradox, she burned to make trial of it before people capable of relishing it, to bring out its psychological originality and to set its epigrammatic brilliance sparkling. No doubt these new opinions embodied as a rule no more truth than the old, often less; but this very element, arbitrary and incalculable, of novelty which they contained conferred on them something intellectual which made the communication of them exciting. Only the patient on whom the Duchess was exercising her psychological skill was generally an intimate friend as to whom those people to whom she longed to hand on her discovery were entirely unaware that he was not still at the apex of her favour; thus the reputation that Mme. de Guermantes had of being an incomparable friend, sentimental, tender and devoted, made it difficult for her to launch the attack herself; she could at the most intervene later on, as though under constraint, by uttering a response to appease, to contradict in appearance but actually to support a partner who had taken it on himself to provoke her; this was precisely the part in which M. de Guermantes excelled.

227

As for social activities, it was yet another form of pleasure, arbitrary and spectacular, that Mme. de Guermantes felt in uttering, with regard to them, those unexpected judgments which pricked with an incessant and exquisite feeling of surprise the Princesse de Parme. But with this one of the Duchess's pleasures it was not so much with the help of literary criticism as by following political life and the reports of parliamentary debates that I tried to understand in what it might consist. The successive and contradictory edicts by which Mme. de Guermantes continually reversed the scale of values among the people of her world no longer sufficing to distract her, she sought also in the manner in which she ordered her own social behaviour, in which she recorded her own most trivial decisions on points of fashion, to taste those artificial emotions, to fulfil those adventitious obligations which stimulate the perceptions of Parliaments and gain hold of the minds of politicians. We know that when a Minister explains to the Chamber that he believed himself to be acting rightly in following a line of conduct which does, as a matter of fact, appear quite straightforward to the commonsense person who next morning in his newspaper reads the report of the sitting, this commonsense reader does nevertheless feel himself suddenly stirred and begins to doubt whether he has been right in approving the Minister's conduct when he sees that the latter's speech was listened to with the accompaniment of a lively agitation and punctuated with expressions of condemnation such as: " It's most serious! " ejaculated by a Deputy whose name and titles are so long, and followed in the report by movements so emphatic that in the whole interruption the words " It's most serious!" occupy less room than a hemistich does in an alexandrine. For instance in the days when M. de Guermantes, Prince des Laumes, sat in the Chamber, one used to read now and then in the Paris newspapers, albeit it was intended primarily for the Méséglise division, to shew the electors there that they had not given their votes to an inactive or voiceless mandatory:

> (Monsieur de Guermantes-Bouillon, Prince des Laumes: "This is serious!" "Hear, hear!" from the Centre and some of the Right benches, loud exclamations from the Extreme Left.)

The commonsense reader still retains a gleam of faith in the sage Minister, but his heart is convulsed with a fresh palpitation by the first words of the speaker who rises to reply:

> "The astonishment, it is not too much to say the stupor" (keen sensation on the Right side of the House) "that I have felt at the words of one who is still, I presume, a member of the Government" (thunder of applause) . . . Several Deputies then crowded round the Ministerial bench. The Under-Secretary of State for Posts and Telegraphs, without rising from his seat, nodded his head in the affirmative.

This "thunder of applause" carries away the last shred of resistance in the mind of the commonsense reader; he discovers to be an insult to the Chamber, monstrous in fact, a course of procedure which in itself is of no importance; it may be some normal action such as arranging that the rich shall pay more than the poor, bringing to light some piece of injustice, preferring peace to war; he will find it scandalous and will see in it an offence to certain principles to which as a matter of fact he had never given a thought, which are not engraved on the human heart, but which move him forcibly by reason of the acclamations which they provoke and the compact majorities which they assemble.

It must at the same time be recognised that this subtlety of the politician which served to explain to me the Guermantes circle, and other groups in society later on, is nothing more than the perversion of a certain fineness of interpretation often described as " reading between the lines ". If in representative assemblies there is absurdity owing to perversion of this quality, there is equally stupidity, through the want of it, in the public who take everything " literally ", who do not suspect a dismissal when a high dignitary is relieved of his office " at his own request ", and say: " He cannot have been dismissed, since it was he who asked leave to retire,"—a defeat when the Russians by a strategic movement withdraw upon a stronger position that has been prepared beforehand, a refusal when, a Province having demanded its independence from the German Emperor, he grants it religious autonomy. It is possible, moreover (to return to these sittings of the Chamber), that when they open the Deputies themselves are like the commonsense person who will read the published report. Learning that certain workers on strike have sent their delegates to confer with a Minister, they may ask one another innocently: " There now, I wonder what they can have been saying; let's hope it's all settled," at the moment when the Minister himself mounts the tribune in a solemn silence which has already brought artificial emotions into play. The first words of the Minister: " There is no necessity for me to inform the Chamber that I have too high a sense of what is the duty of the Government to have received a deputation of which the authority entrusted to me could take no cognisance," produce a dramatic effect, for this was the one hypothesis which the commonsense of the Deputies had not imagined. But precisely because of its dramatic effect it is greeted with such applause that it is only after several minutes have passed that the Minister can succeed in making himself heard, the Minister who will receive on returning to his place on the bench the congratulations of his colleagues. We are as deeply moved as on the day when the same Minister failed to invite to a big official reception the President of the Municipal Council who was supporting the Opposition, and declare that on this occasion as on the other he has acted with true statesmanship.

M. de Guermantes at this period in his life had, to the great scandal of the Courvoisiers, frequently been among the crowd of Deputies who came forward to congratulate the Minister. I have heard it said afterwards that even at a time when he was playing a fairly important part in the Chamber and was being thought of in connexion with Ministerial office or an Embassy he was, when a friend came to ask a favour of him, infinitely more simple, behaved politically a great deal less like the important political personage than anyone else who did not happen to be Duc de Guermantes. For if he said that nobility made no difference, that he regarded his fellow Deputies as equals, he did not believe it for a moment. He sought, pretended to value but really despised political importance, and as he remained in his own eyes M. de Guermantes it did not envelop his person in that dead weight of high office which makes other politicians unapproachable. And in this way his pride guarded against every assault not only his manners which were of an ostentatious familiarity but also such true simplicity as he might actually have.

To return to those artificial and moving decisions such as are made by politicians, Mme. de Guermantes was no less disconcerting to the Guermantes, the Courvoisiers, the Faubourg in general and, more than anyone, the Princesse de Parme by her habit of issuing unaccountable decrees behind which one could feel to be latent principles which impressed one all the more, the less one expected them. If the new Greek Minister gave a fancy dress ball, everyone chose a costume and asked everyone else what the Duchess would wear. One thought that she would appear as the Duchesse de Bourgogne, another suggested as probable the guise of Princess of Dujabar, a third Psyche. Finally, a Courvoisier having asked her: "What are you going to wear, Oriane?" provoked the one response of which nobody had thought: "Why, nothing at all!" which at once set every tongue wagging, as revealing Oriane's opinion as to the true social position of the new Greek Minister and the proper attitude to adopt towards him, that is to say the opinion which ought to have been foreseen, namely that a duchess "was not expected" to attend the fancy dress ball given by this new Minister. "I do not see that there is any necessity to go to the Greek Minister's; I do not know him; I am not a Greek; why should I go to these people's house, I have nothing to do with them?" said the Duchess. "But everybody will be there, they say it's going to be charming!" cried Mme. de Gallardon. "Still, it's just as charming sometimes to sit by one's own fireside," replied Mme. de Guermantes. The Courvoisiers could not get over this, but the Guermantes, without copying it, approved of their cousin's attitude. " Naturally, everybody isn't in a position like Oriane to break with all the conventions. But if you look at it in one way you can't say she was actually wrong in wishing to shew that we are going rather far in flinging ourselves at the feet of all these foreigners who appear from heaven knows where." Naturally, knowing the stream of comment which one or other attitude would not fail to provoke, Mme. de Guermantes took as much pleasure in appearing at a party to which her hostess had not dared to count on her coming as in staying at home or spending the evening at the play with her husband on the night of a party to which " everybody was going ", or, again, when people imagined that she would eclipse the finest diamonds with some historic diadem, by stealing into the room without a single jewel, and in another style of dress than what had been, wrongly, supposed to be essential to the occasion. Albeit she was anti-Dreyfusard (while retaining her belief in the innocence of Dreyfus, just as she spent her life in the social world believing only in abstract ideas) she had created an enormous sensation at a party at the Princesse de Ligne's, first of all by remaining seated after all the ladies had risen to their feet as General Mercier entered the room, and then by getting up and in a loud voice asking for her carriage when a Nationalist orator had begun to address the gathering, thereby shewing that she did not consider that society was meant for talking politics; all heads were turned towards her at a Good Friday concert at which, although a Voltairean, she had not remained because she thought it indecent to bring Christ upon the stage. We know how important, even for the great queens of society, is that moment of the year at which the round of entertainment begins: so much so that the Marquise d'Amoncourt, who, from a need to say something, a form of mania, and also from want of perception, was always making a fool of herself, had actually replied to somebody who had called to condole with her on the death of her father, M. de Montmorency: "What makes it sadder still is that it should come at a time when one's mirror is simply stuffed with cards!" Very well, at this point in the social year, when people invited the Duchesse de Guermantes to dinner, making every effort to see that she was not already engaged, she declined, for the one reason of which nobody in society would ever have thought; she was just starting on a cruise among the Norwegian fjords, which were so interesting. People in society were stupefied, and, without any thought of following the Duchess's example, derived nevertheless from her action that sense of relief which one has in reading Kant when after the most rigorous demonstration of determinism one finds that above the world of necessity there is the world of freedom. Every invention of which no one has ever thought before excites the interest even of people who can derive no benefit from it. That of steam navigation was a small thing compared with the employment of steam navigation at that sedentary time of year called " the season ". The idea that anyone could voluntarily renounce a hundred dinners or luncheons, twice as many afternoon teas, three times as many evening parties, the most brilliant Mondays at the Opera and Tuesdays at the Français to visit the Norwegian fjords seemed to the Courvoisiers no more explicable than the idea of *Twenty Thousand Leagues*

under the Sea, but conveyed to them a similar impression
of independence and charm. So that not a day passed on
which somebody might not be heard to ask, not merely:
" You've heard Oriane's latest joke? " but " You know
Oriane's latest? " and on " Oriane's latest " as on
" Oriane's latest joke " would follow the comment: " How
typical of Oriane! " " Isn't that pure Oriane? " Oriane's
latest might be, for instance, that, having to write on
behalf of a patriotic society to Cardinal X—, Bishop of
Mâcon (whom M. de Guermantes when he spoke of him
invariably called " Monsieur de Mascon," thinking this
to be " old French "), when everyone was trying to
imagine what form the letter would take, and had no
difficulty as to the opening words, the choice lying between " Eminence," and " Monseigneur," but was puzzled
as to the rest, Oriane's letter, to the general astonishment,
began: " Monsieur le Cardinal," following an old aca-
demic form, or: " My Cousin," this term being in use
among the Princes of the Church, the Guermantes and
Crowned Heads, who prayed to God to take each and all
of them into " His fit and holy keeping ". To start people
on the topic of an " Oriane's latest " it was sufficient
that at a performance at which all Paris was present
and a most charming play was being given, when they
looked for Mme. de Guermantes in the boxes of the
Princesse de Parme, the Princesse de Guermantes,
countless other ladies who had invited her, they discovered her sitting by herself, in black, with a tiny hat on
her head, in a stall in which she had arrived before the
curtain rose. " You hear better, when it's a play that's
worth listening to," she explained, to the scandal of the
Courvoisiers and the admiring bewilderment of the Guer-

mantes and the Princesse de Parme, who suddenly discovered that the "fashion" of hearing the beginning of
a play was more up to date, was a proof of greater originality and intelligence (which need not astonish them,
coming from Oriane) than that of arriving for the last
act after a big dinner-party and "going on" somewhere
first. Such were the various kinds of surprise for which
the Princesse de Parme knew that she ought to be prepared if she put a literary or social question to Mme. de
Guermantes, one result of which was that during these
dinner-parties at Oriane's her Royal Highness never ventured upon the slightest topic save with the uneasy and
enraptured prudence of the bather emerging from between
two breakers.

Among the elements which, absent from the three or
four other more or less equivalent drawing-rooms that set
the fashion for the Faubourg Saint-Germain, differenti-
ated from them that of the Duchesse de Guermantes,
just as Leibniz allows that each monad, while reflecting
the entire universe, adds to it something of its own, one
of the least attractive was regularly furnished by one or
two extremely good-looking women who had no title to
be there apart from their beauty and the use that M. de
Guermantes had made of them, and whose presence
revealed at once, as does in other drawing-rooms that of
certain otherwise unaccountable pictures, that in this
household the husband was an ardent appreciator of
feminine graces. They were all more or less alike, for
the Duke had a taste for large women, at once statuesque
and loose-limbed, of a type half-way between the Venus
of Milo and the Samothracian Victory; often fair, rarely
dark, sometimes auburn, like the most recent, who was at

this dinner, that Vicomtesse d'Arpajon whom he had loved so well that for a long time he had obliged her to send him as many as ten telegrams daily (which slightly annoyed the Duchess), corresponded with her by carrier pigeon when he was at Guermantes, and from whom moreover he had long been so incapable of tearing himself away that, one winter which he had had to spend at Parma, he travelled back regularly every week to Paris, spending two days in the train, in order to see her.

As a rule these handsome " supers " had been his mistresses but were no longer (as was Mme. d'Arpajon's case) or were on the point of ceasing to be so. It may well have been that the importance which the Duchess enjoyed in their sight and the hope of being invited to her house, though they themselves came of thoroughly aristocratic, but still not quite first-class stock, had prompted them, even more than the good looks and generosity of the Duke, to yield to his desires. Not that the Duchess would have placed any insuperable obstacle in the way of their crossing her threshold: she was aware that in more than one of them she had found an ally, thanks to whom she had obtained a thousand things which she wanted but which M. de Guermantes pitilessly denied his wife so long as he was not in love with some one else. And so the reason why they were not invited by the Duchess until their intimacy with the Duke was already far advanced lay principally in the fact that he, every time that he had embarked on the deep waters of love, had imagined nothing more than a brief flirtation, as a reward for which he considered an invitation from his wife to be more than adequate. And yet he found himself offering this as the price of far less, for a first kiss in fact, because a resistance upon which he had never reckoned had been brought into play or because there had been no resistance. In love it often happens that gratitude, the desire to give pleasure, makes us generous beyond the limits of what the other person's expectation and self-interest could have anticipated. But then the realisation of this offer was hindered by conflicting circumstances. In the first place, all the women who had responded to M. de Guermantes's love, and sometimes even when they had not yet surrendered themselves to him, he had, one after another, segregated from the world. He no longer allowed them to see anyone, spent almost all his time in their company, looked after the education of their children to whom now and again, if one was to judge by certain speaking likenesses later on, he had occasion to present a little brother or sister. And so if, at the start of the connexion, the prospect of an introduction to Mme. de Guermantes, which had never crossed the mind of the Duke, had entered considerably into the thoughts of his mistress, their connexion had by itself altered the whole of the lady's point of view; the Duke was no longer for her merely the husband of the smartest woman in Paris, but a man with whom his new mistress was in love, a man moreover who had given her the means and the inclination for a more luxurious style of living and had transposed the relative importance in her mind of questions of social and of material advantage; while now and then a composite jealousy, into which all these factors entered, of Mme. de Guermantes animated the Duke's mistresses. But this case was the rarest of all; besides, when the day appointed for the introduction at length arrived (at a point when as a rule the Duke had lost practically all interest in the matter, his actions, like everyone's else, being generally dictated by previous actions the prime motive of which had already ceased to exist), it frequently happened that it was Mme. de Guermantes who had sought the acquaintance of the mistress in whom she hoped, and so greatly needed, to discover, against her dread husband, a valuable ally. This is not to say that, save at rare moments, in their own house, where, when the Duchess talked too much, he let fall a few words or, more dreadful still, preserved a silence which rendered her speechless, M. de Guermantes failed in his outward relations with his wife to observe what are called the forms. People who did not know them might easily misunderstand. Sometimes between the racing at Deauville, the course of waters and the return to Guermantes for the shooting, in the few weeks which people spend in Paris, since the Duchess had a liking for café-concerts, the Duke would go with her to spend the evening at one of these. The audience remarked at once, in one of those little open boxes in which there is just room for two, this Hercules in his "smoking" (for in France we give to everything that is more or less British the one name that it happens not to bear in England), his monocle screwed in his eye, in his plump but finely shaped hand, on the ring-finger of which there glowed a sapphire, a plump cigar from which now and then he drew a puff of smoke, keeping his eyes for the most part on the stage but, when he did let them fall upon the audience in which there was absolutely no one whom he knew, softening them with an air of gentleness, reserve, courtesy and consideration. When a verse struck him as amusing and not too indecent,

the Duke would turn round with a smile to his wife, letting
her share, by a twinkle of good-natured understanding,
the innocent merriment which the new song had aroused
in himself. And the spectators might believe that there
was no better husband in the world than this, nor anyone
more enviable than the Duchess—that woman outside
whom every interest in the Duke's life lay, that woman
with whom he was not in love, to whom he had been con-
sistently unfaithful; when the Duchess felt tired, they
saw M. de Guermantes rise, put on her cloak with his
own hands, arranging her necklaces so that they did not
catch in the lining, and clear a path for her to the street
with an assiduous and respectful attention which she received with the coldness of the woman of the world who
sees in such behaviour simply conventional politeness, at
times even with the slightly ironical bitterness of the dis-
abused spouse who has no illusion left to shatter. But
despite these externals (another element of that politeness
which has made duty evolve from the depths of our being
to the surface, at a period already remote but still continuing for its survivors) the life of the Duchess was by
no means easy. M. de Guermantes never became generous or human save for a new mistress who would take,
as it generally happened, the Duchess's part; the latter
saw becoming possible for her once again generosities
towards inferiors, charities to the poor, even for herself,
later on, a new and sumptuous motor-car. But from the
irritation which developed as a rule pretty rapidly in Mme.
de Guermantes at people whom she found too submissive
the Duke's mistresses were not exempt. Presently the
Duchess grew tired of them. Simultaneously, at this
moment, the Duke's intimacy with Mme. d'Arpajon was

drawing to an end. Another mistress dawned on the horizon.

No doubt the love which M. de Guermantes had had for each of them in succession would begin one day to make itself felt afresh; in the first place, this love in dying bequeathed them, like beautiful marbles—marbles beautiful to the Duke, become thus in part an artist, because he had loved them and was sensitive now to lines which he would not have appreciated without love—which brought into juxtaposition in the Duchess's drawing-room their forms long inimical, devoured by jealousies and quarrels, and finally reconciled in the peace of friendship; besides, this friendship itself was an effect of the love which had made M. de Guermantes observe in those who were his mistresses virtues which exist in every human being but are perceptible only to the sensual eye, so much so that the ex-mistress, become " the best of comrades " who would do anything in the world for one, is as recognised a type as the doctor or father who is not a doctor or a father but a friend. But during a period of transition the woman whom M. de Guermantes was preparing to abandon bewailed her lot, made scenes, shewed herself exacting, appeared indiscreet, became a nuisance. The Duke began to take a dislike to her. Then Mme. de Guermantes had an opportunity to bring into prominence the real or imagined defects of a person who annoyed her. Known as a kind woman, Mme. de Guermantes received the telephone messages, the confidences, the tears of the abandoned mistress and made no complaint. She laughed at them, first with her husband then with a few chosen friends. And imagining that this pity which she shewed for the poor wretch gave her the right to make fun of her, even to her face, whatever the lady might say, provided it could be included among the attributes of the character for absurdity which the Duke and Duchess had recently fabricated for her, Mme. de Guermantes had no hesitation in exchanging with her husband a glance of ironical connivance.

Meanwhile, as she sat down to table, the Princesse de Parme remembered that she had thought of inviting a certain other Princess to the Opera, and, wishing to be assured that this would not in any way offend Mme. de Guermantes, was preparing to sound her. At this moment there entered M. de Grouchy, whose train, owing to some block on the line, had been held up for an hour. He made what excuses he could. His wife, had she been a Courvoisier, would have died of shame. But Mme. de Grouchy was not a Guermantes for nothing. As her husband was apologising for being late:

"I see," she broke in, "that even in little things arriving late is a tradition in your family."

"Sit down, Grouchy, and don't let them pull your leg," said the Duke.

"I hope I move with the times, still I must admit that the Battle of Waterloo had its points, since it brought about the Restoration of the Bourbons, and better still in a way which made them unpopular. But you seem to be a regular Nimrod!"

"Well, as a matter of fact, I have had quite a good bag. I shall take the liberty of sending the Duchess six brace of pheasants to-morrow."

An idea seemed to flicker in the eyes of Mme. de Guermantes. She insisted that M. de Grouchy must not give himself the trouble of sending the pheasants. And

THE DUCHESSE DE GUERMANTES ORDERS
POULLEIN TO FETCH THE PHEASANTS

THE DUCHESSE DE GUERMANTES ORDERS
POULLEIN TO FETCH THE PHEASANTS

making a sign to the betrothed footman with whom I had
exchanged a few words on my way from the Elstir room:

"Poullein," she told him, "you will go to-morrow and
fetch M. le Comte's pheasants and bring them straight
back—you won't mind, will you, Grouchy, if I make a
few little presents. Basin and I can't eat a whole dozen by
ourselves."

"But the day after to-morrow will be soon enough,"
said M. de Grouchy.

"No, to-morrow suits me better," the Duchess insisted.

Poullein had turned pale; his appointment with his
sweetheart would have to be missed. This was quite
enough for the diversion of the Duchess, who liked to
appear to be taking a human interest in everyone. "I
know it's your day out," she went on to Poullein, "all
you've got to do is to change with Georges; he can take
to-morrow off and stay in the day after."

But the day after, Poullein's sweetheart would not be
free. A holiday then was of no account to him. As soon
as he was out of the room, everyone complimented the
Duchess on the interest she took in her servants. "But
I only behave towards them as I like people to behave
to me." "That's just it. They can say they've found a
good place with you." "Oh, nothing so very wonderful.
But I think they all like me. That one is a little annoying
because he's in love. He thinks it incumbent on him to
go about with a long face."

At this point Poullein reappeared. "You're quite right,"
said M. de Grouchy, "he doesn't look much like smiling.
With those fellows one has to be good but not too good."
"I admit I'm not a very dreadful mistress. He'll have
nothing to do all day but call for your pheasants, sit in

the house doing nothing and eat his share of them."
"There are plenty of people who would be glad to be in his place," said M. de Grouchy, for envy makes men blind.

"Oriane," began the Princesse de Parme, "I had a visit the other day from your cousin Heudicourt; of course she's a highly intelligent woman; she's a Guermantes, one can say no more, but they tell me she has a spiteful tongue." The Duke fastened on his wife a slow gaze of deliberate stupefaction. Mme. de Guermantes began to smile. Gradually the Princess became aware of their pantomime. "But . . . do you mean to say . . . you don't agree with me?" she stammered with growing uneasiness. "Really, Ma'am, it's too good of you to pay any attention to Basin's faces. Now, Basin, you're not to hint nasty things about our cousins." "He thinks her too wicked?" inquired the Princess briskly. "Oh, dear me, no!" replied the Duchess. "I don't know who told your Highness that she was spiteful. On the contrary, she's an excellent creature who never said any harm of anyone, or did any harm to any one." "Ah!" sighed Mme. de Parme, greatly relieved. "I must say I never noticed anything myself. But I know it's often difficult not to be a little spiteful when one is so full of wit . . ." "Ah! Now that is a quality of which she has even less." "Less wit?" asked the stupefied Princess. "Come now, Oriane," broke in the Duke in a plaintive tone, casting to right and left of him a glance of amusement, "you heard the Princess tell you that she was a superior woman." "But isn't she?" "Superior in chest measurement, at any rate." "Don't listen to him, Ma'am, he's not sincere; she's as stupid as a (h'm) goose," came in a loud and

rasping voice from Mme. de Guermantes, who, a great
deal more " old French " even than the Duke when he
was not trying, did often deliberately seek to be, but in
a manner the opposite of the lace-neckcloth, deliquescent
style of her husband and in reality far more subtle, by a
sort of almost peasant pronunciation which had a harsh
and delicious flavour of the soil. " But she's the best
woman in the world. Besides, I don't really know that
one can call it stupidity when it's carried to such a point
as that. I don't believe I ever met anyone quite like her;
she's a case for a specialist, there's something pathological
about her, she's a sort of ' innocent ' or ' cretin ' or an
' arrested development ', like the people you see in melo-
dramas, or in *L'Arlésienne*. I always ask myself, when
she comes to see me, whether the moment may not have
arrived at which her intelligence is going to dawn, which
makes me a little nervous always." The Princess was
lost in admiration of these utterances but remained stupefied by the preceding verdict. " She repeated to me—and
so did Mme. d'Epinay—what you said about ' Teaser
Augustus.' It's delicious," she put in.

M. de Guermantes explained the joke to me. I wanted
to tell him that his brother, who pretended not to know
me, was expecting me that same evening at eleven o'clock.
But I had not asked Robert whether I might mention this
engagement, and as the fact that M. de Charlus had practically fixed it with me himself directly contradicted what
he had told the Duchess I judged it more tactful to say
nothing. " ' Teaser Augustus ' was not bad," said M.
de Guermantes, " but Mme. d'Heudicourt probably did
not tell you a far better thing that Oriane said to her the
other day in reply to an invitation to luncheon." "No,

indeed! Do tell me!" "Now Basin, you keep quiet; in the first place, it was a stupid remark, and it will make the Princess think me inferior even to my fool of a cousin. Though I don't know why I should call her my cousin. She's one of Basin's cousins. Still, I believe she is related to me in some sort of way." "Oh!" cried the Princesse de Parme, at the idea that she could possibly think Mme. de Guermantes stupid, and protesting helplessly that nothing could ever lower the Duchess from the place she held in her estimation. "Besides we have already subtracted from her the quality of wit; as what I said to her tends to deny her certain other good qualities also, it seems to me inopportune to repeat it." "'Deny her!' 'Inopportune!' How well she expresses herself!" said the Duke with a pretence of irony, to win admiration for the Duchess. "Now, then, Basin, you're not to make fun of your wife." "I should explain to your Royal Highness," went on the Duke, "that Oriane's cousin may be superior, good, stout, anything you like to mention, but she is not exactly—what shall I say—lavish." "No, I know, she's terribly close-fisted," broke in the Princess. "I should not have ventured to use the expression, but you have hit on exactly the right word. You can see it in her house-keeping, and especially in the cooking, which is excellent, but strictly rationed." "Which leads to some quite amusing scenes," M. de Bréauté interrupted him. "For instance, my dear Basin, I was down at Heudicourt one day when you were expected, Oriane and yourself. They had made the most elaborate preparations when, during the afternoon, a footman brought in a telegram to say that you weren't coming." "That doesn't surprise me!" said the Duchess, who not only was difficult to

secure, but liked people to know as much. "Your cousin
read the telegram, was duly distressed, then immediately,
without losing her head, telling herself that there was no
point in going to unnecessary expense for so unimportant a gentleman as myself, called the footman back.
'Tell the cook not to put on the chicken!' she shouted
after him. And that evening I heard her asking the butler:
'Well? What about the beef that was left over yesterday?
Aren't you going to let us have that?'" "All the same,
one must admit that the cheer you get there is of the very
best," said the Duke, who fancied that in using this language he shewed himself to belong to the old school. "I
don't know any house where one gets better food." "Or
less," put in the Duchess. "It is quite wholesome and
quite enough for what you would call a vulgar yokel like
myself," went on the Duke, "one keeps one's appetite."
"Oh, if it's to be taken as a cure, it's certainly more
hygienic than sumptuous. Not that it's as good as all
that," added Mme. de Guermantes, who was not at all
pleased that the title of "best table in Paris" should be
awarded to any but her own. "With my cousin it's just
the same as with those costive authors who hatch out
every fifteen years a one-act play or a sonnet. The sort
of thing people call a little masterpiece, trifles that are
perfect gems, in fact the one thing I loathe most in the
world. The cooking at Zénaïde's is not bad, but you
would think it more ordinary if she was less parsimonious.
There are some things her cook does quite well, and others
that he spoils. I have had some thoroughly bad dinners
there, as in most houses, only they've done me less harm
there because the stomach is, after all, more sensitive to
quantity than to quality." "Well, to get on with the

story," the Duke concluded, " Zénaïde insisted that Oriane should go to luncheon there, and as my wife is not very fond of going out anywhere she resisted, wanted to be sure that under the pretence of a quiet meal she was not being trapped into some great banquet, and tried in vain to find out who else were to be of the party. ' You must come,' Zénaïde insisted, boasting of all the good things there would be to eat. ' You are going to have a *purée* of chestnuts, I need say no more than that, and there will be seven little *bouchées à la reine*.' ' Seven little *bouchées*! ' cried Oriane, ' that means that we shall be at least eight! ' " There was silence for a few seconds, and then the Princess having seen the point let her laughter explode like a peal of thunder. " Ah! ' Then we shall be eight,'—it's exquisite. How very well phrased! " she said, having by a supreme effort recaptured the expression she had heard used by Mme. d'Epinay, which this time was more appropriate. " Oriane, that was very charming of the Princess, she said your remark was well phrased." " But, my dear, you're telling me nothing new. I know how clever the Princess is," replied Mme. de Guermantes, who readily assimilated a remark when it was uttered at once by a Royal Personage and in praise of her own wit. " I am very proud that Ma'am should appreciate my humble phrasings. I don't remember, though, that I ever did say such a thing, and if I did it must have been to flatter my cousin, for if she had ordered seven ' mouth-fuls ', the mouths, if I may so express myself, would have been a round dozen if not more."

" She used to have all M. de Bornier's manuscripts," went on the Princess, still speaking of Mme. d'Heudicourt, and anxious to make the most of the excellent reasons she might have for associating with that lady. " She must have dreamed it, I don't believe she ever even knew him," said the Duchess. " What is really interesting about him is that he kept up a correspondence with people of different nationalities at the same time," put in the Vicomtesse d'Arpajon who, allied to the principal ducal and even reigning families of Europe, was always glad that people should be reminded of the fact. " Surely, Oriane," said M. de Guermantes, with ulterior purpose, " you can't have forgotten that dinner-party where you had M. de Bornier sitting next to you! " " But, Basin," the Duchess interrupted him, " if you mean to inform me that I knew M. de Bornier, why of course I did, he even called upon me several times, but I could never bring myself to invite him to the house because I should always have been obliged to have it disinfected afterwards with formol. As for the dinner you mean, I remember it only too well, but it was certainly not at Zénaïde's, who never set eyes on Bornier in her life, and would probably think if you spoke to her of the *Fille de Roland* that you meant a Bonaparte Princess who was said at one time to be engaged to the son of the King of Greece; no, it was at the Austrian Embassy. Dear Hoyos imagined he was giving me a great treat by planting on the chair next to mine that pestiferous academician. I quite thought I had a squadron of mounted police sitting beside me. I was obliged to stop my nose as best I could, all through dinner; until the gruyère came round I didn't dare to breathe." M. de Guermantes, whose secret object was attained, made a furtive examination of his guests' faces to judge the effect of the Duchess's pleasantry. " You were speaking of correspondence; I must say, I thought Gambetta's admirable," she went on, to shew that she was not afraid to be found taking an interest in a proletarian and a radical. M. de Bréauté, who fully appreciated the brilliance of this feat of daring, gazed round him with an eye at once flashing and affectionate, after which he wiped his monocle.

"Gad, it's infernally dull that *Fille de Roland*," said M. de Guermantes, with the satisfaction which he derived from the sense of his own superiority to a work which had bored him so, perhaps also from the *suave mari magno* feeling one has in the middle of a good dinner, when one recalls so terrible an evening in the past. "Still, there were some quite good lines in it, and a patriotic sentiment."

I let it be understood that I had no admiration for M. de Bornier. "Indeed! You have some fault to find with him?" the Duke asked with a note of curiosity, for he always imagined when anyone spoke ill of a man that it must be on account of a personal resentment, just as to speak well of a woman marked the beginning of a love-affair. "I see you've got your knife into him. What did he do to you? You must tell us. Why yes, there must be some skeleton in the cupboard or you wouldn't run him down. It's long-winded, the *Fille de Roland*, but it's quite strong in parts." "Strong is just the right word for an author who smelt like that," Mme. de Guermantes broke in sarcastically. "If this poor boy ever found himself face to face with him, I can quite understand that he carried away an impression in his nostrils!" "I must confess, though, to Ma'am," the Duke went on, addressing the Princesse de Parme, "that quite apart from the *Fille de Roland*, in literature and even in music I am

250

terribly old-fashioned; no old nightingale can be too stale for my taste. You won't believe me, perhaps, but in the evenings, if my wife sits down to the piano, I find myself calling for some old tune by Auber or Boïeldieu, or even Beethoven! That's the sort of thing that appeals to me. As for Wagner, he sends me to sleep at once." "You are wrong there," said Mme. de Guermantes, "in spite of his insufferable long-windedness, Wagner was a genius. *Lohengrin* is a masterpiece. Even in *Tristan* there are some amusing passages scattered about. And the Chorus of Spinners in the *Flying Dutchman* is a perfect marvel." "A'n't I right, Babal," said M. de Guermantes, turning to M. de Bréauté, "what we like is:

> Les rendez-vous de noble compagnie
> Se donnent tous en ce charmant séjour.

It's delicious. And *Fra Diavolo,* and the *Magic Flute,* and the *Chalet,* and the *Marriage of Figaro,* and the *Diamants de la Couronne*—there's music for you! It's the same thing in literature. For instance, I adore Balzac, the *Bal de Sceaux,* the *Mohicans de Paris.*" "Oh, my dear, if you are going to begin about Balzac, we-shall never hear the end of it; do wait, keep it for some evening when Mémé's here. He's even better, he knows it all by heart." Irritated by his wife's interruption, the Duke held her for some seconds under the fire of a menacing silence. And his huntsman's eyes reminded me of a brace of loaded pistols. Meanwhile Mme. d'Arpajon had been exchanging with the Princesse de Parme, upon tragic and other kinds of poetry, a series of remarks which did not reach me distinctly until I caught the following from Mme. d'Arpajon: "Oh, Ma'am is sure to be right; I quite admit he makes the world seem ugly, because he's unable to distinguish between ugliness and beauty, or rather because his insufferable vanity makes him believe that everything he says is beautiful; I agree with your Highness that in the piece we are speaking of there are some ridiculous things, quite unintelligible, errors of taste, that it is difficult to understand, that it's as much trouble to read as if it was written in Russian or Chinese, for of course it's anything in the world but French, still when one has taken the trouble, how richly one is rewarded, it's so full of imagination!" Of this little lecture I had missed the opening sentences. I gathered in the end not only that the poet incapable of distinguishing between beauty and ugliness was Victor Hugo, but furthermore that the poem which was as difficult to understand as Chinese or Russian was

> Lorsque l'enfant paraît, le cercle de famille
> Applaudit à grands cris.

a piece dating from the poet's earliest period, and perhaps even nearer to Mme. Deshoulières than to the Victor Hugo of the *Légende des Siècles*. Far from condemning Mme. d'Arpajon as absurd, I saw her (the only one, at that table so matter-of-fact, so nondescript, at which I had sat down with such keen disappointment), I saw her in my mind's eye crowned with that lace cap, with the long spiral ringlets falling from it on either side, which was worn by Mme. de Rémusat, Mme. de Broglie, Mme. de Saint-Aulaire, all those distinguished women who in their fascinating letters quote with so much learning and so aptly passages from Sophocles, Schiller and the *Imitation,* but in whom the earliest poetry of the Romantics induced the alarm and exhaustion inseparable for my grandmother

from the latest verses of Stéphane Mallarmé. " Mme.
d'Arpajon is very fond of poetry," said the Princesse de
Parme to her hostess, impressed by the ardent tone in
which the speech had been delivered. " No; she knows
absolutely nothing about it," replied Mme. de Guermantes
in an undertone, taking advantage of the fact that Mme.
d'Arpajon, who was dealing with an objection raised by
General de Beautreillis, was too much intent upon what
she herself was saying to hear what was being murmured
by the Duchess. " She has become literary since she's
been forsaken. I can tell your Highness that it is I who
have to bear the whole burden of it because it is to me
that she comes in floods of tears whenever Basin hasn't
been to see her, which is practically every day. And yet it
isn't my fault, after all, if she bores him, and I can't force
him to go to her, although I would rather he were a little
more faithful to her, because then I shouldn't see quite
so much of her myself. But she drives him crazy, and
there's nothing extraordinary in that. She isn't a bad sort,
but she's boring to a degree you can't imagine. And all
this because Basin took it into his head for a year or so
to play me false with her. And to have in addition a footman who has fallen in love with a little street-walker and
goes about with a long face if I don't request the young
person to leave her profitable pavement for half an hour
and come to tea with me! Oh! Life really is too tedious ! "
the Duchess languorously concluded. Mme. d'Arpajon
bored M. de Guermantes principally because he had recently fallen in love with another, whom I discovered to
be the Marquise de Surgis-le-Duc. At this moment the
footman who had been deprived of his holiday was waiting at table. And it struck me that, still disconsolate, he

was doing it with a good deal of difficulty, for I noticed that, in handing the dish to M. de Châtellerault, he performed his task so awkwardly that the Duke's elbow came in contact several times with his own. The young Duke was not in the least annoyed with the blushing footman, but looked up at him rather with a smile in his clear blue eyes. This good humour seemed to me on the guest's part to betoken a kindness of heart. But the persistence of his smile led me to think that, aware of the servant's discomfiture, what he felt was perhaps really a malicious joy. "But, my dear, you know you're not revealing any new discovery when you tell us about Victor Hugo," went on the Duchess, this time addressing Mme. d'Arpajon whom she had just seen turn away from the General with a troubled air. "You mustn't expect to launch that young genius. Everybody knows that he has talent. What is utterly detestable is the Victor Hugo of the last stage, the *Légende des Siècles,* I forget all their names. But in the *Feuilles d'Automne,* the *Chants du Crépuscule,* there's a great deal that's the work of a poet, a true poet! Even in the *Contemplations*", went on the Duchess, whom none of her listeners dared to contradict, and with good reason, "there are still some quite pretty things. But I confess that I prefer not to venture farther than the *Crépuscule*! And then in the finer poems of Victor Hugo, and there really are some, one frequently comes across an idea, even a profound idea." And with the right shade of sentiment, bringing out the sorrowful thought with the full strength of her intonation, planting it somewhere beyond the sound of her voice, and fixing straight in front of her a charming, dreamy gaze, the Duchess said slowly: "Take this:

La douleur est un fruit, Dieu ne le fait pas croître
Sur la branche trop faible encor pour le porter.

or, better still:

Les morts durent bien peu.
Hélas, dans le cercueil ils tombent en poussière
Moins vite qu'en nos cœurs ! "

And, while a smile of disillusionment contracted with a
graceful undulation her sorrowing lips, the Duchess fastened on Mme. d'Arpajon the dreaming gaze of her charming, clear blue eyes. I was beginning to know them, as
well as her voice, with its heavy drawl, its harsh savour.
In those eyes and in that voice, I recognised much of the
life of nature round Combray. Certainly, in the affectation with which that voice brought into prominence at
times a rudeness of the soil there was more than one element: the wholly provincial origin of one branch of the
Guermantes family, which had for long remained more
localised, more hardy, wilder, more provoking than the
rest; and also the usage of really distinguished people, and
of witty people who know that distinction does not consist in mincing speech, and the usage of nobles who frater-
nise more readily with their peasants than with the middle
classes; peculiarities all of which the regal position of
Mme. de Guermantes enabled her to display more easily,
to bring out with every sail spread. It appears that the
same voice existed also in certain of her sisters whom she
detested, and who, less intelligent than herself and almost
plebeianly married, if one may coin this adverb to speak
of unions with obscure noblemen, entrenched on their provincial estates, or, in Paris, in a Faubourg Saint-Germain
of no brilliance, possessed this voice also but had bridled

it, corrected it, softened it so far as lay in their power, just as it is very rarely that any of us presumes on his own originality and does not apply himself diligently to copying the most approved models. But Oriane was so much more intelligent, so much richer, above all, so much more in fashion than her sisters, she had so effectively, when Princesse des Laumes, behaved just as she pleased in the company of the Prince of Wales, that she had realised that this discordant voice was an attraction, and had made of it, in the social order, with the courage of originality rewarded by success, what in the theatrical order a Réjane, a Jeanne Granier (which implies no comparison, naturally, between the respective merits and talents of those two actresses) had made of theirs, something admirable and distinctive which possibly certain Réjane and Granier sisters, whom no one has ever known, strove to conceal as a defect.

To all these reasons for displaying her local originality, the favourite writers of Mme. de Guermantes—Mérimée, Meilhac and Halévy—had brought in addition, with the respect for what was natural, a feeling for the prosaic by which she attained to poetry and a spirit purely of society which called up distant landscapes before my eyes. Besides, the Duchess was fully capable, adding to these influences an artistic research of her own, of having chosen for the majority of her words the pronunciation that seemed to her most " Ile-de-France ", most " Champenoise ", since, if not quite to the same extent as her sister-in-law Marsantes, she rarely used anything but the pure vocabulary that might have been employed by an old French writer. And when one was tired of the composite patchwork of modern speech, it was, albeit one was

aware that she expressed far fewer ideas, a thorough re-
laxation to listen to the talk of Mme. de Guermantes—
almost the same feeling, if one was alone with her and
she restrained and clarified still further her flow of words,
as one has on hearing an old song. Then, as I looked at,
as I listened to Mme. de Guermantes, I could see, a
prisoner in the perpetual and quiet afternoon of her eyes,
a sky of the Ile-de-France or of Champagne spread itself,
grey-blue, oblique, with the same angle of inclination as
in the eyes of Saint-Loup.

Thus, by these several formations, Mme. de Guermantes expressed at once the most ancient aristocratic
France, then, from a far later source, the manner in which
the Duchesse de Broglie might have enjoyed and found
fault with Victor Hugo under the July Monarchy, and,
finally, a keen taste for the literature that sprang from
Mérimée and Meilhac. The first of these formations attracted me more than the second, did more to console me
for the disappointments of my pilgrimage to and arrival
in the Faubourg Saint-Germain, so different from what I
had imagined it to be; but even the second I preferred to
the last. For, so long as Mme. de Guermantes was being,
almost spontaneously, a Guermantes and nothing more,
her Pailleronism, her taste for the younger Dumas were
reflected and deliberate. As this taste was the opposite of
my own, she was productive, to my mind, of literature
when she talked to me of the Faubourg Saint-Germain,
and never seemed to me so stupidly Faubourg Saint-Germain as when she was talking literature.

Moved by this last quotation, Mme. d'Arpajon exclaimed: " ' Ces reliques du cœur ont aussi leur poussière! '—Sir, you must write that down for me on my

fan," she said to M. de Guermantes. "Poor woman, I feel sorry for her!" said the Princesse de Parme to Mme. de Guermantes. "No, really, Ma'am, you must not be soft-hearted, she has only got what she deserves." "But —you'll forgive me for saying this to you—she does really love him all the same!" "Oh, not at all; she isn't capable of it; she thinks she loves him just as she thought just now she was quoting Victor Hugo, when she repeated a line from Musset. Listen," the Duchess went on in a tone of melancholy, "nobody would be more touched than myself by any true sentiment. But let me give you an instance. Only yesterday, she made a terrible scene with Basin. Your Highness thinks perhaps that it was because he's in love with other women, because he no longer loves her; not in the least, it was because he won't put her sons down for the Jockey. Does Ma'am call that the behaviour of a woman in love? No; I will go farther;" Mme. de Guermantes added with precision, "she is a person of singular insensibility." Meanwhile it was with an eye sparkling with satisfaction that M. de Guermantes had listened to his wife talking about Victor Hugo "point-blank" and quoting his poetry. The Duchess might frequently annoy him; at moments like this he was proud of her. "Oriane is really extraordinary. She can talk about anything, she has read everything. She could not possibly have guessed that the conversation this evening would turn on Victor Hugo. Whatever subject you take up, she is ready for you, she can hold her own with the most learned scholars. This young man must be quite captivated."

"Do let us change the conversation," Mme. de Guermantes went on, "because she's dreadfully susceptible.

You will think me quite old-fashioned; " she began, turning to me, " I know that nowadays it's considered a weakness to care for ideas in poetry, poetry with some thought in it." " Old-fashioned? " asked the Princesse de Parme, quivering with the slight thrill sent through her by this new wave which she had not expected, albeit she knew that the conversation of the Duchesse de Guermantes always held in store for her these continuous and delightful shocks, that breath-catching panic, that wholesome exhaustion after which her thoughts instinctively turned to the necessity of taking a footbath in a dressing cabin and a brisk walk to " restore her circulation ".

" For my part, no, Oriane," said Mme. de Brissac, " I don't in the least object to Victor Hugo's having ideas, quite the contrary, but I do object to his seeking for them in sheer monstrosities. After all, it was he who accustomed us to ugliness in literature. There are quite enough ugly things already in real life. Why can't we be allowed at least to forget it while we are reading. A distressing spectacle, from which we should turn away in real life, that is what attracts Victor Hugo."

" Victor Hugo is not so realistic as Zola though, surely? " asked the Princesse de Parme. The name of Zola did not stir a muscle on the face of M. de Beautreillis. The General's anti-Dreyfusism was too deep-rooted for him to seek to give expression to it. And his good-natured silence when anyone broached these topics moved the profane heart as a proof of the same delicacy that a priest shews in avoiding any reference to your religious duties, a financier when he takes care not to recommend your investing in the companies which he himself controls, a strong man when he behaves with lamblike gentleness and does not hit you in the jaw. " I know you're related to Admiral Jurien de la Gravière," was murmured to me with an air of connivance by Mme. de Varambon, the lady in waiting to the Princesse de Parme, an excellent but limited woman, procured for the Princess in the past by the Duke's mother. She had not previously uttered a word to me, and I could never afterwards, despite the admonitions of the Princess and my own protestations, get out of her mind the idea that I was in some way connected with the Academician Admiral, who was a complete stranger to me. The obstinate persistence of the Princesse de Parme's lady in waiting in seeing in me a nephew of Admiral Jurien de la Gravière was in itself quite an ordinary form of silliness. But the mistake she made was only a crowning instance of all the other mistakes, less serious, more elaborate, unconscious or deliberate, which accompany one's name on the label which society writes out and attaches to one. I remember that a friend of the Guermantes who had expressed a keen desire to meet me gave me as the reason that I was a great friend of his cousin, Mme. de Chaussegros. " She is a charming person, she's so fond of you." I scrupulously, though quite vainly, insisted on the fact that there must be some mistake, as I did not know Mme. de Chaussegros. " Then it's her sister you know; it comes to the same thing. She met you in Scotland." I had never been in Scotland, and took the futile precaution, in my honesty, of letting my informant know this. It was Mme. de Chaussegros herself who had said that she knew me, and no doubt sincerely believed it, as a result of some initial confusion, for from that time onwards she never failed to hold out her hand to me whenever she saw me. And as, after all, the world in which I moved was precisely that in which Mme. de Chaussegros moved my modesty had neither rhyme nor reason. To say that I was intimate with the Chaussegros was, literally, a mistake, but from the social point of view was to state an equivalent of my position, if one can speak of the social position of so young a man as I then was. It therefore mattered not in the least that this friend of the Guermantes should tell me only things that were false about myself, he neither lowered nor exalted me (from the worldly point of view) in the idea which he continued to hold of me. And when all is said, for those of us who are not professional actors the tedium of living always in the same character is removed for a moment, as if we were to go on the boards, when another person forms a false idea of us, imagines that we are friends with a lady whom we do not know and are reported to have met in the course of a delightful tour of a foreign country which we have never made. Errors that multiply themselves and are harmless when they have not the inflexible rigidity of this one which had been committed, and continued for the rest of her life to be committed, in spite of my denials, by the imbecile lady in waiting to Mme. de Parme, rooted for all time in the belief that I was related to the tiresome Admiral Jurien de la Gravière. " She is not very strong in her head," the Duke confided to me, " and besides, she ought not to indulge in too many libations. I fancy, she's slightly under the influence of Bacchus." As a matter of fact Mme. de Varambon had drunk nothing but water, but the Duke liked to find scope for his favourite figures of speech. " But Zola is not a realist, Ma'am, he's a poet! " said Mme. de Guermantes, drawing inspiration from the critical essays which she had read in recent years and adapting them to her own personal genius. Agreeably buffeted hitherto, in the course of this bath of wit, a bath stirred for herself, which she was taking this evening and which, she considered, must be particularly good for her health, letting herself be swept away by the waves of paradox which curled and broke one after another, before this, the most enormous of them all, the Princesse de Parme jumped for fear of being knocked over. And it was in a choking voice, as though she were quite out of breath, that she now gasped: " Zola a poet! " " Why, yes," answered the Duchess with a laugh, entranced by this display of suffocation. " Your Highness must have remarked how he magnifies everything he touches. You will tell me that he touches just what—perish the thought! But he makes it into something colossal. His is the epic dungheap. He is the Homer of the sewers! He has not enough capitals to print Cambronne's word." Despite the extreme exhaustion which she was beginning to feel, the Princess was enchanted; never had she felt better. She would not have exchanged for an invitation to Schönbrunn, albeit that was the one thing that really flattered her, these divine dinner-parties at Mme. de Guermantes's, made invigorating by so liberal a dose of attic salt. " He writes it with a big ' C '," cried Mme. d'Arpajon. " Surely with a big ' M ', I think, my dear," replied Mme. de Guermantes, exchanging first with her husband a merry glance which implied: " Did you ever hear such an idiot? " " Wait a minute, now," Mme. de Guermantes turned to me, fixing on me a tender, smiling gaze, because, as an accomplished hostess, she was anxious to display her own knowledge of the artist who interested me specially, to give me, if I required it, an opportunity for exhibiting mine. "Wait," she urged me, gently waving her feather fan, so conscious was she at this moment that she was performing in full the duties of hospitality, and, that she might be found wanting in none of them, making a sign also to the servants to help me to more of the asparagus and *mousseline* sauce: "wait, now, I do believe that Zola has actually written an essay on Elstir, the painter whose things you were looking at just now—the only ones of his, really, that I care for," she concluded. As a matter of fact she hated Elstir's work, but found a unique quality in anything that was in her own house. I asked M. de Guermantes if he knew the name of the gentleman in the tall hat who figured in the picture of the crowd and whom I recognised as the same person whose portrait the Guermantes also had and had hung beside the other, both dating more or less from the same early period in which Elstir's personality was not yet completely established and he derived a certain inspiration from Manet. "Good Lord, yes," he replied, " I know it's a fellow who is quite well-known and no fool either, in his own line, but I have no head for names. I have it on the tip of my tongue, Monsieur . . . . Monsieur . . . . oh, well, it doesn't matter, I can't remember it. Swann would be able to tell you, it was he who made Mme. de Guermantes buy all that stuff; she is always too good-natured, afraid of hurting people's feelings if she refuses to do things; between ourselves, I believe he's landed us with a lot of rubbish. What I can tell you is that the gentleman you mean has been a sort of Maecenas to M. Elstir, he started him and has often helped him out of tight places by ordering pictures from him. As a compliment to this man—if you can call that sort of thing a compliment—he has painted him standing about among that crowd, where with his Sunday-go-to-meeting look he creates a distinctly odd effect. He may be a big gun in his own way but he is evidently not aware of the proper time and place for a top hat. With that thing on his head, among all those bare-headed girls, he looks like a little country lawyer on the razzle-dazzle. But tell me, you seem quite gone on his pictures. If I had only known, I should have got up the subject properly. Not that there's any need to rack one's brains over the meaning of M. Elstir's work, as one would for Ingres's *Source* or the *Princes in the Tower* by Paul Delaroche. What one appreciates in his work is that it's shrewdly observed, amusing, Parisian, and then one passes on to the next thing. One doesn't need to be an expert to look at that sort of thing. I know of course that they're merely sketches, still, I don't feel myself that he puts enough work into them. Swann was determined that we should buy a *Bundle of Asparagus.* In fact it was in the house for several days. There was nothing else in the picture, a bundle of asparagus exactly like what you're eating now. But I must say I declined to swallow M. Elstir's asparagus. He asked three hundred francs for them. Three hundred francs for a bundle of asparagus. A louis, that's as much as they're worth, even if they are out of season. I thought it a bit stiff. When he puts real people into his pictures as well, there's something rather caddish, something detrimental about him which does not appeal to me. I am surprised to see a delicate mind, a superior brain like yours admire that sort of thing." " I don't know why you should say that, Basin," interrupted the Duchess, who did not like to hear people run down anything that her rooms contained. " I am by no means prepared to admit that there's nothing distinguished in Elstir's pictures. You have to take it or leave it. But it's not always lacking in talent. And you must admit that the ones I bought are singularly beautiful." " Well, Oriane, in that style of thing I'ld a thousand times rather have the little study by M. Vibert we saw at the water-colour exhibition. There's nothing much in it, if you like, you could take it in the palm of your hand, but you can see the man's clever through and through: that unwashed scarecrow of a missionary standing before the sleek prelate who is making his little dog do tricks, it's a perfect little poem of subtlety, and in fact goes really deep." " I believe you know M. Elstir," the Duchess went on to me, " as a man, he's quite pleasant." " He is intelligent," said the Duke; " one is surprised, when one talks to him, that his painting should be so vulgar." " He is more than intelligent, he is really quite clever," said the Duchess in the confidently critical tone of a person who knew what she was talking about. " Didn't he once start a portrait of you, Oriane? " asked the Princesse de Parme. " Yes, in shrimp pink," replied Mme. de Guermantes, " but that's not going to hand his name down to posterity. It's a ghastly thing; Basin wanted to have it destroyed." This last statement was one which Mme. de Guermantes often made. But at other times her appreciation of the picture was different: " I do not care for his painting, but he did once do a good portrait of me." The former of these judgments was addressed as a rule to people who spoke to the Duchess of her portrait, the other to those who did not refer to it and whom therefore she was anxious to inform of its existence. The former was inspired in her by coquetry, the latter by vanity. "Make a portrait of you look ghastly. Why, then it can't be a portrait, it's a false-hood; I don't know one end of a brush from the other, but I'm sure if I were to paint you, merely putting you down as I see you, I should produce a masterpiece," said the Princesse de Parme ingenuously. "He sees me prob-ably as I see myself, without any allurements," said the Duchesse de Guermantes, with the look, melancholy, modest and coaxing, which seemed to her best calculated to make her appear different from what Elstir had por-trayed. "That portrait ought to appeal to Mme. de Gal-lardon," said the Duke. "Because she knows nothing about pictures?" asked the Princesse de Parme, who knew that Mme. de Guermantes had an infinite contempt for her cousin. "But she's a very good woman, isn't she?" The Duke assumed an air of profound astonishment. "Why, Basin, don't you see the Princess is making fun of you?" (The Princess had never dreamed of doing such a thing.) "She knows as well as you do that Gal-lardonette is an old *poison*," went on Mme. de Guer-mantes, whose vocabulary, limited as a rule to all these old expressions, was as savoury as those dishes which it is possible to come across in the delicious books of Pam-pille, but which have in real life become so rare, dishes where the jellies, the butter, the gravy, the quails are all genuine, permit of no alloy, where even the salt is brought specially from the salt-marshes of Brittany; from her ac-cent, her choice of words, one felt that the basis of the Duchess's conversation came directly from Guermantes. In this way the Duchess differed profoundly from her nephew Saint-Loup, the prey of so many new ideas and expressions; it is difficult, when one's mind is troubled by the ideas of Kant and the longings of Baudelaire, to write the exquisite French of Henri IV, which meant that the very purity of the Duchess's language was a sign of limitation, and that, in her, both her intelligence and her sensibility had remained proof against all innovation. Here again, Mme. de Guermantes's mind attracted me just because of what it excluded (which was exactly the content of my own thoughts) and by everything which, by virtue of that exclusion, it had been able to preserve, that seductive vigour of the supple bodies which no exhausting necessity to think, no moral anxiety or nervous trouble has deformed. Her mind, of a formation so anterior to my own, was for me the equivalent of what had been offered me by the procession of the girls of the little band along the seashore. Mme. de Guermantes offered me, domesticated and held in subjection by her natural courtesy, by the respect due to another person's intellectual worth, all the energy and charm of a cruel little girl of one of the noble families round Combray who from her childhood had been brought up in the saddle, tortured cats, gouged out the eyes of rabbits, and, albeit she had remained a pillar of virtue, might equally well have been, a good few years ago now, the most brilliant mistress of the Prince de Sagan. Only she was incapable of realising what I had sought for in her, the charm of her historic name, and the tiny quantity of it that I had found in her, a rustic survival from Guermantes. Were our relations founded upon a misunderstanding which could not fail to become manifest as soon as my homage, instead of being addressed to the relatively superior woman that she believed herself to be, should be diverted to some other woman of equal mediocrity and breathing the same unconscious charm? A misunderstanding so entirely natural, and one that will always exist between a young dreamer like myself and a woman of the world, one however that profoundly disturbs him, so long as he has not yet discovered the nature of his imaginative faculties and has not acquired his share of the inevitable disappointments which he is destined to find in people, as in the theatre, in his travels and indeed in love. M. de Guermantes having declared (following upon Elstir's asparagus and those that were brought round after the *financière* chicken) that green asparagus grown in the open air, which, as has been so quaintly said by the charming writer who signs himself E. de Clermont-Tonnerre, " have not the impressive rigidity of their sisters," ought to be eaten with eggs: " One man's meat is another man's poison, as they say," replied M. de Bréauté. " In the province of Canton, in China, the greatest delicacy that can be set before one is a dish of ortolan's eggs completely rotten." M. de Bréauté, the author of an essay on the Mormons which had appeared in the *Revue des Deux Mondes,* moved in none but the most aristocratic circles, but among these visited only such as had a certain reputation for intellect, with the result that from his presence, were it at all regular, in a woman's house one could tell that she had a " salon ". He pretended to a loathing of society, and assured each of his duchesses in turn that it was for the sake of her wit and beauty that he came to see her. They all believed him. Whenever, with death in his heart, he resigned himself to attending a big party at the Princesse de Parme's, he summoned them all to accompany him, to keep up his courage, and thus appeared only to be moving in the midst of an intimate group. So that his reputation as an intellectual might

survive his worldly success, applying certain maxims of
the Guermantes spirit, he would set out with ladies of
fashion on long scientific expeditions at the height of the
dancing season, and when a woman who was a snob, and
consequently still without any definite position, began to
go everywhere, he would put a savage obstinacy into his
refusal to know her, to allow himself to be introduced to
her. His hatred of snobs was a derivative of his snobbishness, but made the simpletons (in other words, everyone)
believe that he was immune from snobbishness. " Babal
always knows everything," exclaimed the Duchesse de
Guermantes. " I think it must be charming, a country
where you can be quite sure that your dairyman will
supply you with really rotten eggs, eggs of the year of
the comet. I can see myself dipping my bread and butter
in them. I must say, you get the same thing at aunt
Madeleine's " (Mme. de Villeparisis's) " where everything's served in a state of putrefaction, eggs included."
Then, as Mme. d'Arpajon protested, " But my dear Phili,
you know it as well as I do. You can see the chicken in
the egg. What I can't understand is how they manage not
to fall out. It's not an omelette you get there, it's a poul-
try-yard. You were so wise not to come to dinner there
yesterday, there was a brill cooked in carbolic! I assure
you, it wasn't a dinner-table, it was far more like an
operating-table. Really, Norpois carries loyalty to the
pitch of heroism. He actually asked for more! " " I believe I saw you at dinner there the time she made that
attack on M. Bloch " (M. de Guermantes, perhaps to give
to an Israelite name a more foreign sound, pronounced
the ' ch ' in Bloch not like a ' k ' but as in the German
" hoch ") " when he said about some poit " (poet) " or

other that he was sublime. Châtellerault did his best to break M. Bloch's shins, the fellow didn't understand in the least and thought my nephew's kick was aimed at a young woman sitting opposite him." (At this point, M. de Guermantes coloured slightly.) "He did not realise that he was annoying our aunt by his 'sublimes' chucked about all over the place like that. In short, aunt Madeleine, who doesn't keep her tongue in her pocket, turned on him with: 'Indeed, sir, and what epithet do you keep for M. de Bossuet?'" (M. de Guermantes thought that, when one mentioned a famous name, the use of "Monsieur" and a particle was eminently "old school".) "That put him in his place, all right." "And what answer did this M. Bloch make?" came in a careless tone from Mme. de Guermantes, who, running short for the moment of original ideas, felt that she must copy her husband's teutonic pronunciation. "Ah! I can assure, M. Bloch did not wait for any more, he's still running." "Yes, I remember quite well seeing you there that evening," said Mme. de Guermantes with emphasis as though, coming from her, there must be something in this reminiscence highly flattering to myself. "It is always so interesting at my aunt's. At the last party she gave, which was, of course, when I met you, I meant to ask you whether that old gentleman who went past where we were sitting wasn't François Coppée. You must know who everyone is," she went on, sincerely envious of my relations with poets and poetry, and also out of "consideration" for myself, the wish to establish in a better position in the eyes of her other guests a young man so well versed in literature. I assured the Duchess that I had not observed any celebrities at Mme. de Villeparisis's party. "What!" she re-

plied with a bewilderment which revealed that her respect
for men of letters and her contempt for society were more
superficial than she said, perhaps even than she thought,
" What! There were no famous authors there! You astonish me! Why, I saw all sorts of quite impossible
people! " I remembered the evening in question distinctly
owing to an entirely trivial incident that had occurred at
the party. Mme. de Villeparisis had introduced Bloch to
Mme. Alphonse de Rothschild, but my friend had not
caught the name and, thinking he was talking to an old
English lady who was a trifle mad, had replied only in
monosyllables to the garrulous conversation of the historic
beauty, when Mme. de Villeparisis in making her known
to some one else uttered, quite distinctly this time: " The
Baronne Alphonse de Rothschild." Thereupon there had
coursed suddenly and simultaneously through Bloch's
arteries so many ideas of millions and of social importance, which it would have been more prudent to sub-
divide and separate, that he had undergone, so to speak,
a momentary failure of heart and brain alike, and cried
aloud in the dear old lady's presence: " If I'd only
known! " an exclamation the silliness of which kept him
from sleeping for at least a week afterwards. His remark
was of no great interest, but I remembered it as a proof
that sometimes in this life, under the stress of an exceptional emotion, people do say what is in their minds. " I
fancy Mme. de Villeparisis is not absolutely . . . moral,"
said the Princesse de Parme, who knew that the best
people did not visit the Duchess's aunt, and from what
the Duchess herself had just been saying that one might
speak freely about her. But, Mme. de Guermantes not
seeming to approve of this criticism, she hastened to add:

"Though, of course, intellect carried to that degree excuses everything." "But you take the same view of my aunt that everyone else does," replied the Duchess, "which is, really, quite mistaken. It's just what Mémé was saying to me only yesterday." She blushed; a reminiscence unknown to me filmed her eyes. I formed the supposition that M. de Charlus had asked her to cancel my invitation, as he had sent Robert to ask me not to go to her house. I had the impression that the blush—equally incomprehensible to me—which had tinged the Duke's cheek when he made some reference to his brother could not be attributed to the same cause. "My poor aunt—she will always have the reputation of being a lady of the old school, of sparkling wit and uncontrolled passions. And really there's no more middle-class, serious, commonplace mind in Paris. She will go down as a patron of the arts, which means to say that she was once the mistress of a great painter, though he was never able to make her understand what a picture was; and as for her private life, so far from being a depraved woman, she was so much made for marriage, so conjugal from her cradle that, not having succeeded in keeping a husband, who incidentally was a cad, she has never had a love-affair which she hasn't taken just as seriously as if it were holy matrimony, with the same susceptibilities, the same quarrels, the same fidelity. By which token, those relations are often the most sincere; you'll find, in fact, more inconsolable lovers than husbands." "Yet, Oriane, if you take the case of your brother-in-law Palamède you were speaking about just now; no mistress in the world could ever dream of being mourned as that poor Mme. de Charlus has been." "Ah!" replied the

Duchess, "Your Highness must permit me to be not altogether of her opinion. People don't all like to be mourned in the same way, each of us has his preferences." "Still, he did make a regular cult of her after her death. It is true that people sometimes do for the dead what they would not have done for the living." "For one thing," retorted Mme. de Guermantes in a dreamy tone which belied her teasing purpose, "we go to their funerals, which we never do for the living!" M. de Guermantes gave a sly glance at M. de Bréauté as though to provoke him into laughter at the Duchess's wit. "At the same time I frankly admit," went on Mme. de Guermantes, "that the manner in which I should like to be mourned by a man I loved would not be that adopted by my brother-in-law." The Duke's face darkened. He did not like to hear his wife utter rash judgments, especially about M. de Charlus. "You are very particular. His grief set an example to everyone," he reproved her stiffly. But the Duchess had in dealing with her husband that sort of boldness which animal tamers shew, or people who live with a madman and are not afraid of making him angry: "Oh, very well, just as you like—he does set an example, I never said he didn't, he goes every day to the cemetery to tell her how many people he has had to luncheon, he misses her enormously, but— as he'ld mourn for a cousin, a grandmother, a sister. It is not the grief of a husband. It is true that they were a pair of saints, which makes it all rather exceptional." M. de Guermantes, infuriated by his wife's chatter, fixed on her with a terrible immobility a pair of eyes already loaded. "I don't wish to say anything against poor Mémé, who, by the way, could not come this evening," went on the Duchess, " I quite admit there's no one like him, he's delightful; he has a delicacy, a warmth of heart that you don't as a rule find in men. He has a woman's heart, Mémé has!" " What you say is absurd," M. de Guermantes broke in sharply. " There's nothing effeminate about Mémé, I know nobody so manly as he is." " But I am not suggesting that he's the least bit in the world effeminate. Do at least take the trouble to understand what I say," retorted the Duchess. " He's always like that the moment anyone mentions his brother," she added, turning to the Princesse de Parme. " It's very charming, it's a pleasure to hear him. There's nothing so nice as two brothers who are fond of each other," replied the Princess, as many a humbler person might have replied, for it is possible to belong to a princely race by birth and at the same time to be mentally affiliated to a race that is thoroughly plebeian.

" As we're discussing your family, Oriane," said the Princess, " I saw your nephew Saint-Loup yesterday; I believe he wants to ask you to do something for him." The Duc de Guermantes bent his Olympian brow. When he did not himself care to do a service, he preferred his wife not to assume the responsibility for it, knowing that it would come to the same thing in the end and that the people to whom the Duchess would be obliged to apply would put this concession down to the common account of the household, just as much as if it had been asked of them by the husband alone. " Why didn't he tell me about it himself? " said the Duchess, " he was here yesterday and stayed a couple of hours, and heaven only knows what a bore he managed to make himself. He would be no stupider than anyone else if he had only the sense, like many people we know, to be content with being a fool. It's his veneer of knowledge that's so terrible. He wants to preserve an open mind—open to all the things he doesn't understand. He talks to you about Morocco. It's appalling."

"He can't go back there, because of Rachel," said the Prince de Foix. "Surely, now that they've broken it off," interrupted M. de Bréauté. "So far from breaking it off, I found her a couple of days ago in Robert's rooms, they didn't look at all like people who'd quarrelled, I can assure you," replied the Prince de Foix, who loved to spread abroad every rumour that could damage Robert's chances of marrying, and might for that matter have been misled by one of the intermittent resumptions of a connexion that was practically at an end.

"That Rachel was speaking to me about you, I see her like that in the mornings, on the way to the Champs-Élysées; she's a kind of head-in-air, as you say, what you call ' unlaced ', a sort of ' Dame aux Camélias ', only figuratively speaking, of course." This speech was addressed to me by Prince Von, who liked always to appear conversant with French literature and Parisian catchwords.

"Why, that's just what it was—Morocco!" exclaimed the Princess, flinging herself into this opening. "What on earth can he want in Morocco?" asked M. de Guermantes sternly; "Oriane can do absolutely nothing for him there, as he knows perfectly well." "He thinks he invented strategy," Mme. de Guermantes pursued the theme, " and then he uses impossible words for the most trivial things, which doesn't prevent him from making blots all over his letters. The other day he announced that he'd been given some *sublime* potatoes, and that he'd taken a *sublime* stage box." "He speaks Latin," the Duke went one better. "What! Latin?" the Princess gasped. "'Pon my soul he does! Ma'am can ask Oriane if I'm not telling the truth." "Why, of course, Ma'am; the other day he said to us straight out, without stopping to think: 'I know of no more touching example of *sic transit gloria mundi.*' I can repeat the phrase now to your Highness because, after endless inquiries and by appealing to *linguists,* we succeeded in reconstructing it, but Robert flung it out without pausing for breath, one could hardly make out that there was Latin in it, he was just like a character in the *Malade Imaginaire.* And all this referred simply to the death of the Empress of Austria!" "Poor woman!" cried the Princess, "what a delicious creature she was." "Yes," replied the Duchess, "a trifle mad, a trifle headstrong, but she was a thoroughly good woman, a nice, kind-hearted lunatic; the only thing I could never make out about her was why she had never managed to get her teeth made to fit her; they always came loose half-way through a sentence and she was obliged to stop short or she'ld have swallowed them." "That Rachel was speaking to me about you, she told me that young Saint-Loup worshipped you, that he was fonder of you than he was of her," said Prince Von to me, devouring his food like an ogre as he spoke, his face scarlet, his teeth bared by his perpetual grin. "But in that case she must be jealous of me and hate me," said I. "Not at all, she told me all sorts of nice things about you. The Prince de Foix's mistress would perhaps be jealous if he preferred you to her. You don't understand? Come home with me, and I'll explain it all

to you." " I'm afraid I can't, I'm going on to M. de
Charlus at eleven." "Why, he sent round to me yesterday to ask me to dine with him this evening, but told
me not to come after a quarter to eleven. But if you
must go to him, at least come with me as far as the
Théâtre-Français, you will be in the periphery," said the
Prince, who thought doubtless that this last word meant
" proximity " or possibly " centre ".

But the bulging eyes in his coarse though handsome red
face frightened me and I declined, saying that a friend
was coming to call for me. This reply seemed to me in
no way offensive. The Prince, however, apparently
formed a different impression of it for he did not say
another word to me.

"I really must go and see the Queen of Naples; what
a grief it must be to her," said (or at least appeared to
me to have said) the Princesse de Parme. For her words
had come to me only indistinctly through the intervening
screen of those addressed to me, albeit in an undertone,
by Prince Von, who had doubtless been afraid, if he spoke
louder, of being overheard by the Prince de Foix. "Oh,
dear, no! " replied the Duchess, "I don't believe it has
been any grief at all." "None at all! You do always fly
to extremes so, Oriane," said M. de Guermantes, resuming his part of the cliff which by standing up to the wave
forces it to fling higher its crest of foam. "Basin knows
even better than I that I'm telling the truth," replied the
Duchess, "but he thinks he's obliged to look severe because you are present, Ma'am, and he's afraid of my
shocking you." "Oh, please, no, I beg of you," cried the
Princesse de Parme, dreading the slightest alteration on
her account of these delicious Fridays at the Duchesse

de Guermantes's, this forbidden fruit which the Queen of Sweden herself had not yet acquired the right to taste. "Why, it was Basin himself that she told, when he said to her with a duly sorrowful expression: ' But the Queen is in mourning; for whom, pray, is it a great grief to your Majesty?'—' No, it's not a deep mourning, it's a light mourning, quite a light mourning, it's my sister.' The truth is, she's delighted about it, as Basin knows perfectly well, she invited us to a party that very evening, and gave me two pearls. I wish she could lose a sister every day! So far from weeping for her sister's death, she was in fits of laughter over it. She probably says to herself, like Robert, ' *sic transit*——' I forget how it goes on," she added modestly, knowing how it went on perfectly well.

In saying all this Mme. de Guermantes was only being witty, and with complete insincerity, for the Queen of Naples, like the Duchesse d'Alençon, also doomed to a tragic fate, had the warmest heart in the world and mourned quite sincerely for her kinsfolk. Mme. de Guermantes knew those noble Bavarian sisters, her cousins, too well not to be aware of this. "He would like not to go back to Morocco," said the Princesse de Parme, alighting hurriedly again upon the perch of Robert's name which had been held out to her, quite unintentionally, by Mme. de Guermantes. "I believe you know General de Monserfeuil." "Very slightly," replied the Duchess, who was an intimate friend of the officer in question. The Princess explained what it was that Saint-Loup wanted. "Good gracious, yes, if I see him—it is possible that I may meet him," the Duchess replied, so as not to appear to be refusing, the occasions of her meeting General de

Monserfeuil seeming to extend rapidly farther apart as
soon as it became a question of her asking him for anything. This uncertainty did not, however, satisfy the
Duke, who interrupted his wife: " You know perfectly
well you won't be seeing him, Oriane, and besides you
have already asked him for two things which he hasn't
done. My wife has a passion for doing good turns to
people," he went on, growing more and more furious, in
order to force the Princess to withdraw her request, without there being any question made of his wife's good
nature and so that Mme. de Parme should throw the
blame back upon his own character, which was essentially obstructive. " Robert could get anything he wanted
out of Monserfeuil. Only, as he happens not to know
himself what he wants, he gets us to ask for it because he
knows there's no better way of making the whole thing
fall through. Oriane has asked too many favours of
Monserfeuil. A request from her now would be a reason
for him to refuse." " Oh, in that case, it would be better
if the Duchess did nothing," said Mme. de Parme. " Obviously! " the Duke closed the discussion. " Poor General,
he's been defeated again at the elections," said the Princess, so as to turn the conversation from Robert. " Oh,
it's nothing serious, it's only the seventh time," said the
Duke, who, having been obliged himself to retire from
politics, quite enjoyed hearing of other people's failures
at the polls. " He has consoled himself by giving his wife
another baby." " What! Is that poor Mme. de Monserfeuil in an interesting condition again? " cried the Princess. " Why, of course," replied the Duke, " that's the
one division where the poor General has never failed to
get in."

In the period that followed I was continually to be invited, were it with a small party only, to these repasts at which I had at one time imagined the guests as seated like the Apostles in the Sainte-Chapelle. They did assemble there indeed, like the early Christians, not to partake merely of a material nourishment, which incidentally was exquisite, but in a sort of social Eucharist; so that in the course of a few dinner-parties I assimilated the acquaintance of all the friends of my hosts, friends to whom they presented me with a shade of benevolent patronage so marked (as a person for whom they had always had a sort of parental affection) that there was not one among them who would not have felt himself to be failing in his duty to the Duke and Duchess if he had given a ball without including my name on his list, and at the same time, while I sipped one of those Yquems which lay concealed in the Guermantes cellars, I tasted ortolans dressed according to each of the different recipes which the Duke himself used to elaborate and modified with prudence. However, for one who had already set his knees more than once beneath the mystic board, the consumption of the latter was not indispensable. Old friends of M. and Mme. de Guermantes came in to see them after dinner, " with the tooth-picks ", as Mme. Swann would have said, without being expected, and took in winter a cup of *tilleul* in the lighted warmth of the great drawing-room, in summer a glass of orangeade in the darkness of the little rectangular strip of garden outside. There was no record of anything else, among the Guermantes, in these evenings in the garden, but orangeade. It had a sort of ritual meaning. To have added other refreshments would have seemed to be falsifying the tradition, just as a big at-home in the Faubourg Saint-Germain ceases to be an at-home if there is a play also, or music. You must be supposed to have come simply—though there be five hundred of you—to pay a call on, let us say, the Princesse de Guermantes. People marvelled at my influence because I was able to procure the addition to this orangeade of a jug containing the juice of stewed cherries or stewed pears. I took a dislike on this account to the Prince d'Agrigente, who was like all the people who, lacking in imagination but not in covetousness, take a keen interest in what one is drinking and ask if they may taste a little of it themselves. Which meant that, every time, M. d'Agrigente, by diminishing my ration, spoiled my pleasure. For this fruit juice can never be provided in sufficient quantities to quench one's thirst for it. Nothing is less cloying than these transpositions into flavour of the colour of a fruit which when cooked seems to have travelled backwards to the past season of its blossoming. Blushing like an orchard in spring, or, it may be, colourless and cool like the zephyr beneath the fruit-trees, the juice lets itself be breathed and gazed into one drop by drop, and M. d'Agrigente prevented me, regularly, from taking my fill of it. Despite these distillations the traditional orangeade persisted like the *tilleul*. In these humble kinds, the social communion was none the less administered. In this respect, doubtless, the friends of M. and Mme. de Guermantes had, after all, as I had originally imagined, remained more different from the rest of humanity than their outward appearance might have misled me into supposing. Numbers of elderly men came to receive from the Duchess, together with the invariable drink, a welcome that was often far from cordial. Now this could not have been due to snobbishness, they themselves being of a rank to which there was none superior; nor to love of splendour; they did love it perhaps, but on less stringent social conditions might have been enjoying a glittering example of it, for on these same evenings the charming wife of a colossally rich financier would have given anything in the world to have them among the brilliant shooting-party she was giving for a couple of days for the King of Spain. They had nevertheless declined her invitation, and had come round without fail to inquire whether Mme. de Guermantes was at home. They were not even certain of finding there opinions that conformed entirely with their own, or sentiments of any great warmth; Mme. de Guermantes let fall now and then, on the Dreyfus Case, on the Republic, the Laws against Religion, or even in an undertone on themselves, their weaknesses, the dullness of their conversation, comments which they had to appear not to notice. No doubt, if they kept up their habit of coming there, it was owing to their superfine training as epicures in things worldly, to their clear consciousness of the prime and perfect quality of the social dish, with its familiar, reassuring, sappy savour, free from blend or taint, with the origin and history of which they were as well aware as she who served them with it, remaining more " noble " in this respect than they themselves imagined. Now, on this occasion, among the visitors to whom I was introduced after dinner, it so happened that there was that General de Monserfeuil of whom the Princesse de Parme had been speaking, while Mme. de Guermantes, of whose drawing-room he was one of the regular frequenters, had

not known that he was going to be there that evening.
He bowed before me, on hearing my name, as though
I had been the President of the Supreme War Council.
I had supposed it to be simply from some deep-rooted
unwillingness to oblige, in which the Duke, as in wit
if not in love, was his wife's accomplice, that the Duchess
had practically refused to recommend her nephew to
M. de Monserfeuil. And I saw in this an indifference
all the more blameworthy in that I seemed to have
gathered from a few words let fall by the Princess that
Robert was in a post of danger from which it would be
prudent to have him removed. But it was by the genuine
malice of Mme. de Guermantes that I was revolted when,
the Princesse de Parme having timidly suggested that
she might say something herself and on her own responsibility to the General, the Duchess did everything in
her power to dissuade her. "But Ma'am," she cried,
"Monserfeuil has no sort of standing or influence whatever with the new Government. You would be wasting
your breath." "I think he can hear us," murmured the
Princess, as a hint to the Duchess not to speak so loud.
Without lowering her voice: "Your Highness need not
be afraid, he's as deaf as a post," said the Duchess, every
word reaching the General distinctly. "The thing is, I
believe M. de Saint-Loup is in a place that is not very
safe," said the Princess. "What is one to do?" replied
the Duchess. "He's in the same boat as everybody else,
the only difference being that it was he who originally
asked to be sent there. Besides, no, it's not really dangerous; if it was, you can imagine how anxious I should
be to help. I should have spoken to Saint-Joseph about
it during dinner. He has far more influence, and he's a

real worker. But, as you see, he's gone now. Still, asking him would be less awkward than going to this one, who has three of his sons in Morocco just now and has refused to apply for them to be exchanged; he might raise that as an objection. Since your Highness insists on it, I shall speak to Saint-Joseph—if I see him again, or to Beautreillis. But if I don't see either of them, you mustn't waste your pity on Robert. It was explained to us the other day exactly where he is. I'm sure he couldn't wish for a better place."

"What a pretty flower, I've never seen one like it; there's no one like you, Oriane, for having such marvellous things in your house," said the Princess de Parme, who, fearing that General de Monserfeuil might have overheard the Duchess, sought now to change the conversation. I looked and recognised a plant of the sort that I had watched Elstir painting. "I am so glad you like them; they are charming, do look at their little purple velvet collars; the only thing against them is—as may happen with people who are very pretty and very nicely dressed—they have a hideous name and a horrid smell. In spite of which I am very fond of them. But what is rather sad is that they are dying." "But they're growing in a pot, they aren't cut flowers," said the Princess. "No," answered the Duchess with a smile, "but it comes to the same thing, as they're all ladies. It's a kind of plant where the ladies and the gentlemen don't both grow on the same stalk. I'm like people who keep a lady dog. I have to find a husband for my flowers. Otherwise I shan't have any young ones!" "How very strange. Do you mean to say that in nature . . . ?" "Yes! There are certain insects whose duty it is to bring about the marriage, as they do with Sovereigns, by proxy, without the bride and bridegroom ever having set eyes on one another. And so, I assure you, I always tell my man to put my plant out in the window as often as possible, on the courtyard side and the garden side turn about, in the hope that the necessary insect will arrive. But the odds are too great. Fancy, he has first to have been seen by a person of the same species and the opposite sex, and he must then have taken it into his head to come and leave cards at the house. He hasn't appeared so far, I believe my plant can still qualify for the white flower of a blameless life, but I must say a little immodesty would please me better. It's just the same with that fine tree we have in the courtyard; he will die childless because he belongs to a kind that's very rare in these latitudes. In his case, it's the wind that's responsible for consummating the marriage, but the wall is a trifle high." " By Jove, yes," said M. de Bréauté, " you ought to take just a couple of inches off the top, that will be quite enough. There are certain operations one ought to know how to perform. The flavour of vanilla we tasted in the excellent ice you gave us this evening, Duchess, comes from a plant called the vanilla tree. This plant produces flowers which are both male and female, but a sort of solid wall set up between them prevents any communication. And so we could never get any fruit from them until a young negro, a native of Réunion, by the name of Albins, which by the way is rather an odd name for a black man since it means ' white ', had the happy thought of using the point of a needle to bring the separate organs into contact." " Babal, you're divine, you know everything," cried the Duchess. " But you yourself, Oriane, have told me things I had no idea of," the Princesse de Parme assured her. " I must explain to your Highness that it is Swann who has always talked to me all about botany. Sometimes when we were too bored to go to a tea-party or a concert we would set off for the country, and he would shew me extraordinary marriages between flowers, which was far more amusing than going to human marriages—no wedding-breakfast and no crowd in the sacristy. We never had time to go very far. Now that motor-cars have come in, it would be delightful. Unfortunately, in the interval he himself has made an even more astonishing marriage, which makes everything very difficult. Oh, Ma'am, life is a dreadful business, we spend our whole time doing things that bore us, and when by mere chance we come across somebody with whom we could go and look at something really interesting, he has to make a marriage like Swann's. Faced with the alternatives of giving up my botanical expeditions and being obliged to call upon a degrading person, I chose the former calamity. Besides, when it comes to that, there was no need to go quite so far. It seems that here, in my own little bit of garden, more odd things happen in broad daylight than at midnight—in the Bois de Boulogne! Only they attract no attention, because among flowers it's all done quite simply, you see a little orange shower, or else a very dusty fly coming to wipe its feet or take a bath before crawling into a flower. And that does the trick!" " The cabinet the plant is standing on is splendid, too; it's Empire, I think," said the Princess, who, not being familiar with the works of Darwin and his followers, was unable to grasp the point of the Duchess's pleasantries. " It's lovely,

isn't it? I'm so glad Ma'am likes it," replied the Duchess,
" it's a magnificent piece. I must tell you that I've always
adored the Empire style, even when it wasn't in fashion.
I remember at Guermantes I got into terrible disgrace
with my mother-in-law because I told them to bring
down from the attics all the splendid Empire furniture
Basin had inherited from the Montesquious, and used it
to furnish the wing we lived in." M. de Guermantes
smiled. He must nevertheless have remembered that the
course of events had been totally different. But, the
witticisms of the Princesse des Laumes at the expense of
her mother-in-law's bad taste having been a tradition
during the short time in which the Prince was in love
with his wife, his love for the latter had been outlasted
by a certain contempt for the intellectual inferiority of
the former, a contempt which, however, went hand in hand
with a considerable attachment and respect. " The Iénas
have the same armchair with Wedgwood medallions, it's
a lovely thing, but I prefer my own; " said the Duchess,
with the same air of impartiality as if she had been the
possessor of neither of the articles under discussion. " I
know, of course, that they've some marvellous things
which I haven't got." The Princesse de Parme remained
silent. " But it's quite true; your Highness hasn't seen
their collection. Oh, you ought really to come there one
day with me, it's one of the most magnificent things in
Paris. You'ld say it was a museum come to life." And
since this suggestion was one of the most " Guermantes "
of the Duchess's audacities, inasmuch as the Iénas were
for the Princesse de Parme rank usurpers, their son bearing like her own the title of Duc de Guastalla, Mme. de
Guermantes in thus launching it could not refrain (so

far did the love that she bore for her own originality prevail over the deference due to the Princess de Parme) from
casting at her other guests a smiling glance of amusement. They too made an effort to smile, at once frightened, bewildered, and above all delighted to think that
they were being ear-witnesses of Oriane's very "latest"
and could carry it away with them "red hot". They were
only half shocked, knowing that the Duchess had the knack
of strewing the ground with all the Courvoisier prejudices
to achieve a vital success more thrilling and more enjoy-
able. Had she not, within the last few years, brought
together Princesse Mathilde and that Duc d'Aumale who
had written to the Princess's own brother the famous
letter: "In my family all the men are brave and the
women chaste"? And inasmuch as Princes remain
princely even at those moments when they appear anxious
to forget that they are, the Duc d'Aumale and Princesse
Mathilde had enjoyed themselves so greatly at Mme. de
Guermantes's that they had thereafter formed a defensive
alliance, with that faculty for forgetting the past which
Louis XVIII shewed when he took as his Minister
Fouché, who had voted the death of his brother. Mme.
de Guermantes was now nourishing a similar project of
arranging a meeting between Princesse Murat and the
Queen of Naples. In the meantime, the Princesse de
Parme appeared as embarrassed as might have been
the heirs-apparent to the Thrones of the Netherlands
and Belgium, styled respectively Prince of Orange and
Duke of Brabant, had one offered to present to them
M. de Mailly Nesle, Prince d'Orange, and M. de Charlus,
Duc de Brabant. But, before anything further could
happen, the Duchess, whom Swann and M. de Charlus

between them (albeit the latter was resolute in ignoring the Iénas' existence) had with great difficulty succeeded in making admire the Empire style, exclaimed: "Honestly, Ma'am, I can't tell you how beautiful you will think it! I must confess that the Empire style has always had a fascination for me. But at the Iénas' it is really like a hallucination. That sort of—what shall I say— reflux from the Expedition to Egypt, and also the sweep forward into our own times from Antiquity, all those things that invade our houses, the Sphinxes that come to crouch at the feet of the sofas, the serpents coiled round candelabra, a huge Muse who holds out a little torch for you to play at *bouillotte,* or has quietly climbed on to the mantelpiece and is leaning against your clock; and then all the Pompeian lamps, the little boat-shaped beds which look as if they had been found floating on the Nile so that you expect to see Moses climb out of them, the classical chariots galloping along the bed tables. . . ." "They're not very comfortable to sit in, those Empire chairs," the Princess ventured. "No," the Duchess agreed, "but," she at once added, insisting on the point with a smile: "I like being uncomfortable on those mahogany seats covered with ruby velvet or green silk. I like that discomfort of the warrior who understands nothing but the curule chair and in the middle of his principal drawing-room crosses his fasces and piles his laurels. I can assure you that at the Iénas' one doesn't stop to think for a moment of how comfortable one is, when one sees in front of one a great strapping wench of a Victory painted in fresco on the wall. My husband is going to say that I'm a very bad Royalist, but I'm terribly disaffected, as you know, I can assure you that in those people's house one comes to love all the big 'N's and all the bees. Good gracious, after all for a good many years under our Kings we weren't exactly surfeited with glory, and so these warriors who brought home so many crowns that they stuck them even on the arms of the chairs, I must say I think it's all rather fetching! Your Highness ought really." "Why, my dear, if you think so," said the Princess, " but it seems to me that it won't be easy." "But Ma'am will find that it will all go quite smoothy. They are very good people, and no fools. We took Mme. de Chevreuse there," added the Duchess, knowing the force of this example, " she was enchanted. The son is really very pleasant. I'm going to say something that's not quite proper," she went on, " but he has a bedroom, and more especially a bed in it, in which I should love to sleep—without him! What is even less proper is that I went to see him once when he was ill and lying in it. By his side on the frame of the bed was moulded a long Siren, stretched out at full length, a lovely thing with a mother-of-pearl tail and some sort of lotus flowers in her hand. I assure you," went on Mme. de Guermantes, reducing the speed of her utterances to bring into even bolder relief the words which she had the air of modelling with the pout of her fine lips, drawing them out with her long expressive hands, directing on the Princess as she spoke a gentle, steady and searching gaze, " that with the palms and the golden crown at the side of it was most moving, it was just the arrangement of Gustave Moreau's *Death and the Young Man* (your Highness must know that great work, of course)." The Princesse de Parme, who did not know so much as the painter's name, made violent movements with her head and smiled ardently, in order to manifest her admiration for his picture. But the intensity of her mimicry could not fill the place of that light which is absent from our eyes so long as we do not understand what people are trying to tell us. " A goodlooking boy, I believe? " she asked. " No, for he's just like a tapir. The eyes are a little those of a Queen Hortense on a screen. But he has probably come to the conclusion that it is rather absurd for a man to develop such a resemblance, and it is lost in the encaustic surface of his cheeks which give him really rather a Mameluke appearance. You feel that the polisher must call round every morning. Swann," she went on, reverting to the bed of the young Duke, " was struck by the resemblance between this Siren and Gustave Moreau's *Death*. But apart from that," she added, her speech becoming more rapid though still serious, so as to provoke more laughter, " there was nothing really that could *strike* us, for it was only a cold in the head, and the young man made a marvellous recovery." " They say he's a snob? " put in M. de Bréauté, with a malicious twinkle, expecting to be answered with the same precision as though he had said: " They tell me that he has only four fingers on his right hand; is that so? " " G—ood g—racious, n—o," replied Mme. de Guermantes with a smile of benign indulgence. " Perhaps just the least little bit of a snob in appearance, because he's extremely young, but I should be surprised to hear that he was really, for he's intelligent," she added, as though there were to her mind some absolute incompatibility between snobbishness and intelligence. " He has wit, too, I've known him be quite amusing," she said again, laughing with

291

the air of an epicure and expert, as though the act of declaring that a person could be amusing demanded a certain expression of merriment from the speaker, or as though the Duc de Guastalla's sallies were recurring to her mind as she spoke. "Anyway, as he never goes anywhere, he can't have much field for his snobbishness," she wound up, forgetting that this was hardly encouraging the Princesse de Parme to make overtures. "I cannot help wondering what the Prince de Guermantes, who calls her Mme. Iéna, will say if he hears that I've been to see her." "What!" cried the Duchess with extraordinary vivacity. "Don't you know that it was we who gave up to Gilbert" (she bitterly regretted that surrender now) "a complete card-room done in the Empire style which came to us from Quiou-Quiou, and is an absolute marvel! There was no room for it here, though I think it would look better here than it does with him. It's a thing of sheer beauty, half Etruscan, half Egyptian. . . ." "Egyptian?" queried the Princess, to whom the word Etruscan conveyed little. "Well, really, you know, a little of both. Swann told us that, he explained it all to me, only you know I'm such a dunce. But then, Ma'am, what one has to bear in mind is that the Egypt of the Empire cabinet-makers has nothing to do with the historical Egypt, nor their Roman with the Romans nor their Etruria. . . ." "Indeed," said the Princess. "No, it's like what they used to call a Louis XV costume under the Second Empire, when Anna de Monchy and dear Brigode's mother were girls. Basin was talking to you just now about Beethoven. We heard a thing of his played the other day which was really quite good, though a little stiff, with a Russian theme in it. It's pathetic to

think that he believed it to be Russian. In the same way
as the Chinese painters believed they were copying Bellini. Besides, even in the same country, whenever anybody begins to look at things in a way that is slightly
novel, nine hundred and ninety-nine people out of a thousand are totally incapable of seeing what he puts before
them. It takes at least forty years before they can manage
to make it out." "Forty years!" the Princess cried in
alarm. "Why, yes," went on the Duchess, adding more
and more to her words (which were practically my own,
for I had just been expressing a similar idea to her),
thanks to her way of pronouncing them, the equivalent
of what on the printed page is called italics: "it's like
a sort of first isolated individual of a species which does
not yet exist but is going to multiply in the future, an
individual endowed with a kind of *sense* which the human
race of his generation does not possess. I can hardly
give myself as an instance because I, on the contrary,
have always loved any interesting production from the
very start, however novel it might be. But really, the
other day I was with the Grand Duchess in the Louvre
and we happened to pass before Manet's *Olympia*. Nowadays nobody is in the least surprised by it. It looks just
like an Ingres! And yet, heaven only knows how many
spears I've had to break for that picture, which I don't
altogether like but which is unquestionably the work of
somebody." "And is the Grand Duchess well?" inquired
the Princesse de Parme, to whom the Tsar's aunt was infinitely more familiar than Manet's model. "Yes; we
talked about you. After all," she resumed, clinging to
her idea, "the fact of the matter is, as my brother-in-law
Palamède always says, that one has between oneself

and the rest of the world the barrier of a strange language. Though I admit that there's no one it's quite so true of as Gilbert. If it amuses you to go to the Iénas', you have far too much sense to let your actions be governed by what that poor fellow may think, who is a dear, innocent creature, but really lives in a different world. I feel myself nearer, more akin to my coachman, my horses even, than to a man who keeps on harking back to what people would have thought under Philip the Bold or Louis the Fat. Just fancy, when he goes for a walk in the country, he takes a stick to drive the peasants out of his way, quite in a friendly spirit, saying: 'Get on, clowns!' Really, I'm just as much surprised when he speaks to me as if I heard myself addressed by one of the 'recumbents' on the old gothic tombs. It's all very well that animated gravestone's being my cousin; he frightens me, and the only idea that comes into my head is to let him stay in his Middle Ages. Apart from that, I quite admit that he's never murdered anyone." "I've just been seeing him at dinner at Mme. de Villeparisis's," said the General, but without either smiling at or endorsing the Duchess's pleasantries. "Was M. de Norpois there?" asked Prince Von, whose mind still ran on the Academy of Moral Sciences. "Why, yes;" said the General. "In fact, he was talking about your Emperor." "It seems, the Emperor William is highly intelligent, but he does not care for Elstir's painting. Not that I'm saying this against him," said the Duchess, "I quite share his point of view. Although Elstir has done a fine portrait of me. You don't know it? It's not in the least like me, but it's a remarkable piece of work. He is interesting while one's sitting to him. He has made

me like a little old woman. It's after the style of the
Regents of the Hospital, by Hals. I expect you know those
sublimities, to borrow my nephew's favourite expression,"
the Duchess turned to myself, gently flapping her fan
of black feathers. More than erect on her chair, she flung
her head nobly backwards, for, while always a great lady,
she was a trifle inclined to play the great lady also. I
said that I had been once to Amsterdam and The Hague,
but that to avoid confusing my mind, as my time was
limited, I had left out Haarlem. "Ah! The Hague! What
a gallery!" cried M. de Guermantes. I said to him that
he had doubtless admired Vermeer's *Street in Delft.* But
the Duke was less erudite than arrogant. Accordingly he
contented himself with replying in a tone of sufficiency,
as was his habit whenever anyone spoke to him of a
picture in a gallery, or in the Salon, which he did not
remember having seen. "If it's to be seen, I saw it!"
"What? You've been to Holland, and you never visited
Haarlem!" cried the Duchess. "Why, even if you had
only a quarter of an hour to spend in the place, they're
an extraordinary thing to have seen, those Halses. I don't
mind saying that a person who only caught a passing
glimpse of them from the top of a tramway-car without
stopping, supposing they were hung out to view in the
street, would open his eyes pretty wide." This utterance
shocked me as indicating a misconception of the way in
which artistic impressions are formed in our minds, and
because it seemed to imply that our eye is in that case
simply a recording machine which takes instantaneous
photographs.

M. de Guermantes, rejoicing that she should be speaking to me with so competent a knowledge of the subjects

that interested me, gazed at the illustrious bearing of his wife, listened to what she was saying about Franz Hals, and thought: " She rides rough-shod over everything! Our young friend can go home and say that he's had before his eyes a great lady of the old school, in the full sense of the word, the like of whom couldn't be found anywhere to-day." Thus I beheld the pair of them, withdrawn from that name Guermantes in which long ago I had imagined them leading an unimaginable life, now just like other men and other women, lingering, only, behind their contemporaries a little way, and that not evenly, as in so many households of the Faubourg, where the wife has had the good taste to stop at the golden, the husband the misfortune to come down to the pinch-beck age of history, she remaining still Louis XV while her partner is pompously Louis-Philippe. That Mme. de Guermantes should be like other women had been for me at first a disappointment; it was now, by a natural re-action and with all these good wines to help, almost a miracle. A Don John of Austria, an Isabella d'Este, situated for us in the world of names, have as little com-munication with the great pages of history as the Mésé-glise way had with the Guermantes. Isabella d'Este was no doubt in reality a very minor Princess, similar to those who under Louis XIV obtained no special place at Court. But seeming to us to be of a unique and therefore in-comparable essence, we cannot conceive of her as being any less in greatness, so that a supper-party with Louis XIV would appear to us only to be rather interesting, whereas with Isabella d'Este we should find ourself, were we to meet her, gazing with our own eyes on a supernatural heroine of romance. Well, after we have, in studying Isabella d'Este, in transplanting her patiently from this world of fairyland into that of history, established the fact that her life, her thought contained nothing of that mysterious strangeness which had been suggested to us by her name, once this disappointment is complete we feel a boundless gratitude to this Princess for having had, of Mantegna's paintings, a knowledge almost equal to that, hitherto despised by us and put, as Françoise would have said, lower than the dirt, of M. Lafenestre. After having scaled the inaccessible heights of the name Guermantes, on descending the inner slope of the life of the Duchess, I felt on finding there the names, familiar elsewhere, of Victor Hugo, Franz Hals and, I regret to say, Vibert, the same astonishment that an explorer, after having taken into account, to imagine the singularity of the native customs in some wild valley of Central America or Northern Africa, its geographical remoteness, the strangeness of its flora, feels on discovering, once he has made his way through a hedge of giant aloes or manchineels, inhabitants who (sometimes indeed among the ruins of a Roman theatre and beneath a column dedicated to Venus) are engaged in reading *Mérope* or *Alzire*. And similarly, so remote, so distinct from, so far superior to the educated women of the middle classes whom I had known, the similar culture by which Mme. de Guermantes had made herself, with no ulterior motive, to gratify no ambition, descend to the level of people whom she would never know, had the character—meritorious, almost touching by virtue of being wholly useless —of an erudition in Phoenician antiquities in a politician or a doctor. "I might have shewn you a very fine one," said Mme. de Guermantes, still speaking of Hals, "the finest in existence, some people say, which was left to me by a German cousin. Unfortunately, it turned out to be ' enfeoffed ' in the castle—you don't know the expression, nor I either," she added, with her fondness for making jokes (which made her, she thought, seem modern) at the expense of the old customs to which nevertheless she was unconsciously but keenly attached. " I am glad you have seen my Elstirs, but, I must admit, I should have been a great deal more glad if I could have done you the honours of my Hals, this ' enfeoffed '. picture." " I know the one," said Prince Von, "it's the Grand Duke of Hesse's Hals." " Quite so; his brother married my sister," said M. de Guermantes, " and his mother and Oriane's were first cousins as well." " But so far as M. Elstir is concerned," the Prince went on, " I shall take the liberty of saying, without having any opinion of his work, which I do not know, that the hatred with which the Emperor pursues him ought not, it seems to me, to be counted against him. The Emperor is a man of marvellous intelligence." " Yes, I've met him at dinner twice, once at my aunt Sagan's and once at my aunt Radziwill's, and I must say I found him quite unusual. I didn't find him at all simple! But there is something amusing about him, something ' forced '," she detached the word, " like a green carnation, that is to say a thing that surprises me and does not please me enormously, a thing it is surprising that anyone should have been able to create but which I feel would have been just as well uncreated. I trust I'm not shocking you." " The Emperor is a man of astounding intelligence," resumed the Prince, " he is passionately fond of the arts, he has for works of art a taste that is practically infallible, if a

thing is good he spots it at once and takes a dislike to it.
If he detests anything, there can be no more doubt about
it, the thing is excellent." Everyone smiled. "You set
my mind at rest," said the Duchess. "I should be inclined to compare the Emperor," went on the Prince,
who, not knowing how to pronounce the word archaeologist (that is to say, as though it were spelt "arke-
ologist"), never missed an opportunity of using it, "to an
old archaeologist" (but the Prince said "arsheologist")
"we have in Berlin. If you put him in front of a genuine
Assyrian antique, he weeps. But if it is a modern sham,
if it is not really old, he does not weep. And so, when
they want to know whether an arsheological piece is
really old, they take it to the old arsheologist. If he
weeps, they buy the piece for the Museum. If his eyes
remain dry, they send it back to the dealer, and prosecute
him for fraud. Well, every time I dine at Potsdam, if the
Emperor says to me, of a play: 'Prince, you must see
that, it's a work of genius,' I make a note not to go to it;
and when I hear him fulminating against an exhibition,
I rush to see it at the first possible opportunity." "Norpois is in favour of an Anglo-French understanding, isn't
he?" said M. de Guermantes. "What use would that be
to you?" asked Prince Von, who could not endure the
English, in a tone at once of irritation and cunning. "The
English are so *schtubid*. I know, of course, that it would
not be as soldiers that they would help you. But one
can judge them, all the same, by the stupidity of their
Generals. A friend of mine was talking the other day
to Botha, you know, the Boer leader. He said to my
friend: 'It's terrible, an army like that. I rather like
the English, as a matter of fact, but just imagine that I,

who am only a peasant, have beaten them in every battle. And in the last, when I gave way before a force twenty times the strength of my own, while I myself surrendered, because I had to, I managed to take two thousand prisoners! That was good enough, because I was only commanding an army of farmers, but if those poor fools ever have to stand up against a European army, one trembles to think what may happen to them!' Besides, you have only to see how their King, whom you know as well as I do, passes for a great man in England." I barely listened to these stories, stories of the kind that M. de Norpois used to tell my father; they supplied no food for my favourite train of thought; and besides, even had they possessed the elements which they lacked, they would have had to be of a very exciting quality for my inner life to awaken during those hours in which I dwelt in my skin, my well-brushed hair, my starched shirt-front, in which, that is to say, I could feel nothing of what constituted for me the pleasure of life. "Oh, I don't agree with you at all," said Mme. de Guermantes, who felt that the German Prince was wanting in tact, "I find King Edward charming, so simple, and much cleverer than people think. And the Queen is, even now, the most beautiful thing I've ever seen in the world." "But, Madame la Duchesse," said the Prince, who was losing his temper and did not see that he was giving offence, "You must admit that if the Prince of Wales had been an ordinary person there isn't a club that wouldn't have blackballed him, and nobody would have been willing to shake hands with him. The Queen is charming, exceedingly sweet and limited. But after all there is something shocking about a royal couple who

are literally kept by their subjects, who get the big Jewish
financiers to foot all the bills they ought to pay themselves, and create them Baronets in return. It's like the
Prince of Bulgaria. . . ." " He's our cousin," put in the
Duchess : " He's a clever fellow." "He's mine, too, but we
don't think him a good fellow on that account. No, it
is us you ought to make friends with, it's the Emperor's
dearest wish, but he insists on its coming from the heart.
He says: 'What I want to see is a hand clasped in mine,
not waving a hat in the air.' With that, you would be
invincible. It would be more practical than the Anglo-
French friendship M. de Norpois preaches." " You know
him, of course," the Duchess said, turning to me, so as
not to leave me out of the conversation. Remembering
that M. de Norpois had said that I had once looked as
though I wanted to kiss his hand, thinking that he had
no doubt repeated this story to Mme. de Guermantes,
and in any event could have spoken of me to her only
with malice, since in spite of his friendship with my father
he had not hesitated to make me appear so ridiculous,
I did not do what a man of the world would have done.
He would have said that he detested M. de Norpois, and
had let him see it; he would have said this so as to give
himself the appearance of being the deliberate cause of the
Ambassador's slanders, which would then have been no
more than lying and calculated reprisals. I said, on the
other hand, that, to my great regret, I was afraid that
M. de Norpois did not like me. " You are quite mistaken,"
replied the Duchess, " he likes you very much indeed.
You can ask Basin, for if people give me the reputation
of only saying nice things, he certainly doesn't. He will
tell you that we have never heard Norpois speak about

anyone so kindly as he spoke to us of you. And only the other day he was wanting to give you a fine post at the Ministry. As he knew that you were not very strong and couldn't accept it, he had the delicacy not to speak of his kind thought to your father, for whom he has an unbounded admiration." M. de Norpois was quite the last person whom I should have expected to do me any practical service. The truth was that, his being a mocking and indeed somewhat malicious spirit, those people who had let themselves be taken in as I had by his outward appearance of a Saint Louis delivering justice beneath an oak-tree, by the sounds, easily modulated to pity, that emerged from his somewhat too tuneful lips, believed in a deliberate betrayal when they learned of a slander uttered at their expense by a man who had always seemed to put his whole heart into his speech. These slanders were frequent enough with him. But that did not prevent him from feeling attractions, from praising the people he liked and taking pleasure in shewing that he could be of use to them. " Not that I'm in the least surprised at his appreciating you," said Mme. de Guermantes, " he's an intelligent man. And I can quite understand," she added, for the benefit of the rest of the party, making allusion to a purpose of marriage of which I had heard nothing, " that my aunt, who has long ceased to amuse him as an old mistress, may not seem of very much use to him as a young wife. Especially as I understand that even as a mistress she has ceased for years now to serve any practical purpose, she is more wrapped up in her devotions than anything else. Boaz-Norpois can say, in the words of Victor Hugo:

Voilà longtemps que celle avec qui j'ai dormi,
O Seigneur, a quitté ma couche pour la vôtre !

Really, my poor aunt is like the artists of the advanced
guard who have stood out all their lives against the
Academy, and in the end start a little academy of their
own, or the unfrocked priests who get up a little private
religion. They should either keep their frocks, or not stick
to their profession. And who knows," went on the
Duchess with a meditative air, " it may be in preparation
for her widowhood, there's nothing sadder than the weeds
one's not entitled to wear." " Ah! If Mme. de Villeparisis were to become Mme. de Norpois, I really believe
our cousin Gilbert would take to his bed," said General
de Monserfeuil. " The Prince de Guermantes is a charming man, but he is, really, very much taken up with
questions of birth and manners," said the Princesse de
Parme. " I went down to spend a few days with them in
the country, when the Princess, unfortunately, was ill in
bed. I was accompanied by Petite." (This was a nickname that was given to Mme. d'Hunolstein because she
was enormously stout.) " The Prince came to meet me
at the foot of the steps, and pretended not to see Petite.
We went up to the first floor, to the door into the reception rooms, and then, stepping back to make way for me,
he said: 'Oh, how d'ye do, Mme. d'Hunolsteins?' (he
always calls her that now, since her separation) pretending to have caught sight of Petite for the first time, so
as to shew her that he had not come down to receive
her at the foot of the steps." " That doesn't surprise
me in the least. I don't need to tell you," said the Duke,
who regarded himself as extremely modern, more contemptuous than anyone in the world of mere birth, and

in fact a Republican, " that I have not many ideas in common with my cousin. Ma'am can imagine that we are just about as much agreed on most subjects as day and night. But I must say that if my aunt were to marry Norpois, for once I should be of Gilbert's opinion. To be the daughter of Florimond de Guise, and then to make a marriage like that would be enough, as the saying is, to make a cat laugh; what more can I say?" These last words, which the Duke uttered as a rule in the middle of a sentence, were here quite superfluous. But he felt a perpetual need to be saying them which made him postpone them to the end of a speech if he had found no place for them elsewhere. They were for him, among other things, almost a question of prosody. "Remember, though," he added, " that the Norpois are gallant gentlemen with a good place, of a good stock."

"Listen to me, Basin, it's really not worth your while to poke fun at Gilbert if you're going to speak the same language as he does," said Mme. de Guermantes, for whom the " goodness " of a family, no less than that of a wine, consisted in its age. But, less frank than her cousin and more subtle than her husband, she made a point of never in her conversation playing false to the Guermantes spirit, and despised rank in her speech while ready to honour it by her actions. " But aren't you some sort of cousins? " asked General de Monserfeuil. " I seem to remember that Norpois married a La Rochefoucauld." " Not in that way at all, she belonged to the branch of the Ducs de La Rochefoucauld, my grandmother came from the Ducs de Doudeauville. She was own grandmother to Edouard Coco, the wisest man in the family," replied the Duke, whose views of wisdom were somewhat superficial, "and the two branches haven't intermarried since Louis XIV's time; the connexion would be rather distant." "I say, that's interesting; I never knew that," said the General. "However," went on M. de Guermantes, "his mother, I believe, was the sister of the Duc de Montmorency, and had originally been married to a La Tour d'Auvergne. But as those Montmorencys are barely Montmorencys, while those La Tour d'Auvergnes are not La Tour d'Auvergnes at all, I cannot see that it gives him any very great position. He says— and this should be more to the point—that he's descended from Saintrailles, and as we ourselves are in a direct line of descent. . . ."

There was at Combray a Rue de Saintrailles, to which I had never given another thought. It led from the Rue de la Bretonnerie to the Rue de l'Oiseau. And as Saintrailles, the companion of Joan of Arc, had, by marrying a Guermantes, brought into that family the County of Combray, his arms were quartered with those of Guermantes at the foot of one of the windows in Saint-Hilaire. I saw again a vision of dark sandstone steps, while a modulation of sound brought to my ears that name, Guermantes, in the forgotten tone in which I used to hear it long ago, so different from that in which it was used to signify the genial hosts with whom I was dining this evening. If the name, Duchesse de Guermantes, was for me a collective name, it was so not merely in history, by the accumulation of all the women who had successively borne it, but also in the course of my own short life, which had already seen, in this single Duchesse de Guermantes, so many different women superimpose themselves, each one vanishing as soon as the next had acquired sufficient consistency. Words do not change their meaning as much in centuries as names do for us in the space of a few years. Our memory and our heart are not large enough to be able to remain faithful. We have not room enough, in our mental field, to keep the dead there as well as the living. We are obliged to build over what has gone before and is brought to light only by a chance excavation, such as the name Saintrailles had just wrought in my mind. I felt that it would be useless to explain all this, and indeed a little while earlier I had lied by implication in not answering when M. de Guermantes said to me: " You don't know our old wheedler? " Perhaps he was quite well aware that I did know him, and it was only from good breeding that he did not press the question.

Mme. de Guermantes drew me out of my meditation. " Really, I find all that sort of thing too deadly. Listen, it's not always as boring as this at my parties. I hope that you will soon come and dine again as a compensation, with no pedigrees next time," she murmured, incapable both of appreciating the kind of charm which I could find in her house and of having sufficient humility to be content to appeal to me only as a herbarium, filled with plants of another day.

What Mme. de Guermantes believed to be disappointing my expectations was on the contrary what in the end— for the Duke and the General went on to discuss pedigrees now without stopping—saved my evening from becoming a complete disappointment. How could I have felt otherwise until now? Each of my fellow-guests at dinner, smothering the mysterious name under which I had only at a distance known and dreamed of them with a body and with a mind similar or inferior to those of all the people I knew, had given me the impression of flat vulgarity which the view on entering the Danish port of Elsinore would give to any passionate admirer of *Hamlet*. No doubt those geographical regions and that ancient past which put forest glades and gothic belfries into their names had in a certain measure formed their faces, their intellects and their prejudices, but survived in them only as does the cause in the effect, that is to say as a thing possible for the brain to extract but in no way perceptible to the imagination.

And these old-time prejudices restored in a flash to the friends of M. and Mme. de Guermantes their vanished poetry. Assuredly, the notions in the possession of nobles, which make of them the scholars, the etymologists of the language not of words but of names (and this, moreover, relatively only to the ignorant mass of the middle classes, for if at the same level of mediocrity a devout Catholic would be better able to stand questioning upon the details of the Liturgy than a free-thinker, on the other hand an anti-clerical archaeologist can often give points to his parish priest on everything connected even with the latter's own church), those notions, if we are going to confine ourselves to the truth, that is to say to the spirit, had not for these great gentlemen the charm that they would have had for a man of simple birth. They knew perhaps better than myself that the Duchesse de Guise was Princess of Cleves, of Orleans and of Porcien, and all the rest, but they had known, long before they knew all these names, the face of the Duchesse de Guise which thenceforward the names reflected back to them. I had begun with the fairy—were she fated shortly to perish; they with the woman.

In middle-class families one sometimes sees jealousies spring up if the younger sister is married before the elder. So the aristocratic world, Courvoisiers especially but Guermantes also, reduced its ennobled greatness to simple domestic superiorities, by a system of child's-play which I had met originally (and this gave it for me its sole charm) in books. Is it not just as though Tallemant des Réaux were speaking of the Guermantes, and not of the Rohans, when he relates with evident satisfaction how M. de Guéménée cried to his brother: "You can come in here; this is not the Louvre!" and said of the Chevalier de Rohan (because he was a natural son of the Duc de Clermont): "At any rate, he's a Prince." The only thing that distressed me in all this talk was to find that the absurd stories which were being circulated about the charming Hereditary Grand Duke of Luxembourg found as much credence in this drawing-room as they had among Saint-Loup's friends. Plainly it was an epidemic that would not last longer than perhaps a year or two but had meanwhile infected everyone. People repeated the same old stories, or enriched them with others equally untrue. I gathered that the Princesse de Luxembourg herself, while apparently defending her nephew, supplied weapons for the assault. "You are wrong to stand up for him," M. de Guermantes told me, as Saint-Loup had told me before. "Why, without taking into consideration the opinion of our family, who are unanimous about him, you have only to talk to his servants, and they, after all, are the people who know him best. M. de Luxembourg gave his little negro page to his nephew. The negro came back in tears: 'Grand Duke beaten me; me no bad boy; Grand Duke naughty

man,' it's really too much. And I can speak with some
knowledge, he's Oriane's cousin." I cannot, by the way,
say how many times in the course of this evening I heard
the word " cousin " used. On the one hand, M. de Guermantes, almost at every name that was mentioned, exclaimed: " But he's Oriane's cousin! " with the sudden
joy of a man who, lost in a forest, reads at the ends
of a pair of arrows pointing in opposite directions on
a metal plate, and followed by quite a low number of
kilometres, the words: " Belvédère Casimir-Perier " and
" Croix du Grand-Veneur ", and gathers from them that
he is on the right road. On the other hand the word
cousin was employed in a wholly different connexion
(which was here the exception to the prevailing rule) by
the Turkish Ambassadress, who had come in after dinner.
Devoured by social ambition and endowed with a real
power of assimilating knowledge, she would pick up with
equal facility the story of the Retreat of the Ten Thousand or the details of sexual perversion among birds.
It would have been impossible to " stump " her on any
of the most recent German publications, whether they
dealt with political economy, mental aberrations, the
various forms of onanism, or the philosophy of Epicurus.
She was, incidentally, a dangerous person to listen to,
for, perpetually in error, she would point out to you as
being of the loosest morals women of irreproachable
virtue, would put you on your guard against a gentleman
whose intentions were perfectly honourable, and would
tell you anecdotes of the sort that seem always to have
come out of a book, not so much because they are serious
as because they are so wildly improbable.

She was at this period little received in society. She

had been going for some weeks now to the houses of
women of real social brilliance, such as the Duchesse de
Guermantes, but as a general rule had confined herself,
of necessity, in the noblest families, to obscure scions
whom the Guermantes had ceased to know. She hoped
to give herself a really fashionable air by quoting the
most historic names of the little-known people who were
her friends. At once M. de Guermantes, thinking that
she was referring to people who frequently dined at his
table, quivered with joy at finding himself once more
in sight of a landmark and shouted the rallying-cry: " But
he's Oriane's cousin! I know him as well as I know my
own name. He lives in the Rue Vaneau. His mother was
Mlle. d'Uzès." The Ambassadress was obliged to admit
that her specimen had been drawn from smaller game.
She tried to connect her friends with those of M. de
Guermantes by cutting across his track: " I know quite
well who' you mean. No, it's not those ones, they're
cousins." But this cross-current launched by the unfortunate Ambassadress ran but a little way. For M. de
Guermantes, losing interest, answered: " Oh, then I don't
know who' you're talking about." The Ambassadress
offered no reply, for if she never knew anyone nearer than
the " cousins " of those whom she ought to have known
in person, very often these " cousins " were not even
related at all. Then, from the lips of M. de Guermantes,
would flow a fresh wave of " But she's Oriane's cousin! "
words which seemed to have for the Duke the same practical value as certain epithets, convenient to the Roman
poets because they provided them with dactyls or
spondees for their hexameters. At least the explosion of:
" But she's Oriane's cousin!" appeared to me quite natural

when applied to the Princesse de Guermantes, who was indeed very closely related to the Duchess. The Ambassadress did not seem to care for this Princess. She said to me in an undertone: " She is stupid. No, she is not so beautiful as all that. That claim is usurped. Anyhow," she went on, with an air at once reflective, rejecting and decided, " I find her most uncongenial." But often the cousinship extended a great deal farther than this, Mme. de Guermantes making it a point of honour to address as " Aunt " ladies with whom it would have been impossible to find her an ancestress in common without going back at least to Louis XV; just as, whenever the " hardness " of the times brought it about that a multimillionairess married a prince whose great-great-grandfather had espoused, as had Oriane's also, a daughter of Louvois, one of the chief joys of the fair American was to be able, after a first visit to the Hôtel de Guermantes, where she was, incidentally, more or less coldly received and hotly cross-examined, to say " Aunt " to Mme. de Guermantes, who allowed her to do so with a maternal smile. But little did it concern me what birth meant for M. de Guermantes and M. de Monserfeuil, in the conversations which they held on the subject I sought only for a poetic pleasure. Without being conscious of it themselves, they procured me this pleasure as might a couple of labourers or sailors speaking of the soil or the tides, realities too little detached from their own lives for them to be capable of enjoying the beauty which personally I proceeded to extract from them.

Sometimes rather than of a race it was of a particular fact, of a date that a name reminded me. Hearing M. de Guermantes recall that M. de Bréauté's mother had been

a Choiseul and his grandmother a Lucinge, I fancied
I could see beneath the commonplace shirt with its
plain pearl studs, bleeding still in two globes of crystal,
those august relics, the hearts of Mme. de Praslin and
of the Duc de Berri. Others were more voluptuous;
the fine and flowing hair of Mme. de Tallien or Mme. de
Sabran.

Better informed than his wife as to what their ancestors had been, M. de Guermantes found himself the
possessor of memories which gave to his conversation a
fine air of an ancient mansion stripped of its real treasures but still full of pictures, authentic, indifferent and
majestic, which taken as a whole look remarkably well.
The Prince d'Agrigente having asked why Prince Von
had said, in speaking of the Duc d'Aumale, " my
uncle," M. de Guermantes had replied: " Because his
mother's brother, the Duke of Wurtemberg, married a
daughter of Louis-Philippe." At once I was lost in contemplation of a casket, such as Carpaccio or Memling
used to paint, from its first panel in which the Princess,
at the wedding festivities of her brother the Duc
d'Orléans, appeared wearing a plain garden dress to indicate her resentment at having seen the return, empty-
handed, of the ambassadors who had been sent to sue
on her behalf for the hand of the Prince of Syracuse,
down to the last, in which she had just given birth to a
son, the Duke of Wurtemberg (the first cousin of the
Prince whom I had met at dinner), in that castle called
Fantaisie, one of those places which are as aristocratic
as certain families. They, moreover, outlasting a single
generation of men, see attached to themselves more than
one historical personage. In this one, especially, survive

side by side memories of the Margravine of Bayreuth,
of this other somewhat fantastic Princess (the Duc
d'Orléans's sister), to whom it was said that the name
of her husband's castle made a distinct appeal, of the
King of Bavaria, and finally of Prince Von, to whom
it was simply his own postal address, at which he had
just asked the Duc de Guermantes to write to him,
for he had succeeded to it, and let it only during the
Wagner festivals, to the Prince de Polignac, another delightful " fantasist ". When M. de Guermantes, to explain
how he was related to Mme. d'Arpajon, was obliged, going
so far and so simply, to climb the chain formed by the
joined hands of three or five ancestresses back to Marie-
Louise or Colbert, it was still the same thing in each case;
a great historical event appeared only in passing, masked,
unnatural, reduced, in the name of a property, in the
Christian names of a woman, so selected because she
was the grand-daughter of Louis-Philippe and Marie-
Amélie, considered no longer as King and Queen of the
French, but merely in the extent to which in their capacity as grand-parents they bequeathed a heritage. (We
see for other reasons in a gazetteer of the works of Balzac,
where the most illustrious personages figure only according to their connexion with the *Comédie Humaine,*
Napoleon occupy a space considerably less than that
allotted to Rastignac, and occupy that space solely because he once spoke to the young ladies of Cinq-Cygne.)
Similarly the aristocracy, in its heavy structure, pierced
with rare windows, admitting a scanty daylight, shewing
the same incapacity to soar but also the same massive
and blind force as the architecture of the romanesque
age, embodies all our history, immures it, beetles over it.

Thus the empty spaces of my memory were covered by degrees with names which in taking order, in composing themselves with relation to one another, in linking themselves to one another by an increasingly numerous connexion, resembled those finished works of art in which there is not one touch that is isolated, in which every part in turn receives from the rest a justification which it confers on them.

M. de Luxembourg's name having come up again in the course of the conversation, the Turkish Ambassadress told us how, the young bride's grandfather (he who had made that immense fortune out of flour and cereals) having invited M. de Luxembourg to luncheon, the latter had written to decline, putting on the envelope: " M. So-and-so, Miller," to which the grandfather had replied: " I am all the more disappointed that you were not able to come, my dear friend, because I should have been able to enjoy your society quite intimately, for we were quite an intimate party, just ourselves, and there would have been only the Miller, his Son, and you." This story was not merely utterly distasteful to me, who knew the impossibility of my dear M. de Nassau's writing to the grandfather of his wife (whose fortune, moreover, he was expecting to inherit) and addressing him as " Miller "; but furthermore its stupidity became glaring from the start, the word " Miller " having obviously been dragged in only to lead up to the title of La Fontaine's fable. But there is in the Faubourg Saint-Germain a silliness so great, when it is aggravated by malice, that they all decided that the letter had been sent and that the grandfather, as to whom at once everyone confidently declared that he was a remarkable man, had shewn a prettier wit

than his grandson-in-law. The Duc de Châtellerault tried
to take advantage of this story to tell the one that I had
heard in the café: "Everyone had to lie down!"—but
scarcely had he begun, or reported M. de Luxembourg's
pretension that in his wife's presence M. de Guermantes
ought to stand up, when the Duchess stopped him with
the protest: "No, he is very absurd, but not as bad as
that." I was privately convinced that all these stories at
the expense of M. de Luxembourg were equally untrue,
and that whenever I found myself face to face with any
of the reputed actors or spectators I should hear the same
contradiction. I asked myself, nevertheless, whether the
contradiction just uttered by Mme. de Guermantes had
been inspired by regard for truth or by self-esteem. In
either event the latter quality succumbed to malice, for
she went on, with a laugh: "Not that I haven't had my
little fling at him too, for he invited me to luncheon,
wishing to make me know the Grand Duchess of Luxembourg, which is how he has the good taste to describe his
wife when he's writing to his aunt. I sent a reply expressing my regret, and adding: As for the 'Grand Duchess of
Luxembourg' (in inverted commas), tell her that if she
is coming to see me I am at home every Thursday after
five. I have even had another little fling. Happening to
be at Luxembourg, I telephoned, asking him to ring me
up. His Highness was going to luncheon, had just risen
from luncheon, two hours went by and nothing happened;
so then I employed another method: 'Will you tell the
Comte de Nassau to come and speak to me?' Cut to the
quick, he was at the instrument that very minute." Everyone laughed at the Duchess's story, and at other analogous, that is to say (I am convinced of it) equally

untrue stories, for a man more intelligent, better, more refined, in a word more exquisite than this Luxembourg-Nassau I have never met. The sequel will shew that it was I who was in the right. I must admit that, in the midst of her onslaught, Mme. de Guermantes had still a kind word for him. "He was not always like that," she informed us. "Before he went off his head, like the man in the story-book who thinks he's become king, he was no fool, and indeed in the early days of his engagement he used to speak of it in really quite a nice way, as something he could never have dreamed of: 'It's just like a fairy-tale; I shall have to make my entry into Luxembourg in a fairy coach,' he said to his uncle d'Ornessan, who answered—for you know it's not a very big place, Luxembourg: 'A fairy coach! I'm afraid, my dear fellow, you'ld never get it in. I should suggest that you take a goat carriage.' Not only did this not annoy Nassau, but he was the first to tell us the story, and to laugh at it." "Ornessan is a witty fellow, and he's every reason to be; his mother was a Montjeu. He's in a very bad way now, poor Ornessan." This name had the magic virtue of interrupting the flow of stale witticisms which otherwise would have gone on for ever. In fact, M. de Guermantes had to explain that M. d'Ornessan's great-grandmother had been the sister of Marie de Castille Montjeu, the wife of Timoléon de Lorraine, and consequently Oriane's aunt, with the result that the conversation drifted back to genealogies, while the idiot of a Turkish Ambassadress breathed in my ear: "You appear to be very much in the Duke's good books; have a care!" and, on my demanding an explanation: "I mean to say, you understand what I mean, he's a man to whom one could safely entrust one's daughter, but not one's son." Now if ever, on the contrary, a man existed who was passionately and exclusively a lover of women, it was certainly the Duc de Guermantes. The state of error, the falsehood fatuously believed to be the truth, were for the Ambassadress like a vital element out of which she could not move. "His brother Mémé, who is, as it happens, for other reasons altogether" (he did not bow to her) "profoundly uncongenial to me, is genuinely distressed by the Duke's morals. So is their aunt Villeparisis. Ah, now, her I adore! There is a saint of a woman for you, the true type of the great ladies of the past. It's not only her actual virtue that's so wonderful but her restraint. She still says 'Monsieur' to the Ambassador Norpois whom she sees every day, and who, by the way, left an excellent impression behind him in Turkey."

I did not even reply to the Ambassadress, in order to listen to the genealogies. They were not all of them important. There came up indeed in the course of the conversation one of those unexpected alliances, which, M. de Guermantes informed me, was a misalliance, but not without charm, for, uniting under the July Monarchy the Duc de Guermantes and the Duc de Fezensac with the two irresistible daughters of an eminent navigator, it gave to the two Duchesses the exciting novelty of a grace exotically middle-class, "Louisphilippically" Indian. Or else, under Louis XIV, a Norpois had married the daughter of the Duc de Mortemart, whose illustrious title struck, in the remoteness of that epoch, the name—which I had found colourless and might have supposed to be modern —of Norpois, carving deeply upon it the beauty of an old medal. And in these cases, moreover, it was not only the less well-known name that benefited by the association; the other, grown commonplace by the fact of its lustre, struck me more forcibly in this novel and more obscure aspect, just as among the portraits painted by a brilliant colourist the most striking is sometimes one that is all in black. The sudden mobility with which all these names seemed to me to have been endowed, as they sprang to take their places by the side of others from which I should have supposed them to be remote, was due not to my ignorance alone; the country-dances which they were performing in my mind they had carried out no less spontaneously at those epochs in which a title, being always attached to a piece of land, used to follow it from one family to another, so much so that, for example, in the fine feudal structure that is the title of Duc de Nemours or Duc de Chevreuse, I was able to discover successively hidden, as in the hospitable abode of a hermit-crab, a Guise, a Prince of Savoy, an Orléans, a Luynes. Sometimes several remained in competition for a single shell: for the Principality of Orange the Royal House of the Netherlands and MM. de Mailly-Nesle, for the Duchy of Brabant the Baron de Charlus and the Royal House of Belgium, various others for the titles of Prince of Naples, Duke of Parma, Duke of Reggio. Sometimes it was the other way; the shell had been so long uninhabited by proprietors long since dead that it had never occurred to me that this or that name of a country house could have been, at an epoch which after all was comparatively recent, the name of a family. And so, when M. de Guermantes replied to a question put to him by M. de Monserfeuil: "No, my cousin was a fanatical Royalist; she was the daughter of the Marquis de Féterne, who played

a certain part in the Chouan rising," on seeing this name
Féterne, which had been for me, since my stay at Balbec,
the name of a country house, become, what I had never
dreamed that it could possibly be, a family name, I
felt the same astonishment as in reading a fairy-tale,
where turrets and a terrace come to life and turn into men
and women. In this sense of the words, we may say that
history, even mere family history, gives life to the old
stones of a house. There have been in Parisian society
men who played as considerable a part in it, who were
more sought after for their distinction or for their wit,
who were equally well born as the Duc de Guermantes or
the Duc de La Trémoïlle. They have now fallen into oblivion because, as they left no descendants, their name
which we no longer hear sounds like a name unknown; at
most, the name of a thing beneath which we never think
to discover the name of any person, it survives in some
country house, some remote village. The day is not distant when the traveller who, in the heart of Burgundy,
stops in the little village of Charlus to look at its church,
if he has not sufficient industry or is in too great a hurry
to examine its tombstones, will go away ignorant that this
name, Charlus, was that of a man who ranked with the
highest in the land. This thought reminded me that it
was time to go, and that while I was listening to M. de
Guermantes talking pedigrees, the hour was approaching
at which I had promised to call upon his brother. "Who
knows," I continued to muse, " whether one day Guermantes itself may not appear nothing more than a place-
name, save to the archaeologists who, stopping by chance
at Combray and standing beneath the window of Gilbert
the Bad, have the patience to listen to the account given

them by Théodore's successor or to read the Curé's guide?" But so long as a great name is not extinct it keeps in the full light of day those men and women who bear it; and there can be no doubt that, to a certain extent, the interest which the illustriousness of these families gave them in my eyes lay in the fact that one can, starting from to-day, follow their ascending course, step by step, to a point far beyond the fourteenth century, recover the diaries and correspondence of all the forebears of M. de Charlus, of the Prince d'Agrigente, of the Princesse de Parme, in a past in which an impenetrable night would cloak the origins of a middle-class family, and in which we make out, in the luminous backward projection of a name, the origin and persistence of certain nervous characteristics, certain vices, the disorders of one or another Guermantes. Almost identical pathologically with their namesakes of the present day, they excite from century to century the startled interest of their correspondents, whether these be anterior to the Princess Palatine and Mme. de Motteville, or subsequent to the Prince de Ligne.

However, my historical curiosity was faint in comparison with my aesthetic pleasure. The names cited had the effect of disincarnating the Duchess's guests, whom, for all they might call themselves Prince d'Agrigente or de Cystira, their mask of flesh and of a common intelligence or want of intelligence had transformed into ordinary mortals, so much so that I had made my landing on the ducal door-mat not as upon the threshold (as I had supposed) but as at the farthest confines of the enchanted world of names. The Prince d'Agrigente himself, as soon as I heard that his mother had been a Damas, a grand-daughter of the Duke of Modena, was delivered, as from an unstable chemical alloy, from the face and speech that prevented one from recognising him, and went to form with Damas and Modena, which themselves were only titles, a combination infinitely more seductive. Each name displaced by the attractions of another, with which I had never suspected it of having any affinity, left the unalterable position which it had occupied in my brain, where familiarity had dulled it, and, speeding to join the Mortemarts, the Stuarts or the Bourbons, traced with them branches of the most graceful design and an ever-changing colour. The name Guermantes itself received from all the beautiful names—extinct, and so all the more glowingly rekindled—with which I learned only now that it was connected, a new sense and purpose, purely poetical. At the most, at the extremity of each spray that burgeoned from the exalted stem, I could see it flower in some face of a wise king or illustrious princess, like the sire of Henri IV or the Duchesse de Longueville. But as these faces, different in this respect from those of the party around me, were not discoloured for me by any trace of physical experience or fashionable mediocrity, they remained, in their handsome outlines and rainbow iridescence, homogeneous with those names which at regular intervals, each of a different hue, detached themselves from the genealogical tree of Guermantes, and disturbed with no foreign or opaque matter the buds—pellucid, alternate, many-coloured—which (like, in the old Jesse windows, the ancestors of Jesus) blossomed on either side of the tree of glass.

Already I had made several attempts to slip away, on account, more than for any other reason, of the triviality

which my presence at it imparted to the gathering, albeit
it was one of those which I had long imagined as being
so beautiful—as it would doubtless have been had there
been no inconvenient witness present. At least my departure would permit the other guests, once the profane
intruder was no longer among them, to constitute themselves at length into a secret conclave. They would be
free to celebrate the mysteries for the celebration of which
they had met together, for it could obviously not have been
to talk of Franz Hals or of avarice, and to talk of them in
the same way as people talk in middle-class society. They
uttered nothing but trivialities, doubtless because I was
in the room, and I felt with some compunction, on seeing
all these pretty women kept apart, that I was preventing
them by my presence from carrying on, in the most
precious of its drawing-rooms, the mysterious life of the
Faubourg Saint-Germain. But this departure which I was
trying at every moment to effect, M. and Mme. de Guermantes carried the spirit of self-sacrifice so far as to postpone, by keeping me in the room. A more curious thing
still, several of the ladies who had come hurrying, delighted, beautifully dressed, with constellations of jewels,
to be present at a party which, through my fault only,
differed in no essential point from those that are given
elsewhere than in the Faubourg Saint-Germain, any more
than one feels oneself at Balbec to be in a town that
differs from what one's eyes are accustomed to see—several of these ladies retired not at all disappointed, as they
had every reason to be, but thanking Mme. de Guermantes most effusively for the delightful evening which
they had spent, as though on the other days, those on
which I was not present, nothing more used to occur.

Was it really for the sake of dinners such as this that all these people dressed themselves up and refused to allow the penetration of middle-class women into their so exclusive drawing-rooms—for dinners such as this? The same, had I been absent? The suspicion flashed across my mind for a moment, but it was too absurd. Plain commonsense enabled me to brush it aside. And then, if I had adopted it, what would have been left of the name Guermantes, already so degraded since Combray?

It struck me that these flower-maidens were, to a strange extent, either ready to be pleased with another person or anxious to make that person pleased with them, for more than one of them, to whom I had not uttered, during the whole course of the evening, more than two or three casual remarks, the stupidity of which had left me blushing, made a point, before leaving the drawing-room, of coming to tell me, fastening on me her fine caressing eyes, straightening as she spoke the garland of orchids that followed the curve of her bosom, what an intense pleasure it had been to her to make my acquaintance, and to speak to me—a veiled allusion to an invitation to dinner—of her desire to " arrange something " after she had " fixed a day " with Mme. de Guermantes. None of these flower ladies left the room before the Princesse de Parme. The presence of that lady—one must never depart before Royalty—was one of the two reasons, neither of which I had guessed, for which the Duchess had insisted so strongly on my remaining. As soon as Mme. de Parme had risen, it was like a deliverance. Each of the ladies having made a genuflexion before the Princess, who raised her up from the ground, they received from her, in a kiss, and like a benediction which they had craved kneeling, the permission to ask for their cloaks and carriages. With the result that there followed, at the front door, a sort of stentorian recital of great names from the History of France. The Princesse de Parme had forbidden Mme. de Guermantes to accompany her downstairs to the hall for fear of her catching cold, and the Duke had added: "There, Oriane, since Ma'am gives you leave, remember what the doctor told you."

"I am sure the Princesse de Parme was *most pleased* to take dinner with you." I knew the formula. The Duke had come the whole way across the drawing-room in order to utter it before me with an obliging, concerned air, as though he were handing me a diploma or offering me a plateful of biscuits. And I guessed from the pleasure which he appeared to be feeling as he spoke, and which brought so sweet an expression momentarily into his face that the effort which this represented for him was of the kind which he would continue to make to the very end of his life, like one of those honorific and easy posts which, even when paralytic, one is still allowed to retain.

Just as I was about to leave, the lady in waiting reappeared in the drawing-room, having forgotten to take away some wonderful carnations, sent up from Guermantes, which the Duchess had presented to Mme. de Parme. The lady in waiting was somewhat flushed, one felt that she had just been receiving a scolding, for the Princess, so kind to everyone else, could not contain her impatience at the stupidity of her attendant. And so the latter picked up the flowers and ran quickly, but to preserve her air of ease and independence flung at me as she passed: "The Princess says I'm keeping her waiting; she wants to be gone, and to have the carnations as well.

Good lord! I'm not a little bird, I can't be in two places at once."

Alas! the rule of not leaving before Royalty was not the only one. I could not depart at once, for there was another: this was that the famous lavishness, unknown to the Courvoisiers, with which the Guermantes, whether opulent or practically ruined, excelled in entertaining their friends, was not only a material lavishness, of the kind that I had often experienced with Robert de Saint-Loup, but also a lavish display of charming words, of courteous actions, a whole system of verbal elegance supplied from a positive treasure-house within. But as this last, in the inactivity of fashionable existence, must remain unemployed, it expanded at times, sought an outlet in a sort of fugitive effusion, all the more intense, which might, in Mme. de Guermantes, have led one to suppose a genuine affection for oneself. Which she did, for that matter, feel at the moment when she let it overflow, for she found then in the society of the friend, man or woman, with whom she happened to be a sort of intoxication, in no way sensual, similar to that which music produces in certain people; she would suddenly detach a flower from her bodice, or a medallion, and present it to someone with whom she would have liked to prolong the evening, with a melancholy feeling the while that such a prolongation could have led to nothing but idle talk, into which nothing could have passed of the nervous pleasure, the fleeting emotion, similar to the first warm days of spring in the impression they leave behind them of exhaustion and regret. As for the friend, it did not do for him to put too implicit a faith in the promises, more exhilarating than anything he had ever heard, tendered by these women

325

who, because they feel with so much more force the sweetness of a moment, make of it, with a delicacy, a nobility of which normally constituted creatures are incapable, a compelling masterpiece of grace and goodness, and have no longer anything of themselves left to give when the next moment has arrived. Their affection does not outlive the exaltation that has dictated it; and the subtlety of mind which had then led them to divine all the things that you wished to hear and to say them to you will permit them just as easily, a few days later, to seize hold of your absurdities and use them to entertain another of their visitors with whom they will then be in the act of enjoying one of those " musical moments " which are so brief.

In the hall where I asked a footman for my snowboots which I had brought as a precaution against the snow, several flakes of which had already fallen, to be converted rapidly into slush, not having realised that they were hardly fashionable, I felt, at the contemptuous smile on all sides, a shame which rose to its highest pitch when I saw that Mme. de Parme had not gone and was watching me put on my American " rubbers ". The Princess came towards me. " Oh! What a good idea," she exclaimed, " it's so practical! There's a sensible man for you. Madame, we shall have to get a pair of those," she went on to her lady in waiting, while the mockery of the footmen turned to respect and the other guests crowded round me to inquire where I had managed to find these marvels. " With those on, you will have nothing to fear even if it starts snowing again and you have a long way to go. You're independent of the weather," said the Princess to me. " Oh! If it comes to that, your Royal Highness can

be reassured," broke in the lady in waiting with a knowing air, " it will not snow again." " What do you know
about it, Madame? " came witheringly from the excellent
Princesse de Parme, who alone could succeed in piercing
the thick skin of her lady in waiting. " I can assure your
Royal Highness, it cannot snow again. It is a physical
impossibility." " But why? " " It cannot snow any more,
they have taken the necessary steps to prevent it, they
have put down salt in the streets! " The simple-minded
lady did not observe either the anger of the Princess or
the mirth of the rest of her audience, for instead of remaining silent she said to me with a genial smile, paying
no heed to my repeated denials of any connexion with
Admiral Jurien de la Gravière: " Not that it matters,
after all. This gentleman must have stout sea-legs.
What's bred in the bone! "

Then, having escorted the Princesse de Parme to her
carriage, M. de Guermantes said to me, taking hold of
my greatcoat: " Let me help you into your skin." He had
ceased even to smile when he employed this expression,
for those that were most vulgar had for that very reason,
because of the Guermantes affection of simplicity, become
aristocratic.

An exaltation that sank only into melancholy, because
it was artificial, was what I also, although quite differently from Mme. de Guermantes, felt once I had finally
left her house, in the carriage that was taking me to that
of M. de Charlus. We can at pleasure abandon ourselves
to one or other of two forces, of which one rises in ourselves, emanates from our deepest impressions, the other
comes to us from without. The first carries with it naturally a joy, the joy that springs from the life of the

creator. The other current, that which endeavours to introduce into us the movement by which persons external to ourselves are stirred, is not accompanied by pleasure; but we can add a pleasure to it, by the shock of reaction, in an intoxication so feigned that it turns swiftly into boredom, into melancholy, whence the gloomy faces of so many men of fashion, and all those nervous conditions which may make them end in suicide. Well, in the carriage which was taking me to M. de Charlus, I was a prey to this second sort of exaltation, widely different from that which is given us by a personal impression, such as I had received in other carriages, once at Combray, in Dr. Percepied's gig, from which I had seen painted against the setting sun the spires of Martinville, another day at Balbec, in Mme. de Villeparisis's barouche, when I strove to identify the reminiscence that was suggested to me by an avenue of trees. But in this third carriage, what I had before my mind's eye were those conversations that had seemed to me so tedious at Mme. de Guermantes's dinner-table, for example Prince Von's stories about the German Emperor, General Botha and the British Army. I had slipped them into the frame of the internal stereoscope through the lenses of which, once we are no longer ourselves, once, endowed with the spirit of society, we no longer wish to receive our life save from other people, we cast into relief what they have said and done. Like a tipsy man filled with tender feeling for the waiter who has been serving him, I marvelled at my good fortune, a good fortune not realised by me, it is true, at the actual moment, in having dined with a person who knew William II so well, and had told stories about him that were—upon my word—really witty. And, as I repeated to myself, with the Prince's German accent, the story of General Botha, I laughed out loud, as though this laugh, like certain kinds of applause which increase one's inward admiration, were necessary to the story as a corroboration of its comic element. Through the magnifying lenses even those of Mme. de Guermantes's pronouncements which had struck me as being stupid (as for example that on the Hals pictures which one ought to see from the top of a tramway-car) took on a life, a depth that were extraordinary. And I must say that, even if this exaltation was quick to subside, it was not altogether unreasonable. Just as there may always come a day when we are glad to know the person whom we despise more than anyone in the world because he happens to be connected with a girl with whom we are in love, to whom he can introduce us, and thus offers us both utility and gratification, attributes in each of which we should have supposed him to be entirely lacking, so there is no conversation, any more than there are personal relations, from which we can be certain that we shall not one day derive some benefit. What Mme. de Guermantes had said to me about the pictures which it would be interesting to see, even from a tramway-car, was untrue, but it contained a germ of truth which was of value to me later on.

Similarly the lines of Victor Hugo which I had heard her quote were, it must be admitted, of a period earlier than that in which he became something more than a new man, in which he brought to light, in the order of evolution, a literary species till then unknown, endowed with more complex organs than any then in existence. In these first poems, Victor Hugo is still a thinker, instead of contenting himself, like Nature, with supplying food for thought. His "thoughts" he at that time expressed in the most direct form, almost in the sense in which the Duke employed the word when, feeling it to be out of date and a nuisance that the guests at his big parties at Guermantes should, in the visitors' book, append to their signatures a philosophico-poetical reflexion, he used to warn novices in an appealing tone: "Your name, my dear fellow, but no 'thoughts', please!" Well, it was these "thoughts" of Victor Hugo (almost as entirely absent from the *Légende des Siècles* as "airs", as "melodies" are from Wagner's later manner) that Mme. de Guermantes admired in the early Hugo. Nor was she altogether wrong. They were touching, and already round about them, without their form's having yet the depth which it was to acquire only in later years, the rolling tide of words and of richly articulated rhymes put them beyond comparison with the lines that one might discover in a Corneille, for example, lines in which a Romanticism that is intermittent, restrained and so all the more moving, nevertheless has not at all penetrated to the physical sources of life, modified the unconscious and generalisable organism in which the idea is latent. And so I had been wrong in confining myself, hitherto, to the later volumes of Hugo. Of the earlier, of course, it was only a fractional part that Mme. de Guermantes used to embellish her conversation. But simply by quoting in this way an isolated line one multiplies its power of attraction tenfold. The lines that had entered or returned to my mind during this dinner magnetised in turn, summoned to themselves with such force the poems in the heart of which they were normally embedded, that my magnetised hands could not hold out for longer than forty-eight hours against the force that drew them towards the volume in which were bound up the *Orientales* and the *Chants du Crépuscule*. I cursed Françoise's footman for having made a present to his native village of my copy of the *Feuilles d'Antomne,* and sent him off, with not a moment to be lost, to procure me another. I read these volumes from cover to cover and found peace of mind only when I suddenly came across, awaiting me in the light in which she had bathed them, the lines that I had heard Mme. de Guermantes quote. For all these reasons, conversations with the Duchess resembled the discoveries that we make in the library of a country house, out of date, incomplete, incapable of forming a mind, lacking in almost everything that we value, but offering us now and then some curious scrap of information, for instance the quotation of a fine passage which we did not know and as to which we are glad to remember in after years that we owe our knowledge of it to a stately mansion of the great. We are then, by having found Balzac's preface to the *Chartreuse,* or some unpublished letters of Joubert, tempted to exaggerate the value of the life we led there, the sterile frivolity of which, for this windfall of a single evening, we forget.

From this point of view, if the fashionable world had been unable, at the first moment, to provide what my imagination expected, and must consequently strike me first of all by what it had in common with all the other worlds rather than by its difference, still it revealed itself to me by degrees as something quite distinct. Great noblemen are almost the only people from whom one learns as much as one does from peasants ; their conversation is adorned with everything that concerns the land, houses, as people used to live in them long ago, old customs, everything of which the world of money is profoundly ignorant. Even supposing that the aristocrat most moderate in his aspirations has finally overtaken the period in which he lives, his mother, his uncles, his great-aunts keep him in touch, when he recalls his childhood, with the conditions of a life almost unknown to-day. In the death-chamber of a contemporary corpse Mme. de Guermantes would not have pointed out, but would immediately have perceived all the lapses from the traditional customs. She was shocked to see at a funeral women mingling with the men, when there was a particular ceremony which ought to be celebrated for the women. As for the pall, the use of which Bloch would doubtless have believed to be confined to coffins, on account of the pall bearers of whom one reads in the reports of funerals, M. de Guermantes could remember the time when, as a child, he had seen it borne at the wedding of M. de Mailly-Nesle. While Saint-Loup had sold his priceless "Genealogical Tree", old portraits of the Bouillons, letters of Louis XIII, in order to buy Carrières and furniture in the modern style, M. and Mme. de Guermantes, moved by a sentiment in which the burning love of art may have played only a minor part, and which left them themselves more insignificant than before, had kept their marvellous Boule furniture, which presented a picture attractive in a different way to an artist. A literary man would similarly have been enchanted by their conversation, which would have been for him—for one hungry man has no need of another to keep him company—a living dictionary of all those expressions which every day are becoming more and more forgotten: Saint-Joseph cravats, children dedicated to the Blue, and so forth, which one finds to-day only among those people who have constituted themselves the friendly and benevolent custodians of the past. The pleasure that a writer, more than among other writers, feels among them is not without danger, for there is a risk of his coming to believe that the things of the past have a charm in themselves, of his transferring them bodily into his work, still-born in that case, exhaling a tedium for which he consoles himself with the reflexion: " It is attractive because it's true; that is how people do talk." These aristocratic conversations had moreover the charm, with Mme. de Guermantes, of being couched in excellent French. For this reason they made permissible on the Duchess's part her hilarity at the words " viaticum ", " cosmic ", " pythian ", " pre-eminent ", which Saint-Loup used to employ—as, similarly, at his Bing furniture.

When all was said, very different in this respect from what I had been able to feel before the hawthorns, or when I tasted a crumb of *madeleine,* the stories that I had heard at Mme. de Guermantes's remained alien to me. Entering for a moment into me, who was only physically possessed by them, one would have said that, being of a social, not an individual nature, they were impatient to escape. I writhed in my seat in the carriage like the priestess of an oracle. I looked forward to another dinner-party at which I might myself become a sort of Prince Von to Mme. de Guermantes, and repeat them. In the mean time they made my lips quiver as I stammered them to myself, and I tried in vain to bring back and concentrate a mind that was carried away by a centrifugal force. And so it was with a feverish impatience not to have to bear the whole weight of them any longer by myself in

a carriage where, for that matter, I atoned for the lack
of conversation by soliloquising aloud, that I rang the
bell at M. de Charlus's door, and it was in long monologues with myself, in which I rehearsed everything that
I was going to tell him and gave scarcely a thought to
what he might have to say to me, that I spent the whole
of the time during which I was kept waiting in a drawing-
room into which a footman shewed me and where I was
incidentally too much excited to look at what it contained.
I felt so urgent a need that M. de Charlus should listen
to the stories which I was burning to tell him that I was
bitterly disappointed to think that the master of the
house was perhaps in bed, and that I might have to go
home to sleep off by myself my drunkenness of words. I
had just noticed, in fact, that I had been twenty-five
minutes—that they had perhaps forgotten about me—in
this room of which, despite this long wait, I could at the
most have said that it was very big, greenish in colour,
and contained a large number of portraits. The need to
speak prevents one not merely from listening but from
seeing things, and in this case the absence of any description of my external surroundings is tantamount to a description of my internal state. I was preparing to leave
the room to try to get hold of some one, and if I found
no one to make my way back to the hall and have myself
let out, when, just as I had risen from my chair and
taken a few steps across the mosaic parquet of the floor,
a manservant came in, with a troubled expression: "Monsieur le Baron has been engaged all evening, Sir," he told
me. "There are still several people waiting to see him. I
am doing everything I possibly can to get him to receive
you, I have already telephoned up twice to the secretary."

"No; please don't bother. I had an appointment with M. le Baron, but it is very late already, and if he is busy this evening I can come back another day." "Oh no, Sir, you must not go away," cried the servant. "M. le Baron might be vexed. I will try again." I was reminded of the things I had heard about M. de Charlus's servants and their devotion to their master. One could not quite say of him as of the Prince de Conti that he sought to give pleasure as much to the valet as to the Minister, but he had shewn such skill in making of the least thing that he asked of them a sort of personal favour that at night, when, his body-servants assembled round him at a respectful distance, after running his eye over them he said: "Coignet, the candlestick!" or "Ducret, the nightshirt!" it was with an envious murmur that the rest used to withdraw, jealous of him who had been singled out by his master's favour. Two of them, indeed, who could not abide one another, used to try to snatch the favour each from his rival by going on the most flimsy pretext with a message to the Baron, if he had gone upstairs earlier than usual, in the hope of being invested for the evening with the charge of candlestick or nightshirt. If he addressed a few words directly to one of them on some subject outside the scope of his duty, still more if in winter, in the garden, knowing that one of his coachmen had caught cold, he said to him, after ten minutes: "Put your cap on!" the others would not speak to the fellow again for a fortnight, in their jealousy of the great distinction that had been conferred on him. I waited ten minutes more, and then, after requesting me not to stay too long as M. le Baron was tired and had had to send away several most important people who had made ap-

pointments with him many days before, they admitted
me to his presence. This setting with which M. de Charlus
surrounded himself seemed to me a great deal less impressive than the simplicity of his brother Guermantes,
but already the door stood open, I could see the Baron,
in a Chinese dressing-gown, with his throat bare, lying
upon a sofa. My eye was caught at the same moment
by a tall hat, its nap flashing like a mirror, which had
been left on a chair with a cape, as though the Baron
had but recently come in. The valet withdrew. I supposed that M. de Charlus would rise to greet me. Without moving a muscle he fixed on me a pair of implacable
eyes. I went towards him, I said good evening; he did
not hold out his hand, made no reply, did not ask me
to take a chair. After a moment's silence I asked him, as
one would ask an ill-mannered doctor, whether it was
necessary for me to remain standing. I said this without
any evil intention, but my words seemed only to intensify
the cold fury on M. de Charlus's face. I was not aware,
as it happened, that at home, in the country, at the
Château de Charlus, he was in the habit, after dinner
(so much did he love to play the king), of sprawling in
an armchair in the smoking-room, letting his guests remain standing round him. He would ask for a light from
one, offer a cigar to another and then, after a few minutes' interval, would say: "But Argencourt, why don't
you sit down? Take a chair, my dear fellow," and so
forth, having made a point of keeping them standing
simply to remind them that it was from himself that permission came to them to be seated. "Put yourself in the
Louis XIV seat," he answered me with an imperious air,
as though rather to force me to move away farther from

himself than to invite me to be seated. I took an armchair which was comparatively near. "Ah! so that is what you call a Louis XIV seat, is it? I can see you have been well educated," he cried in derision. I was so much taken aback that I did not move, either to leave the house, as I ought to have done, or to change my seat, as he wished. " Sir," he next said to me, weighing each of his words, to the more impertinent of which he prefixed a double yoke of consonants, " the interview which I have condescended to grant you at the request of a person who desires to be nameless, will mark the final point in our relations. I shall not conceal from you that I had hoped for better things! I should perhaps be forcing the sense of the words a little, which one ought not to do, even with people who are ignorant of their value, simply out of the respect due to oneself, were I to tell you that I had felt a certain *attraction* towards you. I think, however, that *benevolence,* in its most actively protecting sense, would exceed neither what I felt nor what I was proposing to display. I had, immediately on my return to Paris, given you to understand, while you were still at Balbec, that you could count upon me." I who remembered with what a torrent of abuse M. de Charlus had parted from me at Balbec made an instinctive gesture of contradiction. "What!" he cried with fury, and indeed his face, convulsed and white, differed as much from his ordinary face as does the sea when on a morning of storm one finds instead of its customary smiling surface a thousand serpents writhing in spray and foam, " do you mean to pretend that you did not receive my message—almost a declaration—that you were to remember me? What was there in the way of decoration round the cover of the

book that I sent you?" "Some very pretty twined gar-
lands with tooled ornaments," I told him. "Ah!" he
replied, with an air of scorn, "these young Frenchmen
know little of the treasures of our land. What would be
said of a young Berliner who had never heard of the
Walküre? Besides, you must have eyes to see and see not,
since you yourself told me that you had stood for two
hours in front of that particular treasure. I can see that
you know no more about flowers than you do about styles;
don't protest that you know about styles," he cried in a
shrill scream of rage, "you can't even tell me what you
are sitting on. You offer your hindquarters a Directory
chauffeuse as a Louis XIV *bergère.* One of these days
you'll be mistaking Mme. de Villeparisis's knees for the
seat of the rear, and a fine mess you'll make of things
then. It's precisely the same; you didn't even recognise
on the binding of Bergotte's book the lintel of myosotis
over the door of Balbec church. Could there be any
clearer way of saying to you: 'Forget me not!'?"

I looked at M. de Charlus. Undoubtedly his magnificent
head, though repellent, yet far surpassed that of any of
his relatives; you would have called him an Apollo grown
old; but an olive-hued, bilious juice seemed ready to
start from the corners of his evil mouth; as for intellect,
one could not deny that his, over a vast compass, had
taken in many things which must always remain unknown
to his brother Guermantes. But whatever the fine words
with which he coloured all his hatreds, one felt that, even
if there was now an offended pride, now a disappointment
in love, or a rancour, or sadism, a love of teasing, a fixed
obsession, this man was capable of doing murder, and of
proving by force of logic that he had been right in doing

it and was still superior by a hundred cubits in moral stature to his brother, his sister-in-law, or any of the rest. "Just as, in Velazquez's *Lances*," he went on, "the victor advances towards him who is the humbler in rank, as is the duty of every noble nature, since I was everything and you were nothing, it was I who took the first steps towards you. You have made an idiotic reply to what it is not for me to describe as an act of greatness. But I have not allowed myself to be discouraged. Our religion inculcates patience. The patience I have shewn towards you will be counted, I hope, to my credit, and also my having only smiled at what might be denounced as impertinence, were it within your power to offer any impertinence to me who surpass you in stature by so many cubits; but after all, Sir, all this is now neither here nor there. I have subjected you to the test which the one eminent man of our world has ingeniously named the test of excessive friendliness, and which he rightly declares to be the most terrible of all, the only one that can separate the good grain from the tares. I could scarcely reproach you for having undergone it without success, for those who emerge from it triumphant are very few. But at least, and this is the conclusion which I am entitled to draw from the last words that we shall exchange on this earth, at least I intend to hear nothing more of your calumnious fabrications." So far, I had never dreamed that M. de Charlus's rage could have been caused by an unflattering remark which had been repeated to him; I searched my memory; I had not spoken about him to anyone. Some evil-doer had invented the whole thing. I protested to M. de Charlus that I had said absolutely nothing about him. "I don't think I can have annoyed you by saying to Mme. de Guermantes that I was a friend of yours." He gave a disdainful smile, made his voice climb to the supreme pitch of its highest register, and there, without strain, attacking the shrillest and most insolent note: "Oh! Sir," he said, returning by the most gradual stages to a natural intonation, and seeming to revel as he went in the oddities of this descending scale, "I think that you are doing yourself an injustice when you accuse yourself of having said that we were *friends*. I do not look for any great verbal accuracy in anyone who could readily mistake a piece of Chippendale for a rococo *chaire,* but really I do not believe," he went on, with vocal caresses that grew more and more winning and brought to hover over his lips what was actually a charming smile, "I do not believe that you can ever have said, or thought, that we were *friends*! As for your having boasted that you had been *presented* to me, had *talked* to me, *knew* me slightly, had obtained, almost without solicitation, the prospect of coming one day under my *protection,* I find it on the contrary very natural and intelligent of you to have done so. The extreme difference in age that there is between us enables me to recognise without absurdity that that *presentation,* those *talks,* that vague prospect of future *relations* were for you, it is not for me to say an honour, but still, when all is said and done, an advantage as to which I consider that your folly lay not in divulging it but in not having had the sense to keep it. I will go so far as to say," he went on, passing abruptly for a moment from his arrogant wrath to a gentleness so tinged with melancholy that I expected him to burst into tears, "that when you left unanswered the proposal I made to you here in Paris it seemed to me so unheard-of an act on your part, coming from you who had struck me as well brought up and of a good *bourgeois* family," (on this adjective alone his voice sounded a little whistle of impertinence) " that I was foolish enough to imagine all the excuses that never really happen, letters miscarrying, addresses copied down wrong. I can see that on my part it was great foolishness, but Saint Bonaventure preferred to believe that an ox could fly rather than that his brother was capable of lying. Anyhow, that is all finished now, the idea did not attract you, there is no more to be said. It seems to me only that you might have brought yourself," (and there was a genuine sound of weeping in his voice) " were it only out of consideration for my age, to write to me. I had conceived and planned for you certain infinitely seductive things, which I had taken good care not to tell you. You have preferred to refuse without knowing what they were; that is your affair. But, as I tell you, one can always *write*. In your place, and indeed in my own, I should have done so. I like my place, for that reason, better than yours—I say ' for that reason ' because I believe that we are all equal, and I have more fellow-feeling for an intelligent labourer than for many of our dukes. But I can say that I prefer my place to yours, because what you have done, in the whole course of my life, which is beginning now to be a pretty long one, I am conscious that I have never done." His head was turned away from the light, and I could not see if his eyes were dropping tears as I might have supposed from his voice. " I told you that I had taken a hundred steps towards you; the only effect of that has been to make you retire two hundred from me. Now it is for me to withdraw, and we shall know one another no longer. I shall retain not your name but your story, so that at moments when I might be tempted to believe that men have good hearts, good manners, or simply the intelligence not to allow an unparalleled opportunity to escape them, I may remember that that is ranking them too highly. No, that you should have said that you knew me, when it was true—for henceforward it ceases to be true—I regard that as only natural, and I take it as an act of homage, that is to say something pleasant. Unfortunately, elsewhere and in other circumstances, you have uttered remarks of a very different nature." "Sir, I swear to you that I have said nothing that could insult you." "And who says that I am insulted?" he cried with fury, flinging himself into an erect posture on the seat on which hitherto he had been reclining motionless, while, as the pale frothing serpents stiffened in his face, his voice became alternately shrill and grave, like the deafening onrush of a storm. (The force with which he habitually spoke, which used to make strangers turn round in the street, was multiplied an hundredfold, as is a musical *forte* if, instead of being played on the piano, it is played by an orchestra, and changed into a *fortissimo* as well. M. de Charlus roared.) "Do you suppose that it is within your power to insult me? You evidently are not aware to whom you are speaking? Do you imagine that the envenomed spittle of five hundred little gentlemen of your type, heaped one upon another, would succeed in slobbering so much as the tips of my august toes?" A moment before this my desire to persuade M. de Charlus that I had never said, nor heard anyone else say any evil of him had given place to a mad rage, caused by the words which were dictated to him solely, to my mind, by his colossal pride. Perhaps they were indeed the effect, in part at any rate, of this pride. Almost all the rest sprang from a feeling of which I was then still ignorant, and for which I could not therefore be blamed for not making due allowance. I could at least, failing this unknown element, have mingled with his pride, had I remembered the words of Mme. de Guermantes, a trace of madness. But at that moment the idea of madness never even entered my head. There was in him, according to me, only pride, in me there was only fury. This fury (at the moment when M. de Charlus ceased to shout, in order to refer to his august toes, with a majesty that was accompanied by a grimace, a nausea of disgust at his obscure blasphemers), this fury could contain itself no longer. With an impulsive movement, I wanted to strike something, and, a lingering trace of discernment making me respect the person of a man so much older than myself, and even, in view of their dignity as works of art, the pieces of German porcelain that were grouped around him, I flung myself upon the Baron's new silk hat, dashed it to the ground, trampled upon it, began blindly pulling it to pieces, wrenched off the brim, tore the crown in two, without heeding the vociferations of M. de Charlus, which continued to sound, and, crossing the room to leave it, opened the door. One on either side of it, to my intense stupefaction, stood two footmen, who moved slowly away, so as to appear only to have been casually passing in the course of their duty. (I afterwards learned their names; one was called Burnier, the other Charmel.) I was not taken in for a moment by this explanation which their leisurely gait seemed to offer me. It was highly improbable; three others appeared

to me to be less so; one that the Baron sometimes entertained guests against whom, as he might happen to need
assistance (but why?), he deemed it necessary to keep
reinforcements posted close at hand. The second was that,
drawn by curiosity, they had stopped to listen at the
keyhole, not thinking that I should come out so quickly.
The third, that, the whole of the scene which M. de
Charlus had made with me having been prepared and
acted, he had himself told them to listen, from a love of
the spectacular combined, perhaps, with a "*nunc erudim-
ini*" from which each would derive a suitable profit.

My anger had not calmed that of M. de Charlus, my
departure from the room seemed to cause him acute
distress; he called me back, made his servants call me
back, and finally, forgetting that a moment earlier, when
he spoke of his "august toes", he had thought to make
me a witness of his own deification, came running after
me at full speed, overtook me in the hall, and stood
barring the door. "There, now," he said, "don't be
childish; come back for a minute; he that loveth well
chasteneth well, and if I have chastened you well it is
because I love you well." My anger had subsided; I let
the word "chasten" pass, and followed the Baron, who,
summoning a footman, ordered him without a trace of self-
consciousness to clear away the remains of the shattered
hat, which was replaced by another. "If you will tell
me, Sir, who it is that has treacherously maligned me," I
said to M. de Charlus, "I will stay here to learn his
name and to confute the impostor." "Who? Do you not
know? Do you retain no memory of the things you say?
Do you think that the people who do me the service of
informing me of those things do not begin by demanding

secrecy? And do you imagine that I am going to betray a person to whom I have given my promise?" "Sir, is it impossible then for you to tell me?" I asked, racking my brains in a final effort to discover (and discovering no one) to whom I could have spoken about M. de Charlus. "You did not hear me say that I had given a promise of secrecy to my informant?" he said in a snapping voice. "I see that with your fondness for abject utterances you combine one for futile persistence. You ought to have at least the intelligence to profit by a final conversation, and so to speak as to say something that does not mean precisely nothing." "Sir," I replied, moving away from him, "you insult me; I am unarmed, because you are several times my age, we are not equally matched; on the other hand, I cannot convince you; I have already sworn to you that I have said nothing." "I am lying, then, am I?" he cried in a terrifying tone, and with a bound forwards that brought him within a yard of myself. "Some one has misinformed you." Then in a gentle, affectionate, melancholy voice, as in those symphonies which are played without any break between the different movements, in which a graceful *scherzo,* amiable and idyllic, follows the thunder-peals of the opening pages: "It is quite possible," he told me. "Generally speaking, a remark repeated at second hand is rarely true. It is your fault if, not having profited by the opportunities of seeing me which I had held out to you, you have not furnished me, by that open speech of daily intercourse which creates confidence, with the unique and sovereign remedy against a spoken word which made you out a traitor. Either way, true or false, the remark has done its work. I can never again rid myself of the impression it made on me. I cannot even say that he who chasteneth well loveth well, for I have chastened you well enough but I no longer love you." While saying this he had forced me to sit down and had rung the bell. A different footman appeared. " Bring something to drink and order the brougham." I said that I was not thirsty and besides had a carriage waiting. "They have probably paid him and sent him away," he told me, " you needn't worry about that. I am ordering a carriage to take you home. . . . If you're anxious about the time . . . I could have given you a room here. . . ." I said that my mother would be uneasy. "Ah! Of course, yes. Well, true or false, the remark has done its work. My affection, a trifle premature, had flowered too soon, and, like those apple trees of which you spoke so poetically at Balbec, it has been unable to withstand the first frost." If M. de Charlus's affection for me had not been destroyed, he could hardly have acted differently, since, while assuring me that we were no longer acquainted, he made me sit down, drink, asked me to stay the night, and was going now to send me home. He had indeed an air of dreading the moment at which he must part from me and find himself alone, that sort of slightly anxious fear which his sister-in-law and cousin Guermantes had appeared to me to be feeling when she had tried to force me to stay a little longer, with something of the same momentary fondness for myself, of the same effort to prolong the passing minute. " Unfortunately," he went on, " I have not the power to make blossom again what has once been destroyed. My affection for you is quite dead. Nothing can revive it. I believe that it is not unworthy of me to confess that I regret it. I always feel myself to be a little like Victor

Hugo's Boaz: ' I am widowed and alone, and the darkness gathers o'er me.' "

I passed again with him through the big green drawing-room. I told him, speaking quite at random, how beautiful I thought it. "Ain't it?" he replied. "It's a good thing to be fond of something. The woodwork is Bagard. What is rather charming, d'you see, is that it was made to match the Beauvais chairs and the consoles. You observe, it repeats the same decorative design. There used to be only two places where you could see this, the Louvre and M. d'Hinnisdal's house. But naturally, as soon as I had decided to come and live in this street, there cropped up an old family house of the Chimays which nobody had ever seen before because it came here expressly for *me*. On the whole, it's good. It might perhaps be better, but after all it's not bad. Some pretty things, ain't there? These are portraits of my uncles, the King of Poland and the King of England, by Mignard. But why am I telling you all this? You must know it as well as I do, you were waiting in this room. No? Ah, then they must have put you in the blue drawing-room," he said with an air that might have been either impertinence, on the score of my want of interest, or personal superiority, in not having taken the trouble to ask where I had been kept waiting. "Look now, in this cabinet I have all the hats worn by Mlle. Elisabeth, by the Princesse de Lamballe, and by the Queen. They don't interest you, one would think you couldn't see. Perhaps you are suffering from an affection of the optic nerve. If you like this kind of beauty better, here is a rainbow by Turner beginning to shine out between these two Rembrandts, as a sign of our reconciliation. You hear: Beethoven

347

has come to join him." And indeed one could hear the
first chords of the third part of the Pastoral Symphony,
" Joy after the Storm ", performed somewhere not far
away, on the first landing no doubt, by a band of musicians. I innocently inquired how they happened to be
playing that, and who the musicians were. " Ah, well,
one doesn't know. One never does know. They are un-
seen music. Pretty, ain't it? " he said to me in a slightly
impertinent tone, which, nevertheless, suggested somehow
the influence and accent of Swann. " But you care about
as much for it as a fish does for little apples. You want
to go home, regardness of any want of respect for Beethoven or for me. You are uttering your own judgment
and condemnation," he added, with an affectionate and
mournful air, when the moment had come for me to go.
" You will excuse my not accompanying you home, as
good manners ordain that I should," he said to me.
" Since I have decided not to see you again, spending
five minutes more in your company would make very
little difference to me. But I am tired, and I have a great
deal to do." And then, seeing that it was a fine night:
" Very well, yes, I will come in the carriage, there is a
superb moon which I shall go on to admire from the
Bois after I have taken you home. What, you don't know
how to shave; even on a night when you've been dining
out, you have still a few hairs here," he said, taking
my chin between two fingers, so to speak magnetised,
which after a moment's resistance ran up to my ears,
like the fingers of a barber. " Ah! It would be pleasant
to look at the ' blue light of the moon ' in the Bois with
some one like yourself," he said to me with a sudden
and almost involuntary gentleness, then, in a sadder tone:

" For you are nice, all the same; you could be nicer than anyone," he went on, laying his hand in a fatherly way on my shoulder. " Originally, I must say that I found you quite insignificant." I ought to have reflected that he must find me so still. I had only to recall the rage with which he had spoken to me, barely half-an-hour before. In spite of this I had the impression that he was, for the moment, sincere, that his kindness of heart was prevailing over what I regarded as an almost delirious condition of susceptibility and pride. The carriage was waiting beside us, and still he prolonged the conversation. " Come along," he said abruptly, " jump in, in five minutes we shall be at your door. And I shall bid you a good night which will cut short our relations, and for all time. It is better, since we must part for ever, that we should do so, as in music, on a perfect chord." Despite these solemn affirmations that we should never see one another again, I could have sworn that M. de Charlus, annoyed at having forgotten himself earlier in the evening and afraid of having hurt my feelings, would not have been displeased to see me once again. Nor was I mistaken, for, a moment later: " There, now," he said, " if I hadn't forgotten the most important thing of all. In memory of your grandmother, I have had bound for you a curious edition of Mme. de Sévigné. That is what is going to prevent this from being our last meeting. One must console oneself with the reflexion that complicated affairs are rarely settled in a day. Just look how long they took over the Congress of Vienna." " But I could call for it without disturbing you," I said obligingly. " Will you hold your tongue, you little fool," he replied with anger, " and not give yourself the grotesque appearance of regarding as a small matter the honour of being probably (I do not say certainly, for it will perhaps be one of my servants who hands you the volumes) received by me." Then, regaining possession of himself: "I do not wish to part from you on these words. No dissonance, before the eternal silence of the dominant." It was for his own nerves that he seemed to dread an immediate return home after harsh words of dissension. "You would not care to come to the Bois?" he addressed me in a tone not so much interrogative as affirmative, and that not, as it seemed to me, because he did not wish to make me the offer but because he was afraid that his self-esteem might meet with a refusal. "Oh, very well," he went on, still postponing our separation, "it is the moment when, as Whistler says, the *bourgeois* go to bed" (perhaps he wished now to capture me by my self-esteem) "and the right time to begin to look at things. But you don't even know who Whistler was!" I changed the conversation and asked him whether the Princesse d'Iéna was an intelligent person. M. de Charlus stopped me, and, adopting the most contemptuous tone that I had yet heard him use, "Oh! There, Sir," he informed me, "you are alluding to an order of nomenclature with which I have no concern. There is perhaps an aristocracy among the Tahitians, but I must confess that I know nothing about it. The name which you have just mentioned, strangely enough, did sound in my ears only a few days ago. Some one asked me whether I would condescend to allow them to present to me the young Duc de Guastalla. The request astonished me, for the Duc de Guastalla has no need to get himself presented to me, for the simple reason that he is my cousin, and has known me all his life;

he is the son of the Princesse de Parme, and, as a young
kinsman of good upbringing, he never fails to come and
pay his respects to me on New Year's Day. But, on
making inquiries, I discovered that it was not my relative
who was meant but the son of the person in whom you
are interested. As there exists no Princess of that title,
I supposed that my friend was referring to some poor
wanton sleeping under the Pont d'Iéna, who had pic-
turesquely assumed the title of Princesse d'Iéna, just as
one talks about the Panther of the Batignolles, or the
Steel King. But no, the reference was to a rich person who
possesses some remarkable furniture which I had seen
and admired at an exhibition, and which has this advantage over the name of its owner that it is genuine.
As for this self-styled Duc de Guastalla, he, I supposed,
must be my secretary's stockbroker; one can procure so
many things with money. But no; it was the Emperor,
it appears, who amused himself by conferring on these
people a title which simply was not his to give. It was
perhaps a sign of power, or of ignorance, or of malice;
in any case, I consider, it was an exceedingly scurvy trick
to play on these unconscious usurpers. But really, I
cannot help you by throwing any light on the matter;
my knowledge begins and ends with the Faubourg Saint-
Germain, where, among all the Courvoisiers and Gallar-
dons, you will find, if you can manage to secure an introduction, plenty of mangy old cats taken straight out
of Balzac who will amuse you. Naturally, all that has
nothing to do with the position of the Princesse de Guermantes, but without me and my ' Open, Sesame ' her
portals are unapproachable." " It is really very lovely,
isn't it, Sir, the Princesse de Guermantes's mansion? "

"Oh, it's not very lovely. It's the loveliest thing in the world. Next to the Princess herself, of course." "The Princesse de Guermantes is better than the Duchesse de Guermantes?" "Oh! There's no comparison." (It is to be observed that, whenever people in society have the least touch of imagination, they will crown or dethrone, to suit their affections or their quarrels, those whose position appeared most solid and unalterably fixed.)

"The Duchesse de Guermantes" (possibly, in not calling her "Oriane", he wished to set a greater distance between her and myself) "is delightful, far superior to anything you can have guessed. But, after all, she is incommensurable with her cousin. The Princess is exactly what the people in the Markets might imagine Princess Metternich to have been, but old Metternich believed she had started Wagner, because she knew Victor Maurel. The Princesse de Guermantes, or rather her mother, knew the man himself. Which is a distinction, not to mention the incredible beauty of the lady. And the Esther gardens alone!" "One can't see them?" "No, you would have to be invited, but they never invite *anyone* unless I intervene." But at once withdrawing, after casting it at me, the bait of this offer, he held out his hand, for we had reached my door. "My part is played, Sir, I will simply add these few words. Another person will perhaps some day offer you his affection, as I have done. Let the present example serve for your instruction. Do not neglect it. Affection is always precious. What one cannot do by oneself in this life, because there are things which one cannot ask, nor do, nor wish, nor learn by oneself, one can do in company, and without needing to be Thirteen, as in Balzac's story, or Four, as in *The Three Musketeers.*

Good-bye."

He must have been feeling tired and have abandoned the idea of going to look at the moonlight, for he asked me to tell his coachman to drive home. At once he made a sharp movement as though he had changed his mind. But I had already given the order, and, so as not to lose any more time, went across now to ring the bell, without its entering my head that I had been meaning to tell M. de Charlus, about the German Emperor and General Botha, stories which had been an hour ago such an obsession but which his unexpected and crushing reception had sent flying far out of my mind.

On entering my room I saw on my desk a letter which Françoise's young footman had written to one of his friends and had left lying there. Now that my mother was away, there was no liberty which he had the least hesitation in taking; I was the more to blame of the two for taking that of reading the letter which, without an envelope, lay spread out before me and (which was my sole excuse) seemed to offer itself to my eye.

"Dear Friend and Cousin,

"I hope this finds you in good health, and the same with all the young folk, particularly my young godson Joseph whom I have not yet had the pleasure of meeting but whom I prefer to you all as being my godson, these relics of the heart they have their dust also, upon their blest remains let us not lay our hands. Besides dear friend and cousin who can say that to-morrow you and your dear wife my cousin Marie, will not both of you be cast headlong down into the bottom of the sea, like the sailor clinging to the mast on high, for this life is but a dark valley. Dear friend I must tell you that my principal occupation, which will astonish you I am certain, is now poetry which I love passionately, for one must somehow pass the time away. And so dear friend do not be too surprised if I have not answered your last letter before now, in place of pardon let oblivion come. As you are aware, Madame's mother has passed away amid unspeakable sufferings which fairly exhausted her as she saw as many as three doctors. The day of her interment was a great day for all Monsieur's relations came in crowds as well as several Ministers. It took them more than two hours to get to the cemetery, which will make you all open your eyes pretty wide in your village for they certainly won't do as much for mother Michu. So all my life to come can be but one long sob. I am amusing myself enormously with the motorcycle of which I have recently learned. What would you say, my dear friends, if I arrived suddenly like that at full speed at Les Ecorces. But on that head I shall no more keep silence for I feel that the frenzy of grief sweeps its reason away. I am associating with the Duchesse de Guermantes, people whose very names you have never heard in our ignorant villages. Therefore it is with pleasure that I am going to send the works of Racine, of Victor Hugo, of Pages Choisies de Chenedolle, of Alfred de Musset, for I would cure the land in which I saw the light of ignorance which leads unerringly to crime. I can think of nothing more to say to you and send you like the pelican wearied by a long flight my best regards as well as to your wife my godson and your sister Rose. May it never be said of her: And Rose she lived only as live the roses, as has been said by Victor Hugo, the sonnet of Arvers, Alfred de Musset, all those great geniuses who for that cause have had to die upon the blazing scaffold like Jeanne d'Arc. Hoping for your next letter soon, receive my kisses like those of a brother.

"Périgot (Joseph)."

We are attracted by every form of life which represents to us something unknown and strange, by a last illusion still unshattered. In spite of this, the mysterious utterances by means of which M. de Charlus had led me to imagine the Princesse de Guermantes as an extraordinary

creature, different from anyone that I knew, were not
sufficient to account for the stupefaction in which I was
plunged, speedily followed by the fear that I might be
the victim of some bad joke planned by some one who
wanted to send me to the door of a house to which I had
not been invited, when, about two months after my
dinner with the Duchess and while she was at Cannes,
having opened an envelope the appearance of which had
not led me to suppose that it contained anything out of
the common, I read the following words engraved on a
card: "The Princesse de Guermantes, *née* Duchesse en
Bavière, At Home, the ——th." No doubt to be invited
to the Princesse de Guermantes's was perhaps not, from
the social point of view, any more difficult than to dine
with the Duchess, and my slight knowledge of heraldry
had taught me that the title of Prince is not superior to
that of Duke. Besides, I told myself that the intelligence
of a society woman could not be essentially so heterogeneous to that of her congeners as M. de Charlus made out,
nor so heterogeneous to that of any one other woman in
society. But my imagination, like Elstir engaged upon
rendering some effect of perspective without reference
to a knowledge of the laws of nature which he might quite
well possess, depicted for me not what I knew but what
it saw; what it saw, that is to say what the name shewed
it. Now, even before I had met the Duchess, the name
Guermantes preceded by the title of Princess, like a note
or a colour or quantity, profoundly modified from the
surrounding values by the mathematical or aesthetic sign
that governs it, had already suggested to me something
entirely different. With that title one finds one's thoughts
straying instinctively to the memoirs of the days of

Louis XIII and Louis XIV, the English Court, the Queen of Scots, the Duchesse d'Aumale; and I imagined the town house of the Princesse de Guermantes as more or less frequented by the Duchesse de Longueville and the great Condé, whose presence there rendered it highly improbable that I should ever make my way into it.

Many of the things that M. de Charlus had told me had driven a vigorous spur into my imagination and, making it forget how much the reality had disappointed me at Mme. de Guermantes's (people's names are in this respect like the names of places), had swung it towards Oriane's cousin. For that matter, M. de Charlus misled me at times as to the imaginary value and variety of people in society only because he was himself at times misled. And this, perhaps, because he did nothing, did not write, did not paint, did not even read anything in a serious and thorough manner. But, superior by several degrees to the people in society, if it was from them and the spectacle they afforded that he drew the material for his conversation, he was not for that reason understood by them. Speaking as an artist, he could at the most reveal the fallacious charm of people in society. But reveal it to artists alone, with relation to whom he might be said to play the part played by the reindeer among the Esquimaux. This precious animal plucks for them from the barren rocks lichens and mosses which they themselves could neither discover nor utilise, but which, once they have been digested by the reindeer, become for the inhabitants of the far North a nourishing form of food.

To which I may add that the pictures which M. de Charlus drew of society were animated with plenty of life by the blend of his ferocious hatreds and his pas-

356

sionate affections. Hatreds directed mainly against the young men, adoration aroused principally by certain women.

If among these the Princesse de Guermantes was placed by M. de Charlus upon the most exalted throne, his mysterious words about the " unapproachable Aladdin's palace " in which his cousin dwelt were not sufficient to account for my stupefaction. Apart from whatever may be due to the divers subjective points of view, of which I shall have to speak later, in these artificial magnifications, the fact remains that there is a certain objective reality in each of these people, and consequently a difference among them. And how, when it comes to that, could it be otherwise? The humanity with which we consort and which bears so little resemblance to our dreams is, for all that, the same that, in the Memoirs, in the Letters of eminent persons, we have seen described and have felt a desire to know. The old man of complete insignificance whom we met at dinner is the same who wrote that proud letter, which (in a book on the War of 1870) we read with emotion, to Prince Friedrich-Karl. We are bored at a dinner-table because our imagination is absent, and because it is bearing us company we are interested in a book. But the people in question are the same. We should like to have known Mme. de Pompadour, who was so valuable a patron of the arts, and we should have been as much bored in her company as among the modern Egerias, at whose houses we cannot bring ourselves to pay a second call, so uninteresting do we find them. The fact remains, nevertheless, that these differences do exist. People are never exactly similar to one another, their mode of behaviour with regard to ourselves, at, one might say, the same level of friendship, reveals differences which, in the end, offer compensations. When I knew Mme. de Montmorency, she loved to say unpleasant things to me, but if I was in need of a service she would squander, in the hope of obtaining it for me effectively, all the credit at her disposal, without counting the cost. Whereas some other woman, Mme. de Guermantes for example, would never have wished to hurt my feelings, never said anything about me except what might give me pleasure, showered on me all those tokens of friendship which formed the rich manner of living, morally, of the Guermantes, but, had I asked her for the least thing above and beyond that, would not have moved an inch to procure it for me, as in those country houses where one has at one's disposal a motor-car and a special footman, but where it is impossible to obtain a glass of cider, for which no provision has been made in the arrangements for a party. Which was for me the true friend, Mme. de Montmorency, so glad always to annoy me and always so ready to oblige, or Mme. de Guermantes, distressed by the slightest offence that might have been given me and incapable of the slightest effort to be of use to me? The types of the human mind are so varied, so opposite, not only in literature but in society, that Baudelaire and Mérimée are not the only people who have the right to despise one another mutually. These peculiarities continue to form in everyone a system of attitudes, of speech, of actions, so coherent, so despotic, that when we are in the presence of anyone his or her system seems to us superior to the rest. With Mme. de Guermantes, her words, deduced like a theorem from her type of mind, seemed to me the only ones that

could possibly be said. And I was, at heart, of her
opinion when she told me that Mme. de Montmorency
was stupid and kept an open mind towards all the things
she did not understand, or when, having heard of some
spiteful remark by that lady, she said: "That is what
you call a good woman; it is what I call a monster." But
this tyranny of the reality which confronts us, this pre-
ponderance of the lamplight which turns the dawn—
already distant—as pale as the faintest memory, disappeared when I was away from Mme. de Guermantes, and
a different lady said to me, putting herself on my level
and reckoning the Duchess as placed far below either of
us: "Oriane takes no interest, really, in anything or
anybody," or even (what in the presence of Mme. de
Guermantes it would have seemed impossible to believe,
so loudly did she herself proclaim the opposite): "Oriane
is a snob." Seeing that no mathematical process would
have enabled one to convert Mme. d'Arpajon and Mme.
de Montpensier into commensurable quantities, it would
have been impossible for me to reply, had anyone asked
me which of the two seemed to me superior to the other.

Now, among the peculiar characteristics of the drawing-
room of the Princesse de Guermantes, the one most generally quoted was a certain exclusiveness, due in part
to the royal birth of the Princess, but especially to the
almost fossilised rigidity of the aristocratic prejudices of
the Prince, prejudices which, incidentally, the Duke and
Duchess had made no scruple about deriding in front
of me, and which naturally were to make me regard it
as more improbable than ever that I should have been
invited to a party by this man who reckoned only in
royalties and dukes, and at every dinner-party made a

scene because he had not been put in the place to which he would have been entitled under Louis XIV, a place which, thanks to his immense erudition in matters of history and genealogy, he was the only person who knew. For this reason, many of the people in society placed to the credit of the Duke and Duchess the differences which distinguished them from their cousins. " The Duke and Duchess are far more modern, far more intelligent, they don't think of nothing, like the other couple, but how many quarterings one has, their house is three hundred years in advance of their cousins'," were customary remarks, the memory of which made me tremble as I looked at the card of invitation, to which they gave a far greater probability of its having been sent me by some practical joker.

If the Duke and Duchess had not been still at Cannes, I might have tried to find out from them whether the invitation which I had received was genuine. This state of doubt in which I was plunged was not due, as I flattered myself for a time by supposing, to a sentiment which a man of fashion would not have felt and which, consequently, a writer, even if he belonged apart from his writership to the fashionable caste, ought to reproduce in order to be thoroughly " objective " and to depict each class differently. I happened, in fact, only the other day, in a charming volume of memoirs, to come upon the record of uncertainties analogous to those which the Princesse de Guermantes's card made me undergo. " Georges and I " (or " Hély and I ", I have not the book at hand to verify the reference) " were so keen to be asked to Mme. Delessert's that, having received an invitation from her, we thought it prudent, each of us independently, to make

certain that we were not the victims of an April fool."
Now, the writer is none other than the Comte d'Hausson-
ville (he who married the Duc de Broglie's daughter)
and the other young man who "independently" makes
sure that he is not having a practical joke played on him
is, according to whether he is called Georges or Hély,
one or other of the two inseparable friends of M. d'Haus-
sonville, either M. d'Harcourt or the Prince de Chalais.

The day on which the party was to be given at the
Princesse de Guermantes's, I learned that the Duke and
Duchess had just returned to Paris. The Princess's ball
would not have brought them back, but one of their
cousins was seriously ill, and moreover the Duke was
greatly taken up with a revel which was to be held
the same night, and at which he himself was to appear
as Louis XI and his wife as Isabel of Bavaria. And
I determined to go and see her that morning. But,
having gone out early, they had not yet returned; I
watched first of all from a little room, which had seemed
to me to be a good look-out post, for the arrival of their
carriage. As a matter of fact I had made a singularly
bad choice in my observatory from which I could barely
make out our courtyard, but I did see into several others,
and this, though of no value to me, occupied my mind
for a time. It is not only in Venice that one has those
outlooks on to several houses at once which have proved
so tempting to painters; it is just the same in Paris.
Nor do I cite Venice at random. It is of its poorer
quarters that certain poor quarters of Paris make one
think, in the morning, with their tall, wide chimneys to
which the sun imparts the most vivid pinks, the brightest
reds; it is a whole garden that flowers above the houses,

and flowers in such a variety of tints that one would call it, planted on top of the town, the garden of a tulip-fancier of Delft or Haarlem. And then also, the extreme proximity of the houses, with their windows looking opposite one another on to a common courtyard, makes of each casement the frame in which a cook sits dreamily gazing down at the ground below, in which farther off a girl is having her hair combed by an old woman with the face, barely distinguishable in the shadow, of a witch: thus each courtyard provides for the adjoining house, by suppressing all sound in its interval, by leaving visible a series of silent gestures in a series of rectangular frames, glazed by the closing of the windows, an exhibition of a hundred Dutch paintings hung in rows. Certainly from the Hôtel de Guermantes one did not have the same kind of view, but one had curious views also, especially from the strange trigonometrical point at which I had placed myself and from which one's gaze was arrested by nothing nearer than the distant heights formed by the comparatively vague plots of ground which preceded, on a steep slope, the mansion of the Marquise de Plassac and Mme. de Tresmes, cousins (of the most noble category) of M. de Guermantes, whom I did not know. Between me and this house (which was that of their father, M. de Bréquigny) nothing but blocks of buildings of low elevation, facing in every conceivable direction, which, without blocking the view, increased the distance with their diagonal perspective. The red-tiled turret of the coach-house in which the Marquis de Fré-court kept his carriages did indeed end in a spire that rose rather higher, but was so slender that it concealed nothing, and made one think of those picturesque old buildings in

Switzerland which spring up in isolation at the foot
of a mountain. All these vague and divergent points on
which my eyes rested made more distant apparently than
if it had been separated from us by several streets or by
a series of foothills the house of Mme. de Plassac, actually
quite near but chimerically remote as in an Alpine
landscape. When its large paned windows, glittering in
the sunlight like flakes of rock crystal, were thrown open
so as to air the rooms, one felt, in following from one
floor to the next the footmen whom it was impossible to
see clearly but who were visibly shaking carpets, the
same pleasure as when one sees in a landscape by Turner
or Elstir a traveller in a mail-coach, or a guide, at different
degrees of altitude on the Saint-Gothard. But from this
point of view in which I had ensconced myself I should
have been in danger of not seeing M. or Mme. de Guermantes come in, so that when in the afternoon I was free
to resume my survey I simply stood on the staircase,
from which the opening of the carriage-gate could not
escape my notice, and it was on this staircase that I
posted myself, albeit there did not appear there, so en-
trancing with their footmen rendered minute by distance
and busily cleaning, the Alpine beauties of the Bréquigny-
Tresmes mansion. Now this wait on the staircase was to
have for me consequences so considerable, and to reveal
to me a picture no longer Turneresque but ethical, of so
great importance, that it is preferable to postpone the
account of it for a little while by interposing first that
of my visit to the Guermantes when I knew that they
had come home. It was the Duke alone who received me
in the library. As I went in there came out a little man
with snow-white hair, a look of poverty, a little black

neckcloth such as was worn by the lawyer at Combray and by several of my grandfather's friends, but of a more timid aspect than they, who, making me a series of profound bows, refused absolutely to go downstairs until I had passed him. The Duke shouted after him from the library something which I did not understand, and the other responded with further bows, addressed to the wall, for the Duke could not see him, but endlessly repeated nevertheless, like the purposeless smiles on the faces of people who are talking to one over the telephone; he had a falsetto voice, and saluted me afresh with the humility of a man of business. And he might, for that matter, have been a man of business from Combray, so much was he in the style, provincial, out of date and mild, of the small folk, the modest elders of those parts. "You shall see Oriane in a minute," the Duke told me when I had entered the room. "As Swann is coming in presently and bringing her the proofs of his book on the coinage of the Order of Malta, and, what is worse, an immense photograph he has had taken shewing both sides of each of the coins, Oriane preferred to get dressed early so that she can stay with him until it's time to go out to dinner. We have such a heap of things in the house already that we don't know where to put them all, and I ask myself where on earth we are going to stick this photograph. But I have too good-natured a wife, who is too fond of giving people pleasure. She thought it would be polite to ask Swann to let her see side by side on one sheet the heads of all those Grand Masters of the Order whose medals he has found at Rhodes. I said Malta, didn't I, it is Rhodes, but it's all the same Order of Saint John of Jerusalem. As a matter of fact, she is interested in them only because Swann makes a hobby of it. Our family is very much mixed up in the whole story; even at the present day, my brother, whom you know, is one of the highest dignitaries in the Order of Malta. But I might have told all that to Oriane, she simply wouldn't have listened to me. On the other hand, it was quite enough that Swann's researches into the Templars (it's astonishing the passion that people of one religion have for studying others) should have led him on to the history of the Knights of Rhodes, who succeeded the Templars, for Oriane at once to insist on seeing the heads of these Knights. They were very small fry indeed compared with the Lusignans, Kings of Cyprus, from whom we descend in a direct line. But so far, as Swann hasn't taken them up, Oriane doesn't care to hear anything about the Lusignans." I could not at once explain to the Duke why I had come. What happened was that several relatives or friends, including Mme. de Silistrie and the Duchesse de Montrose, came to pay a call on the Duchess, who was often at home before dinner, and not finding her there stayed for a short while with the Duke. The first of these ladies (the Princesse de Silistrie), simply attired, with a dry but friendly manner, carried a stick in her hand. I was afraid at first that she had injured herself, or was a cripple. She was on the contrary most alert. She spoke regretfully to the Duke of a first cousin of his own—not on the Guermantes side, but more illustrious still, were that possible—whose health, which had been in a grave condition for some time past, had grown suddenly worse. But it was evident that the Duke, while full of pity for his cousin's lot, and repeating " Poor Mama! He's such a good fellow!" had formed a favourable prognosis. The fact was that the dinner at which the Duke was to be present amused him, the big party at the Princesse de Guermantes's did not bore him, but above all he was to go on at one o'clock in the morning with his wife to a great supper and costume ball, with a view to which a costume of Louis XI for himself, and one of Isabel of Bavaria for his wife were waiting in readiness. And the Duke was determined not to be disturbed amid all these gaieties by the sufferings of the worthy Amanien d'Osmond. Two other ladies carrying sticks, Mme. de Plassac and Mme. de Tresmes, both daughters of the Comte de Bréquigny, came in next to pay Basin a visit, and declared that cousin Mama's state left no room now for hope. The Duke shrugged his shoulders, and to change the conversation asked whether they were going that evening to Marie-Gilbert's. They replied that they were not, in view of the state of Amanien who was in his last agony, and indeed they had excused themselves from the dinner to which the Duke was going, the other guests at which they proceeded to enumerate: the brother of King Theodosius, the Infanta Maria Concepcion, and so forth. As the Marquis d'Osmond was less nearly related to them than he was to Basin, their " defection " appeared to the Duke to be a sort of indirect reproach aimed at his own conduct. And so, albeit they had come down from the heights of the Bréquigny mansion to see the Duchess (or rather to announce to her the alarming character, incompatible for his relatives with attendance at social gatherings, of their cousin's illness) they did not stay long, and, each armed with her alpenstock, Walpurge and Dorothée (such were the names of the two sisters) retraced the craggy path to their citadel.

I never thought of asking the Guermantes what was the meaning of these sticks, so common in a certain part of the Faubourg Saint-Germain. Possibly, looking upon the whole parish as their domain, and not caring to hire cabs, they were in the habit of taking long walks, for which some old fracture, due to immoderate indulgence in the chase, and to the falls from horseback which are often the fruit of that indulgence, or simply rheumatism caused by the dampness of the left bank and of old country houses made a stick necessary. Perhaps they had not set out upon any such long expedition through the quarter, but, having merely come down into their garden (which lay at no distance from that of the Duchess) to pick the fruit required for stewing, had looked in on their way home to bid good evening to Mme. de Guermantes, though without going so far as to bring a pair of shears or a watering-can into her house. The Duke appeared touched that I should have come to see them so soon after their return to Paris. But his face grew dark when I told him that I had come to ask his wife to find out whether her cousin really had invited me. I had touched upon one of those services which M. and Mme. de Guermantes were not fond of rendering. The Duke explained to me that it was too late, that if the Princess had not sent me an invitation it would make him appear to be asking her for one, that his cousins had refused him one once before, and he had no wish to appear either directly or indirectly to be interfering with their visiting list, be "meddling"; finally, he could not even be sure that he and his wife, who were dining out that evening, would not come straight home afterwards, that in that case their best excuse for not having gone to the

Princess's party would be to conceal from her the fact of their return to Paris, instead of hastening to inform her of it, as they must do if they sent her a note, or spoke to her over the telephone about me, and certainly too late to be of any use, since, in all probability, the Princess's list of guests would be closed by now. "You've not fallen foul of her in any way?" he asked in a suspicious tone, the Guermantes living in a constant fear of not being informed of the latest society quarrels, and so of people's trying to climb back into favour on their shoulders. Finally, as the Duke was in the habit of taking upon himself all decisions that might seem not very good-natured: "Listen, my boy," he said to me suddenly, as though the idea had just come into his head, "I would really rather not mention at all to Oriane that you have been speaking to me about it. You know how kind-hearted she is; besides, she has an enormous regard for you, she would insist on sending to ask her cousin, in spite of anything I might say to the contrary, and if she is tired after dinner, there will be no getting out of it, she will be forced to go to the party. No, decidedly, I shall say nothing to her about it. Anyhow, you will see her yourself in a minute. But not a word about that matter, I beg of you. If you decide to go to the party, I have no need to tell you what a pleasure it will be to us to spend the evening there with you." The motives actuating humanity are too sacred for him before whom they are invoked not to bow to them, whether he believes them to be sincere or not; I did not wish to appear to be weighing in the balance for a moment the relative importance of my invitation and the possible tiredness of Mme. de Guermantes, and I promised not to speak to her of the object of my visit, exactly as though I had been taken in by the little farce which M. de Guermantes had performed for my benefit. I asked him if he thought there was any chance of my seeing Mme. de Stermaria at the Princess's. "Why, no," he replied with the air of an expert; "I know the name you mention, from having seen it in lists of club members, it is not at all the type of person who goes to Gilbert's. You will see nobody there who is not excessively proper and intensely boring, duchesses bearing titles which one thought were extinct years ago and which they have revived for the occasion, all the Ambassadors, heaps of Coburgs, foreign royalties, but you mustn't hope for the ghost of a Stermaria. Gilbert would be taken ill at the mere thought of such a thing.

"Wait now, you're fond of painting, I must shew you a superb picture I bought from my cousin, partly in exchange for the Elstirs, which frankly did not appeal to us. It was sold to me as a Philippe de Champaigne, but I believe myself that it's by some one even greater. Would you like to know my idea? I believe it to be a Velazquez, and of the best period," said the Duke, looking me boldly in the eyes, whether to learn my impression or in the hope of enhancing it. A footman came in. "Mme. la Duchesse has told me to ask M. le Duc if M. le Duc will be so good as to see M. Swann, as Mme. la Duchesse is not quite ready." "Shew M. Swann in," said the Duke, after looking at his watch and seeing that he had still a few minutes before he need go to dress. "Naturally my wife, who told him to come, is not ready. There's no use saying anything before Swann about Marie-Gilbert's party," said the Duke. "I don't know whether he's been invited. Gilbert likes him immensely, because he believes him to be the natural grandson of the Duc de Berri, but that's a long story. (Otherwise, you can imagine! My cousin, who falls in a fit if he sees a Jew a mile off.) But now, don't you see, the Dreyfus case has made things more serious. Swann ought to have realised that he more than anyone must drop all connexion with those fellows, instead of which he says the most offensive things." The Duke called back the footman to know whether the man who had been sent to inquire at cousin Osmond's had returned. His plan was as follows: as he believed, and rightly, that his cousin was dying, he was anxious to obtain news of him before his death, that is to say before he was obliged to go into mourning. Once covered by the official certainty that Amanien was still alive, he could go without a thought to his dinner, to the Prince's party, to the midnight revel at which he would appear as Louis XI, and had made the most exciting assignation with a new mistress, and would make no more inquiries until the following day, when his pleasures would be at an end. Then one would put on mourning if the cousin had passed away in the night. "No, M. le Duc, he is not back yet." "What in the Name of God! Nothing is ever done in this house till the last minute," cried the Duke, at the thought that Amanien might still be in time to "croak" for an evening paper, and so make him miss his revel. He sent for the *Temps*, in which there was nothing. I had not seen Swann for a long time, and asked myself at first whether in the old days he used to clip his moustache, or had not his hair brushed up vertically in front, for I found in him something altered; it was simply

370

that he was indeed greatly "altered" because he was very ill, and illness produces in the face modifications as profound as are created by growing a beard or by changing the line of one's parting. (Swann's illness was the same that had killed his mother, who had been attacked by it at precisely the age which he had now reached. Our existences are in truth, owing to heredity, as full of cabalistic ciphers, of horoscopic castings as if there really were sorcerers in the world. And just as there is a certain duration of life for humanity in general, so there is one for families in particular, that is to say, in any one family, for the members of it who resemble one another.) Swann was dressed with an elegance which, like that of his wife, associated with what he now was what he once had been. Buttoned up in a pearl-grey frock-coat which emphasised the tallness of his figure, slender, his white gloves stitched in black, he carried a grey tall hat of a specially wide shape which Delion had ceased now to make except for him, the Prince de Sagan, the Marquis de Modène, M. Charles Haas and Comte Louis de Turenne. I was surprised at the charming smile and affectionate handclasp with which he replied to my greeting, for I had imagined that after so long an interval he would not recognise me at once; I told him of my astonishment; he received it with a shout of laughter, a trace of indignation and a further grip of my hand, as if it were throwing doubt on the soundness of his brain or the sincerity of his affection to suppose that he did not know me. And yet that was what had happened; he did not identify me, as I learned long afterwards, until several minutes later when he heard my name mentioned. But no change in his face, in his speech, in the things he said to me betrayed the discovery which a chance word from M. de Guermantes had enabled him to make, with such mastery, with such absolute sureness did he play the social game. He brought to it, moreover, that spontaneity in manners and personal initiative, even in his style of dress, which characterised the Guermantes type. Thus it was that the greeting which the old clubman, without recognising me, had given me was not the cold and stiff greeting of the man of the world who was a pure formalist, but a greeting full of a real friendliness, of a true charm, such as the Duchesse de Guermantes, for instance, possessed (carrying it so far as to smile at you first, before you had bowed to her, if she met you in the street), in contrast to the more mechanical greeting customary among the ladies of the Faubourg Saint-Germain. In the same way, again, the hat which, in conformity with a custom that was beginning to disappear, he laid on the floor by his feet, was lined with green leather, a thing not usually done, because, according to him, this kept the hat much cleaner, in reality because it was highly becoming. " Now, Charles, you're a great expert, come and see what I've got to shew you, after which, my boys, I'm going to ask your permission to leave you together for a moment while I go and change my clothes, besides, I expect Oriane won't be long now." And he shewed his " Velazquez " to Swann. " But it seems to me that I know this," said Swann with the grimace of a sick man for whom the mere act of speaking requires an effort. " Yes," said the Duke, turned serious by the time which the expert took in expressing his admiration. " You have probably seen it at Gilbert's." " Oh, yes, of course, I remember." " What do you suppose it is? "

"Oh, well, if it comes from Gilbert's, it is probably one of your *ancestors*," said Swann with a blend of irony and deference towards a form of greatness which he would have felt it impolite and absurd to despise, but to which for reasons of good taste he preferred to make only a playful reference.

"To be sure, it is," said the Duke bluntly. "It's Boson, the I forget how manieth de Guermantes. Not that I care a damn about that. You know I'm not as feudal as my cousin. I've heard the names mentioned of Rigaud, Mignard, Velazquez even!" he went on, fastening on Swann the gaze of an inquisitor and executioner in an attempt at once to read into his mind and to influence his response. "Well," he concluded, for when he was led to provoke artificially an opinion which he desired to hear, he had the faculty, after a few moments, of believing that it had been spontaneously uttered; "come, now, none of your flattery, do you think it's by one of those big masters I've mentioned?" "Nnnnno," said Swann. "But after all, I know nothing about these things, it's not for me to decide who daubed the canvas. But you're a dilettante, a master of the subject, to whom do you attribute it? You're enough of an expert to have some idea. What would you say it was?" Swann hesitated for a moment before the picture, which obviously he thought atrocious. "A bad joke!" he replied, with a smile at the Duke who could not check an impulsive movement of rage. When this had subsided: "Be good fellows, both of you, wait a moment for Oriane, I must go and put on my swallow-tails and then I'll join you. I shall send word to my good woman that you're both waiting for her." I talked for a minute or two with

Swann about the Dreyfus case, and asked him how it was that all the Guermantes were anti-Dreyfusards. "In the first place because at heart all these people are anti-semites," replied Swann, who, all the same, knew very well from experience that certain of them were not, but, like everyone who supports any cause with ardour, preferred, to explain the fact that other people did not share his opinion, to suppose in them a preconceived reason, a prejudice against which there was nothing to be done, rather than reasons which might permit of discussion. Besides, having come to the premature term of his life, like a weary animal that is goaded on, he cried out against these persecutions and was returning to the spiritual fold of his fathers. "Yes, the Prince de Guermantes," I said, "it is true, I've heard that he was anti-semitic." "Oh, that fellow! I wasn't even thinking about him. He carries it to such a point that when he was in the army and had a frightful toothache he preferred to grin and bear it rather than go to the only dentist in the district, who happened to be a Jew, and later on he allowed a wing of his castle which had caught fire to be burned to the ground, because he would have had to send for extinguishers to the place next door, which belongs to the Rothschilds." "Are you going to be there this evening, by any chance?" "Yes," Swann replied, "although I am far too tired. But he sent me a wire to tell me that he has something to say to me. I feel that I shall be too unwell in the next few days to go there or to see him at home; it would upset me, so I prefer to get it over at once." "But the Duc de Guermantes is not anti-semitic?" "You can see quite well that he is, since he's an anti-Dreyfusard," replied Swann, without noticing the logical fallacy. " That doesn't prevent my being very sorry that I disappointed the man—what am I saying? The Duke, I mean—by not admiring his Mignard or whatever he calls it." " But at any rate," I went on, reverting to the Dreyfus case, " the Duchess, she, now, is intelligent." " Yes, she is charming. To my mind, however, she was even more charming when she was still known as the Princesse des Laumes. Her mind has become somehow more angular, it was all much softer in the juvenile great lady, but after all, young or old, men or women, what can you expect, all these people belong to a different race, one can't have a thousand years of feudalism in one's blood with impunity. Naturally they imagine that it counts for nothing in their opinions." " All the same, Robert de Saint-Loup is a Dreyfusard." " Ah! So much the better, all the more as you know that his mother is extremely ' anti '. I had heard that he was, but I wasn't certain of it. That gives me a great deal of pleasure. It doesn't surprise me, he's highly intelligent. It's a great thing, that is."

Dreyfusism had brought to Swann an extraordinary simplicity of mind, and had imparted to his way of looking at things an impulsiveness, an inconsistency more noticeable even than had been the similar effects of his marriage to Odette; this new loss of caste would have been better described as a recasting, and was entirely to his credit, since it made him return to the ways in which his forebears had trodden and from which he had turned aside to mix with the aristocracy. But Swann, just at the very moment when with such lucidity it had been granted to him, thanks to the gifts he had inherited from his race, to perceive a truth that was still hidden from people of fashion, shewed himself nevertheless quite comically blind. He subjected afresh all his admirations and all his contempts to the test of a new criterion, Dreyfusism. That the anti-Dreyfusism of Mme. Bontemps should have made him think her a fool was no more astonishing than that, when he was first married, he should have thought her intelligent. It was not very serious either that the new wave reached also his political judgments and made him lose all memory of having treated as a man with a price, a British spy (this latter was an absurdity of the Guermantes set), Clemenceau, whom he declared now to have always stood up for conscience, to be a man of iron, like Cornély. " No, no, I never told you anything of the sort. You're thinking of some one else." But, sweeping past his political judgments, the wave overthrew in Swann his literary judgments also, and even affected his way of pronouncing them. Barrès had lost all his talent, and even the books of his early days were feeble, one could hardly read them again. " You try, you'll find you can't struggle to the end. What a difference from Clemenceau! Personally, I am not anti-clerical, but when you compare them together you must see that Barrès is invertebrate. He's a very great fellow, is old Clemenceau. How he knows the language!" However, the anti-Dreyfusards were in no position to criticise these follies. They explained that one was a Dreyfusard by one's being of Jewish origin. If a practising Catholic like Saniette stood out also for a fresh trial, that was because he was buttonholed by Mme. Verdurin, who behaved like a wild Radical. She was out above all things against the " frocks ". Saniette was more fool than knave, and had no idea of the harm

that the Mistress was doing him. If you pointed out that
Brichot was equally a friend of Mme. Verdurin and was
a member of the Patrie Française, that was because he
was more intelligent. "You see him occasionally?" I
asked Swann, referring to Saint-Loup. "No, never. He
wrote to me the other day hoping that I would ask the
Duc de Mouchy and various other people to vote for
him at the Jockey, where for that matter he got through
like a letter through the post." "In spite of the Case!"
"The question was never raised. However I must tell
you that since all this business began I never set foot
in the place."

M. de Guermantes returned, and was presently joined
by his wife, all ready now for the evening, tall and proud
in a gown of red satin the skirt of which was bordered
with spangles. She had in her hair a long ostrich feather
dyed purple, and over her shoulders a tulle scarf of the
same red as her dress. "How nice it is to have one's
hat lined with leather," said the Duchess, whom nothing
escaped. "However, with you, Charles, everything is
always charming, whether it's what you wear or what
you say, what you read or what you do." Swann meanwhile, without apparently listening, was considering the
Duchess as he would have studied the canvas of a master,
and then sought her gaze, making with his lips the
grimace which implies: "The devil!" Mme. de Guermantes rippled with laughter. "So my clothes please
you? I'm delighted. But I must say that they don't
please me much," she went on with a sulking air. "Good
Lord, what a bore it is to have to dress up and go out
when one would ever so much rather stay at home!"
"What magnificent rubies!" "Ah! my dear Charles, at

least one can see that you know what you're talking about, you're not like that brute Monserfeuil who asked me if they were real. I must say that I've never seen anything quite like them. They were a present from the Grand Duchess. They're a little too large for my liking, a little too like claret glasses filled to the brim, but I've put them on because we shall be seeing the Grand Duchess this evening at Marie-Gilbert's," added Mme. de Guermantes, never suspecting that this assertion destroyed the force of those previously made by the Duke. "What's on at the Princess's?" inquired Swann. "Practically nothing," the Duke hastened to reply, the question having made him think that Swann was not invited. "What's that, Basin? When all the highways and hedgerows have been scoured? It will be a deathly crush. What will be pretty, though," she went on, looking wistfully at Swann, "if the storm I can feel in the air now doesn't break, will be those marvellous gardens. You know them, of course. I was there a month ago, at the time when the lilacs were in flower, you can't have any idea how lovely they were. And then the fountain, really, it's Versailles in Paris." "What sort of person is the Princess?" I asked. "Why, you know quite well, you've seen her here, she's as beautiful as the day, also rather an idiot. Very nice, in spite of all her Germanic high-and-mightiness, full of good nature and stupid mistakes." Swann was too subtle not to perceive that the Duchess, in this speech, was trying to shew the "Guermantes wit", and at no great cost to herself, for she was only serving up in a less perfect form an old saying of her own. Nevertheless, to prove to the Duchess that he appreciated her intention to be, and as though she had really succeeded in being

funny, he smiled with a slightly forced air, causing me
by this particular form of insincerity the same feeling of
awkwardness that used to disturb me long ago when I
heard my parents discussing with M. Vinteuil the corruption of certain sections of society (when they knew very
well that a corruption far greater sat enthroned at Mont-
jouvain), Legrandin colouring his utterances for the
benefit of fools, choosing delicate epithets which he knew
perfectly well would not be understood by a rich or
smart but illiterate public. " Come now, Oriane, what on
earth are you saying? " broke in M. de Guermantes.
" Marie a fool? Why, she has read everything, she's as
musical as a fiddle." " But, my poor little Basin, you're
as innocent as a new-born babe. As if one could not be
all that, and rather an idiot as well. Idiot is too strong
a word; no, she's in the clouds, she's Hesse-Darmstadt,
Holy Roman Empire, and wa-wa-wa. Her pronunciation
alone makes me tired. But I quite admit that she's a
charming looney. Simply the idea of stepping down from
her German throne to go and marry, in the most middle-
class way, a private citizen. It is true that she chose
him! Yes, it's quite true," she went on, turning to me,
" you don't know Gilbert. Let me give you an idea of him,
he took to his bed once because I had left a card on
Mme. Carnot. . . . But, my little Charles," said the
Duchess, changing the conversation when she saw that
the story of the card left on the Carnots appeared to
irritate M. de Guermantes, " you know, you've never sent
me that photograph of our Knights of Rhodes, whom
I've learned to love through you, and I am so anxious to
make their acquaintance." The Duke meanwhile had not
taken his eyes from his wife's face. " Oriane, you might

at least tell the story properly and not cut out half.
I ought to explain," he corrected, addressing Swann, " that
the British Ambassadress at that time, who was a very
worthy woman, but lived rather in the moon and was in
the habit of making up these odd combinations, conceived
the distinctly quaint idea of inviting us with the President
and his wife. We were—Oriane herself was rather surprised, especially as the Ambassadress knew quite enough
of the people we knew not to invite us, of all things, to
so ill-assorted a gathering. There was a Minister there
who is a swindler, however I pass over all that, we had
not been warned in time, were caught in the trap, and,
I'm bound to admit, all these people behaved most
civilly to us. Only, once was enough. Mme. de Guermantes, who does not often do me the honour of consulting me, felt it incumbent upon her to leave a card
in the course of the following week at the Elysée. Gilbert
may perhaps have gone rather far in regarding it as a
stain upon our name. But it must not be forgotten that,
politics apart, M. Carnot, who for that matter filled his
post quite adequately, was the grandson of a member
of the Revolutionary Tribunal which caused the death
of eleven of our people in a single day." " In that case,
Basin, why did you go every week to dine at Chantilly?
The Duc d'Aumale was just as much the grandson of
a member of the Revolutionary Tribunal, with this
difference, that Carnot was a brave man and Philippe
Egalité a wretched scoundrel." " Excuse my interrupting
you to explain that I did send the photograph," said
Swann. " I can't understand how it hasn't reached you."
" It doesn't altogether surprise me," said the Duchess,
" my servants tell me only what they think fit. They

probably do not approve of the Order of Saint John."
And she rang the bell. "You know, Oriane, that when
I used to go to Chantilly it was without enthusiasm."
"Without enthusiasm, but with a nightshirt in a bag,
in case the Prince asked you to stay, which for that
matter he very rarely did, being a perfect cad like all
the Orléans lot. Do you know who else are to be dining
at Mme. de Saint-Euverte's?" Mme. de Guermantes
asked her husband. "Besides the people you know already, she's asked at the last moment King Theodosius's
brother." At these tidings the Duchess's features breathed
contentment and her speech boredom. "Oh, good
heavens, more princes!" "But that one is well-mannered
and intelligent," Swann suggested. "Not altogether,
though," replied the Duchess, apparently seeking for
words that would give more novelty to the thought expressed. "Have you ever noticed with princes that the
best-mannered among them are not really well-mannered?
They must always have an opinion about everything.
Then, as they have none of their own, they spend the
first half of their lives asking us ours and the other half
serving it up to us second-hand. They positively must
be able to say that one piece has been well played
and the next not so well. When there is no difference.
Listen, this little Theodosius junior (I forget his name)
asked me what one called an orchestral motif. I replied,"
said the Duchess, her eyes sparkling while a laugh broke
from her beautiful red lips: "'One calls it an orchestral
motif.' I don't think he was any too well pleased, really.
Oh, my dear Charles," she went on, "what a bore it
can be, dining out. There are evenings when one would
sooner die! It is true that dying may be perhaps just

as great a bore, because we don't know what it's like."
A servant appeared. It was the young lover who used
to have trouble with the porter, until the Duchess, in
her kindness of heart, brought about an apparent peace
between them. "Am I to go up this evening to inquire
for M. le Marquis d'Osmond?" he asked. "Most certainly not, nothing before to-morrow morning. In fact
I don't want you to remain in the house to-night. The
only thing that will happen will be that his footman, who
knows you, will come to you with the latest report and
send you out after us. Get off, go anywhere you like,
have a woman, sleep out, but I don't want to see you
here before to-morrow morning."An immense joy over-
flowed from the footman's face. He would at last be
able to spend long hours with his lady-love, whom he
had practically ceased to see ever since, after a final
scene with the porter, the Duchess had considerately explained to him that it would be better, to avoid further
conflicts, if he did not go out at all. He floated, at the
thought of having an evening free at last, in a happiness
which the Duchess saw and guessed its reason. She felt,
so to speak, a tightening of the heart and an itching in
all her limbs at the sight of this happiness which an
amorous couple were snatching behind her back, concealing themselves from her, which left her irritated and
jealous. "No, Basin, let him stay here; I say, he's not
to stir out of the house." "But, Oriane, that's absurd, the
house is crammed with servants, and you have the cos-
tumier's people coming as well at twelve to dress us
for this show. There's absolutely nothing for him to do,
and he's the only one who's a friend of Mama's footman; I would a thousand times rather get him right

away from the house." "Listen, Basin, let me do what I want, I shall have a message for him to take in the evening, as it happens, I can't tell yet at what time. In any case you're not to go out of the house for a single instant, do you hear?" she said to the despairing footman. If there were continual quarrels, and if servants did not stay long with the Duchess, the person to whose charge this guerrilla warfare was to be laid was indeed irremovable, but it was not the porter; no doubt for the rougher tasks, for the martyrdoms that it was more tiring to inflict, for the quarrels which ended in blows, the Duchess entrusted the heavier instruments to him; but even then he played his part without the least suspicion that he had been cast for it. Like the household servants, he admired the Duchess for her kindness of heart; and footmen of little discernment who came back, after leaving her service, to visit Françoise used to say that the Duke's house would have been the finest "place" in Paris if it had not been for the porter's lodge. The Duchess "played" the lodge on them, just as at different times clericalism, freemasonry, the Jewish peril have been played on the public. Another footman came into the room. "Why have not they brought up the package that M. Swann sent here? And, by the way (you've heard, Charles, that Mama is seriously ill?), Jules went up to inquire for news of M. le Marquis d'Osmond: has he come back yet?" "He's just come this instant, M. le Duc. They're waiting from one moment to the next for M. le Marquis to pass away." "Ah! He's alive!" exclaimed the Duke with a sigh of relief. "That's all right, that's all right: sold again, Satan! While there's life there's hope," the Duke announced to us with a joyful air. "They've been talking about him as though he were dead and buried. In a week from now he'll be fitter than I am." "It's the Doctors who said that he wouldn't last out the evening. One of them wanted to call again during the night. The head one said it was no use. M. le Marquis would be dead by then; they've only kept him alive by injecting him with camphorated oil." "Hold your tongue, you damned fool," cried the Duke in a paroxysm of rage. "Who the devil asked you to say all that? You haven't understood a word of what they told you." "It wasn't me they told, it was Jules." "Will you hold your tongue!" roared the Duke, and, turning to Swann, "What a blessing he's still alive! He will regain his strength gradually, don't you know. Still alive, after being in such a critical state, that in itself is an excellent sign. One mustn't expect everything at once. It can't be at all unpleasant, a little injection of camphorated oil." He rubbed his hands. "He's alive; what more could anyone want? After going through all that he's gone through, it's a great step forward. Upon my word, I envy him having such a temperament. Ah! these invalids, you know, people do all sorts of little things for them that they don't do for us. Now to-day there was a devil of a cook who sent me up a leg of mutton with *béarnaise* sauce—it was done to a turn, I must admit, but just for that very reason I took so much of it that it's still lying on my stomach. However, that doesn't make people come to inquire for me as they do for dear Amanien. We do too much inquiring. It only tires him. We must let him have room to breathe. They're killing the poor fellow by sending round to him all the time." "Well," said the Duchess to the footman as he was leaving the room, "I gave orders for the envelope containing a photograph which M. Swann sent me to be brought up here." "Madame la Duchesse, it is so large that I didn't know if I could get it through the door. We have left it in the hall. Does Madame la Duchesse wish me to bring it up?" "Oh, in that case, no; they ought to have told me, but if it's so big I shall see it in a moment when I come downstairs." "I forgot to tell Mme. la Duchesse that Mme. la Comtesse Molé left a card this morning for Mme. la Duchesse." "What, this morning?" said the Duchess with an air of disapproval, feeling that so young a woman ought not to take the liberty of leaving cards in the morning. "About ten o'clock, Madame la Duchesse." "Shew me the cards." "In any case, Oriane, when you say that it was a funny idea on Marie's part to marry Gilbert," went on the Duke, reverting to the original topic of conversation, "it is you who have an odd way of writing history. If either of them was a fool, it was Gilbert, for having married of all people a woman so closely related to the King of the Belgians, who has usurped the name of Brabant which belongs to us. To put it briefly, we are of the same blood as the Hesses, and of the elder branch. It is always stupid to talk about oneself," he apologised to me, "but after all, whenever we have been not only at Darmstadt, but even at Cassel and all over Electoral Hesse, the Landgraves have always, all of them, been most courteous in giving us precedence as being of the elder branch." "But really, Basin, you don't mean to tell me that a person who was a Major in every regiment in her country, who had been engaged to the King of Sweden." "Oriane, that is too much; anyone would think that you didn't know that the King of Sweden's grandfather was tilling the soil at Pau when we had been ruling the roost for nine hundred years throughout the whole of Europe." "That doesn't alter the fact that if somebody were to say in the street: 'Hallo, there's the King of Sweden,' everyone would at once rush to see him as far as the Place de la Concorde, and if he said: 'There's M. de Guermantes,' nobody would know who M. de Guermantes was." "What an argument!" "Besides, I never can understand how, once the title of Duke of Brabant has passed to the Belgian Royal Family, you can continue to claim it."

The footman returned with the Comtesse Molé's card, or rather what she had left in place of a card. Alleging that she had none on her, she had taken from her pocket a letter addressed to herself, and keeping the contents had handed in the envelope which bore the inscription: "La Comtesse Molé." As the envelope was rather large, following the fashion in notepaper which prevailed that year, this manuscript "card" was almost twice the size of an ordinary visiting card. "That is what people call Mme. Molé's 'simplicity'," said the Duchess ironically. "She wants to make us think that she had no cards on her, and to shew her originality. But we know all about that, don't we, my little Charles, we are quite old enough and quite original enough ourselves to see through the tricks of a little lady who has only been going about for four years. She is charming, but she doesn't seem to me, all the same, to be quite 'big' enough to imagine that she can take the world by surprise with so little effort as merely leaving an envelope instead of a card and leaving it at ten o'clock in the morning. Her old mother mouse will shew her that she knows a thing or two about that."

386

Swann could not help smiling at the thought that the
Duchess, who was, incidentally, a trifle jealous of Mme.
de Molé's success, would find it quite in accordance
with the "Guermantes wit" to make some impertinent
retort to her visitor. "So far as the title of Duc de
Brabant is concerned, I've told you a hundred times,
Oriane . . ." the Duke continued, but the Duchess,
without listening, cut him short. "But, my little Charles,
I'm longing to see your photograph." "Ah! *Extinctor
draconis latrator Anubis,*" said Swann. "Yes, it was so
charming what you said about that when you were comparing the Saint George at Venice. But I don't understand: why Anubis?" "What's the one like who was an
ancestor of Babal?" asked M. de Guermantes. "You
want to see his bauble?" retorted his wife, dryly, to shew
that she herself scorned the pun. "I want to see them all,"
she added. "Listen, Charles, let us wait downstairs till
the carriage comes," said the Duke; "you can pay your
call on us in the hall, because my wife won't let us have
any peace until she's seen your photograph. I am less
impatient, I must say," he added with a satisfied air. "I
am not easily moved myself, but she would see us all dead
rather than miss it." "I am entirely of your opinion,
Basin," said the Duchess, "let us go into the hall; we
shall at least know why we have come down from your
study, while we shall never know how we have come down
from the Counts of Brabant." "I've told you a hundred
times how the title came into the House of Hesse," said
the Duke (while we were going downstairs to look at the
photograph, and I thought of those that Swann used to
bring me at Combray), "through the marriage of a
Brabant in 1241 with the daughter of the last Landgrave

of Thuringia and Hesse, so that really it is the title of Prince of Hesse that came to the House of Brabant rather than that of Duke of Brabant to the House of Hesse. You will remember that our battle-cry was that of the Dukes of Brabant: 'Limbourg to her conqueror!' until we exchanged the arms of Brabant for those of Guermantes, in which I think myself that we were wrong, and the example of the Gramonts will not make me change my opinion." "But," replied Mme. de Guermantes, "as it is the King of the Belgians who is the conqueror . . . Besides the Belgian Crown Prince calls himself Duc de Brabant." "But, my dear child, your argument will not hold water for a moment. You know as well as I do that there are titles of pretension which can perfectly well exist even if the territory is occupied by usurpers. For instance, the King of Spain describes himself equally as Duke of Brabant, claiming in virtue of a possession less ancient than ours, but more ancient than that of the King of the Belgians. He calls himself also Duke of Burgundy, King of the Indies Occidental and Oriental, and Duke of Milan. Well, he is no more in possession of Burgundy, the Indies or Brabant than I possess Brabant myself, or the Prince of Hesse either, for that matter. The King of Spain likewise proclaims himself King of Jerusalem, as does the Austrian Emperor, and Jerusalem belongs to neither one nor the other." He stopped for a moment with an awkward feeling that the mention of Jerusalem might have embarrassed Swann, in view of " current events ", but only went on more rapidly: "What you said just now might be said of anyone. We were at one time Dukes of Aumale, a duchy that has passed as regularly to the House of France as Joinville and Chevreuse

have to the House of Albert. We make, no more claim
to those titles than to that of Marquis de Noirmoutiers,
which was at one time ours, and became perfectly regularly the appanage of the House of La Trémoïlle, but
because certain cessions are valid, it does not follow that
they all are. For instance," he went on, turning to me,
" my sister-in-law's son bears the title of Prince d'Agrigente, which comes to us from Joan the Mad, as that of
Prince de Tarente comes to the La Trémoïlles. Well,
Napoleon went and gave this title of Tarente to a soldier,
who may have been admirable in the ranks, but in doing
so the Emperor was disposing of what belonged to him
even less than Napoleon III when he created a Duc de
Montmorency, since Périgord had at least a mother who
was a Montmorency, while the Tarente of Napoleon I
had no more Tarente about him than Napoleon's wish
that he should become so. That did not prevent Chaix
d'Est-Ange, alluding to our uncle Condé, from asking the
Procureur Impérial if he had picked up the title of Duc
de Montmorency in the moat of Vincennes."

" Listen, Basin, I ask for nothing better than to follow
you to the moat of Vincennes, or even to Taranto. And
that reminds me, Charles, of what I was going to say to
you when you were telling me about your Saint George at
Venice. We have an idea, Basin and I, of spending next
spring in Italy and Sicily. If you were to come with us,
just think what a difference it would make! I'm not
thinking only of the pleasure of seeing you, but imagine,
after all you've told me so often about the remains of the
Norman Conquest and of ancient history, imagine what
a trip like that would become if you came with us! I
mean to say that even Basin—what am I saying, Gilbert

—would benefit by it, because I feel that even his claims
to the throne of Naples and all that sort of thing would
interest me if they were explained by you in old romanesque churches in little villages perched on hills like
primitive paintings. But now we're going to look at your
photograph. Open the envelope," said the Duchess to a
footman. " Please, Oriane, not this evening; you can look
at it to-morrow," implored the Duke, who had already
been making signs of alarm to me on seeing the huge
size of the photograph. " But I like to look at it with
Charles," said the Duchess, with a smile at once artificially concupiscent and psychologically subtle, for in her
desire to be friendly to Swann she spoke of the pleasure
which she would have in looking at the photograph as
though it were the pleasure an invalid feels he would find
in eating an orange, or as though she had managed to
combine an escapade with her friends with giving information to a biographer as to some of her favourite
pursuits. " All right, he will come again to see you, on
purpose," declared the Duke, to whom his wife was
obliged to yield. " You can spend three hours in front of
it, if that amuses you," he added ironically. " But where
are you going to stick a toy of those dimensions ? " " Why,
in my room, of course. I like to have it before my eyes."
" Oh, just as you please; if it's in your room, probably
I shall never see it," said the Duke, without thinking of
the revelation he was thus blindly making of the negative
character of his conjugal relations. " Very well, you will
undo it with the greatest care," Mme. de Guermantes told
the servant, multiplying her instructions out of politeness
to Swann. " And see that you don't crumple the envelope,
either." " So even the envelope has got to be respected ! "

the Duke murmured to me, raising his eyes to the ceiling. " But, Swann," he added, " I, who am only a poor married man and thoroughly prosaic, what I wonder at is how on earth you managed to find an envelope that size. Where did you pick it up? " " Oh, at the photographer's; they're always sending out things like that. But the man is a fool, for I see he's written on it ' La Duchesse de Guermantes,' without putting ' Madame '." " I'll forgive him for that," said the Duchesse carelessly; then, seeming to be struck by a sudden idea which enlivened her, checked a faint smile; but at once returning to Swann: " Well, you don't say whether you're coming to Italy with us? " " Madame, I am really afraid that it will not be possible." " Indeed! Mme. de Montmorency is more fortunate. You went with her to Venice and Vicenza. She told me that with you one saw things one would never see otherwise, things no one had ever thought of mentioning before, that you shewed her things she had never dreamed of, and that even in the well-known things she had been able to appreciate details which without you she might have passed by a dozen times without ever noticing. Obviously, she has been more highly favoured than we are to be. . . . You will take the big envelope from M. Swann's photograph," she said to the servant, " and you will hand it in, from me, this evening at half past ten at Mme. la Comtesse Molé's." Swann laughed. " I should like to know, all the same," Mme. de Guermantes asked him, " how, ten months before the time, you can tell that a thing will be impossible." " My dear Duchess, I will tell you if you insist upon it, but, first of all, you can see that I am very ill." " Yes, my little Charles, I don't think you look at all well. I'm not pleased with your colour, but I'm not asking you to come with me next week, I ask you to come in ten months. In ten months one has time to get oneself cured, you know." At this point a footman came in to say that the carriage was at the door. " Come, Oriane, to horse," said the Duke, already pawing the ground with impatience as though he were himself one of the horses that stood waiting outside. " Very well, give me in one word the reason why you can't come to Italy," the Duchess put it to Swann as she rose to say good-bye to us. " But, my dear friend, it's because I shall then have been dead for several months. According to the doctors I consulted last winter, the thing I've got— which may, for that matter, carry me off at any moment —won't in any case leave me more than three or four months to live, and even that is a generous estimate," replied Swann with a smile, while the footman opened the glazed door of the hall to let the Duchess out. " What's that you say?" cried the Duchess, stopping for a moment on her way to the carriage, and raising her fine eyes, their melancholy blue clouded by uncertainty. Placed for the first time in her life between two duties as incompatible as getting into her carriage to go out to dinner and shewing pity for a man who was about to die, she could find nothing in the code of conventions that indicated the right line to follow, and, not knowing which to choose, felt it better to make a show of not believing that the latter alternative need be seriously considered, so as to follow the first, which demanded of her at the moment less effort, and thought that the best way of settling the conflict would be to deny that any existed. " You're joking," she said to Swann. " It would be a joke in charming taste," replied he ironically. " I don't know why I

am telling you this; I have never said a word to you before about my illness. But as you asked me, and as now I
may die at any moment . . . But whatever I do I
mustn't make you late; you're dining out, remember," he
added, because he knew that for other people their own
social obligations took precedence of the death of a friend,
and could put himself in her place by dint of his instinctive politeness. But that of the Duchess enabled her also
to perceive in a vague way that the dinner to which she
was going must count for less to Swann than his own
death. And so, while continuing on her way towards the
carriage, she let her shoulders droop, saying: "Don't
worry about our dinner. It's not of any importance!"
But this put the Duke in a bad humour, who exclaimed:
"Come, Oriane, don't stop there chattering like that and
exchanging your jeremiads with Swann; you know very
well that Mme. de Saint-Euverte insists on sitting down
to table at eight o'clock sharp. We must know what you
propose to do; the horses have been waiting for a good
five minutes. I beg your pardon, Charles," he went on,
turning to Swann, "but it's ten minutes to eight already.
Oriane is always late, and it will take us more than five
minutes to get to old Saint-Euverte's."

Mme. de Guermantes advanced resolutely towards the
carriage and uttered a last farewell to Swann. "You
know, we can talk about that another time; I don't believe a word you've been saying, but we must discuss it
quietly. I expect they gave you a dreadful fright, come to
luncheon, whatever day you like," (with Mme. de Guermantes things always resolved themselves into luncheons),
"you will let me know your day and time," and, lifting
her red skirt, she set her foot on the step. She was just

getting into the carriage when, seeing this foot exposed, the Duke cried in a terrifying voice: "Oriane, what have you been thinking of, you wretch? You've kept on your black shoes! With a red dress! Go upstairs quick and put on red shoes, or rather," he said to the footman, "tell the lady's maid at once to bring down a pair of red shoes." "But, my dear," replied the Duchess gently, annoyed to see that Swann, who was leaving the house with me but had stood back to allow the carriage to pass out in front of us, could hear, "since we are late." "No, no, we have plenty of time. It is only ten to; it won't take us ten minutes to get to the Parc Monceau. And, after all, what would it matter? If we turned up at half past eight they'ld have to wait for us, but you can't possibly go there in a red dress and black shoes. Besides, we shan't be the last, I can tell you; the Sassenages are coming, and you know they never arrive before twenty to nine." The Duchess went up to her room. "Well," said M. de Guermantes to Swann and myself, "we poor, down-trodden husbands, people laugh at us, but we are of some use all the same. But for me, Oriane would have been going out to dinner in black shoes." "It's not unbecoming," said Swann, "I noticed the black shoes and they didn't offend me in the least." "I don't say you're wrong," replied the Duke, "but it looks better to have them to match the dress. Besides, you needn't worry, she would no sooner have got there than she'ld have noticed them, and I should have been obliged to come home and fetch the others. I should have had my dinner at nine o'clock. Good-bye, my children," he said, thrusting us gently from the door, "get away, before Oriane comes down again. It's not that she doesn't like seeing you both. On the contrary, she's too fond of your company. If she finds you still here she will start talking again, she is tired out already, she'll reach the dinner-table quite dead. Besides, I tell you frankly, I'm dying of hunger. I had a wretched luncheon this morning when I came from the train. There was the devil of a *béarnaise* sauce, I admit, but in spite of that I sha'nt be at all sorry, not at all sorry to sit down to dinner. Five minutes to eight! Oh, women, women! She'll give us both indigestion before to-morrow. She is not nearly as strong as people think." The Duke felt no compunction at speaking thus of his wife's ailments and his own to a dying man, for the former interested him more, appeared to him more important. And so it was simply from good breeding and good fellowship that, after politely shewing us out, he cried " from off stage ", in a stentorian voice from the porch to Swann, who was already in the courtyard: " You, now, don't let yourself be taken in by the doctors' nonsense, damn them. They're donkeys. You're as strong as the Pont Neuf. You'll live to bury us all! "

THE END

Printed in Great Britain by R. & R. CLARK, LIMITED, *Edinburgh.*